He can't see the restraints, but he can feel them.

One of the men, he's not sure which, removes Darrek's shoes and socks. Darrek is a tall guy at six-foot-six, but when they lock his ankles in restraints as well—just the edges of the heels of his feet resting on tiny footrests, almost like stirrups—his toes and the balls of his feet wiggle and dangle in mid-air. It's not enough contact to do more than keep his legs in place and he's not sure why it unnerves him, but it does. It makes him feel like a child, unsteady and out of his element. He'd feel much better with his feet firmly planted on the ground, but maybe that's the whole point.

"Leg spreader?" the deeper, older sounding one asks Gabe. Darrek can tell from the source of the voice that the man is sitting between his legs. Darrek can sometimes hear the squeak of wheels from that general direction, and imagines that he's sitting on a rolling stool.

"No, not yet. Clothespins first, then the spreader. No neck restraint yet either. I want to see him squirm."

Darrek moans loudly, pulling at the restraints.

"Relax, slave, we haven't even *started* yet," Gabe laughs.

It's an unnerving sound.

Also recommended...

If you enjoy this story, you may also like these other works published by ForbiddenFiction:

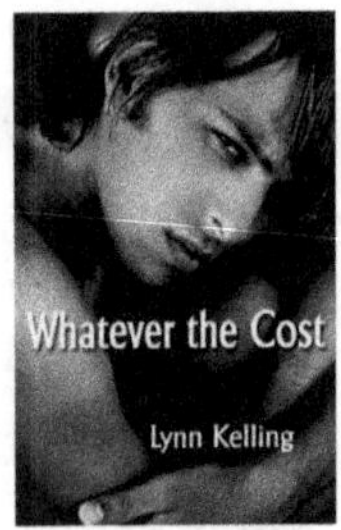

Whatever the Cost by Lynn Kelling
Liam and Jacen are roommates–and elite prostitutes working for a secret organization, The Company. They spend their lives making fantasies come true for spoiled, dangerous clients. In the midst of daily risk of emotional and physical damage, their friendship has been an island of sanity and safety. When The Company orders them to do a job together requiring them to cross the no-sex boundary that has kept them friends, Liam and Jacen must examine how they really feel about each other, and how far they are truly willing to go. Is this the life they want? Used to offering up their bodies without protest to the mercurial whims of others while fiercely guarding their hearts, the true meaning of love and consent is a challenge neither has ever faced before. (M/M)

The Charming by J.A. Jaken
Clayton MacAllister had it all, but the shadow of a past love blinded him until life was slipping through his fingers. Just as Clay is ready to give up on the idea that he might ever be happy, a charming stranger steps into his life like a blessing—or a curse. (M/M+)

Deliver Us

Lynn Kelling

ForbiddenFiction
www.forbiddenfiction.com

an imprint of

Fantastic Fiction Publishing
www.fantasticfictionpub.com

DELIVER US
A Forbidden Fiction book

Fantastic Fiction Publishing
Hayward, California

CREDITS
Editor: Rylan Hunter
Cover Design: DM Atkins
Cover photo: KrisCole - Pixmax
Production Editor: Erika L Firanc
Proofreading: Kailin Morgan

SKU: LK1-000004-02
ISBN: 978-1-62234-068-2

Published in the United States of America

DISCLAIMER

This book is a work of fiction which contains explicit erotic content; it is intended for mature readers. Do not read this if it's not legal for you.

All the characters, locations and events herein are fictional. While elements of existing locations or historical characters or events may be used fictitiously, any resemblance to actual people, places or events is coincidental.

This story may contain descriptions of erotic acts that are immoral, illegal, or unsafe. Do not take the events in this story as proof of the plausibility or safety of any particular practice.

This story depicts fictional BDSM. The characters are not models for the Safe, Sane and Consensual forms embraced by most current practitioners of BDSM. The author takes license with the use of BDSM for dramatic effect. It is not recommended as a manual for how to practice BDSM.

For my readers and my husband,
with profound gratitude.

Contents

Chapter 1
Submission

It all started with Kyle Roth. If Darrek had never told Kyle about the dirty sex he had with Beth, Darrek's life never would have taken the decidedly kinky turn that it did. In all honesty, he had no idea why he told Kyle what happened anyway. The whole thing was obviously none of Kyle's business, and Darrek didn't usually make a habit out of talking about private stuff like that, but then again, he always had poor judgment when it came to knowing when to keep his big mouth shut.

It had only been a couple of dates. Beth seemed nice at first. They always seemed nice at first. Sweet, demure, good manners—a girl his Mama would surely like. But when they'd finally gotten to the point of having *sex*, Darrek had found out firsthand about Beth's adventurous side. And it wasn't a big deal to him. He'd tried weird shit with girls before. He was always up for a good time, and wild sex usually led to a good time for all parties involved, in his experience at least.

So when she spanked him until his ass was red and felt like it was on fire before tying his wrists to the bed and riding him hard, Darrek had liked it. He liked the pain and loss of control —*really* liked it.

And he told Kyle. Again, no fucking idea why.

But Kyle, a blond-haired, blue-eyed, cocky ladies' man, wasn't put off by the intimate information about his childhood best bud at all. In fact, he was excited about it, and was nearly jumping up and down in his eagerness to tell Darrek about a place he heard about from a friend of a friend of a friend. A place you could go to and learn how to be submissive, to be a slave. The friend of a friend of a friend had gone there, and said it was amazing. The best orgasm of his life, he said. But all Kyle could give him was a phone number. Not a name or even a website. Just the phone number, scrawled on a scrap of paper.

And Darrek being Darrek—affable, always up for a good time, willing to try anything once, kind of turned on by the idea of some woman in full-on dominatrix gear spanking his ass and making him beg—called the number. Like an idiot.

Darrek Grealey, a tall, broad-shouldered carpenter with too-long sandy colored hair and soulful brown eyes, arrives at the mysterious place where Kyle had directed him on the day of his appointment, ready to go. He'd followed the instructions of the woman on the phone. Sam had been her name—Sam Cooper. At first Darrek had been kind of freaked out by her instructions, but since this *was* his first time, he just went along with it. Darrek's a pretty easygoing guy.

The address she'd given him was way out in the middle of nowhere, off of the main road, six miles back into farmland, make a left onto a gravel road, go three more miles and stop at the large building over the crest of a big hill.

There are three other cars in the parking lot—an SUV, a truck and a purple sedan. Darrek parks his truck in one of the empty spots and takes a moment to steel himself as he sits behind the wheel before going inside. He takes time to really question his decision. He even questions his sanity, but the allure of the unknown, the challenge that sits before him, the promise of having one of the most erotic sexual experiences of his life, is just too good to pass up.

Staring at the front entrance of the building, Darrek wriggles and shifts slightly in his seat, adjusting himself in his cut-off jeans.

He'd been told not to wear underwear, to shave his genitals completely, and to clean out his ass with this weird douche kit that Sam had recommended. Never claiming to be the brightest, most wary guy in the world, *that* didn't even trigger any alarms in his mind. He just remembered how the guys in the pornos he'd seen had all usually been shaved and really, really clean. It made sense.

But now his balls are rubbing against the rough denim of his shorts. The newly exposed skin around his dick is over-sensitive and distracting him. Grumbling, he shifts again.

"Now or never. Here we fuckin' go," he mutters to himself as he exits the car and heads up the stairs, disappearing through the front door.

A middle-aged woman with a warm smile who nevertheless looks like she could kick an ass or two, the Sam Cooper from the phone call, greets an adorably nervous Darrek in the waiting room. She hands him a clipboard with a form to fill out, and asks him to take a seat. The list on the form intimidates him. There are little checkboxes next to every single item. It's a mind-blowingly comprehensive list of every sexual practice, fetish and perversion he's ever heard of and a whole bunch he hasn't. Darrek has been instructed to check off the things that are absolutely off-limits. They, whoever "they" are, will then use the custom list to choreograph his session, tailoring it to his desires. Darrek examines the list, trying to make sense of what the terms mean, things like CBT and needle play, when his phone vibrates in his pocket.

Cursing, he digs the phone out. Seeing that it's Kyle, Darrek hurriedly turns it off completely.

A cute, young blonde woman appears behind the front desk beside Sam. As the two talk to each other quietly, Darrek struggles to overhear what they say, but only catches something about someone named Gabey being in charge of him, and that they're ready for the next client. Sam turns to Darrek, the only other person present, and asks, "You about done with that form, honey?"

Nowhere near done with the form, Darrek stupidly replies, "Oh. Yeah, sure, ma'am," and almost randomly checks off a few of the things that seem like red flags to him, things like cutting, branding, and strangulation. Not wanting to seem naïve and ask tons of questions about the ones he doesn't understand, he signs the bottom after a number of paragraphs that make up the release portion and hands the form back to Sam with a smile, and without reading it as thoroughly as he probably should.

He will soon come to regret it.

Sam hands the paper off to the young, cute blonde girl, who takes it into the back rooms.

Thinking that 'Gabey' is an interesting and non-intimidating sort of name for a Dominatrix, Darrek gets lost in his own thoughts until he hears, "They're ready for you, Mr. Grealey."

Darrek walks down a flight of dimly lit stairs, into an even darker chamber. Straining his eyes, they start to slowly adjust. Before he can see much of anything besides the bench in the middle of the room, T-shaped with restraints welded onto the frame, a deep, gruff voice says from behind him, "On your knees, slave."

He does it reflexively, going to his knees on the painfully hard concrete floor. As soon as he does, he's instantly uncomfortable as his bones grind against the unforgiving surface.

But it doesn't even matter to him because, see, the *big* problem at the moment is that it's a *male* voice—a very, *very* male voice—low-pitched, rough and alarmingly sensual. He turns his head to look for the source, catching only a flash of full, luscious lips, stark gray-blue eyes framed with thick, almost feminine lashes, a chiseled, bare chest and model-perfect body. Then there's a hand twisted in the back of Darrek's long hair, yanking his head back hard and exposing the thick, long column of his neck.

"I didn't say you could look," the man growls in Darrek's ear, before a blindfold is wrapped over his eyes, tightened at the back of his skull and he can't see *anything*.

A hand pushes down inside the front waistband of his cut-off jeans and closes around his dick. It squeezes slowly up its length and he actually starts to get *hard*.

"What's your safeword?" the voice asks, stroking him up and down and it feels so fucking *good*.

"I... t-think there's been a m-mistake. I was supposed to be with a *woman*, someone named G-Gabe...."

"That's me," the voice interrupts, cutting him off. The unanswered question is repeated, "What's your *safeword*?"

The man—Gabe—releases his cock. Pushing lower, his fingers curl around and grip his balls instead, squeezing them just enough to feel amazing but not enough to hurt.

"I-I don't k-know..." he sputters, confused.

"What kind of vehicle do you drive? What's the model name?"

"T-tundra?"

"That's your safeword. *Use it* if you want us to stop."

"But...."

"*Listen* to me," he growls, punctuating his command with a firm squeeze of his hand. A bolt of heat and pain shoots into Darrek's gut, fire exploding in his balls, his stomach cramping up tightly, but his dick twitches with interest against Gabe's arm.

"I am *very good* at what I do. I will make you feel things that you never even thought *possible* before, things that a *woman* would *never* be able to make you feel. Anything that happens here, in this room, does *not* leave this room. This is between us, and my assistant."

Rubbing his thumb over Darrek's left testicle in small circles, kneading the flesh, he asks, "Do you *want* this?"

"Um... juh... I don't kn...."

"Do you *WANT* this?" the growling voice at his ear asks. Soft, hot lips skim over his neck and throat, over his Adam's apple, sending a shiver down his spine and the hand clenched around his most sensitive body part *tugs* forcefully.

"*Oh, fuck...*" Darrek gasps, tilting his hips instinctively, trying to follow the movement and relieve the pressure. "Yes. Yes! *Shit.*"

"That's all I needed to hear," he purrs, and then the hand is gone—the lips and warm ghost of breath across his neck, as well.

He sharpens his ears, trying to pick up any and all sounds. Soft, padding footsteps—which suggest that Gabe is barefoot—circle him and then recede. Distantly, a door opens and heavier footsteps, someone wearing shoes, possibly boots, approaches.

"Remove your shirt, slave," Gabe commands.

Darrek fumbles a little with it, as the nervousness sets in, but he gets it up and over his head. Someone takes it from his hand before he even has a chance to drop it to the floor. Beginning to tremble, he feels a hand cup his cleft chin, tilting his head up as he's examined.

"I think we'll leave the hood off today. I want to see just how exquisite this face looks when it's begging and screaming," Gabe's voice muses, and then says to the new arrival, "Gag him."

The hand falls away from his chin but he keeps his face tilted to the same angle.

"Open your mouth as wide as you can."

What seems to be a large rubber ball gag is fitted between his teeth. His lips close around it in a perfect 'O' shape. It feels enormous in his mouth. Someone tightens the strap around the back of his head, keeping it snug. Wondering fearfully how he's supposed to say his safeword with the gag in place, Darrek gets even more nervous.

A throaty voice chuckles behind him. Not Gabe, someone else. This voice is somehow even *deeper.* The person that it belongs to sounds intimidating enough to cause Darrek to start clenching and unclenching his fists at his sides, his heart pounding in his chest. Biting down on the gag, he finds that it soothes him, the way his teeth press at the surface. Darrek likes that it will prevent him from saying anything stupid or cowardly in front of these two men to whom he's giving such absolute power over him.

Starting to question the logic of this decision, his safety, the detailed questions on the paperwork about his health insurance information, his existing medical conditions, the legal waiver he's signed absolving them from fault should anything go wrong and he gets seriously hurt....

Oh god, Darrek moans to himself, remembering the form clearly enough that he can almost see it if front of him, and only *just now* realizing that there had been a section that asked if he was averse to anal penetration. He hadn't checked it off. He's left himself in the hands of two Dominants that already have him on his knees on an increasingly painful concrete floor, half-undressed, blindfolded and with a gag in his mouth and he has *NOT* said anything about the fact that he's straight and rather averse to anal penetration. These men have no clue that he's never been interested in gay sex, that he's never let anyone, not even the kinkiest girls he's dated, go *near* his ass with *anything*. He may be easygoing, but he's not *that* easygoing.

He starts to tremble more.

"He's nervous," the deeper of the two voices observes, sounding amused. "Is this your first time, slave?"

Darrek groans and nods his head in affirmation.

"Oh, Gabe. We have ourselves a *virgin* on our hands! I think I'm gonna enjoy this. And *look at him.* Perfect body, pretty-boy face...."

"Wait 'til you feel his balls. They're huge and full. And his cock?" Gabe says to his associate eagerly, literally purring with desire. "...Mmm...."

"That good, huh?"

"That good. Take him to the table. Get him in the restraints. I want to get started."

Chapter 2
Dare to Trust

They guide him to the bench he'd caught a glimpse of before the blindfold had been put in place. It's quite high up in the air, higher than the average dining table. He lies back on it, but it's short and his ass hangs off the end slightly. They tell him to stretch his arms to the sides, perpendicular to his body. There's a narrow beam running crosswise to which they secure his arms. He can't see what the restraints look like or what they are made of, but they feel cold, like metal, and thick. He hears the small sharp snick of a lock clicking into place first on the left side and then the right.

One of the men, he's not sure which, removes Darrek's shoes and socks. Darrek is a tall guy at six-foot-six, but when they lock his ankles in restraints as well—just the edges of the heels of his feet resting on tiny footrests, almost like stirrups—his toes and the balls of his feet wiggle and dangle in mid-air. It's not enough contact to do more than keep his legs in place and he's not sure why it unnerves him, but it does. It makes him feel like a child, unsteady and out of his element. He'd feel much better with his feet firmly planted on the ground, but maybe that's the whole point.

"Leg spreader?" the deeper, older sounding one asks Gabe. Darrek can tell from the source of the voice that the man is sitting between his legs. Darrek can sometimes hear the squeak of wheels from that general direction, and imagines that he's sitting on a rolling stool.

"No, not yet. Clothespins first, then the spreader. No neck restraint yet either. I want to see him squirm."

Darrek moans loudly, pulling at the restraints.

"Relax, slave, we haven't even *started* yet," Gabe laughs.

It's an unnerving sound.

He hears drawers being opened, the clink of metal, the softer tap of other unknown objects being arranged on a surface nearby, and senses the men moving around him. They're deciding what to do to him. They're setting everything out right now, and if he could only *see*, he'd know what was in store for him. Hell, it's all nicely laid out only a few feet away. The fact that the other men know exactly what they're going to do and exactly what they want him to feel, but that *he's* not allowed to know, to say yes or no until it happens, excites him. Darrek is aware that there's always the out of using the safeword, but the position of complete submission he's been put in makes the blood rush to his cock, and he feels it swell even more, pressing at his jeans.

A pair of hands begins to caress lightly over his chest, over the firm, thickly defined muscle there, and then down over his abs and back up to his pectorals. Each hand finds one of his nipples. They rub insistently over them in small circles, stimulating them, and then pinch down and pull. Darrek grunts. He arches a little when he simultaneously feels warm lips close around one of his nipples, sucking at it then biting down, tugging it between teeth as the hand still works at the other one, making the small nubs hard and erect, just as he also feels *another* set of hands grab between his legs, right at his crotch. They seek out and find his balls, tracing the outline of them, pressing at the fabric and gripping them carefully through his jeans.

He makes a series of small grunts, half-words mumbled around the gag and then the first clothespin is attached to his testicles.

The thickness of the fabric covering them dulls the discomfort. It starts as a pinch, but the ache grows, spreads. He starts to breathe harshly through his nose with apprehension, then yelps in surprise when clothespins are attached to first his left nipple and then his right.

Darrek's heart pounds in his chest, especially when what he suspects are Gabe's hands grab his knees and keep him spread wide as the other man attaches more clothespins to his balls.

He counts eight in all.

When they're all attached, Gabe's fingers trace along the outline of Darrek's dick inside his pants. It pulses and strains against them. He dips his hand under the waistband of the tented pants, feathering lightly over Darrek's erection, the proof of his arousal, showing Darrek that he knows how much all of this is turning him on. Darrek moans thickly.

The hand slips free of his pants, and then he's just lying there being closely observed. The pain starts out manageable, concentrated and sharp, but as the seconds turn to minutes, the pain grows exponentially.

Darrek starts to writhe, tries to close his legs like that might help, but it makes it worse. He tries to spread them wider and that makes it worse too as the pins pull and snag at him.

It starts to hit him then—the magnitude of what he agreed to. But he doesn't call it off.

Gabriel watches for a full fifteen minutes, pacing, before he starts to touch the man strapped to the table. Darrek, the paperwork said his name was, squirms and tries every possible variation of position available to him, but he can't escape the pain. It's beautiful to watch, especially because it's only the beginning. Darrek doesn't even know the meaning of the word pain. Yet.

Gabriel nods to his assistant, Trace, a tall, stocky man ten years his senior whose grizzled beard and long hair, typically worn tied back at the nape of his neck, hides strong, handsome features. His dark eyes and piercing gaze punctuate a fearsome personality. At the signal, Trace reaches out and feathers all of the fingers of his right hand rapidly over the clothespins attached to Darrek's testicles. Darrek cries out through the gag and tries to close his legs again. Smiling at the reaction, Trace brushes the clothespins back and forth with his palm and then takes hold of one of the pins. He doesn't squeeze the end to release the grip of the wood at Darrek's flesh, he grips the *top* of the pin, keeping it pinched tight and *pulls*, hard.

Mewling sharply, Darrek flinches, his hips spasm. He tries to turn his hips away from Trace, but Trace's firm hand only grabs Darrek's knee and turns him back toward him. Grabbing a second pin, Trace pulls that one off as well, but does it slowly, to draw out the hurt.

Trace knows well what Darrek is feeling, the instinct to cover the area with your hands, to tuck your hips back and away. He knows the throbbing ache, the feeling of violation, the knowledge that there's someone touching you in your most intimate spots, doing things to you, things you can't see coming or prepare yourself for. You just have to take it and ride out the sensations, trusting in your master. How very much Trace envies Darrek. He would give anything to be where Darrek is, experiencing this for the first time. Smiling, he yanks off another wooden pin, savoring Darrek's low moan and jerking twist on the table.

As the pins continue to come off, Gabriel begins to play with the ones on Darrek's nipples—a simple press against them, tilting the wooden pegs upward or downward elicits delicious whimpers and small pleading sounds from Darrek. He can see how red and inflamed his nipples have gotten, can understand almost perfectly Darrek's mumbled words, from his years of practice at this. He hears, "Please, don't. Don't. It hurts. Shit..." and on and on. But Darrek hasn't used the safeword, so Gabriel keeps going. He twists one of the pins, and Darrek screams, leaning into the touch, trying to follow the motion to make it stop, but Gabriel keeps twisting and then pulls the pin off.

Gabriel strokes over the abused nipple, exposed now, and listens to Darrek begin to cry, sees his tears dampen the blindfold.

His touch is gentle at first, only brushing his palms over the sore, red nub, but even *that* jolts Darrek. Gabriel pulls off the other pin and brushes over that side as well.

Trace is down to two pins. He pulls one of them off, and Darrek bucks his hips, shouting a strangled, "No! No! Fuck!"

"Good boy," Gabriel purrs. "You're doing *so good.* Does it hurt?"

"Yes! Fuck! Yes, it fucking hurts!" Darrek growls viciously around the gag.

Gabriel smiles and tweaks Darrek's nipples, pinching them

hard and twisting them. It gets quite a reaction from him and he thrashes wildly. Leaning down, Gabriel licks over the left one and then sucks on it, feeling the heat of the blood that's rushed to the skin. Darrek gasps and turns into the touch, letting it soothe him a little, but then Gabriel yanks the other nipple with his hand and Darrek starts to cry again.

"Pull the last one. He's had enough," Gabriel says to Trace.

Darrek relaxes visibly at the words, but when the last pin is removed, it makes him growl with pain again. He yanks his arms against the bonds and shuts his legs as much as possible. The clothespins are gone, but he can still feel them anyway like they remain, his flesh tender and on fire.

"Shorts off," Gabriel says, nodding to Trace.

Darrek stills on the table, going quiet and freezing as he tries to process what's happening. The restraints holding his ankles are released and he actually *lifts his hips*, unasked, to help Trace get the shorts off of him. It brings a pleased smile to Gabriel's lips, a clear sign of Darrek's submission and desire.

Even Darrek doesn't really understand why he does it, why he obeys. Why he wants this so badly.

After Trace sets the shorts aside, he starts to attach the leg spreader. Gabriel asks Darrek, leaning down and speaking quietly near his ear, "If I take the gag off, do you promise to behave? I can replace it with a cloth that you can spit out if you need to say something to me."

Darrek thinks for a second then nods vigorously. As the ball gag is unfastened and taken out of his mouth, Trace asks Gabriel, "Legs down or up?"

"Down to start. Then up."

Darrek feels something being strapped to his thighs, just above his knees. When it's attached to both of his legs, he finds that he can't move them at all, that there seems to be a bar stretched between them, keeping them widely open. He feels unspeakably exposed. His genitals are bare now, completely unprotected, even by something as trivial as a pair of jeans. His cock is thick and swollen, lying against his belly. As a blush spreads over Darrek's skin with embarrassment, Trace lifts his ankles to a higher slot than before, so that his legs are bent more sharply than they had been, in order to accommodate the spreader bar.

Knowing that he hasn't been given permission to speak, that he may get punished for talking, Darrek still can't help asking, "What are you going to do to me?"

"Anything I want," Gabriel growls. He pushes the first two fingers of his left hand between Darrek's lips, into his mouth. Reaching far back, he strokes over Darrek's tongue and back into his throat. When Darrek gags on them, Gabriel says, "Relax. Open your throat. Open it wide and relax the muscles."

He makes a concerted effort to follow the instructions, but then a hand closes around his cock and starts jacking him fast and rough, the sound of it obscene in the quiet of the room as pre-come slicks his shaft with each pull and rub.

Struggling not to gag again as Gabriel's fingers push deeper still on each stroke into his mouth, running counter to the strokes at his cock, Darrek loses the battle when yet another hand—Trace's—closes around his sac.

"He does have some big nuts on him, doesn't he?" Trace says with a chuckle.

Trace circles his thumb and index finger around the testicles, letting them rest cradled on his open palm. With his free hand he gently massages them. Darrek groans and bucks up into the touch, which causes him to gag on the fingers.

"Shh... no sound. No noises. You are *not permitted* to make any noises. If you do, there will be punishment. Understand?"

In a moment of insanity, already getting slightly delirious from everything that's happened so far, everything that's *currently* happening, overcome by the fact that two men are fondling him, abusing him and that he's *letting them,* Darrek opens his throat again. He tries to speak and say 'yes'.

Gabriel nods at Trace, releasing his hold on Darrek's dick. The hand circling the testicles closes into a fist and begins to squeeze, gently at first then tighter and tighter and tighter. It takes a few seconds for the sensation to set in. The longer it goes on, the more Darrek's stomach muscles cramp up.

Whimpering and keening, he gags once more on the fingers

fucking his mouth and throat, and starts to retch. Gabriel's fingers withdraw enough to let him recover, but the fist is still squeezing. Stars explode behind his eyes and he writhes freely on the table. The hand compressing his balls releases the pressure for a fraction of a second only to instead begin squeezing in a quick, ruthless rhythm: *squeeze-squeeze-squeeze-squeeze-squeeze.*

"This is what happens when you don't obey the rules," Gabriel says as Darrek arches his neck, his head snapping back as he tries to get away. "When you don't obey, when you talk or make a sound when I tell you *not to,* then you will be punished, and it will be *painful.* If I ask you if you understand, right after telling you not to speak, and you do understand, then you *nod.*"

Gabriel pulls his fingers out of Darrek's mouth only to replace them with a thick wad of cloth.

The squeezing of his testicles stops, but the hand still holds them. Someone starts to jack his cock again, since his erection has wilted slightly due to the pain, and he hardens once more despite everything. They keep jerking him off without pause for almost three full minutes and just when he gets close to his orgasm, feeling it approach despite where he is and who's doing it, he is released, his cock huge and red and dripping wet with pre-come. It pulses, curving up to his stomach. Darrek shudders and moans in disappointment, swallows back a whine.

"Lift your ass," he hears.

Carefully, he obeys, feeling a thick strap slip under his lower back and circle his waist. His over-stimulated dick is taken in hand and forced under the strap, which holds it up against his belly, keeping it pressed tightly there. Fingers idly stroke up and down the velvet-covered steel of its length, over the pulsing veins that run along it. He tries to buck up into the touch, wanting more, wanting release.

Other fingers, Trace's fingers, circle his sac and pull on it, stretching the two reddish-purple orbs of his testicles away from his body as far as they'll go. Darrek pants roughly through his nose. His balls sit poking out of the circle of Trace's thumb and index finger. Trace flicks them with his index finger. *Flick-flick-flick-flick.* Darrek groans and tries to sit up, curling forward as far as he can, stomach muscles rock hard, trying to draw his feet up, but they don't budge.

Gabriel pushes him back down and a strap is quickly fitted across his throat, keeping him restrained. Darrek curses and yells with anger around the gag, and Gabriel just laughs, nodding to Trace.

Drawing back an open hand, Trace starts slapping Darrek's balls, right to left and then backhanded left to right. Again and again and again he slaps them. Each strike provokes a jerk of Darrek's entire body in the bonds and hard, deep grunts from his throat. Trace stops slapping him and pulls. He pulls and pulls and pulls, watching the sac stretch so tight, it looks like it's going to burst and then squeezes his thumb and index finger at the round orb of one of his testicles like it was an oversized grape he's trying to pop.

Darrek screams and starts sobbing.

Gabriel nods to Trace, who stops pulling and squeezing, and just massages him gently instead. Darrek shudders and gasps for air, trembling and riding out the waves of agony radiating through his body. Gabriel pulls a surgical glove from the box nearby, tugging it on and dispensing some lube onto it, spreading it around.

Unlatching Darrek's ankles, Trace raises his submissive's legs, still held widely apart by the spreader bar. He attaches a chain to the bar. The other end of the chain is locked to the bench beside Darrek's head, looping around, underneath the bench, then attached to the bar again. The chain is pulled as tight as he can get it, bending Darrek's legs up to his chest, his lower legs and ankles hanging loose off to either side.

"We're going to flog your balls and your dick now, slave. Your tight little asshole, too. Anybody ever do that to you before?"

Darrek whimpers and shakes his head 'no'.

The flogger rubs over his sac, along his dick, still held under the strap and he arches into the touch, wanting more. Then it snakes down, around and under his balls, over the swell of his ass. It rubs into the crease, starts to stroke and then tap-tap-tap at his hole. Cringing in anticipation and moaning, Darrek becomes more aware of the muscles there, the puckered knot twitching with each touch. It's too personal, too intimate, having these men playing with his orifice like this. And then the strike comes, hard enough to make him want to yell. It comes five times in a row then starts tapping again, lighter, gradually harder and harder. Then WHACK! WHACK! WHACK!

"NO! No! No!" he pleads, spitting out the rag in his mouth. "Don't! *Please* don't! It *hurts*! Don't! Stop!"

The gag is stuffed back in his mouth and the flogger starts to smack at his balls. Trace aims from underneath, flicking his wrist up, watching the soft tissue dance and flop with each slap. He varies his target, moving upward, striking the root of Darrek's cock and then the shaft. Darrek bucks and twists away, but Gabriel moves him back, hearing Darrek continue to beg nonsensically but ignoring it.

Placing his hand at Darrek's perineum, Gabriel pushes his balls up until they're pulled tight, trapped between Gabriel's hand and Darrek's pelvis. Trace knows what to do. He whips them sharply, ten times. Each strike makes Darrek cry out and jerk a little more, but he can't escape.

Keening and whining, his breath hitching with fresh sobs, his head falls to the side. Darrek's hair falls over his face. His chest works hard, hitching with thick emotion. Gabriel releases him and goes to his head.

Leaning over Darrek, brushing the backs of his fingers tenderly over the hollows of Darrek's cheeks, down the side of his neck, Gabriel shushes him and praises him for how good he's doing. His lips skim over Darrek's jaw almost in a kiss as he whispers. It calms Darrek noticeably.

Drinking in Darrek's scent, heady and thick, Gabriel twines his fingers in the long, dusty brown strands of Darrek's hair, and strokes his thumbs over his temples. Gabriel sighs at the rapturous sight of him.

"Gorgeous. So fucking breathtaking. You're doing so well, being so brave. Such a good slave for me," he whispers, and Darrek sighs around the gag in his mouth, savoring the words, attention and gentleness.

Trace steps away, over to the supplies and tools. After a break, and once Darrek is relaxed again, breathing normally, Gabriel asks him, "Better? You ready now?"

"Mm-hmm," Darrek hums.

He pulls the wad of cloth from Darrek's mouth, letting him flex his jaw and work out the stiffness.

"Thank you... sir."

"You're welcome, slave."

Gabriel goes to sit between Darrek's legs, in front of his perfectly presented genitals and ass.

"Now, I've taken out your gag, but you may only speak when spoken to and when I ask you a question. Do you understand?"

"Yes, sir."

"Good. Every time you disobey, if you cry out or shout or curse, I will attach a clothespin to you as punishment. What we're going to do now is fill you up really good. I'm going to finger-fuck your ass and my associate is going to insert a very thin eleven-inch metal rod into your urethra. He's already measured you, to verify that it will fit, and we're using the thinnest one we have, since you're a beginner. It's going to hurt, but once it's in, it will feel very, very good. Now, do you want to watch?"

"Y-y-yes. Y-yes, s-sir," he answers, trembling from head to foot as Trace lifts his dick, taking it out from under the strap, seeing that it's now soft from all of the pain Darrek has just suffered.

"Good. You're nice and soft," Gabriel says as Trace squeezes a water-based lube onto the head, rubbing it into the slit. He walks around the table, removes the blindfold, and unfastens the neck restraint.

It's dark, too dark to see very much. An overhead directional lamp has been turned on, shining down on his crotch. It's the only light in the room. The men are now wearing hoods, concealing their features. He sees a gleam of gray-blue eyes in one of them though, and knows it's 'Gabe,' his Dominant, his Master. The other man is gingerly holding his penis upright, an insanely long metal rod in his other hand. Darrek's Master is coating the metal liberally with lubricant. Darrek is certain that there's absolutely no fucking way that it's ever going to fit inside his penis.

Trace aligns the end with his slit and lets its weight begin to pull it down with the force of gravity alone, letting it begin to sink inside. There's a feeling of pressure as his opening starts to stretch to try to accommodate it and then a sharp burning pain.

"Take a nice deep breath now. Okay? In and out," Gabriel instructs.

Tremors wrack his body as his nervousness gets the best of him. He's all at once certain that this would have been easier if he had been blindfolded, if he hadn't seen the rod, and knows that he made the wrong choice.

A half-inch of the metal disappears into the head of his dick and the man continues to feed it inside, bit by bit.

He whimpers, tilting his hips, fighting not to scream as it feels for all the world like his dick is being split open.

Then it pushes deeper, *so fucking deep* and he *can't* be quiet anymore.

"Ow! Ow!" he yelps, trying to pull away. "Stop!"

Gabriel just sighs and pulls a clothespin from a pocket.

"No, please! Don't! Master, don't! It hurts...."

"No talking," he says, low and insistently, then Darrek feels him pulling a little on the loose skin of his ball sac, stretching it out and then he fastens the pin on it.

Darrek chokes, swallowing a rough yell, his eyes rolling up at the waves of pain, not wanting another pin attached to him though.

Now the torture is radiating from two spots, and he can't watch. His head falls back onto the table as the rod gets deeper, more than halfway in now. His throat works, and he begins to make a choking sound simply because he's fighting so hard to be quiet.

Gabriel adds more lube around the sound, smearing it into Darrek's urethra. The metal keeps slipping inside. It's almost in all the way, only an inch-and-a-half still visible when Gabriel's hand takes hold of the clothespin and pulls on it, watching it stretch out Darrek's sac.

"Aahh!" he screams. He opens his eyes, seeing another pin appear in Gabriel's hand.

"That's not *fair*!" Darrek barks at him, angrily. "That's not...."

The wood clamps down on him in a second spot and then a third time. The sound is inside, the rod not even visible anymore. Trace attaches a device to keep it there, to hold it in place, and rests his fingers lightly on the shaft, keeping it pointing straight up.

Darrek's dick juts out from his body, and he stares at it, curious and fascinated, but he can't seem to care because of the growing ache from the clothespins.

"I wanted to do this part without pain, but I guess it's not going to work out that way. The pins stay on until I'm done. I have a question for you, slave. Have you ever had anyone penetrate your anus before? With anything?"

"N-n-no. No sir."

"Interesting."

He fingers Darrek's entrance, pressing a fingertip inside. Just a fingertip. He rotates it, twisting it in his puckered hole, looking down at it.

Darrek's heart starts to pound in his chest, his mouth going desert-dry. Trace shifts to the side and leans in to watch, and Darrek suddenly feels like he's on display. He tries to close his legs, knowing that it's futile. His toes flex and clench. His feet arch. When the finger penetrates him up to the last knuckle all at once, his legs kick and he bucks his hips, whining loudly.

"Such a tight little pink hole on this straight boy. Can't wait to fuck it and stretch it out until it's wide and gaping and messy. He'll be walking funny for a week," the other man growls.

The finger in his ass is the focus of his attention, the alien, unfamiliar feeling of it overwhelms him as it fucks him deep and rough. A second is quickly added, and they're still staring at his ass, watching Gabriel's fingers get swallowed up by it.

"Please don't do this to me. I didn't *want* this. I didn't *come here* for this," Darrek begs.

"Is that right, slave?" Gabriel asks, sarcastically. "If you don't want this, and you want me to stop, you know what to say. So say it or shut up."

Darrek bites his tongue and squeezes his eyes closed, grunting softly but not saying a word.

Chapter 3
The Renunciation

"Plug," Gabriel says to his associate, holding out his hand. A medium-sized butt plug, already lubed, is set in his hand. With a glance up at Darrek, Gabriel pushes it deep inside, fucking him with it a few times, letting him feel how full he is before leaving it there, completely buried in his body. Darrek's face is beet-red, his lips pursed and his fists clenched tight.

With a hand braced on the spreader bar between his thighs, Gabriel pushes Darrek's legs back even more, bending him in half. With his other, he slaps at Darrek's balls forcefully three times. Darrek shouts and then Gabriel's hand closes around them, clothespins and all. He grips the abused flesh, watching Darrek writhe and buck and curse and scream, but he doesn't let up. Darrek wriggles his ass on the bench, tries to shake Gabriel loose, but he just follows the movement, squeezing him even more.

"T-tundra! *Tundra!* Fuck!"

Gabriel lets go immediately and removes the pins as well.

Darrek sighs in relief.

"Hold his legs," Gabriel orders Trace.

Letting Darrek calm down and catch his breath, Gabriel sits on the stool positioned at the foot of the table. He waits there, brushing his hands over Darrek's thighs until his breathing is steady.

"Okay," Darrek murmurs, almost too soft to hear.

Gabriel leans in and begins licking Darrek's abused sac. Swiping greedily with the flat of his tongue, he laps up over them, moaning hungrily at their taste and heat. The sound vibrates through Darrek's body. He gasps and shudders in response, in pleasure. His dick pulses with need, still stuffed and full. He pulls at the bonds but this time Gabriel knows that it's because he wants to touch himself, not to cover up.

"Please... oh fuck... feels *so... fucking... good....*"

As Gabriel sucks each of Darrek's balls into his mouth, rolling them on his tongue and using gentle suction to pull them back in his mouth, he pushes with a hand at the end of the plug in Darrek's ass, angling it so that it jabs rhythmically at his prostate. Darrek bucks his hips up into Gabriel's mouth with each strike against his sweet spot, whimpering desperately and freely.

Gabriel pulls his mouth away, working the plug still but letting Darrek's sac fall with a soft wet sound from his lips. He watches Darrek, his face working with exquisite bliss. Then he quickly stands.

Gabriel opens his pants and frees his dick. Trace is holding Darrek in position, bent in half, ass out. He shoots Gabriel a sharp look that is soundly ignored and Darrek can't even see what's happening. Pulling the plug slowly out of Darrek's body, Gabriel savors the way his stretched, reddened, wet hole gapes at first then begins to slowly contract once again. He rolls on a condom and coats himself with lube.

Taking his dick in hand, Gabriel taps the head of it repeatedly against Darrek's gaping entrance.

"Can you feel me, slave? That's my dick. I'm going to fuck your virgin ass now, and watch your hungry little hole take my thick cock."

There's not even a pause in which Darrek questions his answer, as Gabriel waits to see if he'll use the safeword again. Darrek just grunts and pleads, "F-fu-fuck! Yeah... *yes,* Master. *Please* fuck me."

"Good boy," he sighs and thrusts inside Darrek in one swift movement, past the tighter outer ring of muscle and into the gripping heat of his body.

"Oh god! Oh my *god...*" Darrek cries, and there's pain there, but the joy, relief and pleasure outshine it.

Gabriel doesn't give him time to adjust, he just grips Darrek's hips and fucks him deep and hard, his hips and balls slapping against Darrek's ass. He circles a hand around Darrek's stuffed cock and starts to stroke him in time with his thrusts. Darrek moans deep and long, arching into the touch.

"More. Please, Master. *Please* more, Master. Thank you...."

Hissing a little at the grip of the too-tight, velvety inner walls of Darrek's body as they squeeze at him in just the right way, not having had a virgin, someone this utterly unbroken in *years*, Gabriel fucks him harder, growling now.

Trace swiftly unhooks the device around the sound. Gabriel's squeezing pumps up the thick, red shaft cause Darrek's body to push the rod out on its own. Trace's fingers close around the metal and he pulls on it, letting it slide against and trigger sensitive nerve endings inside Darrek's penis. Darrek comes suddenly, with a bright, ripping scream of pure, undiluted bliss. The sound is freed from his body just as he unloads, spunk jetting thickly out of the stretched hole, pulsing and spurting in time with the contractions of his body.

Gabriel pounds into him, gasping, his eyes closed as he focuses on nothing but Darrek. He comes quickly, filling the condom, wishing he was filling Darrek instead.

When he pulls out, Gabriel finds Darrek unconscious, limp and unresponsive – knocked out cold with the force of his orgasm.

When Darrek wakes, he's clean, wearing his clothes, and has been covered with a soft cotton blanket. He becomes aware that he is in a small room, lying on a cot, and through the curtained window he can see the large maple tree swaying in the breeze. His whole body aches. It's radiating out strongly from his genitals, though, so he lets his legs fall open wider. He slips a hand down and cups himself, sighing a little.

Then he notices that he's not alone.

There's a man sitting beside the bed, watching him and holding a glass of water. The man is shorter and slighter than Darrek. He has sensuous, full lips, short, dark brown hair that's perfectly tousled, making him look incredibly sexy and like he just got out of bed, and sparkling, pale eyes.

It's his Master.

Darrek sits up with a start, swinging his legs over the side of the bed, ignoring the fresh jolt of pain the sudden movement causes him.

"Hey, take it easy," his Master says, meeting Darrek's stare head-on. "You've been through a lot and you're coming down from a hell of an adrenaline and endorphin rush. Here, drink this. It'll help."

"Master..." Darrek whispers, taking the proffered water and sipping it. He's shocked at how hoarse his voice is. He must have strained his vocal cords with all of the yelling.

"It's Gabriel. You don't have to call me that when we're not in a session," Gabriel tells him, and smiles a little at the way Darrek bites shyly at his lip. "So, are you okay?"

Darrek nods, not sure what to say.

"Will I be seeing you here again?" Gabriel asks.

Shrugging, Darrek lowers his eyes and twists his fingers together.

Leaning in closer, resting an elbow on his knees, Gabriel brushes back a lock of Darrek's hair, tucking it behind his ear. "Did you enjoy it, Darrek?"

The use of his name startles him, so he looks up. "Yes. I enjoyed it, Mas-Gabriel," Darrek says, catching himself, but feeling more than a little weird using the name. It feels more comfortable to just keep calling him Master, and that speaks volumes for how far Darrek's mindset has changed in only the last few hours.

Brushing his thumb over the swell of Darrek's lower lip, and watching the way Darrek's eyes slip softly closed at the touch, the gentle sigh of his breath, Gabriel says quietly, "Good. Good, I'm glad. Since you're new at this, I want you to understand that you're in a recovery phase. Go easy on yourself. You should have something to eat, and keep drinking plenty of fluids. And it's normal to have an emotional crash, too. If you expect it to happen, and accept it for what it is, it'll be that much easier to get past it. It's called subdrop. But, you know, tops go through the same sort of thing. I'm here if you want to talk about our session or how it's making you feel."

"Thanks, uh," Darrek starts. "But I think I just want to head home and rest. A long, lazy lounge on the couch sounds pretty good right now."

"I really enjoyed being your partner today. You were incredible."

Unsure what to say, Darrek's only response is a glance of acknowledgment.

"I can stick around a little longer," Gabriel offers. "As long as you need, to make sure you're okay."

Finishing the water, hands clasped to the glass, self-conscious and out-of-sorts, Darrek says, "That's alright. But I appreciate it."

After waiting another minute to ensure Darrek is telling the truth, and really is fine, Gabriel stands, his hand falling away. He pulls a slip of paper from his pocket, staring at it then folding it over. After a pause, he holds it out to Darrek.

Looking up at Gabriel with wide eyes, Darrek reaches out an unsteady hand and takes it from him.

Gabriel walks to the door, pulling it open. He hesitates, then says over his shoulder, "Don't let anyone else here know that you have that, okay? Put it in your pocket."

"O-okay."

Then he's gone and the door is shut again.

He opens the folded paper, blinking at it and the looping scrawl of letters and numbers:

> *My private number is 340-555-2789.*
>
> *Please call me. No pressure. No rules. No expectations.*
> *I promise.*
>
> – *Gabriel Hunter*

"Oh my god," Darrek gasps. He looks quickly around and carefully refolds the paper, pushing it into his pocket.

His shoes are sitting by the side of the cot. He slips them on and stands, groaning as he does. Walking to the door, Darrek is more than a little bow-legged but he doesn't care in the slightest. He finds his way out of the building and back to his Tundra. Once behind the wheel, he pulls the paper out again, running his fingers over the writing. The business card he'd taken from the front desk, from Sam, is set on the passenger seat, the white cardstock gleaming against the brown leather. The embossed name of the establishment, Diadem, casts shadows in the sunlight. But the paper cradled carefully in his hand, the one that he shouldn't have, but does, is the one that has his attention.

"Gabriel..." he whispers, trying the name out, seeing how it sounds, how it feels in his mouth.

He returns the paper to his pocket and guns the engine, throwing the gearshift into reverse. As he rolls down the gravel road, feeling keenly every bump under the wheels as the unevenness of the surface bounces him a little in his seat, he shifts and writhes, still able to feel vividly the effects of Gabriel's ministrations, the ache in his balls, the soreness in his ass.

Darrek sighs happily and smiles widely.

He turns on the stereo, cranking up the music. Singing along to it, he slides on his aviator sunglasses, shakes the hair out of his face and laughs contentedly to himself as he drives.

Chapter 4

Truth and Spies

"Two lagers, please," Gabriel mutters to the waitress. He's seated in a booth at the back of a local bar, tucked away in a dimly lit corner across from his co-worker and best friend, Ben Knox. Ben's naturally curly, light hair has been buzzed short, only drawing more attention to the mischief constantly brewing in his vivid, royal blue eyes.

It has been a long-ass week, and Gabriel has a lot on his mind. Knowing it's futile, that the interrogation is coming whether he likes it or not, he avoids his friend's all-seeing, probing gaze, and slouches low in his seat.

Once the girl is gone, Ben turns to Gabriel and immediately says, "So, what the fuck, man? What happened with you and that newbie? I *heard* Sam reaming you out. She was pissed!"

"Hey, it's on me. She knows that. My decision. My client. And it's not like it's never happened before," he adds defensively.

"Not with *you*! Sweet little virgin-Dom Gabey," Ben huffs offhandedly. He lounges back casually, stretching his arm out and scoping out the bar. From what he can tell, it seems to be filled mostly with regulars. Some people he recognizes, most he doesn't. They've never come to this particular bar together before, but decided to give it a try, since it's close to their end of town, safely on the outskirts of things. Ben knows it's never too crowded, not too crazy. Just the way they like it.

"Don't fucking call me that. Asshole," Gabriel glares, taking his beer with a badly-plastered-on, polite smile from the waitress when she returns.

"I speak the truth."

"I'm not a fucking *virgin*."

"Oh, really?" Ben sighs, raising an eyebrow in disbelief.

"Yes, really. Aren't we talking about the fact that I fucked a client during a scene?"

"Yeah, but...."

"Or maybe I'm mistaken?"

"Gabe...."

"Or maybe you want to talk to Harry. Get him on the goddamned phone and ask *him* about it?" Gabriel seethes at Ben with his voice lowered.

"Dude! Calm down! What crawled up your ass and died? That's not what I'm fucking talking about and you know it. And I would never throw the Harry shit in your face. Do you really think I'm that much of a heartless bastard?"

"No... Jesus," he groans, rubbing tiredly at his eyes. "I'm sorry. Can we just have a beer, please? And not talk about this shit?"

"Of course. So tell me... total piece of ass?" Ben asks eagerly, eyes twinkly with glee and salivating at the thought. "He was, right? You wouldn't have fucked him otherwise. He had to be something *really* special. What's your type, Gabey? Cute little twink? Or maybe a big muscle-bound dude? Tell me."

"Ben...."

"No way. I am *not* letting this go," he says sternly, his face going sour with frustration. "You're always avoiding shit and being so goddamned secretive and I'm tired of it! Fucking *tell me,* Hunter!"

Gabriel laughs giddily, snorting into his beer, saying sarcastically, "Yes, Master."

That gets Ben laughing too.

"Oops. Wow, you know, I totally did that to a bank teller yesterday. Did I tell you about that? Some chick that was giving me a hard time with a deposit I was trying to make into my money market account. Didn't even realize it until she started to fucking *cower* behind the desk and kept saying, 'Of course, sir.' Totally gave me wood."

"That's alarming."

"I know! Right?!" he says, puzzled. "Maybe I'm becoming bi...

like a late bloomer type of thing. Hmm."

Ben glances up as a decent-looking guy in a button-down shirt and leather jacket approaches the table with his eyes locked on Gabriel like a heat-seeking missile finding its target. Before the guy can even get the first word out, Ben sets his jaw, his eyes sharp as daggers, looking for all the world like the utter picture of 'you-do-not-want-to-fuck-with-me' that's made him so successful in the industry, and says, "He's NOT INTERESTED."

"But...."

"*Leave.*"

Proverbial tail between his legs, the man turns and goes back to his spot at the far end of the bar.

"Hey, I don't need you to be my damn *bodyguard*, Knox. I'm a big boy."

"Oh suck my dick, Gabey. I'm sick of all these pervs trying to get in your pants. It's like we can't even go out anymore." After taking a long sip of his beer, he continues with, "So back to my original question...."

Gabriel rolls his eyes, setting his half-empty beer down on the coaster, and leans forward over the table. Ben leans forward too, just out of impatience to get all the juicy details.

"Well...? How hot was his ass?" Ben prods and kicks Gabriel's foot under the table.

"Okay... first off, he's huge, like six-foot-six, six-foot-seven. Body so fucking tight and tan and toned you just want to lick every inch of him. Just his fucking pecs alone... *god.* Then he's got this long, shoulder-length light brown hair with golden highlights from the sun and little waves in it, like if you got it really wet it'd just be these curly tendrils hanging in his eyes. But he's *beautiful*, too. Literally beautiful, and it's like he doesn't even know it. Immaculate bone structure, and these big, like, almond-shaped eyes, that are this rich burning brown, you could just fall into them."

"*And...?*"

A small smile plays at the corners of his lips, and he admits, "Yeah."

"No shit?"

"No shit."

"Details, Hunter! Details!" he demands, pounding on the table with an open palm. He almost knocks his beer over.

"Totally proportional and then some. Fucking breathtaking. My mouth seriously would not stop watering. *And* the reason why I just *needed* to suck on those huge balls of his right before I fucked his tight virgin ass. God, he screamed so pretty. Fucking begged me to do it, too."

Gabriel takes a sip and gets lost for a moment in the bliss of the memory. Until Ben speaks, that is.

"...My dick is so hard right now," Ben says solemnly.

"Dude!"

"What?! I'm just picturing you sucking on some Greek god's sac with Trace watching the whole damn thing. Of *course* I'm turned on!"

Gabriel has a moment of panic where he's convinced that Ben is going to either loudly applaud him or whip out his cock and just start beating off in the middle of the bar.

"I'm totally not giving you a hand job," Gabriel says, pointing a finger at Ben in warning, his lips wrapping around the bottle again. "That's *all* on you.... Oh... fuck me."

"What?"

"Nothing," Gabriel says quickly, shifting even lower in his seat and sliding a little to the right.

"You're *hiding* for nothing? What the hell is..." Ben says in disbelief, turning to look behind him to where Gabriel is currently sneaking glances. "Oh *HELL* yes. THAT is *mine.*"

"I know. Don't stare!"

"Why? Oh... wait. Is that... Is that *him*?! *THAT* is the client you fucked?!"

Gabriel reaches across the table and smacks Ben upside the head as a few people turn around to look at them.

"Shut up!" he growls. "Shut! *Up!*"

"Shit, I'd fuck that too," Ben smiles. "You got the luck of the draw, baby."

"No, Sam gave him to me because it was his first time and I'm known to be less blatantly cruel than you or Trace. It wasn't luck. And he *has* a name, you know. His name is Darrek," he murmurs, staring at the pair of men at the other end of the room as they enter the bar and find an empty table to sit at. He's enraptured as Darrek removes his jacket and his shirt pulls tight over the muscles of his chest. Gabriel starts brushing the pad of his middle finger back and forth over his bottom lip as he studies Darrek, the way he moves, the way he's dressed, the indescribable smile that lights his face when his friend says something to him.

"Okay, forget the whole fucking-a-client thing...."

"His name is DARREK."

"I'm ignoring that. Since when do you call clients by their first names?"

"How about we talk about the *other* issue we have here?" Gabriel frowns.

"Don't worry, I'll handle it."

"Just don't...."

"I know, not a word to your *precious*. I'll be... subtle."

"Knox! ...*Christ*," he curses, slipping down even lower in the booth as Ben stands and walks up to the bar with a cat-like, intent grin on his face.

Ben grabs a napkin and scribbles a few words on it. Then he folds it twice and hands it to the waitress with a five-dollar bill. After a minute of hushed conversation, she makes a beeline over to the small table by the front window, where two newcomers are sitting.

She hands the shorter, blond one the napkin. After a few words she leaves them. The blond flounders for a minute then excuses himself.

Ben has disappeared, but Gabriel knows right where he is. Sighing with exhaustion and cringing at the tight knot of anxiety in his chest, he watches Darrek flip through the small menu of drinks and snacks. The multicolored lights—pinks, blues and greens—refract and reflect from the neon and glass, illuminating his face and hair. It plays across the hard lines and angles of his brow, cheekbones and jaw, the soft curl of his hair. Transfixed, Gabriel's hand slips beneath the table and he palms his swelling cock as he remembers their one glorious encounter just two days earlier.

He should go over there. He should say something instead of

hiding in the booth and choking on his nerves like one of his clients. But he doesn't.

Trying to be content with the view and the memories, wishing he could just go over there like a normal person, Gabriel curses and drinks his beer.

The rear door to the bar creaks loudly open. Kyle Roth steps through it then lets it swing shut again. Ben crooks a finger, beckoning him.

"Here kitty, kitty, kitty," he sings.

Kyle squeezes his eyes shut, taking a deep, steadying breath and walks over to him, letting Ben guide him back against the brick wall with gentle pressure from fingertips pressing at his chest.

"Good kitty," he smiles. "Pants. Now."

"Y-yes, sir," he sputters.

Kyle unfastens his jeans as quickly as he can and pushes them down slightly on his hips, letting his hands fall away once he's finished.

Pushing his hand inside and wrapping it around Kyle's fully erect cock, Ben starts to stroke him slowly. He knows from years of experience how Kyle likes it.

"Good. Now. What the hell are you doing here? Are you following me?"

"No, Master. I swear, we were just going out, and our job site is near here, that new bank that's going up on Broad and Market..." Kyle sputters then groans as Ben squeezes tighter.

"Okay, let's pretend I believe that. I saw you sitting in there with someone. That your new boyfriend?"

"Darrek? No way! He's a friend, he... *oh fuck,* that feels good...."

"But he makes you hard... or is all this for me?" Ben teases, jacking him rough and fast.

"Oh god..." Kyle moans, bucking his hips.

"*Don't* come. If you come, you will be *severely* punished. Do you understand?"

Whimpering, Kyle nods and manages a quiet, "Yes, sir."

Still pumping his hand along Kyle's shaft, Ben feels him fight back the desperate need to unload. Ben hopes that he loses the battle so that he gets to really sink his claws into his most loyal and obedient slave during their next session. He says, "Admit it. Admit that you're hot for your little 'friend'."

Kyle doesn't respond, but he makes a frustrated little whine.

"*Admit it,* slave," he says threateningly, squeezing harder than is pleasurable on the next stroke.

"Ouch! Fuck! Yeah. Okay! Yes. Yes, sir."

"Did you tell him about us? About our little... arrangement? Has he seen what you do for me?"

"No! Well... I *did* give him the phone number, but I *swear* I didn't say anything. He doesn't know anything. I don't think he's even going to call. There's no way he'd go for this stuff. He's too vanilla... he's too *straight*... he's too... oh god...."

"*Don't* come!" Ben commands him, still stroking him with long squeezing tugs of his hand.

"Shit! Shit! Shit! Please, Master. Please have mercy on me. I've been so good for you, please. Shit!"

Ignoring the begging, Ben says, "That's what you said at first too, remember? You were so *resistant. Defiant.* And *now* look at you...."

Kyle's eyes roll back, his mouth pressed tightly shut as he swallows back a rough yell. But then he can't hold it in anymore. His lips part around a grunting shout, so Ben claps a tight hand over them, muffling the sound. He stops jerking his fist and just rubs in slow circles over the head with his thumb.

"Don't you dare fucking come," he hisses, and Kyle is breathing easier now, calmed by the hand over his mouth.

Releasing Kyle's dick, an angry red, dripping wet with precome, he shifts the hand over Kyle's mouth. Gripping Kyle's face with his thumb and forefingers, pressing the junction of his hand between Kyle's lips, pushing back hard and letting Kyle bite down and lick over the flesh.

Humming with pleasure, Kyle watches as Ben pulls something from his pocket and holds it up in front of him.

"A present to remember me by. Once I put it on, you are *not* to remove it until our session tomorrow. Understand?"

Kyle nods, with Ben's hand still wedged between his teeth. Pinching the small ring in his other hand between his fingers to activate the vibration, Ben slips it over the head of Kyle's dick, letting it sit right there, right under the ridge. It's a tight fit, and it's not going anywhere. As the vibrations tickle down his shaft, stimulating the already over-stimulated nerves, Kyle whimpers and fights to master his urges.

Ben fastens Kyle's pants up for him, one-handed, then finally releases Kyle's mouth as well.

"May I...?" Kyle asks meekly.

"Yes, you may."

He leans forward and gently kisses Ben's lips, whispering a quiet, "Thank you, Master. I love you."

"You're welcome, baby. Go have fun. I'll be watching."

Kyle shuffles back toward the door, hunched over, hands shoved into his pockets to disguise his hard-on. He looks back over his shoulder with a smile before heading back inside.

Chapter 5

Shock and Acceptance

"What's up? You okay?" Darrek asks as Kyle reclaims his seat with a wince. Kyle pushes a hand roughly back through his corn silk hair and straightens his polo shirt.

"Yeah. I... uh... used to date that waitress. She wanted to... 'talk'," Kyle grins smarmily.

Darrek shakes his head and just says, "I need to find you a girlfriend. I think you'd be less of a chauvinistic ass if you were getting laid regularly. I ordered drinks and food, by the way."

"Cool," Kyle sighs, adjusting himself, but careful not to let his hand linger near his crotch too long, knowing that Ben is watching him and that he won't be pleased if he suspects that Kyle is trying to give himself relief. "And I can't deal with girlfriends. You know that. *You're* the girlfriend type, not me."

"Not lately," Darrek mutters. Their food and beers arrive, which provides a welcome distraction for both of them.

"That's why you should call that number I gave you. Blow off some steam...."

"Nah. I think I'm good. I've got a few side projects coming my way. Some special-order pieces. I'm in the middle of building this hope chest out of cherry. It's coming out really nice. It'll all keep me busy for a while, even if the bank job doesn't last too long."

"You can't be hurting for cash, Dare. We haven't been laid off from a job since... what, November?"

"Yeah."

"...and you live like a monk or something. It's bizarre and sad. And work is not a substitute for pussy."

Darrek gives him a disapproving glare, and bites the end off of a fry. "I just like to be busy."

Kyle's face slowly goes blank, and he nurses his beer, gradually paying less and less attention to things as he continues to fight the need to release into his pants in the middle of the bar. Part of him feels a little guilty for ignoring Darrek, but, then, he's not aware that Darrek is ignoring him right back. They sit in silence for a while, eating and drinking, lost in their own thoughts.

"What did you do to that poor kid?" Gabriel asks, watching Kyle make his way back to the table.

"Oh, not much. A little denial, and a little vibrating ring around his pecker. He loves me. You want one? I have extras," Ben offers.

"You just carry vibrating cock rings around in your pocket?" Gabriel laughs.

"You don't?" Ben asks, feigning shock. "Gotta be prepared. Found out about your boy, by the way. My little *pet* is the one that gave Darrek our number, but failed to mention the details about what we do or that he's a client there already. *Or* the fact that he's totally hot for him. Better make your move, Gabey, before someone else gets there first."

Gabriel, the picture of unhappiness, grunts and keeps staring at Darrek.

"Well? What the hell are you waiting for, an engraved invitation?" Ben asks him.

"Something like that," he mutters sadly, and waves over the waitress for another beer.

Darrek is too distracted by his musings about whether or not he's capable of picking up the phone and calling Gabriel to notice that the man in question is less than twenty feet away and staring right at him. It also doesn't help that Kyle has shifted to the side and is doing everything in his power to distract Darrek from looking in the direction of the table where *his* Master is also currently seated and watching them as well. Between Kyle's raging boner and Darrek's forlorn demeanor, they don't stay at the bar longer than it takes to finish their drinks and food.

Ben gives Gabriel hell for not getting up and saying something to Darrek, but in the end, Gabriel is too determined to let Darrek make the next move to do anything himself. The rest of the evening is filled with nothing but heaps of denial and frustration for all parties involved.

"I can't do this. I can't. It's crazy. What do I even *say* to him? I could barely even speak last time I was so nervous. He just... *does* stuff to me. Well, I guess that goes without sayin', but, you know what I mean, right girl? He's different than anyone I've ever met in my life. My tongue gets all tied up in knots and I feel like an idiot. Am I an idiot? Should I just forget it?"

He looks down at Sierra, his golden retriever, her big brown eyes peering up supportively at him. She licks the back of his hand and he sighs, scratching behind her ear.

"I'm sorry, sweetie. I haven't been much fun lately, have I?" he tells her, then realizes that he can't do this. He can't even *attempt* to call Gabriel with a captive audience staring at him, so he says, "C'mere, girl. Good girl. Wanna go outside for a minute? Yeah? There ya go..." and lets her out the back door. She runs out and chases after a rogue squirrel, exploring the bounds of the large, fenced-in yard.

Darrek goes back to the couch and picks up his phone, running his fingers over the tiny buttons.

He can practically feel Gabriel's lips closing over his throat, the point of his tongue licking over his nipple, his purposeful hands sending shockwaves of glorious pain and heartbreaking pleasure shooting through him, his cock pounding mercilessly into his ass. But he also remembers the way Gabriel had so quickly relented when he'd used the safeword, the gentle way he'd touched him to calm him down, the way he'd brushed a fingertip over his lip and told him how good he was.

Gabriel.

He'd taken such good care of him. He'd made Darrek so happy.

Darrek quickly presses the small buttons, dialing Gabriel's number with thick fingers and shaking, clumsy hands.

It starts to ring.

"Yeah?" he hears.

"Uh... this is... um. Well, this is... uh... Darrek. Is this... is this Gabriel?"

"Darrek..." Gabriel says, and Darrek has a moment where he just prays that he doesn't have to explain *which* Darrek he is and how he knows Gabriel.

"Hi, Darrek. Didn't think you were going to call. I'm glad you did."

Darrek lets out a long breath and tries to relax.

Gabriel hears it, can sense Darrek's nerves over the phone, even with the shitty connection.

"Can I see you, Darrek?" he asks, but there's a hint of a demand there—an insistency.

"Yes. Yes, you can see me, M... Ga-Gabriel," he says, and it's almost like he's there already, making him beg and turning him inside out. "Please... I'd... I'd like that."

"Can I see you *today*?"

"Uh... sure? Yes. I... um... I was going to do some work, but...."

"Where do you work?"

"At home. Well, today I'm working at home. In my garage...."

"I'll meet you there. What's your address?"

Darrek recites it to him, and gives him simple directions.

"Perfect. See you soon," Gabriel says with a smile then hangs up.

Darrek stares at the phone in his hands, and realizes that they hadn't discussed a time.

He groans then looks wildly around the space he stands in. The house is clean and neat, thankfully. He's a little compulsive about keeping it that way, but worries briefly what Gabriel will think of it, whether he'll find it too plain and simple. Then he looks down at what he's wearing, beat-up old jeans and a tank top, since he was about to get started on finishing the hope chest.

He considers going to change into something else, but if he's going to be working, and try to get anything accomplished that day, he's not about to ruin one of his nicer outfits. Plus, Gabriel's expecting him to be *working*, not sitting around in a suit, waiting for him to arrive like it's a date or something.

Oh god.

Oh GOD.

Somehow he has managed to avoid realizing what he has been doing, what he has done, until that very moment. It hadn't hit him. Of all things, it was vaguely wondering if he'd made a date or not that has finally flipped the switch of his epiphany.

Darrek's body reacts before his brain can catch up. His gut churns. Bile chases up his throat. He flushes burning hot with a wave of self-consciousness one moment then, too fast, terror drains the blood right out of him, leaving him freezing. Jitters start to shake him, subtly at first but growing in strength as the panic blossoms and he realizes that, without being fully cognizant of the ramifications, he has gotten himself intimately involved with someone of his own gender. Heat bakes from his face, making the skin feel too tight. He rakes his fingers back through his hair and they're like ice.

Scanning the empty house, needing an anchor, needing focus as his world threatens to upend itself, he sees his truck through the front window, parked in the driveway. His Tundra; it's what brought him to Gabriel the one and only time they were together. It's Darrek's physical link to the experience. He stares at it as it reminds him of all the obscene ways his body ached and throbbed after meeting Gabriel.

Because it was the idea of having made a date that began his 'aha' moment, he comes back to that, fixating on it. Did he just make a date? Is he about to have a *date* with another *man?* Or did he simply invite a man over to have sex with him... again?

He had sex with a man.

In another universe far away, where things make sense and all is normal, Sierra barks. The sound manages to carry to him on the wind. The gust whistles through the house, transforming something as harmless as the voice of his beloved pet into human voices instead—those of his family and his friends—judging him.

All are disgusted. All are horrified.

Squeezing his eyes shut against their imagined scorn, Darrek pushes them away, telling himself they aren't real, that it's all in his mind. They don't matter. And Darrek has had plenty of practice at tuning out other's opinions, real or imagined.

Once more it is quiet. The wind ceases to blow and all he's left with are his own ceaselessly revolving thoughts.

He has invited Gabriel to his home.

Gabriel.

Another cold shiver races under his skin, tightening his scalp, making his legs feel unsteady.

He has just invited this man to his home. For a date.

His train of thought abruptly derails, arguing from both sides—pro and con, shock and acceptance.

Why does it even matter if it's a 'date' or not? Hell, he's already had sex with Gabriel. He's submitted to the man in every sense. Shouldn't that make this easier, since they've already gotten that part over with?

He had *sex* with *Gabriel.*

Reflexively, at the memory of penetration, his sphincter clenches shut. And it all boils down to this: Darrek has just invited to his home a man that's already fucked him into unconsciousness once. And there are just so many red flags in that sentence alone, that his head starts to spin.

"What am I doing?" he asks no one in particular, now that even his dog is no longer present to talk to. The sound of his voice echoing in the empty house, the undiluted fear in it makes him even more nauseous. "What the hell did I just do?"

As Darrek works, ears filled with the sound of scratching and scraping, with the static-laced hiss of the music blaring from the old radio nearby, his hands busy, his mind wandering, Darrek figures it out. The shock-induced queasiness has passed. It's not about being straight or being gay. It's not about the mechanics of getting off, or who is penetrating whom in the process. That's all surface, and nothing more.

Disappointment. That's the key. That's the reason. That's the answer to his question regarding *why* he submitted to Gabriel, why he called Gabriel's personal number rather than putting the whole experience behind him and moving on.

He's sick of disappointing people. Darrek is sick to death of not being good enough, not giving enough, seeing that look hiding in someone else's eyes because of something he's done, or *not* done.

Not good enough. That's what he's always been to the people that have really mattered. He's tried to play the game, to play the part and do what he thought was the right thing to do. He tried so very hard. But then they changed the rules on him, and didn't bother to tell him, and he was left with nothing. Nothing but that small sneer and mocking smile.

But with Gabriel, Darrek gives all he has. Gabriel pushes him to the edge, to the boundaries of tolerance and then *further,* but it's okay. Because afterward, Gabriel is *proud* of him. His Master tells him he's *good.* He's *good enough* in that moment—the control, the decisions, taken right out of his hands. He is just left to feel and react and take it.

He can take it. He can take it all. That was never the problem.

What does it matter that Gabriel is a man, when he manages to give Darrek more than any woman ever has? The force between them, as well as the reward, is beyond that, beyond male or female. It's about trust and power, reward and punishment. Simple. Primal.

Darrek wants to trust someone that much. He wants to trust Gabriel, his *Master,* to take care of him, to be proud of him. That's all that matters.

Chapter 6
Work-worn and Wanton

Gabriel pulls up to the driveway, seeing the small, hand-carved sign beside it that reads 'Grealey Carpentry'. He parks on the road in front of the house. It's small, the house—incredibly small, considering the size of the man that lives there. The garage beside it is almost twice as big as the residence itself. There's a fence running along the border of the property, and a golden-brown, medium-sized dog inside it, running around in the distance. If he strains his ears, as he gets out of his SUV, he can just about hear the sound of a radio playing in the garage. He follows the sound of the music, feeling the mid-day sun warm the exposed skin of his arms and neck. It's fairly hot out, for March, and Gabriel muses that the confined space of the garage must be even hotter.

He had been surprised but relieved to get the call from Darrek that morning. It's Sunday, and he was at home with Trace, not doing much of anything—sitting on the front porch with his coffee and listening to his housemate tinker with his beloved classic Chevy. It's where Trace usually is, when he isn't busy doing something else.

It must have taken a lot of guts for Darrek to pick up the phone and call him. But it was necessary for Gabriel to let Darrek be the one to make the call. He has to be sure that Darrek really wants this, and isn't just obeying his orders blindly. Darrek could very easily have just not called, not scheduled any more sessions with him, and that would have been the end of things.

But he didn't. He called. Darrek wants this too.

Smiling widely, he walks up the driveway, and around to the side door of Darrek's garage.

He sees Darrek at a workbench, a tool in hand. Gabriel can't see it clearly, but it looks like it might be an awl. Darrek is using it to dig carefully at the surface of the box in front of him. Skin shiny with sweat, his sleeveless shirt sticking to his back, his jeans dirty and ripped, worn thin from hard use and hanging low on his narrow hips, Darrek doesn't see him standing there. The goggles protecting his eyes might be one reason, because of the way that they narrow his field of vision.

Gabriel watches, the corners of his lips turned up in an eager smile, as Darrek's biceps flex and contract with the movements of his hands over the wood. He flips the hair out of his eyes and shifts his stance, his shirt pulling up a little and showing off the small dimples in his lower back, just above his ass. Darrek runs a thumb over the place on the box's lid where he's carving away thin slivers, and Gabriel notices just how incredibly *big* Darrek's hands are. He thinks of how callused and rough they must be, how they would feel, touching his body, gripping his ass or stroking his cock.

Knowing that it would be bad if he startled Darrek while he has a sharp tool in his hands, Gabriel waits patiently. Licking over his lips, he imagines twisting his fingers in that sweaty, long hair, pulling it hard to expose the thick, long neck of his as he bends Darrek over the bench and fucks him until he's screaming.

As the fantasy becomes more and more vivid in his mind, and he can almost taste the salty moisture on Darrek's skin, can hear the deep thunderous groan in his chest as Gabriel violates his body deeper and deeper and deeper, he decides he can't wait anymore.

Moving carefully and soundlessly across the space, he snakes a hand, unnoticed, around Darrek's waist, and quickly and tightly grips the wrist of the hand holding the scratch awl, preventing Darrek from slipping with it and accidentally hurting himself.

Darrek cries out, beyond startled, and feels his heart leap up into his throat.

"*Oh Jesus Christ,*" he gasps, as his heart pounds against his ribcage. He pulls off the goggles and rubs the back of his left arm over his eyes.

"Nope, just me," Gabriel grins, softening his firm hold on Darrek's arm and running his hand up Darrek's bulging forearm, up the sides of his biceps and triceps, through the light sheen of perspiration. Closing his lips over the tight, tan skin of Darrek's shoulder in a kiss, Gabriel sucks lightly, tasting him with a small moan. His other hand winds around Darrek's waist, his fingers dipping under the waistband, as he growls "You look so good like this—dirty and sweaty and good *god* your *hands*, Darrek. I was watching you from the doorway. I could watch you all day, but then I just wanted to bend your ass over and fuck the hell out of it. I wanted it so bad I could taste it. Would you let me? Would you let me fuck you like that?"

Darrek moans and presses back into Gabriel. "Mmm... Yeah.... Yes."

Swallowing his own groan of desire, Gabriel next presses his lips to the side of Darrek's neck. He pushes his hand into Darrek's pants and grunts against his skin. Darrek's words have gone straight to Gabriel's cock, filling it, and all at once he's as hard as the steel tool in Darrek's hand.

"Okay... okay..." Gabriel whispers, breathing him in, his thumb and forefinger popping open Darrek's fly and then closing around Darrek's cock, easing it free of his pants. He tugs the jeans and boxers down as he circles and squeezes the thick, hot length of him.

Quickly spitting into his free hand, he rubs the moisture into Darrek's hole, his fingers finding it instantly. Darrek trembles in his arms and shifts his feet wider. Just a second earlier, he was lost in concentration as he carved the lid to the hope chest, and now he's got his pants down with Gabriel's fingers rubbing spit into his ass.

"Good, good, yeah... spread your legs nice and wide. Yeah, like that. Now bend over. Wanna see that pretty ass."

Releasing Darrek's cock, now that it's full and heavy, Gabriel watches it bob and twitch with need. He can see Darrek's skin flush with excitement and nerves. But something's wrong. Something is off here, and it gives him pause.

Gabriel's hand stills, and he pulls it away from Darrek's entrance then steps back, questioning himself.

Darrek looks back over his shoulder, ready and willing, eyes dark with lust. He sees Gabriel looking over at him, his face set and hard, but he's too far away, he's... oh god. He's *changing his mind.*

"Please. Gabriel, *please...*" Darrek begs, because if this doesn't happen, if he doesn't feel Gabriel inside of him *right now*, ending all uncertainty, he'll die. "What do you want me to do? I'll do anything... I *need* this. I need you to do this. *Please,* Master."

Then Gabriel is at his back, with one hand gripping his jaw hard enough to bruise, turning his head so that Gabriel can see him more clearly. Forcing two fingers into Darrek's mouth, he commands him, "Suck. Get 'em wet, because in a minute they're going to be up your tight little hole."

Darrek sighs in relief and does as ordered. Then they're gone from his mouth and all at once are being pushed inside his body.

He grunts and blinks, shifting his legs even wider but he can't because his jeans are digging into his thighs. He feels too full and it hurts, but the hurt is good. This is what he wanted. Just this.

Gabriel watches him closely and says, "Keep your hands right in front of you, thumbs touching. If you move them at all, I will punish you and you will *not* like it."

"Yes, sir," Darrek says, moving his hands into position, bracing them against the bench. It's *so much easier* this way. Why is it so much easier this way?

Gabriel works his fingers in Darrek's ass, slow and twisting and pushing deep. The color burns bright on Darrek's cheeks as the feeling of violation, of being *used* washes over him.

"You're blushing," Gabriel tells him. "Do you like the feeling of my fingers up your ass?"

Turning his face away, he says quietly, "Yes, sir."

"No. Look at me. *Look at me*!" He punctuates the command with a hard slap of his open palm to the underside of Darrek's dick. Darrek grunts in pain and tries to tuck his hips back.

Breathing heavily through his nose, he turns his face to the side and glances back at Gabriel through thick lashes.

"That's better. I have to say, though, I'm a little surprised that you begged me for this—that you begged to be *fucked*. You're turning into quite the cock slut."

Darrek bites at the insides of his cheeks, wanting to respond, but not knowing if it's allowed. A third finger presses inside and it hurts again, his nose crinkles up at the feeling and his breath catches once in his throat, his inner muscles tensing up.

"Relax. You *do* want this, don't you? You want to get fucked?"

"Just... just you. Just you. Only... only for you..." Darrek confesses and then the words won't come anymore. He closes his eyes against the world, and waits to see if he'll be punished for it. He's not even breathing.

A single tear leaks from the corner of his eye and he doesn't brush it away.

"What? What did you say?"

Sucking in a breath, he hisses, "Only for you, Gabriel. I would only give this to you."

It's true. Darrek doesn't even realize until it's said, but it's true. Trust is a fragile thing, but he has it here, now. Only Gabriel. Only for Gabriel.

Why? Is the question that sits on the tip of Gabriel's tongue, unasked. He chokes on it.

Just acting, just reacting, he's all at once placing a soft kiss on Darrek's lips, capturing them over his shoulder. It's soft and sweet, the perfect counter to everything else that's happening.

Darrek whines a little, more tears springing free, but he fights through them, needing to feel every part of the kiss, to burn into his memory the loving feel of Gabriel's lips on his.

And then the kiss is over. Gabriel's hand is wrapped around his neck, around his throat, and Gabriel's dick is pushing into his body, sheathing in the clenching heat of him. Darrek groans in satisfaction, at the burn as his body fights to accommodate the intrusion.

Gabriel's hand grips tighter to his throat, and it's so fucking good. He sucks in a breath and holds it as Gabriel restricts his air.

With a hard twitch of his hips, Gabriel forces in the rest of the way and savors the sharp mewl of pain that Darrek chokes down.

"Does it hurt, my beautiful slave?" he asks, scraping his teeth over the skin just under and behind Darrek's ear.

"Not enough," he rasps out.

"Oh *fuck...*" Gabriel moans. He pulls his hips back, tugging mostly free of Darrek's body, the head of his dick catching, and slams back in as hard as he can. It jolts Darrek forward, and his hands grip white-knuckle-tight at the workbench. Gabriel does it again and then again, and he can *see* that it hurts. The veins are standing out on Darrek's neck and his mouth opens, trying to gulp down air, but Gabriel tightens his hand on Darrek's throat, restricts his air even more.

It continues that way, as he pounds harder and harder into Darrek, every single muscle in his body knotting up as he tries to absorb the shock and force of it. His mouth works too, around the grip at his throat, his eyes still leaking tears, but now from the burn in his lungs and the feeling like he's being split open by Gabriel's cock.

The way he's clenching all of his muscles makes it far too good for Gabriel though, and he comes with a rough yell, filling the condom he'd hurriedly rolled on. His hips slap hard against Darrek's bare ass and hold there for a long moment as Gabriel's knees get weak from the force of his orgasm.

He gasps loudly against Darrek's shoulder, and releases his grip at Darrek's neck, seeing the beginnings of faint bruises already appearing. Hoarsely sucking in air, Darrek fights to fill his lungs with blessed oxygen.

Gabriel looks down and sees how huge and red and wet with pre-come Darrek's cock is—how very close he is to release. He touches it lightly, so very lightly, just barely skimming his fingers over it in a gentle tickle. He strokes a thumb feather-light over the head, collecting the wetness there and then bringing it up to Darrek's lips, rubbing his pre-come over them, painting him with it as he still struggles for breath.

Gabriel wants to taste him, *needs* to taste Darrek.

Roughly he turns him around, slams him back against the bench and goes to his knees in front of him. Circling Darrek's balls and the root of his dick with a ruthlessly tight hold, not wanting to allow him to come, Gabriel licks over his lips in anticipation as Darrek whimpers loudly. Gabriel opens wide and closes his mouth around the head of Darrek's cock, his tongue swiping greedily over it, his eyes rolling back in pure pleasure at the flavor of him, at the thick, musky taste. He sucks forcefully at the slick, silky-smooth pink flesh and squeezes his hand even tighter.

"Please! Oh fuck! Gabe-Gabriel! Master, please... oh *Christ...*"

he yells, and then whimpers. He scrabbles for purchase against the workbench as his knees give out, threatening to send him to the floor as well.

Darrek pulls himself back up, but Gabriel just guides his dick back into his throat, along the soft, perfect heat of his tongue and he's still sucking so fucking hard. But Darrek can't come, the hand circling him staving it off, keeping his release at bay.

Taking four hard, deep pulls of Darrek's cock, Gabriel looks up at Darrek. Holding his gaze, he releases his grip and his hand falls away, only to cradle Darrek's balls as they unload and he comes with a shout into Gabriel's mouth.

Once Darrek is spent, Gabriel quickly stands. He grips Darrek's jaw with a firm hand, forcing his mouth open with pressure from his fingers, and seals their lips together.

Darrek grunts, blinking in surprise as Gabriel feeds him his own come, pushing it inside his mouth and chasing the taste of it inside him with an eager tongue.

Gabriel moans deeply as Darrek swallows it down, holding Darrek's face and kissing him almost desperately until they're both gasping and the thick, salty taste is gone. Then the kiss becomes softer, slower, and more careful.

"You okay?" Gabriel asks breathlessly, pulling away and looking into Darrek's half-lidded eyes. "I'm not gonna lose you again, am I?"

"Mmm...I'm...a...I'm oh-okay..." he slurs dizzily, still holding himself up with his vice-like grip on the workbench.

"Really," Gabriel says doubtfully. "Let's go sit you down. Come on. Stay with me, now."

He guides Darrek out of the garage and back to the house.

"You're a carpenter," Gabriel observes, watching Darrek from across the small table. "How very biblical of you."

Darrek takes a sip of his glass of water, and nods. "Yeah, I uh... I like to work with my hands. I like to make things."

"What was that you were working on?"

"Um... a... a hope chest. For a family that lives down the road. They have a little girl, Grace. She's four. I was... I was working on carving her name into the lid, and then I'm going to add some forget-me-nots around it."

Gabriel's heart aches a little at that and he tells him, "You're very good at it—your work. It's a beautiful piece. Listen... Darrek... why did you come to us? Why did you want this? I don't get it. You seem like this wholesome type of guy, a hard worker, honest and sweet. Why would you want to get involved in... in what I do?" Gabriel asks, perplexed. "It doesn't seem to just be a sexual preference with you. It goes deeper than that, doesn't it? You know, I've found, over the years, that some of the people I deal with on a regular basis, through my job, are there because they're lacking something in their lives that they wouldn't be able to get without dominating or submitting. Sometimes there are even darker reasons behind it. They're there because they're having trouble coping with something and the only way they can get past it, the only way for them to be free is to lose themselves in these roles. They're, uh, *troubled*. So I guess I'm trying to figure out what your motives are. Are you troubled, Darrek?"

Darrek smiles but it's mask-like, unreadable, as he says, "You trying to scare me off?"

"Maybe."

"I don't know..." Darrek sighs. "Seemed like it'd be a good time. I was curious. That's all."

"I'm sorry, but I'm not buying it. That might be what you told yourself, but that can't be the whole reason."

"Why do you care? What does it matter? I *belong to you*, Gabriel. I'm yours. I know that now."

Gabriel frowns.

"Fair enough," he says. Reaching across the table, he takes hold of one of Darrek's hands, turning it palm-up and covering it with his own. It is much bigger in size than his hand and its texture is coarse and tough, just like he imagined.

"'M sorry," Darrek apologizes, trying to pull his hand back. Gabriel doesn't let him. "My... my hands are kind of messed up. They're not real nice anymore. I guess it can't be helped, with the work that I do, but...."

"No, they're amazing. You have great hands. Don't be embarrassed."

"Okay."

As Gabriel rubs small circles in the palm of Darrek's hand with his thumbs, massaging them, he says, "I would like to keep seeing you, in whatever capacity you're okay with."

"I'm okay with everything," he says eagerly, eyes wide and open.

"How do you feel about having a private session, just you and me?"

"Yeah... yes. I'd... I'd like that."

"Good," he says, nodding once.

Standing, Gabriel moves around the table. He pulls Darrek's chair back slightly. Gabriel leans over him. Cupping his chin, he stares into his exotic, orange-brown eyes before claiming his mouth in a deep kiss. He licks Darrek's mouth open then thrusts deeply inside, their tongues searching, slipping and twisting together.

"And how do you feel about *this*?" Gabriel asks, his gray-blue eyes wide and piercing, licking again over Darrek's lips and he can still taste traces of come there, at the edges. "I want you. I want all of you. Not just your body. I want to *know* you."

He places a hand on Darrek's chest, over his heart and says it again. "I want to know *you*."

"I want to know you, too," Darrek admits.

Darrek tentatively places one of his large, work-worn hands against the side of Gabriel's face and uses it to bring him back down into another kiss. And Gabriel allows it. Their lips meet again and this time it's Darrek that presses inside. He kisses Gabriel, and his heart skips a beat at the small sigh Gabriel makes into his mouth. His other hand comes up as well and holds on to Gabriel, showing him *exactly* what he feels.

"Does that answer your question?" Darrek asks breathlessly, brushing his thumbs over the smooth skin on either side of Gabriel's mouth, where dimples appear when he smiles.

"Yes it does," Gabriel grins.

Chapter 7
Dangerous Games

"Sam, don't look at me like that," Gabriel says with a scowl over his shoulder, pouring himself a cup of coffee from the communal pot in the back room of Diadem's offices. They've all just arrived for work and are getting ready to start the day. Sam is having a quick breakfast at the table and reviewing the daily schedule.

"Well, at least you didn't scare him off," she allows, looking at him with folded arms. "You know that I gave him to you because I thought you'd go easy on him. How are we supposed to retain clients when you ride 'em that hard their first time? The poor kid passed out, Gabe! And you knew that he was scared shitless, and that he wasn't really okay with some of that. I'm still shocked as hell that you screwed him. Thank god for the legal waiver or I'd be damn sure he'd sue us."

"Isn't it the whole point to push our clients past their limits?" he squints defensively at her over the mug in his hands. "*My* call, Sam. I'm in charge of him, not you. Are we really going to go through this whole thing again? He's coming back. He'll be here later on today. I didn't scare him off."

Ben enters the room, having just surfaced from the building's lower level, and makes right for the coffee as well.

"You gonna help me out on this one, Gabe?" Ben asks.

"Are we talkin' photography or assist?"

"I don't know. Photography definitely, but maybe both. He's a fighter."

"Sure. Afterwards, though, I have to carve some ginger for later. We have some fresh stuff, right? And some of the minced kind?"

"Oh yeah, hon. We've got plenty," Sam nods. "The slivers and the minced supply are in the back of the top shelf in the fridge. Alyssa made some just last night."

"Newbie?" Ben asks Gabriel.

"Yeah."

"Awesome. Can I watch?"

"No way," Gabriel frowns, pointing a warning finger at Ben. "I promised him a private session."

"Aww, buzz-kill. You going to film it?"

"Only if he wants me to, which I can assure you, he probably does not."

"Oh! I just remembered," Ben says happily, his eyes lighting up with excitement. "My ten o'clock thinks you're hot, and he *loves* that degradation shit. Maybe you'll even get to piss on him!"

Gabriel laughs at Ben's enthusiasm and takes a sip. "'Kay. That's Micah?"

"I guess," Ben shrugs.

"Yeah," Sam agrees, checking the appointment book, "Micah is ten o'clock."

"No problem. I've always wanted to piss on Micah," Gabriel admits, adding thoughtfully, "What does that say about me?"

"That you're fucked-up. But we love you for it, hon," Sam chuckles.

"What do you want tomorrow during your session?" Gabriel had asked Darrek over the phone on Monday afternoon, the day after their encounter in Darrek's garage. Gabriel was working the late shift at work, so he'd just been sitting at home when he had decided to call, and Darrek had been taking a break from his carving work on the hope chest. "Now's the time to ask, because once you get there, you have no say."

"Surprise me," Darrek replied, a happy grin hiding in his eyes.

"*Surprise* you... that's kind of a dangerous thing to say, you know. I can be pretty creative."

"Creative is good. The clothespins were pretty creative, and

I've never had anyone stick something inside my dick before. That was... startling. But fantastic."

"You sure about this, Mr. Homegrown-Carpenter?"

"Tell ya what, if I give you free rein to be 'creative,' will you do something... normal... with me? Let me learn a little about you?"

"Like a date?"

Darrek chuckled softly and scuffed his toe on the carpet.

"What?" Gabriel asked. "What are you laughing about?"

"I can hear you smiling."

"No, you can't," he huffed. "You don't know me that well."

"Yeah, I do. I know you... *biblically*."

"Cute."

Darrek laughed again, more freely.

"I'm not smiling!" Gabriel exclaimed defensively.

"Yeah, you are," Darrek said. "And yeah, like a date. I guess. Is that okay?"

"Sounds good to me. Think if I play my cards right I can get a kiss goodnight afterward?"

"Maybe," Darrek told him, pretending to think about it first, adding in a far-too-smoky and sensual tone, "Why, you wanna kiss me, Gabe?"

"Christ, you're such a flirt," Gabriel laughed. "Yeah, I want to kiss you."

"Where?"

"Hey, who's in charge here?"

"Where do you want to kiss me?" he insisted, his voice deeper than normal, almost husky, almost....

Darrek's breath caught and he made a small needful sound through his parted lips, giving himself away.

Jeans unzipped and cock in hand, Darrek heard a rustling through the phone held carefully between his shoulder and his ear, followed by a pause and a small curse from Gabriel.

"Uh... I uh..." Gabriel said slightly breathlessly. "Wanna... I wanna rip the shirt right off of you, see your amazing, tight-as-fuck chest and suck on your nipples. Suck 'em until they're so hard.... Gentle... at first... just brushing them with my lips... with my tongue... and then my teeth.... Bite down on 'em as hard as you could stand it...

and *pull*...."

"Yeah... good... where else? Where else, Gabe?" he asked breathlessly.

"Mmm... um... right... right on the inside of your thighs... spread you out wide under me... hold your legs open... and then just kiss you right there, real high up... and I wouldn't do any more than that... just... just kiss you... feather-light... and you'd beg me... you'd fucking *beg me* to do more ... oh shit... but I wouldn't... cause I *love* to hear you beg... fucking *love* it...."

"Can I kiss you there?" Darrek asked him, "...Just like... *fuck*... just like that... spread you open and kiss you... kiss your bare thighs... kiss 'em real sweet and soft...."

"Dare... Darrek... *oh Jesus*... I uh... gghh... yeah. Yeah... want that... I...."

Gabriel whimpers and then gasps into the phone as he comes over his fist, and it's different this time. So different. He feels bare—naked. Exposed and vulnerable. Out of control.

Then he hears Darrek grunt hard, almost growl as he comes as well, the image of him kissing Gabriel, legs spread wide and inviting, burned into both of their brains.

Gabriel's hand slides in smooth, wet strokes along his shaft as he pulses and shudders with aftershocks, listening to Darrek orgasm.

"I want that too..." Darrek pants.

"Guess so... from the... from the sounds of it. Um... I'll, uh... I'll see you tomorrow."

"Yeah. See ya. 'M looking forward to it."

"Me too."

Darrek arrives a little early, out of both impatience and nerves alike. Sitting in the waiting room, his legs bounce restlessly. Wringing his hands, he averts his eyes when a man he doesn't know leans against the doorway leading to the back rooms. The man stares at Darrek while sipping from a mug held in his hands.

Sam is sitting behind the desk, papers laid out in front of her. She's pressing buttons on the phone and making notes as she listens to the earpiece. She'd asked Darrek if he wanted to review his consent form and change any of his requests or limitations. He'd declined.

After a long period of silence, with only the scratching of Sam's pen, the clicking of buttons, and the faint blare of music from the lower floor the only sounds, Ben says to Darrek, "I know what your Master's got planned for you today."

Darrek's gaze snaps up to him, buzzed-short hair and neatly trimmed goatee, dressed head-to-toe in black, but the fire, intensity and authority in his eyes causes Darrek to look away almost immediately.

"You're in for a treat. Gonna really enjoy hearing you scream, too. Bet we'll be able to hear you all the way at the back of the building."

Swallowing thickly, Darrek wets his lips and scratches at the knees of his pants.

"Leave the boy alone, Ben. Jesus Christ. Don't be an ass," Sam mutters as she takes notes from the voicemail messages.

"Just giving him something to look forward to," he grins before receding back into the shadows.

As soon as he is called, goes downstairs, and sees Gabriel there waiting for him – sees he's wearing only a pair of low-hanging jeans, just like last time—Darrek's heart starts to hammer away in his chest. It's different as soon as they spot each other. Different from Darrek's first session, different even from when they were together in the garage, different than when they spoke on the phone and Darrek told Gabriel that he wanted to spread his legs and kiss the insides of his thighs.

Darrek bows his head and waits for instruction.

"Clothes off. Feet spread and hands clasped behind your back," Gabriel instructs, folding his arms and watching as Darrek does as told as quickly as he can. "One of my rules, slave, since you will *not* be gagged today, is that whenever I address you and you are permitted to speak and respond to me, you will address me in the proper way, and end every statement or question or scream of anguish with *'sir.'* We clear?"

"Yes, sir."

Then he's standing there, completely naked in the dim light, arms held tightly together behind his back. There are a few candles burning on nearby surfaces, and loud, heavy music, thick with bass, thrums from hidden speakers. A nearby metal table is laid out with a number of things that Darrek keeps trying to sneak looks at. He can't make sense of what the objects are, though, the ones that are *uncovered* at least, since there's a black cloth draped over half of the table, hiding many of the objects from view. But he does recognize the long leather strap with a thick handle that sits near the edge. Darrek is quite familiar with such things. He also stares unabashedly at the black and red bench nearby. The top of it is almost like a table, but padded and set at a slight incline, down away from the kneeler, which is also padded in blood-red leather.

Gabriel follows his gaze and asks, "Ever had your ass spanked, slave?"

Getting hard just from the anticipation, the mere thought of Gabriel spanking him, Darrek tries to remain still and fights back a blush as his cock swells between his spread legs. Gabriel steps closer and runs his fingertips up and down Darrek's shaft. It twitches under the touch, curving up now as he gets more erect. Gabriel's eyes flick over to the table and he quickly grabs something from it, fastening a leather cock ring tight enough around the base of Darrek's dick and balls to make him swallow a groan.

Continuing to get even harder under Gabriel's light, tickling touches, now at the head of his cock, he feels the leather bite into his flesh, and knows that he won't be getting any relief until it's removed.

"Ye-yes, sir," Darrek answers, and it's been a delayed response, being so very distracted by Gabriel's hand playing over him.

"Really? Well, did you like it or was it a punishment when you were spanked?"

"I um..."

Images flash through Darrek's mind, initially of himself as a child, then as a teenager, but those are filled with shame and he tries to block them out.

"Go ahead. Honesty, please," Gabriel says, and he sounds almost uninterested in the offhanded way he says it, "I'll know if you're lying."

He goes to the table and picks up something else Darrek doesn't recognize: a small circle of leather that's wider than the cock ring he already wears, imbedded with silver snaps and a smaller, thinner strap looped over the middle of one end.

"Well, my daddy used to give me a whipping with his belt when I was bad," Darrek admits, watching Gabriel turn the item over in his fingers. "That was a punishment, s-sir. But recently, I... uh... I was with a girl...."

"What was her name?" Gabriel interrupts, stepping close to Darrek and beginning to fit the circle of leather around his balls. Darrek holds his breath for a second as Gabriel closes his fingers around his testicles and tugs them far away from his body in order to get the leather snapped into place above them in the space between his balls and where the soft flesh of his sac meets his body. Once fastened it keeps them stretched out.

"I'm waiting," Gabriel prods.

"B-beth? Beth Ryan, sir."

"Go on."

Ache and discomfort radiates from his crotch, and the words aren't there at first, especially when Gabriel brings the thinner leather strap between the orbs of his stretched-out balls, separating them and snapping the divider into place.

"The... the... the girl—Beth—she was... she was pretty kinky," he says a little breathlessly, thinking now that maybe if he just keeps talking it'll distract him. "She spanked me pretty hard... with her hand, and tied my wrists to the headboard. I got... I got off on it. Then, when she s-saw how hard I was, she r-rode me, while I was tied up... like that. That's why... that's why I c-called. That's why I came here. Well, one of the reasons, at least. S-s-sir."

"You know what that means, don't you, slave?" Gabriel asks, brushing the pad of his thumb over the reddening, sensitive surface of Darrek's balls, from where they're forced out between the leather restraints. He sees Darrek's jaw clench and the small sounds he's swallowing back, the veins standing out in his neck.

"No, sir," he admits.

"That means you got off on it when Daddy spanked you, too," he says simply with a dark twinkle in his eyes.

"No!" Darrek barks, frowning at the insinuation, his breathing coming harder.

"Are you sassin' me, boy?" Gabriel hisses, squinting at him.

"No. I'm sorry," Darrek says quietly after a pause, biting his tongue but still retaining defiance in his eyes.

"I'm sorry, *what*?" Gabriel asks with raised eyebrows and a finger to the shell of his ear.

"I'm sorry, *sir*."

"That's better. I'm going to punish you today, slave. I'm going to spank your ass good and hard—until you can't take it anymore and you've had enough, and then I'm just going to keep going. But since you sassed me, and because of this little *revelation* of yours, you're going to call me *Daddy* while I do it. So today you may call me *Daddy* or *sir*, and nothing else. If you call me something else, like 'Master' or, worse, by my first name, you will be punished, and I have some very special ways to punish you today. Understand?"

"Yes, sir. Thank you," Darrek mutters, color high on his cheeks, eyes lowered.

Gabriel rubs the pad of his thumb over the hardened nub of Darrek's left nipple before closing two fingers around it and rolling it between them as his other hand strokes lightly up Darrek's fully-erect shaft. He says in a whisper to Darrek, "I can't wait to get my hands on you. Get my hands on your ass and slap it and beat it until it turns a nice dark pink, taste the heat of it under my tongue...."

Darrek moans thickly, eyes squeezed shut, but clamps his mouth closed quickly at the display of his lust.

"You like that, boy?" Gabriel asks in a fervent whisper near Darrek's ear, tracing circles around the ridge of his cock with his thumb.

"Yes, Daddy," Darrek breathes in response.

Gabriel squeezes his eyes shut, an image bright and stark flashing in his mind. He wants it, wants it so bad his own dick swells painfully in his jeans, just at the very idea. He almost doesn't say it, though.

Almost.

He steps even closer, so close that for a long, blissful moment, their bodies are touching, Darrek's bound cock pressed between them. Gripping Darrek's ass to keep him there, cupping one hand around the back of Darrek's head and bringing him down a little, Gabriel asks, staring at his slave's mouth as he says it, "Want me to ride your cock like that, Darrek? Want to make me take your thick cock and fuck myself onto you like that *whore* did?"

He rocks his hips forward once, grinding his clothed crotch against Darrek's naked one.

"*Oh fucking Christ...* YES. Yes, please, G... sir."

Gabriel doesn't pull away, but Darrek feels him freeze, still as a statue, before growling out, "No. Say it. Come on! *Say my name.* Tell me you want it. *Tell me*!"

It comes out in a fervent rush of words, "I want it, Gabriel. I want to fuck you. I want to feel my cock in your ass, and watch you ride me like that, ride me so hard, watch you bounce on my dick. I know you'd be so tight, so tight just squeezing around me, so much tighter than any of the girls that I've fucked. And I would come so fucking hard, Gabe. So fucking hard I think I'd die from it."

His Master takes a step back, releasing him, his eyes slipped shut.

Gabriel's breathing is rough and ragged, his cheeks flushed, and when he opens his eyes, they're dark, so dark the irises are almost gone, and the sight of him, his plain desire, takes Darrek's breath away too.

"Thank you... slave," Gabriel nods, going back to the table and its implements.

"Sir? Are you going to punish me for saying that?" he asks nervously.

"Of course I am. But I promise you're going to love it. It's gonna hurt *so fucking good,* baby."

Chapter 8

From Inside Out

Gabriel has exploited people's 'daddy issues' before. It's fairly common, and a reliable way to humble his clients, but there's something about doing it to Darrek that makes Gabriel's stomach clench with guilt and nausea. Especially after Darrek's immediate and emotional protest at the suggestion that he enjoyed the spankings.

Mentally berating himself, hoping that he hasn't just made a tremendous error, Gabriel brings Darrek to the bench and prepares to get started.

Darrek kneels on the padded red leather and feels Gabriel circle his neck with a leather collar. After pulling it tight, but not tight enough to greatly restrict his breathing, his wrists are shackled in thick, black leather cuffs. The small clinking sound of the metal chain being attached first to the back of the collar and then to the cuffs is almost delicate, especially with the careful, skilled way Gabriel's fingers work them.

The chain is tight and short, keeping his wrists together and high up near the middle of his back. Gabriel's hand on his left shoulder guides him, bending him forward over the bench. Because of his height, Darrek feels even more exposed, bent over low, his ass in the air behind him. He gets a glimpse of Gabriel as he moves around the front of the bench and clips the front of his collar directly to a metal ring embedded in the wooden surface, no slack in between. The men lock eyes briefly as Darrek tests the give, finding he can't move much at all, save for his legs. It makes him intensely nervous, even given how obviously erotic it is.

"Leg spreader's next and then we'll be ready to get started," Darrek hears from behind him.

He wonders if it's the same one he wore last time, as it's affixed above his knees, spreading him not quite as wide as before. It must be a shorter bar between his legs this time. The cuffs around his thighs are then attached to the legs of the bench, also without any give.

"Try to move," Gabriel tells him, watching closely. Darrek tries, but can only wiggle slightly. "Good. Very good."

Gabriel takes one of the small, teardrop-shaped weights from the tabletop and hooks it carefully to the metal loop on the end of the leather ball stretcher that he'd attached to Darrek. Releasing it, he sees Darrek try to shift his hips, grunting a little, but he can't move, can't go anywhere, can't even ask what Gabriel just did to him.

"That's one weight," he tells Darrek, running his hand over Darrek's backside. "I have plenty more of them, if I need them."

Bringing down his hand once, hard, and savoring the flinch after it lands, the way that Darrek clenches his ass together at the blow, Gabriel smiles. He begins peppering Darrek's behind with sharp slaps from his hand, one after another without ceasing. Darrek groans, lips parted and soft, eyes half-lidded, cock straining in the air below the table and hips wriggling slightly—both to escape the sting from Gabriel's hand as well as the growing ache from his balls.

Pausing, Gabriel grips the muscle of Darrek's ass, kneading it. Darrek's back muscles tense as he arches upward slightly. The hand falls away, and he braces himself, but when the next smack falls, followed by the second and third and forth, it's in a more uneven, unpredictable rhythm. He can't anticipate the blows, and it makes it that much better. And it just keeps going. Minutes pass, his ass gets redder and redder, his cock leaks pre-come and the pleasure builds.

"Daddy..." he moans softly.

"You like that, boy?" Gabriel smirks.

"Yes, Daddy...."

"Your ass is a nice, even pink right now. But this isn't even really a punishment for you, is it? You're enjoying it too much. So I think we'll play with something new."

Darrek's mind flashes back to the strap he'd seen on the table, but even that wouldn't really be a punishment. He wants it though, wants the strap and begs for it unashamedly.

"Please, Daddy... want that...."

Gabriel laughs and fear blooms in Darrek's gut.

A moment later he's standing behind Darrek. With his index finger, he rubs between Darrek's ass cheeks and teases over his hole, not breaching him, just pressing against it, making little circles around the edge.

Literally shuddering with need, Darrek's cock pulses and jumps, waiting, silently willing Gabriel to do more.

"I have a present for you, my slave. Something I made just for you. Carved it myself. And I'm glad you're nice and tight, didn't want to stretch you open at all or prep you first, because I want you to feel my present as much as possible. Ready?"

"Yes, sir..." he agrees warily.

Gabriel presses the narrow end of the tapered, water-slicked ginger root at Darrek's hole, rubbing it over the area first before slowly, oh-so-slowly pushing it inside.

"Wh-what is that? It... it... it burns... sir... please."

The sensation is dull at first, but it gradually builds in intensity.

"What... shit... oh shit...."

The low heat ignites. It blooms and spreads.

"What the *fuck*!"

It feels like he's being branded, like there's actual fire searing the tissues of his body, growing hotter and hotter without sign of stopping. And this fire is being pushed inside his body, radiating deeper inside his rectum, crawling up his back, reaching down his legs. He whimpers then cries out as the object slips even further inside.

"G-Gabriel, please... I don't... I don't *understand*... It, it hurts. It feels like... Are you... are you burning me? Stop! Please, stop! Master!"

Sighing, Gabriel holds the ginger root in place and takes a second weight from his pocket. He hooks it onto the leash around Darrek's balls then repeatedly flicks a finger at the red, exposed orbs of his testicles.

"What did I tell you before we started?" Gabriel growls.

Darrek sobs, fighting hard at his bonds and writhing on the table and he's right on the edge of saying the safeword when Gabriel explains, "I'm putting a carved piece of ginger root in your ass, slave. It's natural, and safe. The oils are reacting with the sensitive membranes of your anus and rectum, producing the burning feeling. It's all in your head. It's not injuring you at all; it just is very, very intense. I wouldn't do anything that would mark you permanently, and I would ask for your permission before doing something like branding you. Okay?"

The ginger twists and pushes deeper. It's almost all the way inside now. Darrek sobs again, as the fire spreads like lava, tears streaming from his eyes. He grits his teeth stubbornly, spitting angrily out, "Yes, *sir*."

Gabriel twists it again, and pushes it in the rest of the way, until the flared end is snug against the outer ring of Darrek's hole. Keeping it there with a fingertip against it, he runs his other hand soothingly over Darrek's sides and flanks as he cries softly.

"Good. Good boy. I know it hurts."

His hand falls away from the root and he simply caresses Darrek's skin, over the backs of his thighs and the curve of his ass. Darrek relaxes slightly, but he's still trying to twist and buck away from the hurt radiating through his body, inescapable. Gabriel is half-expecting Darrek to say the safeword anyway.

Instead, he spits out, "*Fuck you*, Daddy."

Laughing, Gabriel pulls back his hand and spanks Darrek's ass.

"Oh *fuck*! Oh god-fucking-dammit!" Darrek moans.

"See, when I spank you...." *Slap*. "Like this...." *Slap*. "And the ginger...." *Slap*. "Is in your ass...." *Slap*. "You tense up your inner muscles...." *Slap, slap*. "And it makes it burn even more."

"Daddy, please..." Darrek begs, trying not to tense up, but as Gabriel smacks his behind with more force and frequency, it becomes impossible not to.

"Please, don't, sir... please... take it out. Please take it out, Daddy! It fucking hurts! It...."

Gabriel grins mischievously, biting his lower lip, and closes his fingers around the end of the root. As he pulls it slowly out, Darrek sighs, breathing harshly, chest rising and falling rapidly as he's bent over the table.

Then he just pushes it back in, and starts to fuck him with the root.

"No! Shit! Oh god!" Darrek whines and then growls. He shouts until he doesn't have any air left and then just sucks in a rough breath, holding it, the burning spreading and touching new areas of his body whenever it moves over the sensitive tissue.

Once it's once more buried completely in Darrek's body, Gabriel walks back around to his head, crouching down.

"Thank me," he smiles darkly.

"Thank you, you evil son-of-a-bitch, *sir*," Darrek hisses, face covered in sweat, flushed and still grunting with pain.

"You're welcome. And do you know what the best part is? I'm not even *close* to being done with you yet."

Darrek whimpers and closes his eyes.

"You look magnificent like this, by the way. In so much pain, but your cock hasn't lost interest. Can you feel how hard you are, slave?"

Darrek blinks, realizing all at once that he *is* still painfully hard, and that, inexplicably, he's never needed to come so badly in his life. It doesn't make sense to him, but that doesn't make it any less true.

"Do you want me to let you come?" Gabriel asks.

He responds because he's expected to, but also because he can't help himself. "Yes! Yes, please. Please, sir. I'll be good. But please, *please* let me come, sir."

"Just think of how tight your ass would squeeze that root if I let you come right now... if I jerked you off, strapped to the spanking bench just like this. It would burn so fucking bad, but it wouldn't stop you from coming. Your ass would be *blazing* even as you unloaded onto the floor. Think of it. Could you stand it? Should we find out?"

"Jesus," Darrek moans, letting his head fall forward.

Gabriel stands, stroking his fingers through Darrek's hair as he goes. He picks up the strap and runs it over Darrek's body, around the side of his collared neck, down the length of his arms, over his hips and down his legs to his feet, protruding out from the bench.

Tapping the bottom of Darrek's left foot with it, gently at first, as a warning, Gabriel gets gradually more firm with it before striking the foot hard with the narrow swath of leather. Darrek screams and tries to jerk his foot away. It shocks him, how painful it is, and he doesn't like it *at all*. Gabriel just does it again, though—six soft slaps and then three sharp ones.

Darrek's next scream chokes off as pain explodes in his foot, up his leg and out through his body. It hurts so very much more than being hit on his ass that it startles him into holding his breath, waiting for what's to come.

The strap rubs up the back of his left leg, his calf and then his thigh. It rubs over his balls and he moans, shuddering hard on the surface of the bench, but when it makes its way back down his leg to his foot again, he tries to twist his lower leg away.

"No! Please, sir! Please! Gabriel!"

Sighing, Gabriel hooks a third weight onto the leather attached to Darrek's testicles, causing him to whine shrilly. When he twists on the table, Gabriel orders him firmly, "Stay still!"

A shaky gasp of pure fear erupts from him, but he obeys. After only two warning slaps Gabriel strikes his foot three more times. Darrek jerks hard on the table, bucking and pulling so hard on his collar that he starts to choke himself with it.

"Calm down. Hey, hey! Calm down!" Gabriel says forcefully, running a hand over Darrek's back, wrapping his right hand in one of Darrek's, held in the wrist cuffs.

Darrek grips hard at Gabriel's comforting hand, his long fingers twisting desperately around Gabriel's smaller, smoother ones. Trembling and keening, his chest works as he sobs once loudly before getting it under control and falling quiet.

Hearing the sound of quiet, unintelligible murmuring from Darrek, seeing his breathing speed up even more until he seems almost to be close to hyperventilating, Gabriel sets aside the strap and goes to Darrek's head once more.

Darrek turns his face away from him, as much as he can, when he sees Gabriel crouched in front of him.

He's shaking, his lower lip quivering, and he can't catch his breath as he repeats words too quietly for Gabriel to make out until he is only inches away, "I can't do this. I can't. I can't. I can't do this. I can't."

Gabriel leans in, pressing the side of his face to Darrek's, his lips brushing over the skin.

"Do you trust me?" he asks, brushing his fingers over Darrek's lips.

"Yes, but... it's too much... I need to stop. I *can't*...."

"You can. You can do this. You can do this. You're doing wonderfully, my beautiful slave. I'll take care of you. I promise. It's my *job* to take care of you. Okay?"

"O-okay," Darrek nods, turning a little into Gabriel's touch, chasing his lips as they start to pull away.

"Breathe. Just breathe," Gabriel tells him calmly, looking deeply into his eyes.

"Okay... sir."

Hesitating a second, Gabriel leans in and kisses Darrek's lips once before standing and walking back around the bench.

"Thank you, sir," Darrek murmurs, and he's breathing easier now.

"Ready?"

Darrek nods, unable to speak, and still trying not to tense up. When the strap starts to tap in warning against his ass he sighs, because *that* he can handle even with the ginger root still burning away at his body there.

The first real strike of the leather against the thickest part of his behind hurts, but in a way that Darrek completely enjoys. It's more the reflex to clench up around the homemade butt plug that's the real bitch, so as Gabriel spanks him with the strap, Darrek just focuses on not tensing up. And after a series of approximately eight blows, he's mastered it. The surface of his ass is inflamed though, the blood beating under his skin, angry welts forming that he can't see but knows must be there. When Gabriel's short fingernails scratch over them, he really feels it, feels them, and strains up from the table, arching his back and moaning wantonly.

Gabriel smiles and grabs the end of the ginger root, tugging it slowly free of Darrek's body.

Focusing intently on the sensations, trying to figure out what Gabriel is doing, since he's unable to see, unable to hear much over the din of the music as it switches to a loud, pounding electronica song, Darrek feels the root leave his body, cringing and managing to only gasp and grunt as it slides over new parts of his body on the way. It's rubbed up and down in the crease of his ass, and he grits his teeth, trying to wait it out.

Gabriel hears Darrek breathing in fits and starts, trying to anticipate what's coming next. He sets the root aside and pulls on a latex glove, squirts some lubricant onto his hand, coating it and then fingers at Darrek's entrance.

"Does it burn?" he asks, sliding three lubed fingers inside. He searches out Darrek's prostate and rubs over it.

"Oh *shit*.... Geh... mmm..." Darrek pants, eyes rolling back at the tidal wave of pleasure, and it *does* burn, it burns like the root is still there, buried deep, but at the same time it just... feels... so... *good*.

"What's my name? What is my name *today*, boy?" Gabriel asks, watching Darrek buck his hips, searching for some sort of friction against his dick to find a modicum of relief and getting none.

"D-daddy..." he moans thickly.

"What do you want, boy?"

"Want... wanna *come*... want you to let me come, Daddy...."

"Good. Good boy. I think you liked when I spanked your ass and used the strap on you, didn't you?"

"Yes. Yes, Daddy. I liked it. Fucking loved it."

"Gonna use my cane on you now, boy, and then we're going to do something else. Gonna hit your ass with my cane five times, and it's gonna hurt like a bitch, but I think you can take it. Gonna make your ass *bleed*."

"O-okay, Da-daddy... oh fucking *Christ*..." Darrek whines, undulating in time with Gabriel's strokes over his sweet spot.

Gabriel suspects he could make Darrek come just from doing

that, talking dirty to him while milking his prostate, and makes a mental note to try it out sometime. Withdrawing his hand, he laughs at Darrek's mewl of protest while he peels off the glove and tosses it away. He grabs a short stick from the table and brings it around to Darrek's head, pressing it between his teeth.

"Bite down on that. I'm not kidding. You'll need it."

Soft brown eyes flick up to his and Darrek nods a little in agreement.

He lifts the cane from the table and tests it, a flick of his wrist sending it whistling through the air. It's thin, requiring precise movements, and good aim. He runs it lightly over the inflamed skin of Darrek's behind then between his legs over his balls and cock, both of which are still a very angry red, his shaft slicked now with pre-come. It makes Darrek moan and shift his arms restlessly on the table. Gabriel taps his balls gently with it.

Grunting in protest, Darrek shakes his head vigorously.

Gabriel just laughs and brings the cane back to his ass. He sets it against his target and says, "This is one."

The cane is brought back then whistles through the air again, landing true, right on the thick rounded curve of Darrek's ass, leaving a bright red stripe as it bites through the skin. The effect is instantaneous. Darrek screams around the bit in his mouth and bucks on the table, breathing harshly through his nose.

Once he's settled a bit, Gabriel says, "This is two," and brings it down again. "And three."

It lands a third time, both in different spots as Gabriel varies his target slightly. Darrek is almost delirious with the pain and doesn't stop his muffled shouting even as Gabriel taps the cane twice against where the bottom curve of his ass meets his thighs.

"Four," Gabriel warns, striking the target, and Darrek starts to sob around his gag.

"Five," he says, bringing it down two more times against the backs of Darrek's thighs and then throwing the cane aside. He quickly unlocks the thigh spreader and removes the cuffs around Darrek's thighs. Moving to the side of the bench, he next unlocks the collar, not removing it, just unhooking it from the bench.

Grabbing Darrek's shoulders, Gabriel pulls him upright on his knees and then to his feet.

"Look at me. Hey! Hey! Look at me, slave," Gabriel orders him, as Darrek's eyes roll, unfocused. He takes the bit from his mouth and sets that aside as well.

He slaps the side of Darrek's face a few times, and he finally blinks and looks down at Gabriel.

"Hi. Welcome back," he says sarcastically, unhooking the weights on the ball stretcher before removing that as well, unsnapping it and freeing Darrek's testicles from their prison.

"Ohhhh... thank god," he moans in relief. The wrist cuffs are the next things to be unhooked, and he starts to wonder if they're finished, if this is it for the day.

"We're not done, if you're wondering," Gabriel grins up at him, but letting Darrek flex his arms and shake them out for a second, and then does the same with his legs. He's still adorned with the collar and cuffs, though they aren't fastened to anything, and he's still wearing the cock ring.

"Seriously?" he whines. Adding, "Umm... sir?"

"Seriously," Gabriel replies, and Darrek really doesn't like the look on his face as he takes hold of his dick and *pulls* on it, leading him across the room that way, like his dick is his leash. Making him walk faster than is easy or comfortable, Gabriel leads him up to the wall where there are multiple hooks embedded in the concrete at varying heights.

Guiding Darrek's hands up, he attaches them to the wall by the cuffs, above his head on either side.

"Wondering what I'm going to do to you now?" Gabriel asks with a lopsided grin.

"...yeah, actually I am, sir," Darrek squints down at him, until Gabriel kicks his feet farther apart, putting them at equal heights and eye-to-eye.

"That's better," Gabriel says as he next unsnaps the cock ring and sets it aside on another, smaller table. Darrek's eyes skim over the table perfunctorily until he sees something on it—a pale, very thin sliver of something soaking in a dish of fluid. It's the only thing on the tray. "Well, I'll tell you, since you've been good for me so far today."

He wraps his left hand around Darrek's testicles and starts to squeeze.

"I'm going to insert this very special little piece of ginger root into your urethra. But first... I'm going to let you come, mainly because I need you to be soft when I insert it."

Darrek winces loudly, his stomach cramped up and tight, as his balls are gripped tighter and tighter before Gabriel releases them finally. He sighs heavily. Staring at the thin stick of ginger, panic in his eyes, he's unable to think of anything else until Gabriel's fist closes around his shaft and begins to jack him in a relentless, brutally fast pace.

"G... Ga... oh god... oh my fucking, fucking *god*... oh sh-*shit*.... *SHIT!*"

He shouts as he comes, hot and thick over Gabriel's hand, shuddering, his knees giving out, but he's held up by his wrists until the strength comes back to his legs, and Gabriel's still pumping his cock. Darrek's head leans back against the wall, his eyes closing, just savoring the feeling of Gabriel's hand sliding through the mess of his spunk as he comes back down from his orgasm.

Not stopping even after it's moved past pleasurable and started to become painful, Gabriel squeezes up and down his shaft until he's totally soft and limp in his hand. Darrek winces again and follows the movement of Gabriel's right hand with his eyes as it plucks the matchstick of ginger from the dish. Not hesitating or saying a word, Gabriel presses it at the slit in the head of his dick.

Darrek's opening his mouth to say something in protest, he's not sure *what* exactly, but surely *something*, when it's all at once inside his wet opening and sliding deeply into his cock. And JESUS CHRIST does it burn.

Gabriel slides it in, until only a small bit, enough to grab hold of, is sticking out.

He's not surprised when Darrek starts yelling, and takes a few steps away, grabbing some black tape. He rips off a length of it and seals Darrek's mouth shut with it, quieting him.

Eyes flashing with fear and then anger, Darrek glares at him so Gabriel explains, "If you were going to use the safeword, you would have done it by now. And I don't want to hear your complaining or protests. I just want you to *feel* this."

He pulls out a blindfold from a drawer in the table and secures it over Darrek's eyes next.

"I'm just going to leave you here, your dick on fire from the ginger, and let you really enjoy it. It's been soaking in a solution with some minced ginger root for about twenty-four hours now, and is really very potent. Your ass and your dick are going to burn like this all day and possibly tomorrow too. The effects are very long-lasting."

Darrek pulls on the wrist cuffs and alternately draws one leg up to his body then the other, but it doesn't help at all, of course. He moans and grunts and cries and yells. For a few long minutes he doesn't hear Gabriel, doesn't even feel him nearby.

Then, fingers stroke up his shaft, grasping him just under the ridge of the head and squeezing there, putting pressure on the ginger inside his dick.

Shouting through the tape, Darrek shakes his head as fire blooms and explodes in his loins.

A finger rubs in circles around the head as the squeezing doesn't let up.

Gabriel holds Darrek's dick still, watching him get hugely erect again, and grips the ginger slice between two fingers of his other hand. Slowly, he begins to pull it out, and Darrek arches his hips, going up on his toes and pulling ferociously hard on the wrist cuffs. He's still yelling but it's nothing compared to when Gabriel starts to slide the ginger back inside, and doesn't pull it free like Darrek expects him to.

Once it's back inside, Gabriel steps away again and just watches him for a full ten minutes.

By the end, Darrek's covered in a thick, fresh layer of sweat, and close to hyperventilating again. The ginger is pulled quickly free and the blindfold and tape removed. Darrek doesn't seem to see him though, and when the wrist cuffs are unlocked, he falls to his knees, cupping himself and curling forward.

He's gasping for air, and doesn't look up as he asks in a meek, wrecked, hoarse voice, "May I... may I come, sir?"

"You may, slave."

Darrek half-sighs, half-moans and straightens up, quickly jerking himself off, needing to relieve the aching hard-on. It doesn't take long. After he's unloaded onto his fist and stomach, he collapses forward once more and goes back to cupping himself.

"Come on, Dare, let's get you cleaned up," Gabriel smiles.

Chapter 9

The Devil You Know

"He can't drive himself home; he's still too woozy and shit. I'm going to drop him and come back," Gabriel tells Ben. "I don't have another appointment for an hour and a half anyway."

"Are you two *dating* now?!" Ben gushes.

"Maybe. Shut up," Gabriel scowls.

"You can't date your sub."

"Says who?"

"Me. Sam. Trace. *The world.*"

"Fuck you. I'll be back." Gabriel grabs his keys and heads out of the back office to get Darrek.

"You're pouting."

"Yeah, I'm pouting. My butt is on fire, not to mention the inside of my penis. I want to take a bath in milk or something," he complains, curled up in a ball in the passenger seat of Gabriel's SUV. After a pause he asks, "That wouldn't help, would it?"

Gabriel laughs and says, "I don't know, man. Might be worth a try. I'll drop your truck off later, okay? When Trace and I get off we'll swing by with it."

"So, I think I was very tolerant of the 'creativity' today. I think that means I get a *date* with you," he says, glancing sideways at Gabriel as they drive down his street and approach his house.

"Oh really? Is that what you think?" Gabriel teases.

"Yes. I think I've earned that much, at least. Possibly several thousand sexual favors as well," he continues to pout.

"Yeah? I don't think so. I saw how much that turned you on. You can't honestly tell me you didn't relish every single second of what I did to you today," he says as he pulls into the driveway and cuts the engine.

Darrek gives him an evasive little sideways glance and doesn't respond.

"Is that how we're going to play it?" Gabriel asks. In a flash he's over the center console and straddling Darrek's lap in the passenger seat. He grinds down, rubbing his ass hard enough to hurt on Darrek's sore cock, a wicked smile in his eyes, lips parted and soft as he looks down his nose at Darrek.

"Okay! Yes! Yes, I liked everything. *Everything*. You were right, the pain was good. Really fucking good. I'd do anything for you, Master. Anything..." Darrek moans.

After a second, when Gabriel doesn't leave, and just stays where he is, breathing and watching him, Darrek dares to slip his hand under Gabriel's shirt and rub over smooth skin and the ripples of his abdominal muscles. Then his hands stroke around back his waist and down over the curve of Gabriel's ass, squeezing the firm muscle.

"God, you're beautiful. I'd do anything for you. Anything," Darrek admits. Their lips almost touch and Darrek chases Gabriel's mouth, wanting to kiss him, but Gabriel just pushes him back against the seat with a hand gripped lightly around Darrek's neck, just under his jaw.

"What? Gabe...?"

"Shh..." Gabriel purrs, unsmiling and intent.

He tenses his thigh muscles and rears up, starting to work himself on Darrek's lap in a steady, easy rhythm. He grinds and moves in small circles on Darrek's crotch, his ass perfectly outlined in his jeans, pulled tight with the way he's sitting. Darrek's hands are still on him, and Darrek pushes his cock up against Gabriel on every thrust he makes down onto Darrek's tented pants.

It feels so real, like Darrek is really fucking him, the only thing separating them insignificant layers of clothing, as Gabriel moves in little dips and figure eights with his narrow hips. He's graceful and gorgeous, breathtaking.

Transfixed, Darrek watches, searching Gabriel's haunted eyes, knowing his desire and lust must be painted clearly on his own face. Darrek attempts to lean forward again, wanting to kiss him, but Gabriel's hand tightens more on his throat.

"Please. Please let me," he pleads softly. "Don't you trust me?"

Gabriel stops moving. His hand falls away from Darrek's neck.

"Oh my god. You *don't*. You don't *trust* me," Darrek frowns, looking hurt.

"Darrek... I want to. I want to trust you. That's a lot more than anyone's gotten from me in a long time. Just... give me some time. Please?"

He can see that Darrek wants to escape since his feelings have been bruised, but Gabriel doesn't allow it, and stays firmly seated on his lap.

"Let's have our date," Gabriel says. "Tomorrow night. I'll pick you up. And then we'll... we'll go from there."

"You asked me the other day if I'm troubled. You asked me if that's why I came to you," Darrek asks in a whisper, running his hands gently over Gabriel's back. "Are *you* troubled, Gabriel?"

Gabriel smiles, finally, but it's full of pain.

"Yeah. Yeah, I'm troubled."

His crystal-clear, shining eyes appear to be a richer blue in the shadowy light. They fall closed, and he seems so far away, even though he's sitting right there.

"Do you still want me? Even if... even if I'm really messed up?" Gabriel asks. It's the first time he's seemed fragile to Darrek, and terrifyingly so. "Tell me now if you don't. If it's... a problem."

Darrek pushes forward and claims Gabriel's lips in a kiss.

"Of course I want you. I'm *yours*, remember? We're all messed-up. We're all in pain. It's not going to scare me off if you have issues. It just makes you human," Darrek assures him. "I can handle human."

"So, it's a date?" Gabriel smiles, and this time it's tinged with hope.

"It's a date," Darrek agrees.

Kyle walks out the side door of Darrek's garage, belt sander in hand. He's pulling his car keys from his pocket when he freezes after seeing what's currently happening in the driveway.

It's Darrek, and he's with someone, another *man* whom Kyle doesn't recognize at first. They're standing by the side of a black SUV, and kissing. The sight of Darrek with another man's tongue evidently shoved so far back in his throat—to the point where Kyle is amazed that he's even managing to breathe—is the cause for his initial shock. Never having hinted before that he's even been slightly attracted to another man, it's perplexing enough, but when Kyle sees that it's *Gabriel Hunter* that is kissing his best friend, it makes it even worse.

"Holy fucking shit on a stick," he mutters, nearly dropping the belt sander.

The next thing to hit him is a powerful surge of protectiveness for Darrek, knowing the type of guy that Gabriel is, the cold-hearted bastard that he's always been during Kyle's sessions with Ben.

At first when Gabriel was only handling the photography and technical aspects of the videos and webcasts that he'd been doing for almost half-a-year now as Ben's slave, Kyle had been fairly indifferent to him. It was when Gabriel started to assist once in a while with the torture that Kyle felt he saw who Gabriel *really* was, the sick pleasure he got out of dominating people, the blank, angry look in his eyes while he did it, like he was getting off on other people's misery.

Kyle gets a different vibe from Ben, which is why he's been so devoted to him. Ben always takes care of him, knows what he needs and rewards him greatly for being obedient. And even when Ben is causing him blissfully intense pain and pleasure, he always sees the intent clearly shining in Ben's eyes, the attention that he pays to his slaves, his respect for their boundaries, and the deep, unspoken affection he has for them. Kyle has heard that Gabriel's personal limits and the extent of what he does with his submissives is usually more restrained than with Ben or Trace, but it doesn't even seem to matter in the long run, not when Gabriel seems like such a spiteful, heartless bastard while he's doing it.

Gabriel breaks the kiss and says something quietly to Darrek that Kyle can't hear. Then he gets back in the vehicle and drives away.

When Darrek turns and starts to head to the house, Kyle sees immediately his exaggerated limp, his sickly pallor and the tightness in his expression, speaking clearly of his underlying torment and discomfort. Kyle runs over to him.

"Dare! Dare, are you alright man?" he asks, honestly concerned, setting the tool in his hand aside so that his hands are free to help Darrek up the few steps leading to his front door. Kyle knows what it means, that Darrek has gone to see Gabriel for his professional services. That's not what bothers him. Hell, Kyle's been actively encouraging him to call and do it for the release he knows it could provide him. Gabriel is not who Kyle expected Diadem to pair Darrek with, but it's not Kyle's call to make. That's not what bothers him either. It's the fact that Gabriel was *kissing* him, that Gabriel *brought Darrek home*. It means that things have gotten mixed up, that lines have been crossed, and Kyle doesn't like it one bit.

Darrek freezes when he sees Kyle, guilt washing over his expression at being caught by his best friend in the world, standing in front of his house locking lips with another dude. It doesn't last long. Without any more fight or strength left in him, Darrek sighs heavily, deflating. "Um, Look. I'm really not up for company, man. You borrowing the sander?"

"Yeah... the sander," Kyle says distractedly. "Dare, did you call that number? Did you...?"

"I don't want to talk about it, Kyle. Not right now. I just... I just want to go inside and *rest*. I don't feel so hot..." he mutters, and then blushes when he realizes what he said.

"I'm not... I just want to help. Here, let me get the door open," Kyle says, grabbing the keys from Darrek and using a firm grip on his friend's elbow to get him up the steps and inside. "Sit the hell down. What do you need? What can I do?"

Kyle shuts the door behind them then goes to the kitchen to get a beer or three for Darrek, knowing from personal experience that he's going to need them. He returns with them and sets the bottles on the table near where Darrek is lying carefully down on the couch.

"I just need rest. I'm cool. You don't have to be my nurse, dude," Darrek mutters, shifting with a grimace.

After a brief but admittedly intensely psychotic urge to brush the hair out of Darrek's eyes, to kiss his pouting mouth, Kyle instead hands Darrek the TV remote. Worrying at his lower lip, Kyle runs a hand back through his hair, saying, "You look like shit. I'm just... worried about you. Who was that guy that I saw you with? I saw you two kissing, Darrek. Since when do you kiss *guys*?"

"I don't need your permission to live my life," Darrek tells him defensively, unable to meet Kyle's searching gaze.

"I'm not judging! I'm not! I swear. It's just kind of new for you, to say the least. Are you... are you, like, *dating* him?"

Darrek turns away and turns on the television.

"Kind of. Yeah," he mutters, flipping through channels rapidly before throwing the remote aside and rubbing a hand over his eyes. "Fine. I, I like him. He likes me. It's not... it doesn't have anything to do with the fact that he's a *guy*, it's just... it's about how we *are* together. I don't go around kissing guys. I just kiss Gabriel."

"His name is Gabriel?" Kyle asks quietly.

"Yeah."

"And you like him."

"Yeah."

"Is he a douchebag?"

"Do you think I'd like him if he were a douchebag?"

"Well, you like me. I can be a douchebag sometimes," Kyle allows.

"I don't like you the way that I like Gabriel. And neither of you are douchebags. He's... he just gets me. Look, I'm not really comfortable talking about this with you."

"We talk about chicks all the time, man. Same thing," Kyle frowns. "We talked about Beth, about Sara. You can trust me. I think I've proven that to you by now."

"Fair enough."

"He gets you, huh?"

"Yeah. He does."

"If he hurts you ... I mean *really* hurts you, I swear to god...."

"Gonna protect me?" Darrek smiles.

"Hell-fucking-yes. I know how you are, you're too goddamned forgiving of the assholes in the world. You let people do shit to you that they have no right doing. Just promise me that you'll stand up for yourself and what you want. What *YOU* want, Darrek."

"I want Gabriel."

The blood slowly drains from Kyle's face as he fully realizes what he's gotten his best friend in the world involved in. The combination of Darrek's issues from his past, his baffling tolerance of secretly cruel-hearted people, the way that he lets people in all the way before bothering to check if they have his best interests at heart, all melded in the worst ways when he encountered Gabriel. Kyle doesn't trust Gabriel with Darrek. Not on the level of a loved-one. In the dungeon, perhaps, but not in life. Not in his bedroom and as a lover.

"Please, promise me that you will *not* let this guy fuck you over," Kyle pleads. "Just tell me you're going to ask the questions that need to be asked and protect yourself. Please."

"Okay. I promise," Darrek frowns. "What's this all about? Is there something you're not telling me here?"

Kyle grabs one of the beers that Darrek hasn't touched, let alone looked at, and pops the cap off on his belt before handing it right to Darrek.

"Nah, man. Just, I can see that you got major shit happening here. You're dating a *dude,* for Christ's sake. You come home looking like you've literally been through hell. I'm just concerned. I care about you, you know that, right?"

Darrek smiles, turning the bottle in his hands.

"Yeah, I know that. Thanks."

"No problem," Kyle tells him. "You good or do you need me to stick around?"

"I think I'm good."

"Call me if you're not. I'm serious."

"I'm good."

"No, I'm really serious, Dare."

"Okay. You're serious. It's good to know. It's good to have you on my side. You taking the sander?"

"Yeah, I'll bring it back in a day or two. See you in the morning at work, I guess."

"See ya," Darrek says, watching Kyle let himself out, new thoughts swirling restlessly in both of their heads.

Chapter 10

Curtain Closed, Masks Down

Kyle arrives on time, as usual, and goes right past Sam at the front desk with a smile and a hello, heading for the lower level and Ben. As soon as he's down the steps and drops his bag, he can see the set-up on the far end of the room, the swing and the rolling metal cart loaded with paraphernalia. Ben and Gabriel exchange a knowing glance before Ben hurries over to Kyle.

"Hey... hey. No way. No. Varese," Kyle quickly says, reversing a few steps until his back bumps up against the wall near the exit. In the huge space filled with every kind of bizarre furniture, hooks, chains, equipment, tools tacked to the walls, heavy curtains and secret rooms, all he can see is the small table in the circle of light near Gabriel and the camera, the various sized-dildos laid out and ready on it, and in particular the largest one which is almost as big as a man's arm.

"You can't safeword out when we haven't even *started* yet," Ben frowns, planting a hand beside Kyle's head and laying his other hand, fingers splayed, on Kyle's chest.

Kyle is determined though, finding hidden reserves of courage and resilience out of pure fear.

"We talked about this," he says quietly. Gabriel glances over at the pair of them as he readies the camera and checks the web feed. Kyle continues with, "I told you...."

He doesn't finish. Ben knows what he's referring to—the specific arrangement between them, the list of his specified limits in his signed paperwork which sits in the filing cabinet at Sam's desk. The list that states that penetration with anything larger than a small butt plug is not permitted under *any* circumstances during a scene unless clearly stated beforehand by him. He's allowed Ben to fuck him in the past, but only during private sessions, free of any sort of audience. Now Ben is expecting him to get into the swing, spread his legs and get fucked with a variety of sex toys in front of countless online viewers.

"You will be wearing the hood. They won't be able to see who you are. I promise," Ben says very quietly in his ear. "If you do this for me, I will *reward* you greatly. They want it. They want to see the preppy straight boy get fucked by a monster dildo... even if the straight boy's just *pretending* to not be gay. All that matters is that they believe it and pay shitloads of money for it. I'll make it good for you, baby. Stretch you out nice and slow and easy."

Gesturing past him, Kyle murmurs in response, "That... *thing*... is as big as my damn arm... sir. And does *he* have to be here? I thought Trace was going to be doing the camerawork this week."

He makes an effort not to pout, but is fairly sure he doesn't succeed, just from the wicked cat-got-the-canary grin on Ben's face.

"*Trace* is making a house call with one of his clients. Scheduling conflict. Gabriel is just following my orders here, you know that. Ignore him. And there's a reason why it's almost as big as your arm. After I fuck you with it, and your ass is wide open, I'm gonna stick my hand inside you, ease it in *really* slow and then fuck you with my fist. It's the big finish. Didn't want to ruin the surprise, but since you used your safeword just at the *sight* of my toys, I figure it's only fair."

Clearly still wildly unconvinced and very much afraid, Kyle keeps staring at the far end of the room, imagining what's in store for him. Ben decides to change tactics.

"How's your little boyfriend doing? The big one from the bar. Darrek, right? While I pound your ass with those huge fake cocks, why don't you pretend it's *him* fucking you. I'm sure what he's packin' is pretty comparable. And if you're good today, I'll see if I can arrange a double session – us with Darrek and *his* Master," Ben murmurs, ghosting his lips over Kyle's and feeling him inhale a shaky breath. He presses his thigh against Kyle's crotch and says, "Would you like that, kitty?"

He can clearly feel the hard line of Kyle's cock inside his pants, pressed against his leg and chuckles darkly, grinding a little against it, relishing the way Kyle bites hard at his lip and closes his steely blue eyes.

"I think you do," Ben teases.

"Yeah..." Kyle agrees with a longing sigh.

But there's more in Kyle's face besides desire. He's thinking about something, *worrying* about something, letting it make him angry, defiant. Ben knows it's better to get it out than let him hold on to it and bring it with him into the session. Staring hard at Kyle, not missing a thing, Ben asks, "What? Say it."

Kyle lowers his eyes and it comes out in a grumble.

"You know they're dating now?" he says, nodding toward Gabriel.

Figuring Kyle found out somehow from Darrek, and knowing how *he* feels about the whole thing, Ben can only assume Kyle's take on it.

He goads Kyle with, "Jealous?"

"Maybe," Kyle admits, his eyes sharp and clear as they flick up at Ben.

There's a pause where they're both just breathing, standing flush together against the wall, Ben's lips still brushing over Kyle's every so often.

"You wanna date me, Kyle?" Ben asks simply.

It jolts and startles Kyle, for a few reasons, the biggest one being that he can count on one hand the number of times Ben has said his name.

Ben continues with, "You could have me next to you in your bed at night, in the morning, fucking your sweet ass into next week. Giving you orders. Telling you what to do. That sound like a good time to you?"

"That's not fair, sir. You know how I feel about you," Kyle frowns sadly, hurt by the jest.

"How about I make my own house call then? This weekend. Off the books, just you and me."

His thumb brushes in the hollow of Kyle's jaw and he still looks so damn *sad*, it's infuriating.

"I mean it. I'm not dicking you around," Ben insists.

"Then yes. Please. I'd like that, sir," Kyle nods, brightening noticeably but trying to be cool and play it off.

"Okay then. Get your pretty little ass in there," he tells him, spanking him playfully as he goes, watching Kyle pull his shirt off on the way.

Watching Ben and Kyle interact is usually like watching a cat play with a very clever mouse. The cat thinks it's the shit, the tough guy, thinking that he can just wait out the mouse or overpower it, but in the end, the mouse is too quick, too skittish and too driven by pure need and wit. The mouse always wins.

Gabriel has a good feeling that even *they* don't realize this. Ben thinks he has Kyle eating out of his hand, that he's the one in control.

He's not.

It was Kyle's idea to do the live webcam, it's him that winds up giving into everything that Ben throws at him, managing to play it all off like he's the one being taken advantage of, the poor, innocent victim, the ultimate submissive. But really, if you step back and see it from an outsider's point of view, Kyle gets off on the whole thing. He's in the closet to every single person in his life. He needs this, needs Ben, in order to stay sane. So, he figures out a way to get it, to get *Ben*, the ultimate commitment-phobe, to be with him on a regular basis. And Ben, a professional Dom, even gets swindled out of having Kyle pay him for it.

Because of the terms of their agreement, Kyle does not have to pay the usual fee for his sessions because of the services he provides Diadem in the form of his appearances in the streaming videos. He even gets some residuals off of the videos for sale on Diadem's website and the modeling rights attached to the photography he appears in that sometimes runs in a few select pornographic magazines. In the end, Kyle not only gets his sub sessions for free, he gets *paid*, and in the process, tricks Ben into making a commitment to him.

It's the reason why Gabriel walks a harder line with Kyle. He doesn't play his games or take his shit. When Gabriel is in control, or is at least one of the people in control, he doesn't give any leeway. And Kyle *hates* it. Gabriel knows this. He knows that Kyle hates him. He's fine with that.

Gabriel honestly has nothing against Kyle. He seems like a cool guy, someone who gets what he wants, on his terms, and Gabriel respects him for that.

He's not surprised at all when Kyle eventually caves to Ben's plan for the day, even though it's true that Kyle has never before agreed to take part in the kind of sexual torture that they have planned for him. Gabriel overhears enough to witness Kyle getting everything he could want out of the deal: a date with Ben—a *real* date; the glimmer of hope for a double session with Gabriel and Darrek; and the chance to fantasize about Darrek working him over. It all rubs Gabriel the wrong way, especially the parts concerning himself and/or Darrek, but it doesn't matter anyway. Neither he nor Darrek will do anything that they're not both okay with. Whatever it takes, whatever empty promises that are made to get Kyle's ass in the swing so that they can get the show on the road are fine with him.

Kyle is usually unnervingly apt at playing things up for the camera, and giving a damn good show. There's a reason why they've been using him so long. And the same is true today. Kyle screams and bucks and pleads for mercy. He plays the part of the nervous straight boy getting fucked wide open. It's amusing to watch, just for the sake of the nuances in his performance.

It does surprise Gabriel when Kyle goes still, when he gets quiet and stops performing.

This happens a short time after they manage to get the biggest, oversized dildo into Kyle's ass. When Ben steps away and walks around to Kyle's head, Gabriel doesn't need to be asked, he holds the sex toy in place and carefully blocks the shot of the small camera at his back, making sure that no one who happens to be tuning in can see Kyle or Ben for the moment.

With a glance at the camera, seeing that they're not in frame due to where Gabriel is standing, Ben pulls back his hood and then Kyle's hood as well when he doesn't respond to questions or prompts.

Kyle turns his face away when he's uncovered, his face wet with salty tears, eyes red, nose running, and when he opens his mouth to say, "'M fine. Keep going, sir," Ben can see the blood in his mouth and staining his lips. He's obviously been crying for a while.

"Hey, what the hell?" Ben asks, shaken. "You're bleeding."

He grabs a clean towel and dabs at Kyle's mouth with it.

"Bit my tongue. Fucking hurts, you know, and I'm not talking about my tongue," Kyle mumbles, adding, "with all due respect, sir. But I'm fine. Keep going."

"We're taking a break," Ben tells Gabriel. "Cut the feed."

Gabriel doesn't hesitate; he just turns and pushes a few buttons. The light on the camera goes dark.

"I didn't say the safeword, Master," Kyle frowns stubbornly. "I didn't want...."

"Shut up," Ben says sharply. "We're taking a break."

"I'm sorry, sir. Yes, sir."

Gabriel removes the toy with a low groan from Kyle, and Ben helps Kyle sit up a little and drink from a glass of water.

Watching the concerned expression on his friend's face, the way that Ben touches Kyle, soothes him, and wipes away the moisture on his face, Gabriel smiles to himself and starts to pack away the equipment, even before Ben tells him that they're stopping for the day.

When he makes a trip back into the supply closet, he catches a glimpse of Kyle standing next to Ben, and the loving kiss that they share before Ben goes with Kyle to the showers.

Approximately an hour later, Gabriel is getting in his vehicle, ready to drive to Darrek's to pick him up for their date. He feels strange going from a session with Darrek's friend to a date with Darrek when Darrek has no idea what he's been doing. As far as Gabriel knows, Darrek has not been informed about Kyle's involvement in Diadem. Aware that it's not his place to reveal Kyle's secrets though, Gabriel makes a mental note instead to encourage Darrek to talk to the other man and find out the truth on his own.

He glows with happiness at the thought of seeing Darrek, and the promise of getting to know him better. Gabriel has been enraptured with him almost from first sight. Not even sure exactly what it is, Gabriel wonders if perhaps it's his utter confidence and his faithful willingness to abide and trust. There's a purity to Darrek that fascinates him. There are no hidden motives, no expectations. The way that Darrek seems to need whatever Gabriel gives him, and then the sweetness he embodies outside of their sessions, how he can make Gabriel smile and cause his world-weary heart to swell with affection has made Gabriel unable to get Darrek out of his head from morning to night.

That old familiar fear of his has been missing so far in his encounters with Darrek. However, when Gabriel had been on Darrek's lap, showing him how it could be, showing *himself* how it could be, and Darrek tried to kiss him, the alarms had still gone off in Gabriel's head. After a decade and a half, it's something he can't help anymore, the need for distance. Giving himself to Darrek like that, even if it wasn't real, and it was just Gabriel moving against him, like a dance, and allowing Darrek to touch him while he did it, there was no way he could also let Darrek kiss him. That would be letting him in all the way, taking down all the walls. Gabriel is not ready for that.

He knows he needs to explain, that Darrek deserves to know about him, deserves honesty. It's not fair to demand so much and not give back.

But no matter how much Gabriel wants, how much he desires and hopes, when he gets to the intersection of Thistle Way and Route 78, with Darrek's house lying in one direction and his and Trace's house in the other, Gabriel freezes, unable to move. He sits there for possibly as long as ten minutes on the little-used road, engine idling, his foot a lead weight, keeping the brake pedal pressed down to the floor, his hands at ten and two, until a car comes up behind him.

Even then, he can't go, so he pulls off of the road, onto the shoulder and cuts the engine, taking his hands off the wheel.

He's going to be late. Darrek is going to wonder where he is, and Gabriel's phone lies right there on the passenger seat.

He can't touch it.

He wishes he smoked so that he could have a cigarette, wishes he had something strong to drink to give him courage. The void in his heart fills with anger, anger at his past, at how he still lets it all get to him and affect his life. He yells roughly, his low-pitched voice reverberating and filling the SUV.

When Ben rolls by, on his way home after making sure Kyle has gotten on his way with no trouble, he pulls off right beside Gabriel and walks over to his window.

"What the hell? You been sitting here the whole time?" Ben asks.

"I'm an asshole," Gabriel sighs. "I practically begged him to give me a chance, to let me show him that I trust him, and I can't even drive to his damn house."

"Look, I'm not going to start telling you how to live your life, but this shit's been keeping you from being happy for a long fucking time, man. You really want to go home to Trace right now when you could be going to see Darrek and get yourself a piece of that ass?"

"No," he admits sullenly.

"Then go see Darrek. He seems like a decent guy. You gotta trust someone, you know."

Gabriel scowls and smacks the dashboard, venting some of his frustration.

"I'm so fucking mad!" He yells, clutching the wheel in a death-grip, "I just... I wanna *kill* him. I want to drive down there right now and find the bastard and kill him for doing this to me, for making me so goddamned fucked-up. *He* did this! And I just wanna... I just wanna *kill him*!"

"Hey, I offered," Ben says evenly. He's heard all this before from Gabriel, many times. "I know a guy who knows a guy that can take care of it for you. One phone call. That's all it would take."

"No. My problem," Gabriel says resignedly. "But thank you anyway."

"Give me your phone," Ben says, reaching through the window.

Gabriel doesn't react or respond, but keeps staring straight ahead at the road he can't bring himself to go down.

"Give me your phone, asshole! Give it!" Ben barks at him harshly.

"Fine," Gabriel huffs, rolling his eyes and handing it over.

Ben presses a few buttons then places the phone to his ear.

"This Darrek?" he says when the other end is picked up. "This is Gabriel's friend, Ben. He's on his way. There was an emergency at work that he had to help me with, but he'll be there soon. No worries, man. Later."

He hangs up and hands it back to Gabriel.

"Fuck you."

"You're welcome," Ben grins. "Go on. Stop being so dramatic and emotional like a damn girl having her period. Go, Hunter, go! Your boyfriend is waiting for you! He wants you to fuck him! Go! Hurry!"

"...not my boyfriend..." Gabriel grumbles with a slow blush.

"Oh yes he is, he's your *boyfriend,*" Ben laughs. "Stop being an idiot. Go. Or I'll drive you there myself and shove your shiny, perfect ass out of the car and onto the dirt when we get there. Ooh! Think of all the stories I could tell our Darrek about you! Maybe I *should* drive. Get out of the car."

"Kiss my ass, Knox," Gabriel grins, putting the key back in the ignition and shifting into drive.

"With pleasure," he replies, then waves cheerfully from the roadside as Gabriel drives away, flipping him off through the opened window.

Chapter 11
Show Your Hand

Darrek opens the door after hearing the doorbell to find Gabriel standing on the stoop. For a fleeting, strange moment he looks almost like he's lost and doesn't quite know where he is or how he got there. But then it passes; Gabriel is just Gabriel, leaving Darrek to assume he's imagining things.

"Gabriel?" Darrek squints with a smirk.

"I'm a douchebag," Gabriel tells him seriously, a small wrinkle of concern forming between his eyebrows as he says it.

Darrek laughs. It's surprised out of him, but when Gabriel remains grimly apologetic Darrek can't seem to stop.

"What?" Gabriel asks, frowning even more.

"Nothing..." he says, recovering slightly. "Sorry. Just something Kyle said to me.... It's a long story. Why are you a douchebag?"

"I'm so late...."

"For a very important date?" Darrek giggles.

Gabriel rolls his eyes and waits out the fit patiently. He walks past Darrek and sits on the couch. When Darrek gets himself slightly under control, he looks over at Gabriel who happens to be checking his wristwatch and starts laughing again.

"What's so damn funny?!" Gabriel asks, mildly offended.

"I keep picturing you with big white ears and a fuzzy bunny tail. And maybe a little vest so you have somewhere to put your pocket watch," Darrek cries, wiping tears from his cheeks.

"My pocket watch? Are you insane?" Gabriel asks with a quirked eyebrow.

"Have you never seen *Alice in Wonderland*?" Darrek gasps in shock.

"Have you noticed that I'm not a *girl*?" he retorts. "Everyone's calling me a girl today."

"Yes, I've noticed that you're not a girl. It might have occurred to me, what with the lack of breasts and the fact that you've fucked me up the ass with your dick. Twice. And I'll have you know that *boys* like *Alice in Wonderland*, too."

"The gay ones, maybe," Gabriel huffs.

"Hey!" Darrek frowns, crossing his arms over his broad chest. "I was gay after you were gay. You're more gay than me."

"Why are we talking about this?"

"Because you were late...."

"...for a very important date," Gabriel finishes, watching Darrek's giddiness with fascination.

"See! You admit it!" Darrek cries eagerly jabbing a finger in the air at him.

"Admit what?"

"That you are the white rabbit!" he exclaims.

"Have you been drinking?" Gabriel squints, looking him over more closely.

"No... there has been lots of candy though. I eat it compulsively whenever I'm bored. Or nervous. I'm kind of a little buzzed," Darrek admits.

"Obviously."

"So, Ben said there was an emergency at work. Is everything okay?"

"Yeah. Fine," Gabriel tells him, rubbing a hand over the back of his head, the gesture betraying his discomfort and slight lie. "I am sorry, though. I had reservations for us at a restaurant downtown, but it was for, like, a half hour ago. They wouldn't have kept the table this long, and I really wanted to take you somewhere nice."

"Gabe, we don't need to go somewhere fancy. I just wanted to spend time with you, get to talk to you a little. There's a pub a few blocks away. It's nothing special, just a neighborhood place. But we could walk there, and they have decent food. Good beer."

"That sounds great, actually," Gabriel smiles.

On the walk over, Gabriel asks about what Darrek did that day, so Darrek obliges and fills him in, explaining how his crew was framing out the bank's structure, and how he has to get up early to walk the dog before getting over to the job site when it's still near dawn. It allows him to get home around mid-afternoon though, giving him time to work on his other side-projects. He's starting to build a set of Adirondack chairs and bought the lumber for them that afternoon.

Gabriel keeps itching to touch Darrek, to hold his hand or something. He fights the urge. It's clear that Darrek is uncertain of what to do. With his hands shoved into his pockets, shoulders hunched, and talking a mile a minute, it's pretty clear that he's nervous as well. Being that it's his first date with a guy, it's really no surprise that he's mildly discombobulated by it.

They stroll and talk, gazing up at the stars and at the lights twinkling on the porches and through the windows of houses in the rural neighborhood. The air is still, unmoving, but brisk. They welcome it though, as it cools them when their blood starts pumping from both the exercise and anticipation.

Gabriel watches Darrek's face, the way his hair swings into his eyes, and the smile that lights his expression. He has missed that smile when they've been together in session. Darrek never smiles when he's being dominated, and Gabriel realizes that that makes sense, but he craves that gleaming, perfect grin when he doesn't have it.

He misses it.

He misses Darrek.

Wishing he could admit it, that he could just blurt it out in the middle of Darrek's ramblings, and just say, '*I missed you, Darrek. I missed you so much, even though I just saw you yesterday, and now that I have you with me, I want the night not to end. But I also want to not see your face when I tell you more about me, the disappointment or disgust that might appear there, for completely valid reasons.*'

The brighter lights of what seems to be the pub appear in the distance, cars parked in clusters out front, bugs and mosquitoes buzzing and arcing through the air, another sure sign of the approaching spring.

"Wait," Gabriel says suddenly, grabbing Darrek's arm. "Wait. Please, Dare."

Darrek stops and turns to Gabriel with a question in his eyes, but Gabriel just reaches up for Darrek's face, his fingers twining back in his hair and pulling him down. He kisses him softly and unhurriedly.

"What was that for?" Darrek asks, adding, "Not that I'm complaining or anything."

"I wanted to kiss you before we go inside, and before we talk. In case you change your mind about me. And I've needed that kiss all day."

"Really?" Darrek smiles. "You needed me?"

"Yeah," Gabriel sighs, touching Darrek's lips.

"I'm not gonna change my mind, you know."

We'll see about that, Gabriel thinks to himself, and says, "Come on. I'm starving."

They order drinks right away, opting for rum and cokes over beer at Darrek's suggestion. Darrek drinks his too quickly, unable to think of much else besides Kyle's warnings about Gabriel from the previous day and Gabriel admitting, perhaps not in so many words, that he didn't trust Darrek.

It doesn't help that Gabriel looks so good in his tight jeans and button-down white shirt, the top two buttons undone to reveal a swath of his tan chest and the sleeves rolled up to the elbows due to the heat in the thick air of the small, crowded space.

As Darrek finishes off his first drink, Gabriel waves over the waitress for a second while Darrek asks him, "So why 'Diadem,' anyway? Why's it called that?"

"Oh, that was Ben's idea. Once Trace talked him out of wanting to call the business 'Whips and Chains, Incorporated'... no, I swear to God," he adds, laughing softly after Darrek starts giggling. "He had business cards printed and everything with a watermark of a big, swollen, veiny... never mind. What was I saying?"

"Diadem?" Darrek offers with a grin.

"Thank you. So after that, he went in the complete opposite direction, wanting to be all subtle and sly with the name, so that you could talk about the company around anyone, freely, in public, and no one would suspect it was a BDSM business unless they were in the know. I think he got the idea from all the porn he orders, how it comes in those plain boxes in the mail. Diadem is associated with power. It's traditionally a type of crown, so it's like a metal band, an adornment that marks you with distinction, and the word's origin translates as 'to bind across.' Ben was all proud when he told Trace and Sam all of this. Gave a little presentation and everything, or so I've heard. That was before my time. He's not usually one to whip out the ol' dictionary, so...."

Still smiling, Darrek says, "Big improvement over Whips and Chains, Inc."

"Isn't it though?"

"How did you get into this line of work? I've never met anyone who did this kind of thing professionally, or, like, full-time."

"Well..." Gabriel sighs, "I have a bunch of different responsibilities at Diadem. It's kind of like a partnership between the four of us. Ben, Trace and I are like independent contractors working together under the umbrella of the company. Sam runs the business side of things, coordinating shit and all. Alyssa does office work, janitorial stuff, just whatever the hell we need help with. I um... I started out in janitorial, and worked my way up. Ben kind of took me under his wing, training me, showing me what to do, and when he saw how much I love photography, got me involved in doing the glamour shots that we run in magazines sometimes. I do most of the video now, and I'm the webmaster for our site. I have a guy that helps me out on the more complex programming side of things, but I keep it all running."

"I had no idea," Darrek admits. "I haven't even looked at the site yet. You really take video and all of sessions?"

"Yeah. It's another revenue stream. Ben and Trace star in the videos with some select clients who express an interest in it. Some of the videos are duplicated and put up for sale on the site, and others are webcast to our paid subscribers. I... I only really started doing the Dom stuff a few years ago. Had a knack for it I guess, but I have a lot more limits than the others do. I... uh..." Gabriel laughs nervously, taking a long sip of his drink before continuing. "I never... and I mean *never,* had sex with a client during a scene before you. I don't even touch them unless I'm wearing gloves, and even then, not so much. I don't even do hand releases at the end for people, like other Doms do. Never kiss; never touch them with my mouth. But with you... it sounds lame, but I had to taste you. I had to feel you and take you and make you mine. But I need you to know that, Darrek. I don't go around whoring myself out all the time. I'm not that guy. If I had my way, I'd get into mainstream photography or photo journalism instead. That's my dream. But you gotta do what you're good at, I guess. And I'm really fucking good at my job. Or so they tell me."

"But how did you... how did you even *find* Diadem. Why work as a janitor for them, and not for an office company or whatever?" Darrek asks, dragging his finger through the condensation on his glass and the ring of it gathering on the tabletop.

Gabriel sighs, and throws back his drink, his mouth puckering up slightly at the taste as he mentally prepares himself for what he has to say next.

His hand going still on the table, Darrek asks, "What, Gabe? You look freaked."

Gabriel rubs a palm over his mouth, his eyes darting around as he decides. Then he says, "I'm gonna answer, just... just let me... give me a second."

"Okay."

Darrek watches the wheels turn in Gabriel's head, the way he keeps looking at the door, the exit, like he's considering darting through it and out into the night.

Eventually he says quietly, "I left home, or... well, okay more like *ran away* from home when I was seventeen. I hitchhiked north through a few states, and then I kind of was sleeping in a bus station for a little while. I had nowhere to go. I saw in one of the papers lying around that there was a company nearby that was looking for help, and I took a chance. It was Diadem. Sam... she figured out that I was underage. She's pretty fucking sharp, man—watch out for her. But she knew. It was illegal for me to work there, but she also figured out that I was homeless, that I needed the job and a place to live. She gave me that. They all did. Trace let me have the spare room in his house. I had a job. Ben warmed up to me real fast and he's been my best friend ever since. That's how it all started. That's my story."

"My god," Darrek frowns, reaching across the table and taking Gabriel's hand in both of his. "I'm so sorry. Why did you run away like that if you had nowhere to go?"

"Darrek... this isn't... this isn't shit I talk about..." Gabriel tells him, not meeting his eyes, but also not pulling his hand free.

"You can trust me with this. I have bad stuff in my past, too. I'll tell you my sob story if you tell me yours. Promise."

"It's... it's just *stupid*. It's so fucking cliché! It's almost laughable. Fucking pathetic and... I just can't... fine. I'll just say it."

His heart hammers against his ribcage so hard he feels like it's going to break right through the bone, rip through the skin and muscle and fall with a splat onto the worn wooden table between them. Gabriel actually pauses for a second to wait and see if it'll really happen. He can almost see it there, pulsing and bleeding.

"My stepfather molested me. Started when I was fourteen and never stopped. So I left. End of story."

Gabriel wishes desperately for another drink, and when Darrek pushes his closer to Gabriel's side of the table, Gabriel takes it gratefully and downs it in one gulp.

"Thanks," he hisses, "Really needed that."

"I'm glad you told me," Darrek says quietly. "Sorry is too small of a word for what I want to say in response to that."

"You don't have to say anything. That's not why I told you. And anyway, it's done. Past. Explains a lot, though, doesn't it? I'm no psychoanalyst, but I think it makes sense why I enjoy torturing people sexually for a living. They don't get to touch me, but I get to hurt the fuck out of them, and they pay me handsomely for it."

It's quiet between them and Gabriel can feel Darrek looking at him, can feel the words even before he says them, like he's gone suddenly psychic or something.

"May I hug you?" Darrek asks softly. The formality of *sir* or

Master hangs unspoken in the air between them, potent enough that it may very well have been said anyway. And Darrek understands. He knows now why it feels right to have this dynamic between them—the power and distance of Gabriel, the Dominant and Master, and the loyalty, reverence and obedience of himself, the submissive and slave. Gabriel craves the power, needs the distance to survive. Darrek in turn needs to be validated and cared-for.

"Sure," Gabriel nods, head bowed.

Darrek stands, walking around the small table and pulls Gabriel up out of his chair and into a hug. Burying his face in Gabriel's neck, listening to him take a long, shaky breath, Darrek whispers, "I'm sorry, Gabriel. I'm so damn sorry. But thank you for trusting me with that."

Gabriel pulls away and rubs at his eyes with the heels of his hands and says with a sad laugh, "Can we not talk about it anymore? Let's talk about you instead. Why are *you* troubled, Darrek Grealey? Come on, it's sharing and caring hour at the town pub. Lay it all out and we'll drink it away."

Darrek sits back down. The waitress appears again and they order some steak sandwiches and more drinks.

Once she's gone he admits, "Well... okay. It's either a very long story or a very short story. Here's the short version, since you gave me yours: I fell in love. Hard. Found the love of my life—little birds and hearts floating around my head like in those old cartoons when people get hit with cupid's arrow. The day before our wedding I walked in on her fucking my brother."

"Jesus...."

"Oh, and my daddy's a preacher—the worst kind. Beats his kids, tells 'em they're going to hell for being lousy people, *sinners*. Always hated me, and I mean *hated* me. Told me I wasn't man enough for Sara, and that's why she ran off with my brother, Steven. It was *my* fault. I'm the screw up, the disappointment, so it *must've* been my fault, right?" Darrek scratches restlessly at the table, feeling the old anger and shame flood him again. "And hey, he'll be real proud when he finds out I've gone queer. Just added fuel to the fire with that one."

"When did this happen? With Sara?" Gabriel asks, taking

Darrek's hands in his, stilling them and brushing his thumbs soothingly over them.

"June," he mutters.

"June?!" Gabriel exclaims.

"Yeah. But I got the hell out of there right away. Moved close to Kyle. Started working under his foreman. I'd been doing carpentry in my hometown; I just bought my house and set up shop here instead."

"So this, like, *just* happened to you..." Gabriel gasps.

"No. It happened millions of years ago. Another lifetime. Might as well have been, anyway."

Their sandwiches arrive and another round of drinks.

"Good thing we're walking home," Darrek murmurs, grabbing the new, full glass tightly, like a man who's been dying of thirst.

"How pathetic are we? We should go be on Oprah or something, man," Gabriel sighs, shaking his head. Darrek giggles into his drink. "Are you drunk already or is this the sugar rush thing again?"

"Probably drunk. I don't drink much. Daddy didn't allow the 'devil's nectar' in his house. Can't really hold my liquor," Darrek mutters, taking a bite of his sandwich and hoping that it soaks up some of the rum in his stomach.

"But you're so... big," Gabriel squints. "How can you be drunk off of, like, two rum and cokes?"

"Just another example of how pathetic I am, I guess. So, you don't talk to your family at all? Not even your mom? Got any siblings?"

"Nah. And it's better this way. For all of us. But yeah, I've got siblings... somewhere. I'm sure they left home, too. Fuck it," he grumbles, drinking more. "How 'bout you?"

"Mom calls once in a while. Don't talk to Steven anymore. *Obviously*. The prick. Oughta cut his dick off...."

"Listen to the violence from Mr. Homegrown-Carpenter," Gabriel laughs. "I'm shocked."

"Cut your stepdad's dick off too," he squints, pointing a finger. "I can start a collection."

Gabriel laughs harder, his head buzzing with the rum. "Go

right-the-fuck ahead, Dare. But that's what serial killers do, you know. They collect shit. Are you a serial killer?"

"I'm not gonna *kill 'em*, Gabey, I just wanna cut their *dicks* off. You don't *die* from that."

"How do you know?"

"The Discovery Channel told me," Darrek says seriously, like he's conveying a great secret.

Gabriel chuckles, "Man... I gotta start watching cable more."

"You should. You learn things," Darrek tells him earnestly before taking another bite of food.

"Ooh! We could do it with one of those fancy saws you have in the garage!" Gabriel exclaims excitedly. "Those are pretty sharp."

"Gonna help me?" Darrek smiles with a wink, "You could be my accomplice."

Gabriel takes a huge bite of his sandwich and moans around it. He waves it at Darrek and mumbles, "This is an awesome cheese steak!"

"I know!" Darrek agrees, washing down another bite with more rum. "Kyle gets all the credit, though. He discovered them. I never went out much at all until he started dragging me to places like this against my will in an attempt to make me less miserable and get my sorry ass a life."

"He's the one that gave you our number, right?" Gabriel asks, his face losing its smile.

"Yeah."

"Did you tell him you called Diadem? That you've been seeing me?"

"I haven't really told him much," Darrek admits. "I don't know why. I tell him about everything else. He'd probably understand."

"You should talk to him. Seriously. Be honest with him," Gabriel insists.

"You think so?"

"Yes. I do. So will you? Talk to him, I mean...."

"I guess so. Sure," Darrek relents, squinting at Gabriel over his sandwich and trying to figure out the cause of the intense look on his face.

Chapter 12
Pay the Price

By the time they've walked back to Darrek's house, the alcohol has mostly worn off, their drunken giddiness long gone. Darrek opens his door, fitting the key into the lock with Gabriel at his back. The sound of eager dog barking from inside is the only noise in the dark, cold night. As soon as the door is open, Sierra pounces on Darrek with happiness. He scratches behind her ears and hugs her before leading her to the back door and outside into the yard.

Returning to the front door, he sees Gabriel stepping inside and shutting the door behind him.

"Are you... staying?" Darrek asks, watching Gabriel unbutton his shirt slowly, top to bottom. It hypnotizes him as gradually more and more skin is revealed.

"I'm staying," he nods, stepping closer.

Darrek tugs his shirt over his head in a swift, fluid movement, releasing it and letting it fall to the floor as Gabriel gets the last button slipped free of its hole and shrugs the shirt from his shoulders.

His hands restless by his sides, buzzing like electricity is surging through them, Darrek tries to keep them there, and still, as his eyes skim helplessly over Gabriel's chest and arms, hungry, drinking him in.

"Touch me," Gabriel tells him. "It's okay. Go ahead."

"Thank you," he whispers in response, capturing Gabriel's mouth in a kiss and pressing their bodies together, with one hand palming the curve of Gabriel's ass and the other stroking up over his chest, mapping the contours and lines, the firm muscle, the silky-soft skin.

They breathe into each other, moaning softly. As Gabriel kisses him back, pushes deeper, his tongue slipping between parted lips, he guides Darrek back in the direction of the stairs, leading up to the bedroom.

With one hand on the railing, Gabriel murmurs, "Come on."

"Wait. I don't know if I can do this," Darrek confesses breathlessly, his face flushed. "I'm probably an idiot for saying this, but... I think I want it too much. I want *you* too much. It's... it's so much easier when you're making me do it, when it's out of my control and I'm just following orders. To have you... like *this*... I can't go back from this. It changes things...."

"You think I'm going to run out on you like Sara did," Gabriel frowns, kissing him again, simply because he can't help it, he can't *not* be kissing Darrek.

"I have a knack for destructive relationships," he admits. "I know that now. And... I don't want to let myself care about you if you *can't* care about me back. So, if you *can't*... then I think you should go."

Darrek steps backward, up onto the first stair, putting distance between them.

After a long pause filled with fidgeting, his thoughts surging and blaring in his mind, Gabriel responds, laughing sadly. "Honestly, I don't want to care about you, Darrek. I've trained myself not to care about people. Not like *that*... but... god. It's too late. That's... that's why I was late tonight. There *was* no emergency. Ben lied. I lied. I was on my way over here, and I froze. I couldn't go any further at first, and just parked on the side of the road for a full hour because I *do* care about you. I already do! And it scares the fuck out of me! You have no idea... I was so hard on you, so rough and cruel to you during our sessions because I wanted to push you away. I know we joked about it, but I *did* want to scare you away. I wanted you to hate me, to be afraid of me. But it didn't... it didn't fucking *work*! You're too strong, too stubborn, too damn resilient. So, I don't have a choice anymore. Don't you see? I'm fucked! You were supposed to be the one that belonged to *me*. That's the way it works. I call the shots. I make the rules. I keep things in control. I'm not in control anymore. I don't know the rules. Please, make me leave, Darrek.

Tell me to get the fuck out. Tell me I'm a horrible person, that I don't deserve you and your sweetness, that I'm sick and perverted and disgusting. I want you to. Please! Please make me leave, because I *can't.*"

A muscle in his jaw twitches, and he looks up defiantly at Darrek with shining eyes.

Darrek grabs his hand and pulls him up onto the step with him, kissing him.

"Don't do this..." Gabriel begs. "Please... you should be with someone better than me. You're a *good person*. I'm *not* a good person."

"Make love to me. That's what I want. I want you to love me," he whispers against his lips.

Gabriel presses their foreheads together, teeth clenched and swallowing a hiss of pain. Then he hugs Darrek with his arms looped around his neck.

"I don't want to hurt you. I'm, like, infecting your new life with these dark, horrible things. I should go," Gabriel insists. "I'm gonna go."

"You're not going anywhere. My eyes are open, Gabriel. Let's go to bed."

Darrek tugs at his hand as he begins to climb the staircase.

Gabriel doesn't budge.

"You were right," Gabriel says quietly with his feet planted. "This *will* change things."

"Things have already changed. If you feel that way about me, then it's too late to go back to the way things were. This is really happening and it's okay."

"Yeah."

"You know what happens at the end of the movie *Alice in Wonderland*? She has this world build up around her. And it seems good at first—exciting and exotic. But it's not *real*. No matter how good it seems, it's just a daydream and under the surface it's all twisted up anyway. It all falls apart, and she wakes up."

"I'm still not a girl," Gabriel tells him.

"It's a metaphor!" Darrek says, exasperated. "You can't hide from reality forever. Eventually you have to wake up and live. You might even find out that it's not as scary as you thought it'd be."

"So, I went from being a rabbit to being a girl?"

"I'll carry your ass upstairs if I have to. I am bigger than you, you know," he warns.

"Hey, who's in charge here?" Gabriel frowns mock-seriously. "And I'd like to see you try."

"*Nobody's* in charge. That's the whole point. And okay," he shrugs, ducking and grabbing Gabriel's legs, throwing him over his shoulder, ass in the air.

"Put me down, Grealey!" Gabriel yells, swatting at his back. "Darrek! I can fucking *walk*, you know! Okay! I get it! You're strong as an ox. Now put me down!"

"Sorry, Master. Just following orders," he laughs as he carries him up to the bedroom with ease.

It's still very early and close to dawn when Darrek sneaks back into bed wearing only his boxer shorts. He's tired, but not sleepy. Smiling, he savors the aches radiating throughout his body, knowing that Gabriel is the one that put them there and that they are proof of his lover's attentions and affection.

Turning onto his side, he watches Gabriel sleep. He's naked and stretched out on his stomach with only the thin sheet covering him. Darrek watches for a long time, enjoying the vulnerable softness in the delicate, ivory skin of Gabriel's face, and the sight of him with all of his many defenses down.

When he had let Sierra out, Darrek had also brought back something with him, selected and plucked from the untended garden beside the rear entrance of the house. Darrek trails the petals of the violet-colored daisy over the gentle curves of Gabriel's supple lips, over the small cleft in his chin, down over his neck and arm.

Gabriel does not stir; he just twitches his nose when Darrek tickles it with the flower. Darrek chuckles at the reaction. The rays of the sun, filtered through the curtained window, slant and shift as minutes and then hours slip by.

Finally, an uncertain amount of time later, Gabriel sighs and peeks open his eyes.

"Morning!" Darrek grins widely from beside him, biting eagerly at his bottom lip, the points of his gleaming-white teeth pressing small dents in the rosy flesh.

"God. You're a morning person, aren't you?"

Gabriel stretches and groans, rolling onto his left side so that he faces Darrek. Darrek shifts closer and momentarily places an oversized hand on Gabriel's bare hip, brushing long fingers over the silky-smooth, sleep-warmed skin. He had laid the flower aside a while ago, but now he picks it up again and trails it down the center of Gabriel's chest. As it moves lower and skims to the side, over his taut abdomen and the ridge of his hipbone, along his thickly muscled thigh, Gabriel's eyes slip closed.

He tries not to smile as he asks, "Why do you have a flower?"

"I had to get up and let my girl out earlier," Darrek confesses. "I picked this for you from the garden while I was outside. It was there when I bought the place—the garden. I don't have much of a green thumb, so it's kind of gotten overgrown lately. I was tickling you with this. You didn't wake up, though."

"I'm a heavy sleeper, or so I've been told," he replies, suppressing a shiver when Darrek strokes the silken edge of the purple petals across the length of Gabriel's morning erection and down between his legs. "How come I'm naked and you're not?"

"Because I had to go outside and you've been in bed sleeping half the day," Darrek whispers back. "I have to admit, I kind of like it this way."

He captures Gabriel's lips with his, reaching across Gabriel and laying the flower on the nightstand. Using a hand on Gabriel's side, Darrek rolls Gabriel onto his back and straddles him quickly with a slide of his leg. He can see the realization in Gabriel's eyes when he finds himself on the bottom, with Darrek heavily on top of him, trapping him. His lips purse, the amusement in them fading fast and his eyes going wide with a cold flash of panic.

"Darrek...."

"Relax. You can tell me to stop anytime," he assures him, brushing the back of his hand down the side of Gabriel's neck, shifting his hips so that he can better feel the line of Gabriel's dick against his belly, his own member nudging against Gabriel's left hip. "I just want to make you feel good. I never get to see you, or touch you. That's all I want to do. Nothing scary, and no more than that. May I? Please?"

The previous night they'd made love for hours, but it was almost pitch dark the whole time with not a light on throughout the whole second floor at Gabriel's insistence, and even when they had been face-to-face, with Darrek's legs hooked over Gabriel's shoulders, Gabriel had kept Darrek's hands pinned down above his head, unable to touch or do anything but take it.

"Please, Gabe," Darrek asks more softly, brushing a hand over Gabriel's tensed jaw, willing away the mistrust in his eyes.

Gabriel nods, a faint pink flush starting to color his fair cheeks.

Darrek kisses him first, though. Their lips parted, they press together, breathing into one another. The point of Darrek's tongue breaches the gap first, finding the heated softness of Gabriel's. Eyes locked, hands roaming, exploring, Darrek dives down, opening wide and sucking Gabriel's tongue, licking back into the cavern of his mouth, under his tongue, along his teeth. Pulling back, he catches Gabriel's lower lip in a gentle bite and tugs on it with a grin. He's playing with him, trying to tease away the darkness lurking at the back of Gabriel's eyes.

Inching downward, he brushes his mouth down the arcing line of Gabriel's neck, over his collarbone and the slight curve of his heaving chest. Gabriel's breath is coming in rapid gasps, his hands tangling in the cascading waves of Darrek's hair. Moving to one side, Darrek seals his lips around each of his nipples in turn, the left and then the right, licking over the dark, hardening nubs with the flat of his tongue before releasing them and going lower. Kissing a line down the center of his body, between his abdominal muscles, his tongue delves down into Gabriel's navel. Sliding to the right, Darrek scrapes his teeth over the place just above the ridge of his hipbone and glances up at Gabriel's face.

With his arm now slung over his eyes, Gabriel's lips are parted, his chest rising and falling quickly. He gasps and arches up off the bed when Darrek encircles his full, heavy cock with a firm, callused hand. It jumps and swells more under the touch and Gabriel rocks his hips up into Darrek's fist, searching for friction and relief. Darrek can't see his eyes, though. He wants to see them, but they are well-hidden by Gabriel's forearm.

Refocusing his attention, Darrek takes in the sight before him, the thick, curved line of Gabriel's cock, lying up against his belly, the pulsing vein running along the shaft, the soft nest of curls at the base. His mouth watering in anticipation of having Gabriel's cock in his mouth for the first time, Darrek licks over his lips to moisten them, preparing to wrap them around Gabriel's flesh.

That's when he sees it.

And he realizes why Gabriel is hiding his eyes.

"Is this... is this what I think it is?" Darrek asks, his voice sounding strange in his own ears—uneven, lilting and hushed.

He touches the spot in question carefully with the pad of his thumb and Gabriel twists his left leg inward, attempting to turn his hips away and hide.

Darrek can hear Gabriel muttering to himself, too low to make out the words.

"Gabriel?"

Taking Gabriel by the knee, he guides him open so that he's exposed again, his bent legs fallen widely apart, the covers all thrown back. Gabriel lets him, and lies there, motionless, naked, no longer attempting to hide. It's too late for that now. He knows it.

Darrek just stares at the mark, suddenly buffeted by thoughts, reactions and emotions.

"Say something," Darrek rasps.

"This is why I don't let people..." he mumbles, trailing off. Then curses sharply, punching the bed with a closed fist, "*Shit*! Shit, shit, shit!"

Darrek blinks dumbly at him.

"Look, it's not a big deal," Gabriel grunts, marginally recovering himself. "It's been there since I was a kid, okay? I've had it since... forever."

Darrek traces the perfect circle of the scar with his fingertip, the raised, marred skin, about the size of a pencil eraser. It's easy to miss unless you're looking closely, since it sits very close to the base of Gabriel's penis and is partially covered by the soft curls of hair there.

"He did this to you?" Darrek hisses.

"Can't we just forget it? It doesn't matter anymore."

"Someone burned you with a cigarette, Gabriel. Why the fuck would someone burn you here with a cigarette?"

"Because Harry is a sick bastard, that's why. Surprise!" Gabriel says sarcastically and somewhat maliciously. "What, you think a man that enjoys fucking a little boy that's supposed to be his son wouldn't get off on putting a cigarette out on his genitals, too?"

"Hey...."

"I *told*, okay? I told my mom what he did to me. And he found out that I told her, so he was angry. That's all. He was trying to scare me."

"You told her?"

"Yeah, I told her. Of course I told her. I wanted it to stop! I wanted her to help and *believe* me!"

"She didn't *believe you*?" Darrek gasps.

Gabriel loops his other arm over his face as well and his words get harder to hear, even in the perfect silence of the house.

The only thing he can make out is, "...thought I was just jealous of her new husband."

Shifting up the bed, Darrek pulls Gabriel's arms away. He brushes away the wetness around his lover's eyes, the color of storm clouds, teardrops caught in the curls of his dark eyelashes. Cupping Gabriel's face in his hands, he says to him, knowing there are not really words for this, "I'm so sorry. No one should have to suffer that sort of nightmare, least of all a defenseless, innocent child. You deserved better from your parents. That's... the saddest thing I ever heard. No wonder you ran away."

"Yeah..." he murmurs, eyes lowered.

"Your mom never found out what Harry was doing to you?"

"Christ, I hope not! I hope she was just blind and stupid. It's kind of the least horrifying option."

"Did he—did Harry ever... with your siblings?"

"I don't think so. I was kind of his favorite," Gabriel says and then, picking up the flower from the nightstand, spins it between his fingers and asks, "Can we stop talking about it now?"

"Yeah."

Chapter 13
Bared and Burned

They lay together for a while, and Darrek gives Gabriel time—as much time as he needs. Slowly Gabriel seems to refocus on the present instead of the past, and the hand that had been playing over Darrek's body all at once grabs hold of the long, light brown hair streaked with gold at the nape of Darrek's neck and pulls him over for a kiss. Plundering Darrek's mouth, Gabriel guides Darrek's hand down to his re-swelling cock. Darrek takes the hint and strokes Gabriel into hardness.

"Still wanna taste you," he breathes when Gabriel momentarily releases his lips, one of his hands squeezing hard at the rounded, muscular swell of Darrek's ass.

"Do it, then," Gabriel grunts, now thrusting slowly, rhythmically, into Darrek's fist.

"Yeah?"

"Yeah. Do it. Fucking do it."

Wrapping his hands around the tops of each of Darrek's shoulders, Gabriel pushes him down along the length of his body. Then he grabs hold of Darrek's head with both of his hands, watching as Darrek slips an opened hand under his dick, circling the base of it with his thumb and index finger, and guides it to his mouth. Taking it in and sealing his lips under the ridge, he licks experimentally over the silky-smooth pink flesh of the head, salty drops of precome leaking out onto his tongue.

"Come on, Dare," Gabriel groans impatiently, "Don't fucking tease me, just suck my cock. As hard as you can, okay? Remember when I had my fingers in your mouth and down your throat? How you relaxed and opened up for me? Open up just like that."

"Mm-hmm," he hums, his eyes locked to Gabriel's as Gabriel's hands on the sides of his head—tangled in the hair at his temples—guide him down, the length of him sliding back between Darrek's lips, over his tongue and into the perfect glove of his throat, deeper and deeper. There's a moment of mild panic, with Darrek breathing heavily through his nose with nervousness, when his oxygen is cut off and he feels the head of Gabriel's cock lodge in his throat. He fights back a strong urge to buck and gag.

"No, just relax, baby. Just relax and stay nice and open for me," Gabriel croons as Darrek blinks away the wetness gathering at the corners of his eyes. He slowly guides Darrek's mouth back up, Gabriel's reddened dick withdrawing, sliding back out from between Darrek's spit-slick and shiny lips which are still pressed in a tight seal around his throbbing flesh.

"Good. Yeah, just like that," he groans as he feels Darrek give in a little more and Gabriel thrusts back up into his mouth. He doesn't gag this time, so they gradually speed up the pace as Gabriel uses Darrek's mouth, violating it with smooth, tilted thrusts of his hips.

Gabriel stays in control, holding Darrek still as he fucks up into him faster and faster. Groaning loudly, he feels Darrek suck harder and swipe his tongue up over the heated flesh stuffed inside of him whenever it dislodges from his throat and pulls out until the ridge of the head catches at his lips.

Darrek cups Gabriel's balls and rolls them in his hand. He's not even sure Gabriel is consciously aware that Darrek is doing it, perhaps too focused on the other ways he is being stimulated, but his legs begin to open more, almost automatically, as he does. Planting his feet more firmly on the bed, angling his thrusts, Gabriel is spread wide under Darrek.

It makes Darrek think fleetingly of the phone call they'd shared the other day, and his promises to spread Gabriel out, just like this, and kiss him. The hand not braced on the bed moves and caresses the downy, soft curls of hair covering Gabriel's inner thighs.

Gabriel moans long and deep, his head thrown back and eyes squeezed shut as he chases his orgasm.

Acting on instinct alone, Darrek's hand slides up to where

Gabriel's right thigh joins with his body, tracing the curve of his ass. His thumb rubs over the spot just behind Gabriel's balls. It gets a strong reaction from him. Gabriel's breath catches and he makes a swallowed back mewling cry. So Darrek presses harder there, at the small patch of skin, and then rubs down across his clenched hole and up into the crease of his ass. Then back down, finding then slowly circling his opening.

"Dare... Darrek..." he whimpers, the rhythm of his hips' movements faltering and slowing. "*Fuck....*"

As Darrek just teases back and forth over the puckered ring of muscle, Gabriel's entire body vibrates with a shudder. He slams back hard into Darrek's mouth as he loses control. Now the tears are streaming from Darrek's eyes. It becomes harder for him to focus on how he's touching Gabriel as he struggles just to breathe.

He doesn't realize his fingertip is slowly pressing into Gabriel's body until Gabriel cries out brokenly. Darrek freezes and looks quickly up at him. He wants to ask if Gabriel is okay, but with his mouth and throat otherwise occupied, he just has to trust in Gabriel to tell him what to do and when to stop.

Darrek pulls his finger out and away, but Gabriel just growls roughly, "No! Do it. I want you to. Go on. Finger me."

His index finger slides back to the spot, to the opening in Gabriel's body and at first just presses lightly. Eyes locked to Gabriel's face, or at least what he can see of it with the way his head is thrown back and his eyes blurry with tears, Darrek gradually, steadily, pushes it inside.

The walls of Gabriel's body squeeze his dry finger tightly, and he can feel his pulse, the throbbing and fluttering of his muscles as Gabriel attempts to unclench and relax.

Darrek tugs his finger back out until it's freed then pushes right back inside, past the outer ring and in to the last knuckle, crooking his finger and stroking gently over the soft walls lining the cavity of Gabriel's body. Gabriel bucks off the bed, Darrek's finger buried completely inside him and chokes out a jagged, keening cry. His dick is hard as steel on Darrek's tongue, though, and Darrek knows he's close.

"F-faster. Faster..." Gabriel gasps.

Finger-fucking Gabriel rapidly, Darrek hums with pleasure around the flesh filling his mouth. The only sounds in the room—besides the desperate ones currently purring from Gabriel—are slick, wet and obscene. Gabriel's cock, coated thickly with pre-come and saliva, moves in and out between Darrek's now equally wet lips.

"Dare... pull off," he chokes out and guides Darrek's mouth up and off with his hands, his dick slipping free of Darrek's lips, a glistening strand of wetness joining them. Gabriel releases his hold on Darrek's head and instead squeezes up his cock with hard pulls of his hand. Then he's coming, thick jets of spunk spurting from him, moaning brokenly. Darrek catches some of it in his opened mouth as he dips his head, moving to take the cockhead back between his lips. Gabriel keeps stroking up his shaft as Darrek carefully sucks him clean, swallowing down every drop that pulses free, just as his finger keeps working in the clenched vessel of his body. He angles his wrist and tugs his finger in slower movements as Gabriel comes down.

When he's through it, Gabriel's hand falls away. Darrek pulls his mouth off and frees his finger from Gabriel's still-tight hole. Moving back up the bed, he grins at the deep, hot flush covering Gabriel's face, neck and chest, his ears red and eyes bright.

Darrek giggles and says, "You look so cute like this. Wow. God, I love being able to see you after you come. You're all pink and your hair's fuzzy. It's kind of awesome."

"I'm glad you're entertained," he says with a tiny twitch of his pursed lips that could be a smile.

"Thank you for letting me do that," he whispers, tangling himself up in Gabriel's arms which take him right in, laying his hand over Gabriel's still-rapidly-beating heart. "I guess that was kind of a big deal for you, right?"

"Yeah. I don't... I don't let anyone touch me like that anymore."

"Except me?" Darrek ventures.

"Except you," he nods in agreement. "Because I trust you."

"You really trust me?" Darrek asks, shifting to get a clearer look at Gabriel's face.

"Yeah. I guess I do. It's... not something I, like, *decided*. I just do,

I guess."

"I'm really glad to hear that," Darrek admits.

"But... I kind of need some time to work up to doing... more. I don't bottom. Ever. It has too many... psychological... um... *problems,* for me. It's just something that has never been appealing. I'm guessing you want to fuck me eventually, though, right?"

"Hey... I get that you're conflicted about stuff because of how you were abused. I'm not going to push you to do something you don't want to do, but I won't lie. I do want to be with you like that. I would like you to trust me that much."

"That's what I thought."

"Is it a problem?"

"No. But it's not going to be easy for me to go there, and I need you to be really patient with me. And maybe someday... maybe someday I'll be ready."

"Okay. Fair enough."

Later that day, Darrek is sitting alone in the house, nursing his third beer and staring at the lifeless, blank screen of his computer. Gabriel left and has gone off to work, saying he has a client to meet with and is also scheduled to assist Trace that night.

After they had gotten out of bed and cleaned up, Gabriel had become more and more distant. He seemed almost eager to leave and be away from Darrek. The news that he was leaving to go to work was blurted out in a very clipped and cold way. After a brief kiss at the door, Gabriel was gone, without even a promise to call Darrek later.

Darrek had understood. He still does. Gabriel is clearly just battling his own demons, and it's to be expected, with his history. But for the first time, the idea of Gabriel's profession is not sitting quite right with Darrek. He doesn't like that Gabriel is off with some other man, interacting in incredibly intimate ways with him while Darrek is sitting at home alone and questioning where their relationship is headed.

Darrek trusts Gabriel completely when it comes to the two of them together, but the standoffish vibe he gets from Gabriel sometimes, the sharply evident suspicion in his eyes, the defensiveness, all hurts more than he thought it would and makes Darrek uneasy.

He realizes that it is not technically cheating, that Gabriel is not letting his submissives touch him, but the plain fact is that he is giving other men pleasure. He is giving them sexual services, and with Darrek's history, with the betrayal he has already suffered at the hands of Sara and Steven, he is having a hard time reconciling it.

He had asked Gabriel about who he would be with that night, and what he would be doing, but Gabriel told him only that he couldn't talk about it due to a privacy clause in their contracts. After the almost loving intimacy of the morning, it has all become a thorn in his side and made their parting strained.

And there is no easy solution.

This is Gabriel's job. This is his life, and who is Darrek to ask him to suddenly change his life for him? How can he expect Gabriel to trust him so completely after the violent trauma of his adolescence when Darrek is himself having trouble trusting Gabriel in return, at least in this respect?

So, he stares at the monitor and pouts, sipping his beer. Stuck halfway between real happiness, the possibility of *love* and total loneliness, both of their trust issues are like a cement wall standing solidly in their way.

He wants to look at Diadem's website. He wants to see Gabriel interacting in the videos and pictures with other people, to see what feelings it stirs in him, and to see if he can handle it.

But he's afraid. He's afraid that it will not be okay, and that it will drive him to ask things of his new lover and Master that he has no right to ask for.

There's a knock on the door.

"Come in," he calls, not getting up. He has been expecting Kyle to show up after a brief phone call during which Darrek told Kyle that they needed to talk. "It's open."

Kyle steps inside, glancing around the silent, darkening house—not a light on though the sun is almost completely set. Sierra is curled up and forlorn at Darrek's feet. Her ears perk up as she sees Kyle. After a quick sniff at the air, she bows her head again and lays it back down on her paws.

"Wow, who died?" Kyle asks, falling into a nearby chair, watching Darrek watch the blank screen.

Darrek sighs heavily and takes a long drink from his beer.

"I have something to tell you, man," Darrek confesses.

"Yeah?"

"Yeah, um... that number you gave me? I called it. I actually..." he pauses, picking at the paper label on the glass bottle. "I've been there twice already. And that guy... Gabriel... he's the person I've been seeing there. He's... he's kind of in charge of me."

Kyle gets very still for a second, going deathly pale, then catches himself, trying to shake off the reaction. He wants to not appear overly guilty, but knows that his face in that moment must look unspeakably so. He brushes his fingers back through his hair and thinks fast for what to do. He had not planned on this—on complete *honesty*.

Darrek's hands skim over the keyboard and he hits the power button. The computer starts to boot up and the screen glows brightly in the dim space. They both stare at it, fixated.

"What are you doing?" Kyle asks, his voice hushed, a knot of fear coiling in the pit of his stomach. Suddenly, with Darrek's confession, with the look on Darrek's face, the trust he's showing in Kyle by admitting to his secrets, everything is coming apart. Everything is threatening to be revealed. All of his defenses are slipping from between his fingers. He could lose it all. He could lose it all right here in the next few minutes.

"I'm going to check out their website. It's called Diadem. I want to see... I don't know. Everything, I guess. I want to know the whole picture."

Kyle speaks even before he knows he is going to.

"Don't!" he cries out, sitting up straight and stiff-as-a-board in the soft chair.

Darrek looks confusedly at him. His large hands still making their restless movements at the peeled-back edge of the label.

"Shit..." Kyle curses, crumpling forward and rubbing a palm over his lips. "Okay. I have a confession, too."

"A confession?"

"Yeah. And it's kind of a doozy, so you have to promise that you won't hate me if I tell you."

He jumps off of the chair and grabs a pad of paper and a pen from the desk. Handing them to Darrek, he says, "Here. You have to write 'I swear that I won't hate Kyle,' and then sign your name."

"Are you shitting me?" Darrek laughs.

"No! I'm not. This is important. You're my best friend, Dare, and I am not losing your friendship over this shit. Please just humor me?"

Still laughing, Darrek writes and speaks aloud as he does, "I solemnly swear that I won't hate Kyle. Love, Darrek."

"Don't joke about this, dude."

"What's going on, man? You're being weird. Or, well, weirder than normal. You're... skittish. Jumpy."

Kyle grabs one of the chairs from the kitchen table and brings it over, setting it in front of Darrek's chair by the desk. Kyle sits at it, knee-to-knee, face-to-face with Darrek.

"You'll probably understand why in a minute. Trust me."

The words jolt Darrek, because he realizes that he *does* trust Kyle. He trusts him much more than he trusts Gabriel with his clients and it's a pain the burns through his heart.

"I do. I trust you," Darrek says seriously, his smile and laughter long gone.

Kyle's face relaxes at the words and the no-nonsense tone in Darrek's voice.

"I'm just gonna say it, okay?" Kyle tells him.

He pushes the paper with the promise scrawled on it over the surface of the desk and more toward Darrek's hand. The paper's edge nudges gently against it and Darrek lays his hand on top of it. Then Kyle twists his fingers together, his heart hammering away and his words sticking in his throat.

"Please don't hate me, Dare," he whispers desperately.

Darrek can see Kyle's usual smart-ass façade stripped away. His lip starts to quiver. His eyes slowly redden and fill with tears.

"Holy shit, Kyle. What's wrong?"

He answers simply, with three little words.

"I love you."

"I love you too, man," Darrek responds at once.

"No, you don't understand. *I love you.* I've loved you for years."

"What? Are you serious? ...Oh my god. You are, aren't you?"

"I warned you that I'm a douchebag. And I'm sorry, but I can't help it. I tried not to feel this way, and just be a friend to you, but I've been lying for a long time here. I've accepted that you'll never feel *that way* about me. I really have. I get it. But, I just want to be totally honest with you now. I want to tell you everything. You deserve that."

"Okay," Darrek nods.

"There's more," Kyle warns. "Do you hate me yet?"

"No I don't hate you," Darrek scoffs. "Stop it. I'm not going to hate you."

"Well, for a long time, I didn't want anyone else. No one but you. I got a little obsessed. But then I just... I needed *something*, you know? And I hated myself for not being honest with you, and for feeling the way that I did. I felt like such a crappy friend, a crappy *person*. So I started going to a Dom. I became a submissive. His name is Ben."

"Ben..." Darrek murmurs, and it all starts to make sense.

"And I liked that he made me hurt, because I *wanted* to hurt. I wanted pain and to be punished. I just hated myself so much. I deserved it all. I deserved everything he could dish out."

"When did this start?"

"Over a year ago. Almost two years, actually, now that I think about it. Before you even moved up here with me. And it's kind of... escalated. I've been doing BDSM videos and live webcam stuff. They pay me for it. I'm a professional sub now. And I've let Ben—my Master—I've let him do things to me. I was trying to save some stuff, some parts of myself, for you, even though, logically, I knew I'd never have you. It was something that was mine, you know? It was special. But then... I couldn't wait anymore. I let Ben have sex with me a few times, and I do care about him. He cares about me too, but I don't *love* him. Not like I love you, Darrek. And I just... I just want you not to hate me. Please? That's all I'm askin' here. I just want to be able to stop lying and still be your friend, because I don't think I could bear it if I lost you completely."

Darrek reaches out and takes one of Kyle's hands, tears pricking at his own eyes as he looks into Kyle's vibrantly blue ones, at the rivers streaming down his cheeks, at the openness of his expression.

Kyle laughs brokenly and claps his other hand over Darrek's, squeezing it gratefully.

"I still don't hate you," Darrek says softly.

Ignoring the words, not believing that they could be true, Kyle continues with what he needs to say. "I know you're dating Gabriel now, and I have to say, just as your friend, that he does *NOT* deserve you. You deserve a total commitment and real love. *You* are the most amazing person I've ever known, Dare, and you've been through so much shit. I just want you to know that if someday you could ever care about me like that, I would devote myself to you completely. I would be *yours*. In whatever way you wanted me. I love you so much, and... *god*... it feels so good to finally say this stuff out loud. I just want you to be *happy*. That's all. Whatever I can do to make you happy, I'll do it. So... I apologize, again, for lying. There were never any girlfriends. There were no women. It was an act. I've known that I'm gay for a while now, I just couldn't tell anyone because I'm a coward and a fake."

Kyle stares down at where Darrek's fingers are brushing lightly over his, and the kindness in the gesture is almost too much for him when he had expected disgust and anger and nothing more.

"End of sappy speech. That's all I've got. Um... I'll go. You probably want me to go now."

"So, you knew Gabriel, didn't you? Before I did."

"Hell, yeah. I've known Gabriel for a long time. He assists Ben with me a lot more than I'd like. He runs all the video shit. If you go on the website, you'll see him in most of my stuff. I don't like him, Dare. I won't lie about that either. The dude is closed-off and cruel. And maybe I just don't know him like you do, so feel free to ignore me completely. It's just my opinion. But, I mean, come on! He busts balls for a *living*, man. That really the person you want to *date*?"

"Why did you give me the number?" Darrek asks quietly, still lightly brushing Kyle's hands and handing him a tissue from the box on the desk.

Kyle takes the tissue and wipes at his face with it.

"I thought it might help you. They're starting to train Alyssa to be a Dominatrix, so I thought they might let you have a go with her. Figured she'd go pretty easy on you. I didn't think they'd give you to Gabe."

There's a moment of silence, where they're just touching. Kyle's confessions seem to fill the air around them, invisible but heavy and thick.

"I can't really handle you being nice like this to me," Kyle whispers. "It'd be easier if you were pissed off."

"You really love me?"

Kyle looks plaintively up at him, and there's such heartbroken urgency in his face that it destroys Darrek a little.

"Yeah. I do. I love you so much, Darrek. Always will."

Kyle can tell this is going in a way he didn't foresee at all. It's out of control. Something snaps in him then, and he presses his lips closed to hold in a weak sob, jumping out of his chair.

Kyle almost bolts for the door, but Darrek grabs his shoulder and keeps him there.

Turning back to face Darrek, Kyle pleads shamelessly through gritted teeth, "Just let me go, okay? I can't do this. It's too hard and it's not fair to you or Gabriel. Let me go. You don't need me. Nobody needs me. I'm like this leech just taking shit and infecting people's lives. I don't want my problems messing up your life. I'm just messing everything up."

What happens next is the last thing he expects, at least on a surface level. Underneath, deep down in his heart, he knows it has always been leading here.

The selfish part of him is glad.

Darrek curls one of his strong hands around the back of Kyle's neck, into his short blond hair, and brings him in as he closes the distance and claims Kyle's mouth in a kiss. After a small, pained whine, Kyle grabs Darrek with both hands, licking over his lips eagerly then deeply into his mouth, kissing him back fiercely with a year's worth of need and want pouring into it. It goes on and on, and when Kyle finally pulls away, Darrek's lips are tingling, swollen and hot, his head spinning.

"Thank you," Kyle whispers against his cheek, "I'm sorry."

Then he turns, dashes through the door, and is gone before Darrek can even blink.

Chapter 14
The Trouble With Honesty

"Come on..." Darrek groans, dialing for the fifteenth time. It goes right to voicemail.

He's been trying to get hold of both Kyle and Gabriel for what seems like forever. Kyle is not picking up and Gabriel is probably still working and unable to answer.

He's angry. He's angry with himself for kissing Kyle and turning into the thing he hates most—a cheater. He's angry with Kyle for leaving so abruptly, like he was doing Darrek a favor by taking off right after hitting him with all of these revelations and turning his world upside-down.

He's angry with Gabriel.

His anger with Gabriel is harder to define. It is partly because Gabriel knew about Kyle and did not let Darrek know, other than to urge him vaguely to 'talk' to Kyle. He is also upset that Gabriel has been personally responsible for a good majority of Kyle's pain and pleasure for such a long period of time. It just underlies his feelings from before Kyle had appeared at his door, his mistrust in Gabriel's job and his doubt in the fact that the two of them can have a healthy relationship despite it.

Darrek keeps envisioning Kyle, Ben and Gabriel together in Diadem's dungeon. The images his mind supplies make his stomach churn. He glares at the glowing computer screen, the opened browser window and wants to see for himself, but it's the buttons of his phone that he keeps touching, his connection to the two men so very much on his mind. He has left them both multiple voicemails. The waiting is hard, though.

Two more hours pass with nothing, and he is about to lose his mind when the phone rings in his hand. Fumbling with it, he answers with a hurried, "Yeah? Hello?" before even looking to see who it is.

"You have to stop calling," is the almost begging and sullen reply.

"I want to make sure you're okay! Are you okay? You were so upset... I've never seen you like that."

"Are you looking at it? You're looking at the website, aren't you?"

"No. I'm not," Darrek insists, adding, "Why, do you want me to?"

"I don't know if I can handle you seeing that shit. I asked Ben if he could set up a double session for me and you, but it wasn't real then, you know? Now... after what I told you... I don't think I can stand the thought of you seeing everything they've done to me."

"Wait... you asked Ben for a double session?"

"Yeah. But that was before. Just a fucked-up fantasy or something. Look... I'm sorry. I didn't want you to know. I wanted to just keep this all to myself and I didn't want to make things weird for you and Gabe. I meant it when I said that I just want you to be happy. So, stop calling, okay? Go be with Gabe."

"Kyle... I'm trying to be sorry about kissing you, because I know it's not fair to Gabriel, but... I'm not. I'm not sorry at all."

There is a rustling at the other end of the line and Darrek says loudly into the phone, "Don't hang up!"

"This *isn't fair* to me, Darrek!" Kyle yells, "I'm trying to be honest with you! Don't take advantage of that and, like... lead me on or something. Just don't."

"I'm not trying to lead you on," he insists. "I'm trying to be honest, too. I don't know what's going on right now. I'm... confused."

"I can tell."

There is a long moment of quiet between them then Kyle adds, "You told me that you don't like me the way that you like Gabriel. I could tell that you meant that. You've never seemed to be attracted to me, Dare, so I have no idea what's going on here. Did Gabe hurt you or something? Are you just acting out by kissing me?"

"I don't know... I *don't* feel the same way about you guys. Kyle, you're the best friend I've ever had in my life. I trust you and I *do* love you as a friend. I feel like there's something happening here with us. Seeing this side of you and how much you care about me... I don't know. It changes things for me. I just keep thinking about that kiss, about how it felt to kiss you and how *good* it was, but I have feelings for Gabriel too. I feel like I *could* love him—*really* love him—if we could each get past the shit holding us back. But I don't know if that's even possible. Maybe Gabe and I work best when we're just Dom and sub. Maybe it shouldn't be more than that."

"Okay. You need to stop and take a breath. Talk to Gabriel. You sound like you're trying to talk yourself into this. I don't want you to talk yourself into wanting me. Do me a favor and don't call me for a few days. Take some time to sort this shit out."

"But I want to *see you*, Kyle," he argues softly. "Can I come over there and see you?"

The worst part is that Kyle can hear the implication of what would happen between them if Darrek *did* come over to see him. He can hear the naked desire in Darrek's voice, and can feel his own fragile defenses and resolutions to do what is right melting away. The knowledge is like salvation and damnation all wrapped up in one neat package. He can almost see it; almost feel how it would be.

Darrek hears a small cry of pain then a hissed, "Fuck you, Dare. Go to hell. I can't fucking believe you."

The line goes dead.

Sometime later, the phone rings on the desk.

Darrek stares at it, at Gabriel's number glowing like a spark of warmth and life on the tiny screen in the darkened house.

Pushing his chair back from the desk, he leaves it there, unanswered. Heading to the house's back door he walks outside into the pitch black of the night. Shutting the door tightly behind him, he's glad when he can no longer hear the faint ringing from inside.

Approximately a half hour later, Darrek is systematically marking and then cutting lumber with a hand saw in the garage, channeling his frustration and anger into the movements of his hands and the exertions of his muscles. His shirt discarded, forgotten on the dirty floor, ear buds in place, he drowns out the world with the music blasting from his iPod, tucked carefully into his back pocket. As he slices repeatedly into the wood, focusing on the digging back-and-forth motion of the blade, Darrek lets it fill his mind and drown everything else out. It makes him feel better. He could go all night like this and probably will. It's a distraction, it's *real* and the last thing he wants right now is to dream.

His hand cramps up and arm muscles burn as the pile of trimmed boards grows next to him, but he welcomes it. He wants more hurt, more pain.

When a hand grabs him from behind, this time he's marginally more prepared for it, though it still catches him off-guard.

Dropping the saw onto the workbench, ear buds tugging free, Darrek is spun around by Gabriel's firm grip on his shoulder. All he sees is the fist headed for his face. It connects with his jaw. Pain blooms and explodes up through his skull, knocking him backward.

"I trusted you, you son of a bitch!" Gabriel screams. "I *trusted* you!"

Darrek's vision had darkened at the edges but now it gradually starts to clear. He feels hands shoving at his bare chest and prepares himself for further blows that do not come.

"How dare you?! How *dare you* kiss him?! And you weren't even sorry about it! Goddamn it! Goddamn it you son of a bitch! I trusted you, Darrek! Do you know how big a deal that is for me, you asshole?!"

Blinking, Darrek's eyes clear, and then he can see. He sees the tears running down Gabriel's face, the betrayal and hurt burning in his eyes. For someone who's usually so stoic and emotionally withdrawn, the sight of Gabriel's raw pain is jolting to Darrek, even more jolting that Kyle's confession had been.

Gabriel's breath catches in a whine and he stumbles over a piece of wood littering the cluttered floor. He nearly falls over, and Darrek reaches out to catch him.

"Don't touch me! Don't fucking touch me!" Gabriel cries, pushing him off and steadying himself, and it's the weakness and frailness in his voice that causes Darrek to fall to his knees in front of him.

"I'm sorry," he begs. "I'm sorry for hurting you. I didn't go looking for this, I swear. He just laid this all on me and he was so upset... I just wanted to...."

"Shut up! Just shut up!" Gabriel spouts, rubbing the back of his arm across his damp face. "And fucking stand up! Stand up, you jerk!"

Still on his knees, Darrek bows his head and clasps his hands behind his back.

"Go ahead," he urges. "Please. Hurt me. I want you to. I deserve it."

It's far too tempting, and Gabriel knows that Darrek would let him. He would let him do anything and they are surrounded by all sorts of cruel implements that Gabriel simply itches to pick up and wield against him.

Gabriel yells, fists clenched, and kicks a small chunk of pine across the garage. It ricochets off the side wall and gets lost in a dark corner.

"God damn you," Gabriel hisses, "why would you do this? Why *today*? After what happened, after what we *did*, what I *told you*? How could you?!"

Head still bowed, Darrek says quietly, "Because I was scared, okay? I could feel myself falling in love with you, and it scared the shit out of me, because I still wasn't sure if you could ever love me back. And I can't let myself fall for someone that can't love me. I did that once already and it nearly killed me. So, yeah, maybe I saw Kyle as an out. And I'm a shitty person for doing that to him and to you, but I do love him as a friend. He's always been there for me, and I've never doubted that about him. It's never been an issue."

"But you think *I'm* not going to be there for you," Gabriel scowls, stepping up to him. Grabbing a fistful of Darrek's long hair, he yanks his head back, forcing him to meet his eyes as he spits out, "You think I'm gonna fuck and run? I told you that I don't let myself be with people! I *told you* that I care about you. I told you that! I asked you to tell me to leave! I asked you that because I didn't want it to go this far! And fuck you for not telling me to leave! So... what? Because I'm scared to let you fuck me, you're calling it off? Seriously, Darrek? If I bend over right here, and let you fuck the hell out of my ass, that gonna change your mind? You really controlled that much by your dick?"

Releasing him roughly, Gabriel still wants to slap him, to smack that pitiful expression off of Darrek's face. Instead his hands go to his own pants, to his buckle. He begins to undo it.

Darrek grabs Gabriel's legs and says, "Stop, Gabe. That's not true..." even as Gabriel gets the buckle undone and goes to unzip his fly, still sobbing and sniffling back tears. "*Don't*!"

"No, obviously, this is the only way you're going to believe me," Gabriel chokes out, hitching his pants down on his hips. "Come on and fuck me, Dare. I'm used to crying when I get fucked, anyway. It'll be like old times."

Darrek struggles to his feet and tugs Gabriel's pants back up, a scowl of his own on his face.

"If you hate me so much, Gabriel, then leave. Why are you here if you hate me this much?" he asks.

"Why am I here?!" Gabriel laughs, wiping at his incredibly red, puffy, and tired-looking eyes again. "Because I'm an idiot! I am a stupid fucking idiot."

Gabriel turns away and crosses his arms over his chest, hugging himself. Then he sighs heavily and digs something out of his front pocket. He closes his fingers around it and throws it to the dirty floor.

It's a crumpled purple flower.

"Oh god... Gabe..." Darrek gasps, stung and almost knocked off his feet by the sight of it.

He steps forward and takes Gabriel in his arms, looping them around Gabriel's chest and feeling the hitches as he chokes back his emotions.

"Get off of me," Gabriel grunts, trying to shake Darrek off, but he's not really trying. Darrek holds on tighter and presses his face into Gabriel's hair.

"No," Darrek tells him. "I'm not letting you go."

"I was ready to give you my heart. And then you broke it. Fucking *stomped* on it. Do you know what it was like to get that call from Kyle? Or when you wouldn't even pick up your goddamned phone?"

"Kyle called you?"

"Of course he called me! He's madder at you than I am!"

"I told you that I tend to disappoint people. I always have. I'm a fuck-up."

They stand there together for a few minutes as Gabriel catches his breath and Darrek berates himself silently.

"I'd stay the hell away from Ben for a while," Gabriel warns. "He wants to cut off your dick and nail it to the wall."

"I'm not surprised," Darrek sighs. "I *am* surprised that you took the flower...."

"Yeah, well... like I said. I'm an idiot. No one's ever given me a flower before," he confesses almost soundlessly.

"Look, I have issues with your job, Gabe. I didn't realize it until you took off earlier to go be with some other guy. I know that you wouldn't do anything with them, but it... it bothers me. And if we're being honest here, then you need to hear that."

"Okay."

"I don't want to lose you. I'm... well, I'm really fucking shocked that you care this much. I had no idea. I thought it was me holding on again to something that wasn't meant to be. Maybe we *are* meant to be. Could you ever forgive me for Kyle?"

"I don't care about the kiss. It was one stupid kiss. And we never said we're in some monogamous relationship or anything," Gabriel says. "It's more that you were ready to throw everything away at the drop of a hat, throw *me* away, and go be with *him* instead. Kyle is really good at manipulating people. He's really good at getting what he wants. And he might think I'm some kind of heartless bastard, but he doesn't *know me*, Darrek. Not like you do. I'm sure he does love you. I don't doubt that. But you need to ask yourself who you want to be with. This is the only chance you get. This is the only one I can give you."

Darrek lets him go and backs away. Gabriel turns and blinks confusedly up at him.

"Wait here, okay? Give me one second," Darrek says before dashing through the garage door.

He returns a second later. Jogging back over to Gabriel, he pulls from behind his back a perfect, unspoiled purple daisy.

Holding it out to Gabriel, Darrek says, "Um... I'm falling in love with you, Gabriel Hunter. I'm sorry for letting that scare me so bad, for doubting you and being the biggest douchebag in the world. *Please* let me have another chance?"

"Second biggest douchebag," Gabriel murmurs, taking the flower and holding it gently between his fingers. "Or maybe the fourth biggest, but you're definitely top five."

Darrek smiles and hugs Gabriel close.

"Agreed," he nods.

"I don't know what to tell you about the job thing, though," Gabriel tells him. "I can see why it would bother you, but it's my *job*. I can't just quit. It's kind of my whole life. Can you give me time to figure it out? Or we can figure it out together?"

"I'd like that," Darrek grins. "Want to come inside? I'll fix you something to eat. You hungry?"

"A little. I didn't really eat anything since I left here this afternoon."

"Then come in," Darrek urges, tugging on Gabriel's hand and leading him to the door. "And you can stay over if you want. It's pretty late."

"Well, it *was* kind of fun to wake up next to you today," Gabriel allows.

"Likewise," Darrek laughs, clicking off the garage light and guiding Gabriel to the door of the house. As it opens, Sierra bounds eagerly through it, sniffing frantically at Gabriel, who just scratches behind her ears and smiles as she licks at his hand. Satisfied, Sierra sneaks past them and off into the yard, snapping at the fireflies hovering in the calm springtime air as the two men pass through the doorway and the lights suddenly begin to glow warmly from inside the home's curtained windows.

They don't even discuss it. It just happens naturally.

Darrek washes his hands thoroughly at the sink and then cooks Gabriel a simple dinner of pasta and steamed vegetables.

He sets it out for him at the table; the purple flower placed in a small vase filled with water and set above the plate of food.

Gabriel takes his seat and Darrek falls to his knees again by Gabriel's left side.

He stays there as Gabriel eats, sitting on his heels, head bowed once more, fingers twined loosely together behind him. Once in a while Gabriel feeds him small scraps of food from his right hand which Darrek takes gratefully, carefully taking each morsel between his teeth and kissing Gabriel's fingers clean.

Every now and then Gabriel rests his left hand on Darrek's shoulder or gently touches his hair. Whenever it happens, Darrek's heart swells with pride and utter contentment.

They don't speak. They don't need to. It's all been said.

When Gabriel is finished with dinner, he wipes his mouth with a napkin and, without looking over, says, "Upstairs. Clothes off. I'll meet you there."

"Yes, Master. Thank you," Darrek whispers happily.

When he moves to stand, Gabriel stops him, his strong hand clamping down on Darrek's shoulder and tells him with a shake of his head, clearly enunciating each word, "No. *Crawl.*"

A tingling shiver runs through Darrek's body, spiraling outward from his gut, and a surge of blood rushes to his cock, making it swell and press painfully against his jeans.

"Yes, sir," he nods, and obeys as a blush heats his face.

Gabriel watches him carefully as he goes. Biting thoughtfully at the pad of his thumb, he takes in the sight of the sweat- and dirt-covered muscles of Darrek's back, arms, and chest working as he slowly crawls up the steps on his hands and knees, his hair fallen forward and obscuring his face.

As he concocts Darrek's punishment, Gabriel's lips curl up at the ends, small dimples denting his cheeks. Once he hears Darrek move into the bedroom, Gabriel pivots on his heel and walks purposefully out through the back door in the direction of the garage and the plentiful bounty of tools and supplies waiting there for him.

He knows he is *really* going to enjoy this.

Chapter 15
Good Boy

The span of time between when Gabriel orders Darrek to crawl upstairs, and when Gabriel finally appears in the bedroom's doorway is long enough that Darrek's initial purely-lustful anticipation has turned a corner and, after pondering the circumstances he finds himself in, has become instead a nerve-rattling, stomach-clenching, chilled acquiescence.

After setting down an armful of supplies outside the door's frame, out of Darrek's line of sight, Gabriel looks down his nose at his naked, guilt-ridden lover, kneeling and ready before him.

"You know what this is, right?" Gabriel asks, the amusement long-fled from his voice as well. "This is punishment. It's not play and it's not intended to be in any way pleasurable for you. In fact, I'm going to make sure you're *not* enjoying it, and if I find that you *are*, I will immediately change tactics and do something even less appealing. If you want out, say so now, and I'll leave. We can break things off right here. It will be hard for both of us, but I need you to be a perfectly clear and willing part of this. This isn't something I'm going to make you do or force you into. But if you take this punishment, and are truly sorry for what you've done wrong today, then I *will* forgive you. I'll forgive you completely and we will never have to speak of it again. You'll never have to apologize after this. It will be completely resolved; we can move on and start fresh."

Darrek swallows thickly and Gabriel watches his face. He glances up hesitantly, unsure whether he's allowed to look.

"Go ahead. You may speak," Gabriel tells him.

"I'll do it. I'll take my penance. I want to make things right between us, and I would do *anything* to earn your forgiveness."

"You sure about that?"

"Yes. I want to earn your trust again. I want to be good for you and obedient. I want to deserve you. *Please,* Master."

"And you understand that this will be unpleasant? You have a fairly high tolerance for pain, Dare. I'm a little shocked at how vast your limits are. Hell, you enjoyed the ginger root even though you seem to have a keen sensitivity to it. Some people don't even feel much of a burn, but you did. You were in real pain and you not only bore it, but were highly aroused by it. So I'm going to have to think outside the box right now, especially since I have no supplies of my own here. We may have to change that. Maybe... maybe I'll bring some of my things over here... if I'm going to be here so often, and if you *are* interested in making this commitment to me. Do you want that?"

"Yes!" Darrek says eagerly. "Please. Let me prove myself to you. I'm ready. I promise."

"Okay," he nods, and strangely, seems simultaneously both sad and contented.

It makes Darrek afraid.

"Crawl to the bathroom, kneel in the tub and we'll get started."

Darrek doesn't know what he's so afraid of. The only things Gabriel has brought into the room and piled by the door are: a length of rope; a small, approximately twelve-inch length of a pine two-by-four; a small piece of a plastic tarp; two bottles of water; and a few odds and ends. None of these things alone is much cause for trepidation, but perhaps the sum of them, the grinding pain of his knees against the porcelain tub, the sorrow in Gabriel's eyes and turn of his mouth is what does it.

"Drink these," Gabriel says, handing him the water.

Unable to meet his Master's eyes, his heart hammering in his chest, Darrek finds his breathing sounds overly loud in the small room. Gabriel is standing beside the tub, an arm across his chest, one finger of his right hand tracing the outline of his lips, his expression thoughtful and far away.

Darrek finishes the first bottle and sets it aside, taking up the second. He has no idea where this is going, or what Gabriel could possibly have planned for him, and he doesn't even realize how far his panic has ratcheted up until he swallows down a large gulp from the second water bottle and makes a low whine in the back of his throat. The sound of it surprises him, and he tries to cover it up, to turn it into a cough. Gabriel sees right through it though.

"Are you afraid?" he asks quietly.

Eyes darting around, he turns the bottle in his hands as he nods and murmurs, "Yeah. Yes... sir. I'm sorry."

"Don't be sorry. It's good that you are afraid. It shows that you're taking this seriously. And honestly, Darrek, I don't want to do this to you. I'm not enjoying this either, but I have hope that things will be better, afterward, for both of us. We can both put what happened today behind us, and it won't drag us down or spoil the relationship we could have, given time. I see this as a healthy way to resolve the problem of your sense of guilt, and my hurt over your betrayal, but believe me when I say that I want nothing more than for this to be the last time I ever have to punish you for something."

Darrek nods in absolute agreement with Gabriel's words and resumes drinking. He wants to ask why he's being made to drink water. His mind won't even supply him with suggestions, but he thinks that perhaps it's better that way. It may be better not to know.

"The reason that I am punishing you tonight, slave," Gabriel begins to say in a disturbingly authoritative voice, "is for your actions this afternoon. In the interest of most effectively correcting this behavior, and penalizing you for it, you will be punished right here and now, and you will apologize to me. Today you kissed another man and expressed an interest in doing much more with him, all without my knowledge or approval. Do you deny this?"

"No, Master. I did it. I admit to it."

"You don't deny that you would have gone ahead and been *intimate* with Kyle Roth, if given the chance?"

"I don't deny it. I'm so sorry, Gabriel. I deserve this. I hate myself for what I've done to you. There's nothing worse than someone who betrays the people they love. I know how much it hurts to find out that someone you care about has done something behind your back and cheated on you. Please believe me that I *never* wanted to turn into that kind of monster. I was thoughtless and weak and cruel. I accept my punishment, whatever it is, completely. I trust you, Master."

"You can't use your safeword to get out of this, slave. I'm telling you that ahead of time. This is over when I say it is. But when it's over, it's *over* and is something we will never need to discuss again. It will be *done*. Understood?"

"Yes, sir."

"Because I am still learning what you do *not* enjoy, I'm going back to the basics, to what I know is generally found to be unpleasant. I'm going to tie you up with this rope, lay you down in the tub you are currently kneeling in, and then urinate on you and that mouth that you were so fucking eager to share with Kyle. Essentially, I'm marking my territory. Your mouth is now *my* territory, my property, and I can do with it whatever the hell I want. Bite it, spit on it, piss on it —*anything*. And in case you were not previously aware of the fact, let me assure you that urine is a sterile substance. It will *not* make you ill if you ingest it.

"I will also be spreading your legs with this piece of wood in order to keep an eye on your genitals and make sure you are not getting off on this. If I discover that you *are* becoming erect, I will begin whipping the undersides of your feet with my belt until your dick is once more soft. You will stay in the tub, face down, until you relieve yourself and empty your bladder. Then you will lay there until I release you. *That* is your punishment. Understood?"

Head bowed to the point where his chin is almost resting on his chest, and turned away, Darrek nods.

"Look at me! Look at me and say you understand!"

Darrek turns toward Gabriel, cheeks stained with tears already, nose running and sniffling, Darrek whispers, "I understand. Okay... okay, Master."

He hears the air rush out of Gabriel's lungs, sees him press hard at his left eye with the heel of his left hand as his breath hitches when he tries to inhale. Closing his eyes against the sight, because it only makes this so much harder, Darrek resigns himself for what's to come.

The first thing Gabriel does is tie Darrek's hair back from his face with a rubber band found in the downstairs desk. Next, he has him lie down on his stomach and get into position—legs bent so that his calves are pressed to the backs of his thighs, ankles crossed, arms behind his back and wrists crossed as well. Gabriel loops the rope multiple times around each wrist, each ankle, before securing them together, wrist-to-wrist and ankle-to ankle before tightly connecting ankles to wrists with a short length of the rope. Every so often his gaze rests on Darrek's face, lying flush against the smooth, white porcelain. He's still crying soundlessly, face fully exposed with his hair fastened back, and looks very much the sweet boy aching with remorse, desperate for daddy's approval, a hug or a smile—forgiveness.

Gabriel wrenches his eyes away, wanting to just get this over with as fast as possible so he can take Darrek in his arms and make everything better.

With the ropes secure and Darrek in position, Gabriel takes up the small piece of wood he had found in the pile of scraps in Darrek's garage and trimmed down with the circular saw. Gabriel had thoroughly sanded the ends to rid them of jagged edges and splinters, but just in case, also cut the piece of tarp now at hand. Wrapping the plastic tightly around the wood to protect Darrek's skin, Gabriel just hopes that it fits.

Sitting down on the side of the tub, Gabriel nudges Darrek's knees apart with a hand. Darrek takes the hint and opens his legs as wide as he can in the confined space. Fitting the wood in place, it turns out to be just the right size, keeping Darrek's knees apart and pressed tightly to the walls of the tub.

Trembling from head to toe with nerves, eyes and lips squeezed shut; Darrek sucks in a rough breath. Gabriel itches to touch him, to kiss away his tears, but restrains himself with effort. He stands and goes to the medicine cabinet above the sink. He finds what he needs inside it and goes back to Darrek's head, kneeling down on the bathroom's tile floor.

Twisting the cotton balls between his fingers, reshaping them to be narrow and long, he catches Darrek's eyes for a second after he glances at Gabriel's hands and sees what he's doing. The question is in his eyes, if not on his lips. His obedience and restraint continues to amaze Gabriel.

Reaching over the lip of the tub, cupping Darrek's face, he explains as he works, "I'm putting these inside your nostrils to prevent you from breathing through your nose and to force you to keep your mouth open. I have a special gag that's designed to do that as well, but since I don't have it with me, this will have to do. The good news is that it might help dull the smell for you."

He gets the first one in, pushing it deep, and then the second. Darrek's lips part instantly and he breathes softly through them. The fear is still darkening his eyes, but there's strength there too—determination, resiliency.

Quick enough to badly startle Darrek, Gabriel gets to his feet and rapidly works open his belt, whipping it from his belt loops and tossing it to the floor. He unsnaps his jeans and lowers the zipper, hitching them down on his hips. Darrek's eyes are locked to his crotch.

As he tugs his dick free, cradling it in one hand and stepping up into position over Darrek, he warns, "You may close your eyes but if you close your lips I will be *very* displeased."

A keening whimper of pure, unadulterated fear rips from Darrek's chest and then it's happening.

A shower of warmth rains on his head, trickles over his cheeks and down into his mouth. A jet of it falls right onto his tongue and it's acidic and bitter, stinging his nose even with the cotton there. For a second he forgets and starts to close his mouth to keep it out, even if that means he can't breathe. He catches himself just before his lips touch, and forces himself to open back up. Darrek does have his eyes shut, so is forced to imagine what this must look like, the sight of Gabriel's dick above him as he washes Darrek with his piss.

It's over before he knows it, and he blinks his eyes open. He hadn't seen Gabriel close the drain, but he obviously has, since the liquid is not draining away. It pools under Darrek's body, under his head, since he's lying with his face only inches from the tub's metal drain. He can taste it on his tongue.

He feels ashamed, dirty, but there's more than that—much more. Darrek knows that it's wrong, that he's lying in Gabriel's urine, but at the same time, it's still part of *Gabriel*.

He hears Gabriel sigh with disappointment.

"*Goddamn it,*" Gabriel hisses, and Darrek knows why.

There's a hand at his crotch, gently moving his dick so that it's pointing away from his body and not trapped between his belly and the tub.

Darrek is getting hard.

He wants to apologize but the words won't come. Once more fright bubbles up in his gut, clawing and manic.

"I didn't want to *do this* to you," Gabriel almost whines, anger and disappointment coloring his impenetrable facade.

He picks up the belt and doubles it over, holding it tightly in his fist, drawing his arm back.

"Don't! Please! Please, I'm sorry! I can't help it!"

The blows start to fall, and it's so much worse than before, when he had been in the dungeon. Then he'd had other pain to distract him, other pleasure. Now, his ankles bound together and hog-tied in the tub as he is, the bottoms of both his feet get whipped at the same time and he can't even buck or writhe away. He's trapped.

Darrek is fairly sure that nothing has ever hurt this much as fire explodes up his ankles, shins, through his knees and thighs, burning through his muscles and skin, radiating through his body. Daggers, sharp and cutting, bite into tender flesh. Getting lost in it, he doesn't hear himself screaming, doesn't feel himself choking on Gabriel's piss until the leather strap of the belt stops landing with the regular, rapid lashes that Gabriel had been dealing him.

The sound tearing from his chest fades away, echoes off the walls. He coughs and spits, turning his mouth as far away from the sour aroma of the wetness beneath him as he can.

When he opens his eyes, he sees Gabriel covering his face with both his hands, the belt discarded, and there's a crazy moment when

Darrek wants to comfort *him.*

His pleasure gone now, the thrill of receiving a golden shower from Gabriel is overwhelmed by the throbbing ache in his feet.

Gabriel sits heavily on the closed lid of the toilet, and says, "This'll be over sooner if you just do it."

"...I don't... I don't know if I *can*... sir," Darrek admits quietly, and his voice sounds more raw and high-pitched with simple, primal vulnerability than he'd expected it to.

"When's the last time you took a leak?"

"Um... I guess... sometime this afternoon. A while ago. But... with you watching like this... I just can't. I'm sorry."

"You *can* and you're not getting out of there until you empty your bladder, slave. You will lie in my piss. It will get cold and congeal to your skin and every five minutes that pass will earn you five lashes from my belt. That sound like fun to you?"

"No."

It comes out as a sharp whine, almost childish, and Darrek's humiliation grows.

"No, what?" Gabriel barks.

"No, *sir*."

"Then do it! Piss on yourself and *then* we'll see how much Kyle wants you!"

"I'm *sorry*, Gabe," Darrek cries.

"Don't you fucking *DARE* say my name!"

"I'm sorry! I'm sorry, Master," he wails.

Gabriel's over to him in a flash, pushing his face down, pressing his lips into the mess.

"Lick it! Lick it up!" he barks. "You like me peeing in your mouth so much, then LICK IT UP! *NOW*!"

He only struggles for a second or two before getting control over himself, getting control over the urge. Tears sting his eyes, his opened mouth held against the cold surface of the tub, urine seeping through, into him, coating his teeth, soaking into the cotton in his nose. Trying to be silent, small, grunting, desperate sounds slip through his defenses as he sticks out his tongue and licks.

"Good boy," Gabriel says maliciously, releasing him.

A half hour later, Gabriel stands watch, arms folded, by the side of the bathtub. Darrek has turned his face away from him, and Gabriel hears it before he sees it. There's a small splashing sound as Darrek finally lets go and begins to urinate on himself. Gabriel had gotten momentarily lost in his tangled thoughts but it jerks him right back to reality.

Darrek begins to cry softly as the golden, hot liquid fills the tub even more.

After suffering a total of six more rounds of lashings, his throat is now scraped-raw from his screams, his feet an angry, swollen red.

A full hour passes. His entire body throbbing or numb, his muscles are knotted up so badly that he's not sure he could get out of his current position even if the ropes were no longer there. Darrek is dizzy with pain, exhaustion, and the pungent odor of the mess he's been laying in for far too long, and therefore doesn't feel Gabriel cut the ropes. He doesn't hear Gabriel flip the switch on the drain to let the urine drain away.

"Come on, baby, let's get you up," Gabriel hushes to him.

Darrek blinks, but doesn't move—can't move. Untwining the ropes, Gabriel guides Darrek's arms to his sides, one by one, grips his hands and pulls.

"Come on. Stand up. Let's get you on your feet, okay?"

"Don't touch me. I'm disgusting. Just leave. Please," Darrek rasps vacantly. His muscles quake as he gets his knees under him, and when he begins to stand, he screams again as pins and needles set-in to his previously numb feet, legs, hands, and arms.

"No way. I'm not leaving," Gabriel argues. "I'm *never* leaving you, Dare."

He pulls the curtain closed, the metal rings scraping along the bar, and turns on the water. When it gets warm enough, he pulls the lever and the water shoots out from the showerhead onto Darrek's body. Still gripping Gabriel's hands tightly enough to bruise, Darrek is silently grateful when Gabriel steps into the tub with him and holds him up.

Not even consciously aware of when Gabriel had shed his own clothes, Darrek shivers even with nearly scalding-hot water pouring over him, his legs threatening to give out from under him.

"I've got you," Gabriel assures him. Turning Darrek around, Gabriel faces him toward the water, and loops an arm around Darrek's waist, pinning their bodies together as Darrek's knees *DO* give out. Quickly catching himself, though, Darrek presses his hands clumsily to the walls and opens his mouth, letting the clean, fresh water fill him. He swishes it around before spitting it back out in a jet against the far wall. He does it again and again, washing out the sour taste.

After moving to grab a washcloth so that he can use it to begin to wash himself off with soap, Darrek realizes the impossibility of the idea when as soon as he lets go of the wall, and takes his full weight onto his feet, his legs give out again immediately. Collapsing in Gabriel's arms as his muscles turn to mush, he grabs the wall again while Gabriel guides him back upward.

"Let me help you," Gabriel insists, a plaintive but unyielding edge to his voice. "You just stay on your feet and *I'll* wash you off."

"Yes, sir," he responds automatically.

Gabriel does a thorough job, soaping him up, rinsing him down then repeating the process, even brushing Darrek's teeth for him.

Each gentle touch, each caress of the washcloth over his skin, the particular way Gabriel keeps an arm slung protectively around him at all times, the feel of Gabriel's fingers brushing the tangles out of his hair overwhelms Darrek. His grateful tears mix with the spray of water from above, trickling over his skin and washing the salty drops away.

When the water is shut off and the curtain tugged aside, Gabriel helps him step out and onto the carpet, Darrek's muscles still weak, and his face pale and drawn with tiredness.

"Let's get you in bed. Get you warm," Gabriel tells him, wrapping him in towels and leading him out to the other room. Lowering Darrek down onto the bed, Gabriel dries his hair for him then gets two extra blankets from the hall closet.

Darrek falls back onto the bed at Gabriel's urging. Gabriel

climbs in as well, wrapping his arms and legs around him. Sharing his body heat, he covers them both in the blankets and rubs the warmth back into Darrek's chilled flesh.

His eyes close almost immediately. Tucking himself further into Gabriel's embrace, breathing him in, Darrek hears his Master say lovingly to him, "I forgive you, baby. It's all over now. Sleep. Sleep and I'll be right here with you."

"Sierra..." Darrek mutters sleepily, frowning.

"I'll let her in. Don't worry. I'm taking care of you first, though."

"Thanks, Gabe," he whispers, hugging onto him tight.

Darrek is asleep as soon as the words leave his lips. Gabriel stays long after the shivering has stopped and Darrek's breathing has become deep and regular, his snores a soft tickling rumble against his chest. He presses soft kisses to Darrek's skin as he sleeps, and wants to never let go.

Eventually he does, and slips away to clean up the bathroom and take care of Sierra. He returns, though, and wraps himself right back into Darrek's wonderfully smothering embrace.

Chapter 16
Sobering Up

Across town, ready to pick the front door's lock in order to get inside, Ben wishes he knew where a spare key might be hiding. He soon discovers that it will not be necessary to go so far as to attempt breaking and entering. The door swings open with a push of his hand, without even touching the knob. Storming through the house like a furious force of nature, bursting into each room, one by one, it doesn't take long before he finds who he's looking for.

Kyle is in the bathroom off of the main bedroom upstairs, swaying as he stands over the sink, pressing the dulled edge of a steak knife's blade into the flesh of his forearm.

"Hey!" Ben shouts, "Knock it off," smacking the knife away.

It clatters to the floor.

Grabbing Kyle's chin, Ben forces him to look at him. Pupils dilated and visibly dazed, it's clear that he's taken something, but what, exactly, that might be, Ben has no idea.

"What the fuck did you *take*, dumbass?!"

Kyle blinks and tries to push him away, slurring his words as he says, "Get off. I'm allowed. Get off me."

"What the fuck did you *TAKE*?!" Ben bellows.

Kyle squints stubbornly at him, silent, so Ben slaps him hard across the face with the back of his hand.

"Fucking hell!" Kyle cries, his hand going to where his lip has now been split open and is starting to bleed, "Prick!"

Ben pulls his arm back, ready to hit him again, when Kyle throws his hands up in surrender and confesses, "Okay! I had a couple shots of somethin', and I bought some tablets off of some dude at the bar down the road. I don't know what it was. Don't fucking care."

"I care!" Ben spits at him.

He twists Kyle's arm into a better position in order to get a closer look at the wound. Luckily Ben had gotten there before Kyle could do serious damage to himself. The cut is not deep and the blood merely trickles out, rather than gushing. He roughly tears away Kyle's clothes, yanking his shirt up over his head, pulling his pants and underwear down.

"In the tub!" he shouts, putting all the force he can muster behind the words.

Kyle scowls but obeys without protest. He's too well-trained not to, no matter how defiant he may be feeling.

Ben turns the knob and ice-cold water sprays onto Kyle's naked body. Yelping, he tries to jump away, complaining, "It's *cold*!"

"Fuck you! Get under the water, slave! We gotta sober you up."

Pulling the nozzle free of its holder, Ben sprays Kyle down. When he sees his eyes start to clear, it's a huge relief to Ben.

Shutting the water off, he pulls Kyle out of the tub. Pointing to the toilet seat, he barks, "Sit!"

Ben rummages in the linen closet and the drawers under the sink. When he finds what he's looking for, he brings it over to Kyle. Wrapping his fingers in a vice-like grip around the wrist of Kyle's injured arm, Ben holds him still as he quickly pours some hydrogen-peroxide over the cut.

Kyle shrieks as it burns into him, and tries to yank free.

"Hurts, don't it? Man up, ya damn baby! Maybe you shouldn't have cut open your fucking arm, huh?"

"Why do you *care* if I cut my arm? *You've* cut me before! Why can't *I* do it? It's *MY* body!" he spouts defiantly.

"When *I* do it, it's with sterile equipment in a controlled environment and I'm not drugged up. You could have really hurt yourself! If you'd nicked a main artery, you could have died," Ben growls at him.

He wraps the disinfected arm tightly with gauze then tapes the end down.

"Maybe I want to die."

"Oh, don't be so dramatic," Ben sighs, "You really that upset about your little boyfriend?"

"Stop calling him that!" Kyle licks over his lips, worrying at the cut with the point of his tongue and pinching the bridge of his nose between his index finger and thumb. Confused, the defiance temporarily gone from his voice, he asks Ben, "You know what happened with me and Darrek?"

"Yeah. *Duh*."

"How?"

"You called me."

"Oh. Oops."

"Yeah. Oops," Ben scowls, rolling his eyes. "Don't remember that, huh? Such a fucking drunk-dialer."

He yanks Kyle up and pushes him forward in front of him into the hallway, where Kyle trips over his own feet.

"Kitchen! You need coffee. *Lots* of coffee. Then we teach your ass a lesson."

After three cups of black coffee and heaps of tense silence, Kyle finds himself beside his bed, on his knees at his Master's feet, dressed in the first thing he could find—loose-fitting pajama pants and a shirt. Unlike Darrek, Kyle's house is well stocked with a plentiful and wide variety of sex toys and gear. Ben has perused the collection and chosen a few items that have been laid out on the bed and are ready to go.

"You know what I think?" Ben tells him, finally breaking what seems like hours of unbroken and maddening quiet, Kyle's eyes obediently locked to his. "I think you're clinging so fucking hard to your 'love' for Darrek because it's *SAFE*. It's safe because you thought he would never feel the same way as you do. You could just love him in secret, and have the fantasy all worked out perfectly in your precious little head. Poor baby, aren'tcha? So fucking *tragic*, with your perfect unrequited love. You're the ultimate victim. So damn *noble*. But you are so full of *shit*. *You* are just afraid of *real-*

ity! You couldn't handle it when Darrek wasn't disgusted by you. Ruined your plans, didn't he?"

Kyle juts out his jaw in stubbornness but doesn't say a word. He doesn't move, doesn't blink.

Ben crouches down and gets in his face.

"Do you love Darrek?" he demands.

"Yes, sir," Kyle mumbles.

"Did you tell him you love him for purely selfish reasons?"

"...Yes, sir."

"Is there anything you want to add in explanation of your behavior today?"

"Well... yeah... I'm also upset because Darrek was all ready to just fuck me, you know? Dare's supposed to be the good guy. He's not supposed to fuck around and be a cheater. He's supposed to be better than that."

"Better than you?"

"Yeah."

"Spoiled your perfect little picture of him, did he? *Nobody's* perfect. Not even lover boy *Darrek*."

"I'm sorry," Kyle sighs. "I'm really sorry. God. I'm such an ass. I want to be better for you, sir. Let's do this. I'm ready."

"What is this to you, Kyle?" Ben asks curiously. He almost smiles at the flinch Kyle makes at the sound of his name. "You think you're playing me? Looking for me to hurt you so you can revel in the pain and feel better about yourself?"

"I don't know," he shrugs, looking away.

"Don't play dumb with me. You are *not* dumb. You are the furthest thing from dumb." Ben tilts Kyle's chin up with his index finger, so that they're eye-to-eye, "Did it freak you out that we were going to have a date? That we were going to move past the D/s shit? Is this you acting out so that you get a good, hard punishment from me? So that I'm good and angry at you instead?"

Kyle's gaze slips away, eyes closing over.

"Look at me," Ben hisses to him. Kyle complies after a pause. "I love you, Kyle."

Flinching again, he breathes, "Shut up. Shut the fuck up."

"No. Tough shit. I love you, Kyle, and I'm here only because I know that now. If I didn't care, I wouldn't have come. You *are* important to me and I want whatever this is between us. I'm going to do this, and punish you, because I know you need it, and because you deserve it. But I'm also doing it because I care about you. I'm sorry I couldn't say it earlier. I'm a little... *resistant*... sometimes."

Kyle doesn't respond. He goes still as a statue and absolutely silent.

"Hmm..." Ben hums thoughtfully. "Fine then. Maybe I should leave. Maybe this isn't gonna work. I think it's time for us to take a nice, long break."

He stands and walks to the door.

"What are you doing?" Kyle says with dread. "Stop! *Stop!*"

Ben doesn't stop, though, so Kyle scrambles to his feet and chases after him.

"Ben, stop! Don't leave! Don't leave me!"

Running down the steps and catching him at the door, Kyle crumples at Ben's feet and holds desperately to his ankles, begging, "Please, Master. I'll be good for you. I'll be the best slave you ever had—real loyal and obedient. I'll be so damn good. I'll stop... you know... trying to get things from you. I'll just *obey*. No more fucking around. You were right, okay? I'm chicken shit! I've been trying to get you to care about me for so long. It was like a game, you know? But it's *NOT* a game. It's so fucking *NOT* a game, and *I know that* now. And I'm scared. I've never been so scared. I thought it'd be better this way. I thought it could go back to the way it was."

Ben shakes him loose and grabs the door handle.

"*NO*! Oh god, *PLEASE*, master! Don't do this!" Kyle cries, grasping pathetically at Ben's feet.

Ignoring him, Ben pulls open the door even as Kyle tries to push it closed. He steps outside and begins walking down the path, out to the street where he's parked. Kyle runs after him, still pleading shamelessly, trying to stand in his way. He falls to his knees in front of Ben again and wraps himself around Ben's legs.

All Kyle gets is a cold scowl as Ben kicks him away like a stray dog. As Ben digs his keys from his pocket, Kyle is sobbing openly now, his wails surely waking his neighbors with their piercing volume.

Ben pulls the handle and opens the truck's door, muttering tonelessly, "Maybe you'll be able to find a new Dom somewhere that's more compatible with you. You never know. Good luck with that."

Crawling on the cracked asphalt, Kyle grips the hem of Ben's pants, choking on tears, unable to get any more words out.

After one sharp, swift kick to Kyle's chest that sends him sprawling back on his ass, Ben pulls the door closed and starts the engine.

"NO!" Kyle screams. He dives in front of the truck's front end, using his body as a barrier, curling himself over the hood. "You'll have to run me over first. You can't leave me! I need you, Ben! I need YOU. You have to believe me! I'm telling the truth now! I love you too, okay? It's just so fucking hard to say it to you like this because it feels like I'm ripping my goddamned heart out of my chest for you. I'm not saying it to get anything, I just MEAN it. And *I'M SORRY*. Please! Please! Don't do this to me! *PLEASE!*"

Ben actually revs the engine once, foot still firmly on the brake. Thinking in that moment that Ben really is going to hit him with his truck, it scares Kyle so badly that he retches. Stumbling backward and doubling over, he throws up his three cups of coffee and the remnants of the pills and booze out onto the road in front of Ben's truck. Curling up in a ball, kneeling there, Kyle prepares himself for the impact. He's got nothing left to lose.

When the engine shuts off, he's confused.

There's the creaking sound of the driver's side door opening. Kyle scrambles to his feet, wiping his mouth with the back of his sleeved arm.

Ben appears in front of him and Kyle falls into his arms, hiding his face against the side of Ben's neck, wrecked and whimpering weakly with thick tears.

"I forgive you," Ben whispers to him and kisses his hair, hugging him close.

Kyle clutches to him, making small noises, shaken to the core.

Chapter 17
Declawed and Collared

After a shower and brushing his teeth about fifteen times, Kyle reappears in the bedroom where Ben is sprawled on the bed, ankles crossed and hands laced behind his head.

"That was my punishment, huh?" Kyle mutters, tiredly. "I didn't like it. You scared the fuck out of me."

Sitting perched on the edge of the bed, he holds his head in his hands, elbows propped on his knees, and groans.

"You aren't supposed to like it, babe," Ben tells him. "Think of it as another way I needed to sober you up."

He sits up and palms the pair of leather handcuffs nearby. Looping an arm around Kyle, he draws him backward and up the bed, kissing over his neck.

"Would you really have left me?" Kyle asks a little fearfully as he lays back. Ben pushes the pillows away and starts to draw Kyle's hands above his head.

"Yeah, I would. If that's what it took. If that was the right thing to do."

Watching as Ben fits the leather around his wrists, enjoying how it holds them flush together, restricting him, putting him at Ben's mercy, Kyle relaxes for the first time all day.

This is going to happen, Kyle realizes. He's going to get to have this. And this time, it's not a game at all. This time it's all real—just him and Ben, his Master. His heart beats faster and he clears his throat, shifting a little on the bed as his whole body starts to jitter with desire and the most delicious and familiar sort of fear.

Ben smiles as, gradually, the tension in Kyle's body grows noticeably, even as his face softens and the worry lines disappear. Pulling Kyle's hands up tight, fully extending his arms, he affixes the cuffs to the headboard.

Glancing down, he sees how aroused Kyle is getting, at his thin cotton pajama pants tenting in the front. Brushing his palm featherlight over the erection, Ben watches Kyle arch his back, pushing up against the hand, head thrown back and eyes shut.

"You want this so bad, don't you, kitty?" Ben laughs darkly.

"Shit, yeah. Please, Master? Play with me?"

Smoky blue eyes wide and innocent, gaze up at him from between arms bound tightly in the leather, begging shamelessly for whatever Ben wants to give him; the words go straight to his dick.

"You're gonna be the fucking death of me with how stupidly sexy you are," Ben groans, catching Kyle's lips in a kiss before commanding him, "Turn the fuck over. On your belly."

Kyle wriggles over, turning his face to the side as he breathes hot against his arm.

Ben moves away. It's a sign that it's starting, that it's *happening*, and Kyle can't contain his need. It dizzies him—every inch of flesh, every nerve ending in his body tingling with anticipation, ready to explode at the slightest touch or sensation.

He hears a length of tape get unwound and ripped from the roll. Ben stretches it across Kyle's eyes and presses it tightly down, blinding him.

"Mmm... what are you gonna... do to me, sir?"

"It's a surprise," Ben lilts, laughing as he pulls Kyle's legs straight, holding them together as he fastens ankle cuffs to them and then attaches the cuffs to the footboard. Kyle is stretched out in a line on the mattress, pulled tightly enough at either end that he can't move much at all, can't even thrust his hips or wriggle away.

Another piece of tape is ripped off and this one goes over his mouth, keeping him quiet. His dick is painfully erect now, squeezed by the weight of his body against the mattress. Testing the give, he finds he can't move, can't relieve the pressure in his balls and get off. It's perfect. It's just how he likes it. Even if it's just this, and Ben leaves him like this all night, if Ben just watches him, and lets Kyle *know* he's being watched, it would be enough.

He's still wearing pants and he wonders why, until he feels Ben slowly ease them down to mid-thigh, baring the curve of his ass. It makes Kyle feel more exposed, somehow, than if he was simply naked, and he moans behind the gag. The sound chokes off as Ben breaches him suddenly with a dry finger down to the last knuckle. His body automatically clenches up around it and his inner muscles squeeze tight as Ben crooks the finger and digs deep. He's still not used to this, even after almost two years as Ben's submissive. It feels foreign and startling, and the utter violation of it disturbs him on a base level.

"You breathing, kitty?" Ben asks knowingly, stroking over Kyle's silky-soft inner walls. "Relax."

The held breath is let out all at once through his nose, loudly, before he sucks back in a lungful of oxygen and focuses on breathing regularly and unclenching.

"We've gotta get you past these issues, Kyle. I've got you. Okay?"

"Mm-hmm," he nods.

Angling his wrist, Ben curls the finger and rubs deliberately over Kyle's prostate in a steady, gentle rhythm.

He moans through the gag. It turns into a whimper as his hips twitch and snap against the bed with nowhere to go, no way to escape. All he can do is twist to the side, and even then Ben just follows the movement, not relenting or easing up. The whimper breaks and turns into a small mewling purr, the very sound that earned Kyle his nickname months and months ago.

"You know I love it when you do that, kitty. Gonna be my kitten? Gonna purr for me?"

He keeps fingering the sweet spot, and as the sensations overload in Kyle, the pressure builds even more. The purrs become desperate. Ben imagines the pre-come that must be milking from Kyle's cock and decides he has to check, has to *know*, so he forces his other hand between Kyle's belly and the bed. It slips into the slickness pooling near the head of his cock.

"God, you're so wet, kitten. You made a mess of the bed. I think you're a bad, bad, kitty," he teases as more spunk seeps out onto his hand. Shifting his hand with effort, he closes his fingers around the throbbing member; his index finger and thumb grip around the sensitive, spongy head, and his thumb presses right at the bundle of nerves under the ridge as he starts to squeeze.

The purrs turn to whines of pain. Kyle is trapped between the finger entering him from behind, and the hand squeezing and pulling at his dick. He bucks and wriggles with renewed force, but knows it's useless. He rides it out, lets it wash over him, and good fucking *god* does it hurt. It hurts and it feels horribly, unbearably good all at the same time. The ecstasy goes on and on and then, all at once, stops.

The finger withdraws. The hand slides away. He waits for the feeling of Ben wiping his soiled hand off on him, sure that he'll do it.

He doesn't.

Then there's a small, satisfied moan from Ben as he says, "Mmm... god, you taste good, kitten. Makes me want to lick your dick clean like I just licked my hand clean. Wanna lap up that milky-white jizz and suck every drop off of you."

Kyle groans loudly, the sound vibrating through his chest, and he just wants that so badly. It would be amazing, especially if it was *Ben* doing it, but he knows it's not going to happen, that it's a tease. But at least it's a good tease.

There's the soft, padding sound of footsteps receding, of Ben walking away, and Kyle realizes that he *is* leaving him there. Ben is leaving him half-spent, nerves jangling and firing, cock rock-hard, ass throbbing from the slight burn left by Ben's dry finger.

An untold amount of time later, Ben reappears. Kyle hears the soft footsteps again on the carpeting, notes the dip and shift of weight on the bed as Ben climbs on and straddles his legs, sitting down on them, restraining him even more.

He doesn't say a word. Ben just sits there, watching Kyle listen to him, watching his ribs expand and contract with each breath.

Grabbing the round globes of Kyle's ass cheeks, one in each hand, he spreads him wide, watches his pink hole twitch, knowing well that it bothers Kyle to be observed like this. There have been countless sessions with him where the only thing Ben did to him was expose him in this way. And whether it was just the two of them, or it was the two of them and one of Ben's assistants, or even during the streaming videos with untold numbers of people watching, it always has done things to Kyle and set him on edge more than anything else in Ben's arsenal. He makes a mental note to try using a speculum on him soon.

Keeping him spread, he presses his thumbs at the hole, pulling it open. As just the tips of them dip inside, prying him apart, Kyle cries out and snaps his hips. Then he shakes his ass from side to side, like he's trying to throw Ben off.

Ben laughs mischievously.

"I haven't even gotten to the good part," he chuckles, adding sarcastically, "I'm sorry, is this making you uncomfortable?"

Kyle growls through the gag and Ben can tell he's cursing him out. It amuses him immensely.

Adjusting his left hand, he keeps Kyle's hole open with only those fingers and grabs an ice cube from the dish he'd brought up with him from the kitchen. Careful not to drip onto Kyle's skin or touch him anywhere with it, not wanting to give any warning for what's coming, Ben aligns it with his target and then quickly pushes it through the outer ring of muscles in Kyle's anus and down into his rectum.

Kyle wails and cries out sharply as Ben chases the cube with two fingers, pushing it down as far as he can reach. Savoring each sound, each struggle, Ben plucks a second cube from the bowl. This one he takes more time with, now that Kyle knows what's happening. He runs it up and down the crease of his ass, the heat of him quickly starting to melt it, before pushing it inside his opening as well. A third cube is forced deep as Kyle tries clenching his ass shut in an effort to stop Ben.

"Getting cold?" Ben asks solemnly.

"Mmfghh!" Kyle growls, his brow creased in anger. A hard shudder runs through his body and his fury slowly dies as his discomfort grows and grows.

The tight, hot walls of the inside of his body steadily melt the ice, but the burn from the cold stays. It hurts in a different way that anything else he's ever experienced and it's almost like he wants to jump right out of his skin to escape it. It's unbearable. And as the ice warms, turning to water, it trickles even further into him. It's like a slow, torturous enema.

Three more cubes are inserted into his body before he loses count altogether. He can feel himself crying, but the tears have nowhere to go because of the tape. Pooling over his eyelids, they find a weakness in the adhesive and trickle out, down his face.

To distract himself, he digs his fingernails into his hands. His ass feels so full. Ben keeps prodding into him with his fingers, and as the cubes farthest into him melt, slipping far down and getting lost in him. He just pushes the larger pieces into their place and keeps feeding more into his body.

It's never going to stop. Ben's just going to keep filling him with ice until he passes out or succumbs to hypothermia. Kyle is sure of it.

Kyle is resigning himself with noble stoicism to this hopelessly tragic fate when Ben's weight is suddenly gone from his legs.

It's a worrisome thing.

"Lift your hips, slave!" he barks.

It startles Kyle into obedience and he does it instantly. There's a crumpling, rustling sound and then cold as what feels and sounds like plastic is slid under him.

That's a worrisome thing as well.

"I'm going to turn you onto your side now," Ben warns, "But you need to keep that tight little asshole clamped shut. Keep the water inside. Got it?"

Kyle whimpers but nods.

Then he's being turned. As the air hits his dick and balls, now exposed, no longer hidden by his body, he starts to feel the suffocating tidal wave of panic drench him.

Knowing it's useless, but unable to stop, he begs through the gag, wordlessly, mumbling and humming the sounds.

A hand circles his balls, cradling them, before another, holding more ice, closes down over them. The ice presses against his sac and Ben squeezes. The combination of freezing, burning, penetrating and terrible cold and crushing pressure causes him to scream shrilly. He tries to wriggle away, but loses his concentration and forgets to keep his ass shut tight. Some water dribbles down his crack, runs over his leg onto the plastic.

Ben doesn't relent until the cubes are melted away. By the time they have, Kyle has fallen silent, has stopped moving, so Ben goes to his head and slaps his cheek.

"Hey!" he calls, "You with me?"

Kyle's only response is a sighing exhale, so Ben rips off the tape on his mouth and eyes.

"Baby, look at me," he urges, watching Kyle's eyes roll. "Come on. Kyle? Hey! Kyle!"

"Ye-yeah..." he sighs, eyes still unfocused, starting to shiver. "So fucking cold.... We done already? It's over?"

"Yeah, it's over," Ben assures him, kissing him softly before rapidly unfastening the bonds on his wrists and ankles. He scoops Kyle up in his arms and carries him the ten paces or so from the bed to the toilet, setting him carefully down onto it.

"Let it go. Let the water out," Ben tells him.

"I don't wanna," Kyle pouts, eyes still mostly closed over.

"Stubborn ass," Ben sighs. He places a hand on Kyle's taut lower belly and another right above the crack of his ass and pushes with both.

Kyle gasps as the water is forced out. It's not that much, not as much as a full enema, but it's still embarrassing, and he feels himself blushing beet red.

"You know I don't like you being here for this part," he complains.

"I don't fucking *care* if you like it. You aren't in charge. You done?"

"Yeah."

Ben unfastens both sets of cuffs and helps him stand, guiding him to the shower. He rinses Kyle off with warm water, and makes sure he's clean. He can see the exhaustion setting in, so he guides Kyle right back to bed, stripping the plastic sheet from it first and folding it up to be disposed of.

"Still cold?" Ben asks, as Kyle lies back on the pillows, and gazes curiously up at him.

"Yeah," he admits. "Why?"

"I'll warm you up," he offers.

Kyle watches as Ben rips open a condom wrapper with his teeth. Pulling out the circle of latex, he rolls it onto his aching, huge erection. Kyle feels the low, niggling tickle of terror grip his stomach again as Ben spreads him open and guides his legs back. With one hard push at the clenched rim of his entrance, Ben's dick forces through all resistance until he bottoms out, fitted in the perfect, fascinatingly-cool-from-the-ice glove of Kyle's body.

Leaning down over him, Ben kisses him tenderly, suckling at his pouting lips and brushing a hand over his creased brow. His thrusts are slow and gentle, and Kyle kisses him back fervently. Kyle grips at Ben's ass, pulling him impossibly closer, but there's still pain sparked-bright in his eyes.

"You all right?" Ben asks in a gasp, his hand going to Kyle's cock to stroke him off twice as fast as his deep, easy pushes into Kyle's body.

"I'm scared," he admits, biting down on his own lip but arching up into the touch. He starts to make that small mewling sound back in his throat again as Ben's cock jabs at his prostate on each push, and it warms Ben's heart.

Kyle's head snaps back and he gets lost in the feelings, but it's so intense, too intimate, and the intimacy *hurts*.

"Don't be scared," Ben tells him, kissing along his neck, over his pulse point and Adam's apple. "This is just me loving you."

"That's what scares me," he gasps. He comes suddenly, with a sharp cry, over Ben's fist.

Ben rides out the fluttering, pulsing grip of Kyle's body reacting to the orgasm. Pushing harder now, his hips slap audibly against the smooth, firm curved muscle of Kyle's ass. With a long, rough, grunting moan, Ben fills the condom.

Stripping it off, and disposing of it, he crawls back onto Kyle, and smiles when Kyle wraps his legs around him, and twines his fingers around the back of his head, brushing through his short hair. Kyle pulls Ben down against him and whispers next to his ear, "Look... this is serious to me, okay? I trust you with my body. You know that. But if I give you this part of me, too, then you have to *swear* to take it seriously. You have to *swear* not to fuck me over with it. And please don't *ever* lie to me. I might come off like a cocky bastard sometimes, but that's only because underneath I break kind of easy."

"Yeah, I've figured that out. I'll protect you," Ben vows, "I'll protect you in every possible way. Don't you get it? That's what this *means*. I'm responsible for your *well-being* now, in every sense. Your job is to obey me, and *my* job is to take care of you completely."

"That sounds kind of perfect," he sighs.

"Good."

Chapter 18
First Steps

"Mornin' sleepyhead," Darrek hears through the fog of slumber clouding his senses, as he rouses from weird dreams.

"Gabe?" he croaks, still hoarse from the previous night. Trying to crane his neck around to see him, Darrek feels a nerve pinch and curses with pain.

"Don't try to move," Gabriel warns him. "You're stiff, right?"

"Yeah..." Darrek groans.

A weight settles onto the backs of his thighs and, as hands start to work at his muscles, slowly and gently un-knotting them. Darrek hears, "I know I should have done this last night, but I saw how tired you were. I don't think you moved once all night, so that probably didn't help, either."

Gabriel continues to massage him, starting at the top near his neck and shoulders, working steadily downward, knuckles and palms, fingers and fists digging in circular motions. They get to his lower back and Darrek moans with pleasure.

"So good..." he sighs. "I wanna wake up like this every day. Well, not with the muscle pain, but the massage is nice; really, really nice."

"You'd probably get tired of me after a while," Gabriel responds quietly.

"I don't think so. I liked what you said last night, you know, about keeping your stuff here. If you're still interested... I would like that. I'd like you to stay here. And stay for as long as you want...."

Smiling, Gabriel starts to work at Darrek's left arm, the muscles in his bicep and triceps just as clenched as those in his back.

"I can hear you smiling," Darrek chuckles.

"How in the fucking world can you *hear* me smiling? Seriously, how?"

"You are, aren't you? You didn't deny it. I bet you're still smiling. I wanna see. Can I see?"

"I'll be smiling again later, after I fix you."

"You're fixing me?"

"Yeah. I guess you don't have to go to work today, right? Because yesterday you were home."

"Nah. No work. Our crew got laid off from the bank job. It happens. We'll probably be hired for a new job in a few days. No biggie. In the meantime, I'll just work on my other projects."

"Good."

"Sierra... is she...?"

"She's fine. I fed her already and let her outside to run around. She was ready to break down the door to get out there if she had to."

"Yeah, she's got a lot of energy to burn off. That's one of the reasons I liked this place and bought it. It has a nice, big yard for her. She's always calmer after running around for a while."

"Sounds like you and she have similar personalities," Gabriel says.

Darrek chuckles and agrees. "Only I don't burn off my energy by running around in circles and chasing squirrels. I like my way of calming down better, even if it is a little... unconventional."

"Me too. Are you calm now?"

"Yeah, I am. It's... strange."

"I, um... I've been thinking, while you were asleep. I have some thoughts I want to share with you."

"Okay. Lay 'em on me."

"I'm going to tell Sam that I'll be restricting my future involvement in Diadem to the videography side of things, and running their website. I might offer to train Alyssa and anyone else they would be bringing in to replace me as a Dom—whoever would be taking over my current clients, besides you, of course. No one else gets to touch you. But, as of today, once I talk to Sam, I will have no more clients, and will not be doing any more assisting either. And that will leave me with enough free time to explore... other avenues."

There is a brief pause and then Darrek asks, "Really? That's... that's a *big* deal."

"I know. But, I want you to trust me. If I'm expecting you to trust me completely, then I have to reciprocate, you know? And, this idea... it appeals to me. I can get into doing other kinds of video production; I can work on my craft instead of staying stuck in the professional Dominant side of things. Because I realize now, that if I ever want more than that, if I want someone... well, okay, if I want *you* to be in a fully exclusive and committed relationship with me, then I have to give it up."

"Gabriel... I have to see you. May I see you, please? Can I get up and..." Darrek says almost desperately, still face down on the bed with Gabriel's body and his seized-up muscles keeping him pinned.

Gabriel just moves off of him in response and lies down next to Darrek, so that they are face-to-face and nose-to-nose.

Darrek cups the side of Gabriel's face with one large hand, his own face creased with frown lines. His voice is hushed as he says, "That means so much to me, that you would do that... that you would change your whole life around like that. I could never... I would *never* ask you to do that."

"I know. That's why I'm not waiting for you to ask. It's my decision. It's as good as done. I'm doing this. It'll be all wrapped up today."

"And you said... you said that we're in a...."

"Committed relationship," Gabriel finishes for him.

"Oh my god..." Darrek breathes. "*Thank you*, Gabe. I don't even know what to say.... Um.... Yes. I guess I'll say yes."

Gabriel moves closer, pressing his lips to the tousled mess of Darrek's hair, and soundlessly mouths three little words to him, meaning them in every possible way, even if he is not yet able to let Darrek hear them.

The fullness of his rose-colored lips urgently form the words, 'I love you.'

After a thorough massage, Gabriel makes sure that Darrek can move around unassisted and without discomfort. Satisfied, Gabriel leaves him to go and make breakfast downstairs while Darrek gets washed up and dressed.

Once he finishes getting ready, Darrek appears at the bottom of the stairs, eagerly following the enticing aroma of coffee and bacon with a growling stomach, eyes alight. Ravenous with hunger, Darrek gratefully devours the hearty, filling meal laid out by Gabriel, the delicate purple flower from the night before still sitting in its vase between them.

Gabriel smiles happily the whole time, nursing a huge mug of coffee, and seemingly unable to take his eyes off of Darrek.

"I guess you've gotta go into the office?" Darrek asks between bites.

"Yeah, just to talk to Sam and work some things out. I'm going to swing by Trace's place too, and grab some of my stuff. If you're going to be in the garage all day working on those chairs, it'll help to keep me occupied so I'm not just gawking at your ridiculously sexy ass all day. When, um... when I get finished with that, I thought I might clean up your garden. Do some weeding...."

Darrek grins widely up at him and takes a sip of his coffee.

"What?" Gabriel asks at the twinkling in Darrek's eyes. As he blushes slightly, Gabriel adds in his own defense, "I like to work with my hands, too."

"Oh, I *know*," Darrek assures him, chuckling a little. Lowering his eyes, he asks, "You always gonna clean up my messes?"

"I hope so," Gabriel replies, a small smile playing at the edges of his mouth.

They finish their breakfasts and clear the table.

Both of them are keenly aware when the moment of their parting approaches. Needing to broach another, more difficult topic before he goes, Gabriel leans against the counter next to where Darrek is rinsing and loading plates, silverware, and glasses into the dishwasher. His voice lowers a little as he says, "I... uh... I talked to Ben earlier. It turns out that Kyle called me last night because he was really fucking wasted. He called Ben too and actually tried to hurt himself, but Ben got there in time to stop him from doing any real damage. They... well, they worked things out between themselves kind of the way we did. They're together now. Ben's keeping a close eye on Kyle, and he's taking good care of him. It's so bizarre, but I've never seen Ben care about someone to the extent he cares about Kyle, even in all the years we've been friends. So... I guess I'm telling you all of this because I want to assure you that Kyle is okay and that he's not as big of an asshole as he appeared to be last night."

Darrek has shut off the water, and set down the dish in his hand. He struggles momentarily with a fairly uncontrollable desire to go to his knees before Gabriel again, just because of the kindness in the way Gabriel is talking about the very man that caused him so much heartache and pain. The fact that Gabriel obviously really *has* forgiven him, and Kyle as well, has Darrek reeling with near-delirious joy and gratitude. His eyes close and a shiver runs down his spine at the tone in his lover and Master's voice.

After a moment or two, he gives in to the urge and gets down onto his knees, curling his arms around Gabriel's body. Sighing with relief once he does, feeling better already for having done so, he rests his forehead against Gabriel's hip and shivers again when Gabriel's fingers curl into his hair, brushing gently over his scalp.

He has never felt as loved as he does in that one small moment.

Gabriel continues speaking, after taking a second to clear his throat and tame his own wild desire to show Darrek with actions as well as words how much he truly feels.

"Ben and I discussed the fact that you and Kyle work together. We realize how much your friendship means to you both, and we want to help each of you resolve this shit and salvage that friendship. The best way, in our opinion, for you to take that first step is for you both to apologize for how you've hurt one another. Would you like us to help you do that? Is that something you want?"

"Yes. God, yes. Thank you," Darrek sighs, curling his hands around the backs of Gabriel's knees, the side of his face resting against Gabriel's pelvis. "Thank you. I'd *really* like that. Kyle... he's been there for me through so much, and when no one else was. He deserves an apology."

"Good. I thought you'd say something like that. How long has he been your best friend?"

"I don't even know... forever, maybe. As far back as I can remember at least. I can't speak for *him*, obviously, but... I need to apologize to him for how I behaved. I don't want to lose his friendship over this. Even if he doesn't want anything to do with me anymore, I still need to tell him that and, I know that you'll help me find a way. But, honestly... just the fact that you would be *willing* to help me and help *him* after what happened... I can't even wrap my mind around it."

"Well, I don't want you to worry about any of that today. Just do what you need to do. I'm going to go do what *I* need to do, run some errands, and I'll be back later," Gabriel tells him, fingers stroking down the side of Darrek's face, around and under his chin and lifting it so that he can look into his trusting brown eyes. They catch the sunlight and turn golden. "I'd like to have you later, Darrek. I want to get my hands on you and make you feel everything and anything you want to feel. You tell me how far or how much, but I just... I need to have you. I want to take you right now, bent over the fucking table, or hell, on top of the table... but I think it'll be even better if we have to wait all day for it. Would you let me?"

"Fuck yes," Darrek breathes, holding even tighter to Gabriel's legs, inhaling his scent while he still can. "God, the things you do to me. They're like air, I need them so goddamned bad. Please. Please... you can take me any way you want me."

"I just wasn't sure if you wanted to take a break, or, you know... take it easy today. I wasn't sure you'd want to."

"Gabe... I don't think I've ever needed you more. It's like... it's like after what happened last night... I just want to be with you."

"Why?"

"Because... because I care about you and I know now that you *really do* care about me too. I have you under my skin now. When I'm with you, whether we're having sex, or you're just touching me, making me feel and react, or if we're just doing the damn dishes... I've never felt so lo...." He chokes on the word, not knowing if he's gone too far, meaning it, but just because he *means it* doesn't mean it's alright to say. Gabriel's eyes beg him to finish though, so he does, without any further hesitation. "I've *never* felt so loved. Not with *anyone*. That you could forgive me, even after I was shitty to you—*really* forgive me... no one's ever done something that big for me. I'm convinced. I'm committed. I would do absolutely *anything* for you, and I want to make you so fucking proud of me. I just want the chance to show you how much I mean those words. Nothing has ever been more important to me than just being worthy of you. I need you to take me, or fuck me, or hurt me, or punish me, or make love to me. I need anything you think I deserve."

"Come here," Gabriel breathes, pulling Darrek to his feet, wrapping the younger man's tall, muscular body in his arms, enclosing him in a gentle hug. They stand like that for long minutes, until Gabriel murmurs against Darrek's chest, "Now I don't wanna leave."

"Do your errands. It's okay... as long as you come right back."

Darrek feels Gabriel's lips moving soundlessly against his body, forming unspoken words.

"Me too," Darrek whispers into Gabriel's tousled hair.

After hours spent arranging his new contract with Diadem, Gabriel has reassigned his clients and made some very difficult phone calls. He has also stopped by the house to gather some of his belongings, and just missed running into Trace. Aware that it looks like he is moving out, or at least beginning to move in with Darrek, Gabriel is not at all ready to defend his choices to Trace.

His errands completed, and his life in as much order as it is going to get, Gabriel stands in the darkened doorway and watches Darrek work in the garage.

It makes Darrek self-conscious, feeling the weight of Gabriel's stare on him. Every move he makes, every time he bends over the workbench to sand down the far end of the planks he is readying, every time he brushes sweaty strands of hair out of his face, he knows Gabriel is watching. Gabriel is staring at his shifting body, the muscles working under his clothes. Feeling like he is on display, a flush of heat simmers up through his body, starting in the pit of his stomach, racing up his spine, tickling up the back of his neck and around, reaching to the tips of his ears, coloring his cheeks. As his dick swells and presses against the front of his jeans, he becomes self-conscious of that as well, just hoping that Gabriel does not notice how easy it is for him to affect him.

When Gabriel appears behind him, though, and; reaching around Darrek's body; rubs the palm of his right hand over the pulled-taut front of his pants, Darrek bites his tongue, sets his jaw, and goes very still. Gabriel chuckles, as he traces the outline of Darrek's cock with careful, light fingers, playing and squeezing over the head until Darrek exhales a shaky breath.

Gabriel says low in his ear, "I'm going to borrow some of your gardening tools until I pick up some of my own."

"Mmn... okay. Yeah... okay," Darrek nods. He's unable to think or function with Gabriel's fingertips rubbing small circles at the tip of his cock.

"Thanks," he says in response then is gone, tools in hand.

Fifteen minutes later, after finally calming down enough to trust himself around the power tools, Darrek goes back to work.

After dusk has begun to fall, Gabriel reappears once more in the doorway, hands washed clean, and changed into fresh clothes, as the ones he had been wearing were soiled with dirt from his efforts in the flowerbeds.

Darrek pauses in his work immediately. Frozen in place, he follows Gabriel out of the corner of his eye. Gabriel sees him doing it and chuckles, saying, "You look like a scared rabbit waiting for some big scary dog to come and try to sink its teeth into you. All that's missing is the pink, twitching nose. You've already got the perky little ass ready to leap into action and the raring sex drive."

"Are you... gonna watch some more... or...."

Masking his expression, Gabriel strides over to him again. Stepping up to Darrek's left side, he presses his thigh against Darrek's, cupping his crotch with a hand. With the other, he rubs a fingertip firmly up the crease in the seat of his pants, and asks, "Would you like me to watch?"

Darrek exhales sharply.

Gabriel represses a smile. Now rubbing back and forth over the particular spot that most interests him in the crevice of Darrek's ass, Gabriel continues with, "Actually, I wanted to ask if it's okay with you if I install some... hardware... in the bedroom. Just a few strategically placed hooks above the headboard, maybe one in the ceiling. You have a couple of screw eye hooks in a jar over there that'd work really well, and are big enough for a chain to be fed through. And, I see you have a stud finder. I'll make sure they're firmly anchored so they don't pull out of the wallboard and they'd be easy enough to patch up with...."

"Yes!" Darrek gasps impatiently, eyes closed.

Smiling at the outburst, Gabriel falls quiet, licking his lips.

"You interrupted me," he says quietly.

"I'm sorry!" Darrek says, still breathless. "I'm really sorry, sir."

"Maybe I should discipline you for that...."

Darrek swallows thickly and Gabriel feels Darrek's cock jump, pulsing hot inside his pants, moving against his hand.

"Yes, sir," Darrek agrees.

"Okay. I'll be right back. Don't move from this spot."

Just a minute or so later, Darrek hears footsteps leading from the back door of the house to the garage, and then up behind him. Darrek doesn't turn around, he stays perfectly still and opens wide as Gabriel fits a gag between his lips, pushing the hard red rubber ball back between his upper and lower teeth, lips stretched and pressed around it, and secures the straps tightly behind his head.

As he works, Gabriel explains at Darrek's ear, his deep, authoritative voice stirring an insistent tickle of lust low in Darrek's belly and making the blood pulse and throb even more in his over-filled dick.

"That's to teach you to be quiet while I'm talking to you, to hold your tongue and be respectful of me, and wait to respond until it is appropriate for you to do so. I'll remove it when you're done working. When you're finished in here, meet me upstairs in the bedroom. I'll be waiting for you."

Darrek moans, but when Gabriel's hand slips under the front of his shirt and his fingers push down inside the front of his jeans, over hot, tight skin and farther down still, inside his boxers, he hurriedly bites off the sound.

"You're wet, my beautiful slave. Your dick is leaking all over your underwear. Perhaps I should get you a chastity device as well so you don't keep soiling your clothes."

Gabriel's hand forces its way lower and his fingers curl and squeeze around his shaft and balls. He doesn't move the hand; he just squeezes with steady pressure, and is more than a little surprised when Darrek makes a low grunt and comes in his pants. Hips twitching, pushing forward into the grip of Gabriel's hand, Darrek's pelvic and stomach muscles all contract as he spills hot and wet over his underwear and Gabriel's fingers as well.

"Jesus, you were more worked up than I thought," Gabriel admits. "Well, I guess there's a second part to your lesson about *control* today. No cleaning up or getting changed. You can work in your come-filled pants as well as the gag."

Nodding and flushed, Darrek shudders a little with aftershocks.

Pulling his hand free, Gabriel wipes it clean with the edge of Darrek's shirt. Turning away, he gathers some more supplies—a hammer, cordless drill, anchors, a handful of the screw eye hooks, the stud finder, and a few other things—before heading back to the house.

Chapter 19

Just a Pinch

An hour later, Darrek appears in the doorway to the bedroom. The gag is still snug between his dehydrated, stretched-wide lips. His jaw aches, and the front of his pants displays a large, drying stain. As Gabriel approaches, Darrek keeps his eyes averted, his head lowered and fingers laced behind his back.

Immediately removing the gag with quick work of his fingers at the straps, he pulls it from Darrek's mouth. Gossamer-like strings of saliva connect it to his mouth as Gabriel pulls it away. Darrek licks his lips, rubs the back of a hand over his mouth and flexes his jaw, working the stiffness out of it with a quiet sigh.

"Are you ready to start or do you need to eat something first?" Gabriel asks. "Be honest."

"The truth is that I'm going to explode if we don't start right the fuck now—with all due respect... Master."

He is jittering with nerves and eager anticipation, and Gabriel can see that his slave's words are true from the look in his pleading eyes.

"Okay. I want to start by prepping you, so follow me into the bathroom."

Walking into the room, Darrek trails right behind him. Gabriel gathers shaving cream, a new, unused razor, and a towel, placing it all on the counter. Then, he closes the sink's drain and fills it with warm water, saying, "Remove all of your clothing and step into the tub. Wash your genitals off with soap, rinse well and then dry off."

He sits down on the closed lid of the toilet and watches Darrek follow his instructions, pleased that Darrek knows better than to try to close the curtain and block the view. Darrek uses the showerhead to wet himself down then lathers up his fully hard dick and balls, reaching between his legs as well to wash his ass. Then he rinses off and steps out of the tub, in front of Gabriel.

"Good," Gabriel tells him, picking up the shaving cream.

"Obviously your pubic hair has grown back in a little since our last session at Diadem, so I'm going to shave you completely now. Does that make you nervous?"

"Um... a little... sir."

"All right, well let me assure you that I'll be careful, and that I've done this many times before, okay?"

Darrek nods and mumbles, "Yes, sir," as Gabriel fills his hand with shaving cream and then proceeds to carefully cover Darrek with it – his balls and shaft and anywhere on his pelvis that has some of the short, dark hair, smearing the excess back between Darrek's legs.

Interlocking his fingers, clasping his hands tightly behind his back to steady them, and trying not to move, Darrek watches Gabriel pick up the gleaming razor and, without hesitation, begin to drag it over the patch of skin just below his navel. After a few swipes, he rinses it off in the water in the sink and goes back to work. Once the hair has been removed from the area above the base of his cock, Gabriel moves to the sides, scraping off the short, scratchy hairs with determined sweeps of the sharp implement.

The most unnerving part of the whole thing is how quickly Gabriel is working, how fast he's swiping the blade over Darrek's delicate flesh. Darrek silently prays that Gabriel slows down a little when he begins doing his balls.

As soon as the thought is through his head, he sees Gabriel bring the washed-off razor to his testicles, after cradling them in his left hand. Not even pausing or glancing up at Darrek, he just as quickly cuts away the pubic hair from his sac with precise gentle presses of the razor. Darrek can feel the tremors growing in strength in his knees and fights to control them, to keep as still as he can as the sharp edge glides over the soft, wrinkled skin. Luckily, the fact that Gabriel is going so heart-stoppingly fast also means that he is done that much sooner.

Rinsing off the blade again, he takes hold of Darrek's swollen cock next, gripping it with fingertips pressed around the head.

Now he *does* take a moment to glance up, only to say to Darrek severely, "Don't come."

"Okay," he gasps, nodding.

Positioning the razor at the base, he slowly drags it up the shaft. As it scratches at the over-sensitive skin of Darrek's dick, Gabriel listens to Darrek exhale shakily and says to him, "Obviously you don't have any hair here. This part I'm doing just because I *can*, and because I want to. The blade creates an interesting sensation, moving over the surface of the penis, especially when you're this erect. There's also the fear of being cut. Makes it more exciting, don't you think?"

"Yes, sir," he replies meekly, his steely hard-on proof enough of his interest, despite the tone of his voice.

The blade has stopped just before the ridge of his cock head, one inch-wide swath of cream now removed. Dipping the razor in the water and tapping it on the rim of the sink, it goes once more to the base of Darrek's dick and starts to work its way back up his length. Gabriel keeps Darrek's dick pulled down at a ninety-degree angle to his body instead of where it wants to curve up against his belly.

Darrek's gaze darts down, examining himself before it snaps back up to the spot on the wall above Gabriel's head.

"You're not bleeding, if that's what you're wondering," Gabriel tells him, beginning a third pass.

Heart beating fast and wildly in his chest, stomach knotted and the entire length of his legs practically vibrating with nervous energy, somehow he survives Gabriel shaving-clean his dick.

Just when Darrek thinks they're done, Gabriel says, "Turn around, spread your legs, and grab your ankles."

"Umm..." Darrek grunts, too surprised to move.

Gabriel blinks up at him once before Darrek quickly obeys.

Assuming the position, he feels Gabriel spreading shaving cream over his ass, into his crack, and over the smooth patch of skin between his balls and asshole.

"Oh god..." he groans, hearing the quiet swishing, splashing sound of Gabriel cleaning the razor.

It is deeply humiliating, being bent over like this, letting someone else shave bare his most intimate areas, but the fact that it is *Gabriel* doing it, knowing how much he *does* trust Gabriel, only makes Darrek confused. The embarrassment becomes laced with dread of being cut with the razor, which mingles with the undeniable force of his lust and his surprise at the fact that some part of him is deeply enjoying this whole process.

Gabriel speedily shaves clean the globes of his cheeks and works inward, doing the crease of his ass last. When Gabriel swipes the blade repeatedly over his hole, Darrek knows it's more to torture him than to take away any hard-to-reach hair. He does the patch of skin behind Darrek's balls last, and Gabriel grins as he sees a shiver race down Darrek's spine at the feeling of the blade pressing over the skin and sees goose bumps rise on his skin.

Using the towel to wipe away any lingering residue of foam, Gabriel admires his handiwork, satisfied.

"Okay. You're ready," he tells Darrek.

As he stands back up and turns around, Darrek locks eyes with Gabriel, who tells him, "You know, the best part about shaving you right before I start working you over is that right now your skin is at its *most* sensitive—newly exposed and slightly raw from the blade scraping at it. You'll feel everything I do that much more."

"Mmm," Darrek hums, still overly aware of how exposed and turned on he is, still unable to speak.

Taking his hand, Gabriel feels Darrek curl his fingers tenderly and closely around his, taking comfort from the contact. Gabriel leads Darrek back to the bedroom.

As Darrek lays down on the bed at Gabriel's urging, he stares raptly at the new hooks attached and anchored securely to the ceiling and wall. Gabriel guides his arms up and apart, securing his wrists with thick cuffs connected to chains that are fed back through the gaps in the headboard and then looped through the new hardware in the wall. Next, his feet are brought up, knees slightly bent, as far back and wide apart as Darrek's body will let them go. He is in as much of a split as he will ever manage and his legs are as close to the wall as Gabriel can pull them, the thick ankle cuffs Gabriel fits him with secured to the opposite ends of the chains that hold his wrists.

It leaves him fairly unable to move and his genitals, ass and torso utterly exposed to Gabriel.

Darrek thinks it is *glorious.*

Already fully hard, Darrek is aware of his cock leaking pre-come, further evidence of how he is incredibly turned on by the position he is in, and the knowledge that Gabriel could do anything to him right now and Darrek would not only let him, but would probably enjoy the fuck out of it.

Gabriel walks away, gathering supplies and laying things out on the surface of the dresser nearby, somewhat out of Darrek's line of sight.

Darrek sees him pick up a dish of tiny multicolored things and bring it back to the bed. Settling between Darrek's spread legs, right in front of his ass, Gabriel picks one of the brightly colored objects and holds it up, showing it to him.

"It's a tiny clip," Gabriel explains, pinching the clips ends to demonstrate how they open and close. It looks like an itty bitty clothespin, which, of course, makes Darrek instantly nervous. "I have hundreds of them. I like these a *lot* because they can fit in *very* small places."

The plastic clip is no more than three-quarters of an inch long. Darrek can see that Gabriel really does seem to have an endless supply of them. Before he can even begin to imagine where they are going to go, Gabriel's hand is on his ass, spreading him out. One of the tiny clothespin-like things is attached to the lip of skin of his asshole.

"Oh fucking *hell...*" Darrek moans, head falling back as Gabriel clips on one after another after another to the spot, ringing his opening with them. He counts eleven in total. As he clenches up reflexively, he sees Gabriel watching him squirm, watching his opening twitch.

Next Gabriel circles Darrek's dick with careful fingers, not touching it more than he has to, and steadies it as he attaches the first clip to the ridge of the head.

"Ga-*Gabe...*" he gasps, hips bucking at the sharp pinch, and gets a hard swat at his balls in response.

As Darrek writhes from the smack, Gabriel asks severely, "What did you call me?"

Choking out a small cry and twisting away, he croaks out, "I'm sorry, Master."

"That's better."

The next clip is attached to the opposite side of the edge of his cock head, followed by six more. They are torturously intense, focused stings that never let up; they only grow with strength, the ache spreading down his shaft, cramping his belly. The pinching at his asshole throbs out across his glutes, down his legs and radiates up along his spine.

Selecting a blue one next, Gabriel lifts Darrek's cock even more and slowly, carefully attaches it to a bit of skin at the slit in his dick. Pulling the clip to the side to make room for a second on the other side, stretching out the opening there in the process, Darrek whimpers brokenly, his hips coming up off the bed. A green one is attached on the other side and Gabriel lets him go, watches his dick bob and move in the air, ringed with colorful plastic.

Then he carefully grips the blue clip and the green one and twists them in opposite directions.

"Ahh! Fuck! Ouch! *Oh fucking....*"

He stops twisting them and instead pulls them apart, watching as the hole in the crown of Darrek's dick gapes open.

Darrek grunts thickly, hips chasing the feeling, coming up off the bed again like that could possibly help at all.

"You know..." Gabriel says softly. His voice is calm and hushed as he makes his fingers into a circle around Darrek's shaft, bringing them upward, pushing all the tiny clips attached to the head up, each one twisting and pulling at the sensitive flesh it's attached to, "The thing I like most about these, besides the fact that they're small enough to do *this....*"

He moves his hand and next pushes all of the circling clips back down almost flush against Darrek's shaft. Darrek makes a sharp mewling cry, as Gabriel uses his other hand to grip a few of the clips attached to Darrek's ass and twists them sharply clockwise, saying, "...when I take these off..." he twists the clips counterclockwise, "...it's going to hurt a *hell* of a fucking lot more than it does right now...."

Taking hold of only one of the clips at Darrek's entrance, he pulls it, stretching the skin away from his body before the clip gives way and plucks off.

"*OH. FUCK*!" Darrek cries, wiggling his ass away from Gabriel; muscles of his sphincter spasm as the ache spreads and multiplies, radiating in a shockwave. He has an overpowering urge to cover the area and rub it with a hand to try to soothe the hurt, so the chains rattle and clink as he tugs his arms at the bonds.

"Want me to take 'em off, slave?" Gabriel asks with a smile.

"*No, sir*! No, sir! Please no, sir!" Darrek says hurriedly.

"They're going to have to come off at some point. I have other plans for your ass and dick tonight, you know."

Darrek's eyes flick down to all of the multicolored specks he can see, imagining all the ones he can feel on his ass, and moans, head lolling back. He feels a hand close gently around his sac, rolling his balls, and it all turns a corner. The pain shifts to pleasure. It hurts just as much, it even hurts *more*, but it's not enough.

It's not nearly enough.

His dick weeping pre-come, slicking the bits of plastic clamped down on it, Darrek moans, "More, please. More, please, Master. Thank you."

Gabriel shifts up the bed, carefully moving one leg then the other so that he is straddling Darrek's splayed body, with his knees on either side of Darrek's waist and his legs extended under Darrek's thighs. Staying upright so that he doesn't put any pressure on Darrek's bound and splayed legs, he reaches down and closes his fingers around each of Darrek's hardened nipples. Pinching down firmly on the dark pink flesh, he watches Darrek's face. Next, he begins pulling them away from his body, stretching out the skin as far as it will go. Arching his back, Darrek comes up off the bed, but the clips on his dick brush against the denim of Gabriel's jeans and he shouts at the sudden wonderful sensation of pain there.

Not letting up at all, Gabriel twists the nubs of flesh in his fingers, pinching them harder still.

"Ahh! Ah-ha... ahhh... *shit*..." Darrek curses, writhing and coming up even more, his head curled forward now like he is trying to sit up, but his arms will not let him.

Gabriel twists them in the opposite direction.

"Master! Master, it hurts! *Oh god*...."

"Shhh...."

Releasing him, Gabriel begins plucking them, pulling them as far as they will go before his fingers just tug free, only to do it again and again. The nipples are red now, and Gabriel can feel the blood beating under the skin. Darrek is flushed pink from head to toe, slick with new sweat.

Gabriel leans down over him, bracing one hand on the bed beside Darrek's head, bending forward at the waist as he takes hold of one of Darrek's nipples between his thumb and forefinger, crushing it with rapid, pulsing squeezes, and says, "Look at me."

Staring up with black, lust-filled eyes, Darrek complies, breathing hard, his head resting against the soft pillow behind it.

"More..." Darrek rasps. "Please, sir."

Smiling, Gabriel climbs off of him, pausing only to kiss Darrek's lips in a soft, tender kiss.

Chapter 20
Feeling It

"I'm telling you right now..." Gabriel explains, yanking the miniature clips off one by one by one, as Darrek screams and fights to stay quiet all at the same time, bucking and twisting on the bed.

"...I'm not letting you come for a while. I plan to enjoy myself first, and if you behave, and are a very obedient slave for me, then *maybe* I will allow you to come. Otherwise, you'll be forced to sleep with your erection, and believe me when I tell you that I will check the weight of your balls in the morning, and am perfectly able to tell if you have jerked off or not. Understood?"

"Yes, Master. *Fuck!* Goddamn it! You evil fucking son-of-a-bitch, sir..." he cries weakly as the last clip comes off, one of the two that are attached to the tip of his dick.

"Hurts?"

"Fuck yeah... it's fantastic...."

Gabriel laughs and squirts a large amount of lube onto his hand, covered in a latex glove. He sees that Darrek is still feeling the effects of the clips, still fighting against sources of pain that are no longer there, still trying not to scream and lose control. Gabriel continues anyway and jabs two slick fingers into his asshole, fucking him roughly with them.

Darrek grunts, ass clamping down around Gabriel's probing hand, squeezing down on it like he could possibly keep him out.

"Just relax..." Gabriel says soothingly – far too soothingly.

On the next jabbing penetration of Darrek's baby-smooth ass, Gabriel uses the whole of his hand, fingertips tight together, hand closed in a tapered point. It does not get very far in, but he just keeps thrusting back in, forcing the hole wider, squeezing the gel of the lubricant on his own hand to slick the way more.

"What... what are you... Master? I'm... I'm..." Darrek asks fearfully.

"It's just my hand. It's important for you to relax right now, okay? Just listen to my voice and let go of the tension. Keep your muscles loose and it'll be much easier for you. I'm not going to do anything your body won't let me do."

"Okay..." Darrek whimpers, ass burning and throbbing as Gabriel's hand works deeper, stretches him out impossibly far.

It goes on and on. Darrek loses track of time.

Corkscrewing his hand on the next few pushes, Gabriel tries to coax Darrek's body into letting him in. The force of Gabriel's hand, combined with Darrek's initial fear has caused him to shift back an inch or two on the bed, even with the restraints. He can hear Darrek whining softly back in his throat. His hand is in almost to the last knuckle and the widest part. Just a little more and the whole of his fist will be inside.

Twisting his arm, pushing in one last time, he then pulls out, watching Darrek's reddened entrance, shiny-wet from lube, slowly closing back up. Inserting his fingers once more, this time without his thumb, the four of them go in easily so he digs in as far as he can reach.

"Ahhh!"

"I've got you baby, stay relaxed for me. You've got four fingers in you right now. I'm going to try to fit my whole hand, but if you can't do it, I'll stop."

Rotating his wrist, he rubs over the spongy bundle of nerves of Darrek's prostate. Hips coming far up off the bed, Darrek cries out, voice breaking, inner muscles fluttering and convulsing at the touch. A jet of come oozes down Darrek's shaft as Gabriel milks his prostate. Darrek seems to be in a frenzy of over-stimulation, unable to stop bucking his hips and writhing. Gabriel moves with him, tapping the bundle of nerves faster. Two more jets of come erupt from him, and Darrek's body finally goes still, every muscle tight and tensed, the only movement being Gabriel's hand working furiously in his ass.

"Breathe, Dare," he says. "Keep breathing."

He eases up on Darrek's prostate, and resumes fucking him with the whole of his pointed hand, thrusting in as far as it will go then pushing intently at his entrance for a moment before pulling back and doing it again.

Darrek has suddenly gone limp as a noodle, the only exception being the steely length of his red dick, coated now with all of the milked-out pre-come. Listening to him breathe softly, Gabriel realizes it's not going to happen, that he can't quite get the widest part of his hand past the outer ring of muscle.

He gets up off the bed and pulls off the glove as Darrek moans desperately with disappointment, watching him leave.

"Gonna try something else," Gabriel tells him. "One of my other favorites."

Grabbing an object, he brings it back to the bed. Afraid to look or ask, Darrek waits with closed eyes, his head against the pillow, ass gaping and wide, wet with lube and now unbearably empty of Gabriel's hand. He doesn't have to wait long before what feels like a more than twelve-inch-long smooth object is slid into his ass.

Focusing on staying loose, he concentrates on the sensations, and the feel of Gabriel fucking him with it.

Gabriel presses the inflatable dildo in until it is completely swallowed up by Darrek's hole. As his outer ring of muscles clear the end and close back up around the narrow tube trailing from the end of the dildo and out of his body, Darrek groans, shifting on the bed as his body automatically begins to force the object right back out. Gabriel does not let it out though, and just thrusts it back inside with two fingers on the end. He pushes at it until it is an inch inside Darrek's hole then keeps it there with steady pressure.

"Keep it in. Hold it inside," Gabriel tells him.

"It's too big! It's too goddamn big! I can't! I can't take it! Please, Gabe... oh *fuck*...."

He knows it's coming and braces for it. He's more afraid though, when Gabriel's hand is no longer at his ass and he, opens his eyes to see Gabriel circling his dick and balls with a length of rope. Working the ends into a knot, he pulls it tight with a tug. The rope constricts around him, biting into his body, and just when he cannot take anymore, when it is too fucking much, Gabriel pulls it even tighter. He loops the ends around him, three times around the base of his cock, and about thirteen times around his sac, forcing his testicles far away from his body, as well as keeping them in their crushing hold.

Gabriel watches Darrek's balls and dick slowly turn from dark red to purple.

"Well, now we know you're not going to come," he smiles.

The end of the rope trails between his legs like a leash and Gabriel pulls on it.

"Don't! Don't!" he begs, knowing it is useless but unable not to.

"You know what I think?" Gabriel asks, tugging the rope steadily with one hand while his other begins to rub at the reddish-purple orbs of Darrek's testicles. Darrek begins to cry as Gabriel says, "I think you do it, that you say my name like that on purpose. I think you want to feel this pain... that you need it, as a distraction or maybe just because you get off on it."

He stops tugging on the rope and curls his hand around Darrek's shaft instead, stroking it lightly, tormenting him with pleasure now that he cannot release.

"Tell me you don't want this. Tell me I'm wrong."

"I can't. You know I can't."

"Want me to stop?"

"No, Master. Please don't stop. Please, sir. Give me more...."

Gabriel releases him, leaves his over-filled member where it is trapped, encased in rope, and goes back to the inflatable cock inside his body.

"I see you were able to keep it inside. Good job. Now let's see what else you can do."

Keeping two fingers on the base of the dildo, Gabriel squeezes the bulb at the end of the tube, slowly pumping it and filling the dildo with more air. It gradually expands in Darrek's body, and it tries to force its way back out, easier for his ass to expel the object than to stretch to fit something of its girth and thickness.

Darrek moans loud and long, his legs flexing, muscles contracting, toes curling.

It starts to slide out and Gabriel lets it, only to push it hard right back inside until it is fully engulfed by Darrek's body. Darrek instantly comes up off the bed, crying out.

Gabriel lets it slide almost completely out by itself, only keeping the tapering end inside. Darrek's cry turns to a groan of ecstasy as the dildo pulls free. Not giving him time enough to close back up, Gabriel pushes it back inside. At first, it won't go, and Darrek flinches with pain. Gabriel stops then tries again. Bucking on the bed, Darrek's back arches as it disappears inside his hole.

Beginning to fuck him very slowly with it, now that he can get it inside, Gabriel watches Darrek's blissful expression. Gabriel's free hand rubs gently over his constricted balls and the head of his dick.

"This is the biggest thing you've ever taken, my amazing, gorgeous slave. Bigger than my cock, as big as... well... as big as my fist, actually."

Rubbing the pre-come in circles on his dick, working the black air-filled dildo in and out, so, so slowly, Gabriel's fingers stroke over the edge of Darrek's opening, at the pink outer ring of his asshole, stretched so widely opened, getting filled up again and again, tug and thrust, tug and thrust.

Darrek pulls on the cuffs on his wrists, head snapped so far back Gabriel is only able to see Darrek's chin.

Just as slowly, he lets Darrek's body force-out the dildo until it is free of him. Holding it up, Gabriel says, "Look."

Darrek's face comes back into view, staring open-mouthed and panting at the thing in Gabriel's hand. It's bigger than Gabriel's *arm*.

Slicking his hand and then his wrist with plenty of lube Darrek watches Gabriel with fascination. Moving close to Darrek, hooking his left arm over Darrek's leg and propping it on the bed by Darrek's side, Gabriel locks eyes with him as he begins to work his pointed hand once inside. It goes right in. His knuckles squeeze through the lip of the outer edge of Darrek's opening. The heated muscles of his sphincter press tightly at him on all sides before he's through and in, enclosed in the silky-soft heat of him.

Darrek's lower lip is quivering, and Gabriel sees the words, three words, sitting there on the tip of his slave and lover's tongue, he can see them in his eyes. It is evident that he wants so very badly to say them.

Gabriel just pushes farther in, up to his wrist, deeper and deeper.

Darrek falls back, unable to maintain contact with Gabriel's eyes as he gives small weeping cries.

Unable to quite believe that Darrek was able to give him this, to let his body go this far, Gabriel sees himself untying the rope with his left hand even before he knows he has decided to. Once it is unknotted, he unwinds it, unwraps Darrek, loop by loop, even as his right hand and part of his forearm thrust gently in and out of his body, and then the rope is free, his fingers picking at and then undoing the last remaining knot.

Pulling his hand back until he finds Darrek's sweet spot again, Gabriel leans down and takes Darrek's dick between licked-moist parted lips. He lets it slide over his tongue and back into his throat. Swallowing just as he starts to stroke over the bundle of nerves in Darrek's body, Darrek comes—soundlessly, but every single muscle in his body strung as tight as a rubber band—down Gabriel's throat. Breathing heavily through his nose, Gabriel does not release him, but sucks and rubs for long minutes. He continues until Darrek's prostate is milked completely and he is just pulsing dry, *still* orgasming, nerves still exploding and firing.

Gabriel pulls off, lets the softening cock fall from his mouth, and slides his hand free. Quickly unlocking Darrek's ankles first, Gabriel guides his legs down to the bed before undoing his wrists as well.

Darrek is unsurprisingly out like a light. Gabriel's sharp ears listen to him breathing regularly as he cleans him off with a warm cloth, and rubs down the muscles in his legs and arms. He checks to make sure Darrek's opening has contracted before putting all of the gear away and shutting off the room's lights. Changing into his soft, flannel pajama pants, Gabriel climbs in bed next to Darrek and covers them both with blankets.

Advil in hand, as well as a tall, cool glass of water, Gabriel lightly taps Darrek's face with the back of his hand, saying, "Hey. Wake up for me, baby. Come on. Open your eyes. You had a nice little nap, but I need you to take these now. Come on, Dare. Open those beautiful eyes."

After a moment, Darrek blinks at him, dazed but awake.

"Take these," Gabriel says, slipping the pills into his mouth and helping him sip at the water. "I can't believe you didn't stop me and say the safeword," he confesses.

"Why would I *stop* you? I've never felt that much... that *amazing*... in my whole fucking life! That was the best orgasm I have ever—no, *WILL* ever have. *Ever*. It's un-top-able."

"I love you," Gabriel smiles and then the smile is gone and he freezes, realizing what he has said.

Seeing the fear creep into his widened, painfully beautiful eyes, Darrek says quickly, "I love you too. I wanted to say it before... I almost did anyway... but.... I thought... I don't know. That you wouldn't believe me, maybe."

"I believe you," Gabriel says softly.

"Me too," Darrek smiles back. "And it's a damn good thing I made so much progress on those chairs today, and don't have work tomorrow, because I have a feeling I won't be standing *or* sitting for a while."

"I guess that means I get to take care of you. Cook your meals, feed you, bring you cold drinks and keep you stocked with horribly bad movies to watch and the sports section of the paper to read..."

"God, now I really love you," Darrek sighs. "Even more than when you fist-fucked me."

Laughing, Gabriel says, "Oh, shut up."

"I can't believe you really fist-fucked me. My *ass* tells me it's true, but still. That's unreal. I'm so... so *proud*!"

"You're such a kinky bastard," Gabriel grins, still chuckling.

"Oh, you know you love me for it."

"I do," he agrees.

"Plus, it really is all your fault. You're not just my master, you're my *enabler*." Pausing a second to think, he asks, "My ass is going to go back to normal, right? 'Cause I still need you to fuck me and I really want to be able to... you know... *FEEL* it."

"Yes, it'll go back to normal, but no fucking for a day or so."

"Aw... bummer."

"Well, at least no sex with *your* ass."

"You don't mean...."

"I don't know. Maybe I do."

"I love you, Gabe."

"I love you too, Dare."

Chapter 21
Father of Mine

Darrek walks downstairs after getting washed up for dinner. He smiles, seeing Gabriel at the sink. Gabriel is busy washing out pots and pans as well as a few of his favorite coffee mugs that he has started to keep on the bottom shelf of the cabinet above the coffee-maker. The simple fact that Gabriel's coffee mugs have a home in his little house warms Darrek's heart, and he loves Gabriel so much in that moment that he feels like he's bursting with it.

Certain that Gabriel must have heard him coming down the squeaky stairs, his heavy footsteps perfectly audible on the hard-wood floor, Darrek walks up behind him and places a hand on Gabriel's waist, leaning in to kiss his neck.

"*NO!*" Gabriel gasps, going instantly pale, his body instantaneously rigid from head to toe, and his hand shooting out, too fast to see, to grab a knife from the drying rack. Spinning on his heels, he wields it at Darrek. He freezes, seeing the look on Darrek's face.

"Gabe! Hey! What the..." Darrek frowns, grabbing the wrist holding the knife. He pries it out of Gabriel's hand and sets it aside.

"*Shit*... I'm sorry," Gabriel says breathlessly, his hands going to his face, "I'm so *sorry*, Dare."

"I really scared you that bad?"

"No. Well, yes. I was... remembering something... and...."

"And...?"

"Never mind."

"No, don't do that. You keep doing that. Tell me. Please tell me. I can handle it. Why the hell would you grab the knife like that?"

"You don't wanna know."

"I do. I *do* want to know. I want to *know* about this stuff. I want you to be able to tell me so I can help you feel better."

"I need some air," he sighs, "I can't breathe in here. Can we go outside?"

"Yeah. Okay."

They head out through the back door and sit on the back stoop, watching Sierra dash after a robin pecking for worms, hopping around under a tree.

"This is better," Gabriel says, taking a deep breath. "Much better."

He was almost finished with the pile of dishes from supper, enough for five people, stacked neatly next to the sink, each piece of china washed thoroughly by hand. It was his main chore—washing the dishes—and he only had the big copper pot left to do that night. He could hear the crickets chirping outside and the radio was quietly playing the local independent rock station. They had been taking a break to do the weather report and station identification when Gabriel was suddenly knocked forward. Bent sharply in half over the sink, his t-shirt pressed against the small puddles of water on the counter's edge, becoming damp and heavy.

"It was just one of those times of day when he knew he could get to me," Gabriel explains. "My sister and brother would go out to meet with friends. My mom would go run errands or visit with the neighbors. It would just be him and me. And doing the dishes was my job, so... sometimes... I would *not* do them, and try to wait until everyone else went to sleep and then sneak downstairs to finish up. My mom didn't like that though. Said I was slacking off."

"No! Don't...don't touch me." It sounded even more desperate that he'd intended it to.

A gnarled hand, vein-riddled but smooth since his stepfather had never done a hard day's work in his life, reached out and pulled the large, pointed knife from the drying rack. Going instantly still at the sight of it in Harry's hand, Gabriel squeezed his eyes tightly shut at the feeling of hands on his jeans.

"He would sneak up behind me, pull my pants down. A few times, he'd grab a knife just to make sure I wouldn't fight back. Just the sight of it in his hand... knowing what he did with it... what he kept threatening to do...."

"Such a little whore, Gabey. Couldn't even fit the tip of my pinky in here this morning. Now yer takin' three fingers no problem."

It was always over after just a few sloppy ruts, before he was even fully seated. Gabriel would just listen to the radio and pretend he was somewhere else.

Just when he thought it was over, he saw the knife move, as it caught the light from overhead and shone brightly in his peripheral vision. A hand moved and cradled his testicles. The other brought the knife around in front of him. He felt the blade press between his legs, dragged forward until it could go no further. Gabriel was sure it was cutting into him.

"Say thank you," demanded the voice at his ear.

"No."

"Say it, you little bitch. Think I won't do it? Wanna try me? Or maybe you want to be a girl. Wanna be my girl, Gabri*elle*?"

Then it really was cutting him, and he yelped, "Stop! Okay! Th-th-thank you."

"See? That wasn't so difficult, was it? Manners are important."

"What did he do with the knife?" Darrek asks fearfully.

The reply he gets is quick and to the point. "Threatened to cut my balls off if I didn't thank him for fucking me. Cut me pretty good, but, obviously, never did more than that. Just another way he liked to scare me. But that's why I grabbed the knife in there when you surprised me, I guess. Just an instinct. Didn't think about it."

Gabriel laughs miserably, staring out into the yard, squinting up into the dying sunlight. Quietly, he confesses, "Sick thing is, that wasn't even the worst part. I knew he'd never really do that anyway. No way he'd get away with it."

Processing Gabriel's words, Darrek gapes at him, "You're kidding, right? What the hell could be *worse* than that?"

Gabriel shakes his head, falling quiet.

Taking Gabriel's hand in both of his, Darrek waits, holding on.

"I don't like talking about his shit. I don't like it," Gabriel tells him, shaking his head.

"I know."

Sierra finds a broken-off tree limb and starts to play with it, snapping at leaves and barking excitedly.

"God, I wish I was a dog. Look how happy she is about a branch. That's incredible."

"Gabe...."

"I'll get there. I will. You should know the whole truth; the whole thing. Just... give me a minute, okay?"

Sierra rips off a bunch of leaves and bounds over to them. She brings them right to Gabriel, dropping the clump of leaves, still attached to a stick, in his lap. Smiling, he scratches behind her ears, hugging her head.

"Good dog. Such a pretty girl," he says softly. Darrek hears him sniff once, and looks over to see a tear fall down onto Sierra's head. Gabriel kisses the golden fur then tosses the stick away. Sierra chases it, barking with happiness.

After taking a deep breath, Gabriel says out into the air, "He would make me finish washing the dishes with my pants around my ankles, and he'd just sit there... staring at me, and touching himself. I know it doesn't sound that bad, compared to... well... but..." he rolls his eyes then keeps speaking, "His... his... you know... would start to... I would try to hold it inside... but some would... leak out of me. He'd come back over to me, scrape it off with the knife... make me lick it clean."

Drawing his knees up to his chest, he presses his forehead to his knees and says, "I was sixteen, Darrek. *Sixteen years old.* He was... he was supposed to be my *dad*."

Their relatively sedate afternoon is disturbed when a fist begins to pound heavily on the house's front door. Gabriel walks to the front window and, through the sheer curtain, sees the large black truck parked outside.

"Gabriel Hunter, open the fuck up! I need to talk to you! Come on. Not leaving 'til you do, ya stubborn ass."

Gabriel sighs, telling Darrek, who is behind him and lying on the couch, "Stay there. I've got this."

"'Kay," Darrek frowns.

He opens the front door and steps through, shutting it behind him, hands going deeply into his pockets.

"What?" he asks, squinting up at Trace.

"The fuck is going on with you, Gabriel? You cut back at Diadem, move more than half your shit out of the house and then avoid my calls. Benny won't tell me anything... You living with this jerk now?"

"He's not a jerk," Gabriel protests, pulling his hands out and crossing his arms over his chest instead.

"No, he's a *client*."

"Not anymore."

"Nice, Gabe. After what, thirteen goddamned years, this is all the explanation I get?" Trace scowls, throwing his arms wide, clearly very pissed off.

The words have a powerful effect on Gabriel. He is instantly taken aback, face softening, head bowed, and Trace looks highly satisfied at the reaction.

Gabriel explains quietly to him after clearing his throat, "Fine. You want an explanation? This is my decision. I'm happy with

Darrek. He makes me *happy*. So yes. Yes, I'm living here. It just... kind of happened. I was going to talk to you... I just hadn't gotten around to it."

Laughing a little maliciously, Trace asks, "What, you love him or something? 'Cause he lets you fuck him over? Real healthy, Gabe."

"That's not fair."

"I'm sorry. Christ. I'm sorry, I'm just... angry."

"I can tell."

"But do you? Love him?"

"Yeah, I love him."

"He's your *sub*," Trace argues, almost pleading with him. "What kind of life are you gonna have with him? Is this like a power trip for you?"

"That's not what this is about. I mean... yes... fine...he is still my sub. That's just part of it though. That's not why I..." he trails off, sighing, scratching and picking at his shirt sleeve.

"He treats you good?"

"Yeah," Gabriel frowns, like it should be obvious. "Of *course*! Of course he does. I wouldn't... I wouldn't be here if he didn't."

Trace's voice gets quieter, glancing around, as he says, "I thought you didn't like... you know... being with guys that were bigger than you. This Darrek guy is a *lot* bigger than you. He could...."

"No. No. He wouldn't do anything to hurt me. He's not like that."

"You really know him that well? How long's it been? A few *weeks?* If he tries anything... if he does *ANYTHING* to hurt you, I swear to fucking *god*, Gabriel, I will come over here and string him up from the nearest tree myself."

"Which is why I never told you where to find Harry. You're too goddamned impulsive. You're even worse than Knox," Gabriel accuses.

"I'm still waiting for that. One day... one of these days I'll get you or Benny to tell me, and then there's gonna be one more body rotting in the sewers."

"Yeah, yeah, tough guy. So many tough guys around here."

"I wanna talk to him. Let me talk to him."

"Who? Darrek?"

"Yes, Darrek! Unless you're gonna give me Harry's phone number. I'd like to talk to him too."

"I don't want you talking to Darrek. He's my responsibility. No one gets to threaten him or touch him or come near him."

"Fuck you. Let me talk to him."

"No."

"Gabriel. I am not fucking kidding."

"Neither am I."

"I promise to be... nice."

"No."

Trace growls with frustration, pursing his lips, running a hand back through his hair.

"I don't trust him with you! I don't *trust him*!" he exclaims, jabbing a finger at the house.

"*I* do. I trust him, and believe me, I have pretty high standards."

"Look, you can keep stuff at the house. That room will always be yours, you know that. So if you need to... whatever... change your mind, or have somewhere to crash...."

"I know. Thanks. I mean it. Thank you, Trace."

Pacing in front of Gabriel like a riled-up dog, Trace tries one more time, "Please let me talk to him? Two minutes? Can I just look him in the eye once, so I'm able to sleep tonight?"

Gabriel rolls his eyes, and sighs, "Fine. You can say hello and that's it."

"Thank you."

Opening the door, Gabriel calls inside, "Dare? C'mere a second."

A moment later, he appears in the doorway, blinking into the sunlight.

"Hey. You're Trace, right?" Darrek says politely, extending a hand. He has a few brief flashes of memory as he looks Trace over, remembering his first experience at Diadem, and the many, many things Trace did to him under Gabriel's instruction.

"Yeah. That's me," Trace says gruffly, and it's there in *his* eyes as well—a dark amusement, an intense inspection, and the silent acknowledgment of all that came between them before.

Part of Darrek is still back there, bound and helpless, violated and stimulated. Remembered old screams and moans of ecstasy reverberate in both of their minds as Trace takes Darrek's hand. He pumps it twice then keeps it gripped in his own, looking hard into Darrek's eyes before releasing him.

"Nice to officially meet you, Darrek."

"Likewise. And, um... I have a feeling I know why you're here. I just want to assure you... I love Gabriel. I trust him with my life, and I promise that I will take good care of him, too."

"Good. Glad to hear that," Trace nods.

"Happy now? See? It's fine. I'm *fine,*" Gabriel says to Trace. "And yes, he knows."

"Seriously?" Trace asks, his doubt and surprise apparent.

"Yes. Of course! In fact, now he knows more than you do. So, *please* chill out."

"Well, maybe if you *talked to me* sooner, I'd be less freaked."

"He has a point," Darrek admits, turning to Gabriel. "You do tend to shut people out."

"Okay. We are not going to psychoanalyze me and you two are definitely not allowed to discuss me and, like, compare notes. Goodbye Trace. I'll see you at work. If you can behave yourself, maybe we'll have you over soon for dinner or something."

After one more piercing, protective glare of warning at Darrek, Trace leans in and kisses the side of Gabriel's face before turning and walking back to his truck.

Chapter 22
Paying For It

They watch him leave then head back inside as Gabriel groans with weariness. He slumps down onto the couch and lets his head fall back. Darrek stands in the middle of the room watching through the window as Trace drives away.

"How much of that did you hear?" Gabriel asks.

"A good amount. Were you guys... was Trace someone that you... you know...."

"It's complicated," he sighs. "Look... you have to understand something. With our line of work... doing what we do... did... every fuckin' day... for years upon *years*... you get kind of desensitized to some stuff. Not the important stuff, but... I've always had trouble finding people I trust to be with. I have needs, though. Everyone needs... *affection*... once in a while."

"So, you were 'affectionate' with Trace?"

"In a way... it's not like I love him or like he was my boyfriend. He's... he's Trace. He's a good, loyal friend. But yeah... I mean... we're just talking like a hand release here and there. A couple of blow jobs. And some kissing. That's it."

"Was it just Trace or...."

Running his hands over his face, Gabriel sighs and says, "No. Of course not."

"Ben *too*?"

"Darrek, it's just something we did to stay sane. It didn't *mean* anything."

"No, I understand. I do. I admit I don't *like* it. At all. Especially the thought of them touching you like that. Kind of makes me really fucking nauseous, but... at least it's obvious that they care about you. You deserve to have people care about you."

"Come here," Gabriel murmurs, waving him closer. He sits forward, elbows rested on knees, as Darrek kneels at his feet. Cupping his face, Gabriel brings him in for a kiss. It's soft and slow, and then he says urgently, "I *love* you."

Darrek places his hands over Gabriel's arms, holding on to Gabriel holding on to him. Gabriel recedes back into his mind, getting farther away by the second. Images start playing there, rising from the murky depths of Gabriel's memory, and he grips Darrek tightly as they come, unbidden.

It all boils down to one incident in particular, one that sums up all of his personal sexual encounters with Trace absolutely perfectly.

Gabriel is just getting home after a long day with three clients booked one after the other with hardly any breaks in between. Climbing out of his Land Rover Discovery, he slams the door hard enough to shake the SUV on its frame. He's wired and dizzy with it all, every muscle strung tight and vibrating—angry, riled-up, mean and needy. Hands restless, his breath comes quick, blood beating in his temples, in his chest, in his hard and aching dick.

He sees Trace in the garage, sorting through wrenches; hands dirty, shirtless and sweaty.

"Trace! Need you! Inside. Fuckin' now," Gabriel pants, sounding hoarse and god, but it's getting worse.

They lock eyes and Trace sees it in his face, in his posture and the darkness of his expression.

Gabriel doesn't stop to see if he is coming or not. Stumbling through the front door, he flings aside his keys, which skitter noisily across the floor. Grimacing, teeth bared, eyes closing over, he leans back against the wall with hips canted forward as he fumbles with his buckle, getting it open, hitching his shirt up with annoyance, trying to get at the button-fly.

Trace appears in the doorway, wiping his hands carelessly on a rag. Stepping forward, as calm as could be; a stark contrast in control to Gabriel; he wraps a steady hand around Gabriel's jaw, gently brushes a rough thumb over the place just under the pouting curl of his lower lip.

Grunting, Gabriel pushes him away with a hard slap to his left shoulder. Laughing, Trace grabs his arm when it winds back to deliver another blow. He smoothly pulls it up over Gabriel's head, holding it to the wall even as the younger man continues to fumble with his fly, fingers unsteady and clumsy, just pushing, needing to get free of the constricting clothing. Taking that hand too, Trace brings it up and pins it with the other one.

There is a tense pause, then Gabriel bucks in the hold, tugging at his arms when Trace doesn't move fast enough for his liking.

"Hush. I've gotcha," he smirks, tugging the jeans down, one-handed, on Gabriel's hips. As the younger man's achingly full and reddened cock springs free, Trace chuckles darkly, just watching Gabriel fight.

"Hate you. Hate you when you pull this shit..." Gabriel spits at Trace's patience and complacency.

Trace's dirt-smeared hand closes tightly around Gabriel's pulsating flesh, so fucking tight that Gabriel can't stand it, but it's perfect. He fights not to whimper, to show weakness, as Trace strokes quick and easily, squeezing out drop after drop of thin clear fluid from the slit. Pushing into the hand, helpless not to, Gabriel undulates in front of him. When Trace suddenly shifts his grip, circling around and rubbing under the crown, gathering pre-come to slick the way, Gabriel can't hold it in anymore.

Glassy eyes stare up at the ceiling as he lets out a frail, plaintive whimper. Hanging from his wrists, he finally pulls hard enough to get them free. His fingers scratch, claw and dig at Trace's shoulders, leaving red marks and welts on the skin.

His gravelly voice like thunder rolling in, Trace says low and quiet to him, "Come on, Gabey. Come on, baby boy. It's okay." Gabriel shakes his head once in answer.

"No! No, no..." Gabriel hisses, hips coming forward even more sharply, head thrown back, as Trace's fist moves at a bruising pace, a tight glove around his overfilled dick.

Then Trace just presses their bodies together, takes Gabriel's lip between his teeth and bites down. The metallic tang of blood spills over their tongues. Gabriel cries out, coming hard, splashing hot and thick over Trace's stomach and hand.

"C'mon.... C'mon...."

Shaking his head again in negation, tightly once back and forth, Gabriel gasps, chest rising and falling rapidly. Trace angles his hand with his wide thumb planted firmly just under the ridge on the underside, his other fingers squeezing still, milking him dry.

Gabriel's right hand shifts, rubbing over Trace's torso. Moving down, it splays wide over the center of his chest. Trying to swallow back another whimper, he forces it deeper and turns it into a growl. Darting forward, he kisses Trace. Instantly, Trace's free hand forces Gabriel's mouth open wide with gentle pressure at his jaw, tongue-fucking him through the aftershocks. As soon as Gabriel starts to go soft in his hand, the palm on his chest pushes hard. Knocked back two steps, Trace watches as Gabriel straightens up. Short hair almost black, his intoxicating pale eyes catching the light from the sunset filtering through the opened door, eyelashes thick, lips full and blood red, skin flushed from his orgasm, body lean and toned, he's a breathtaking sight. Running the back of his arm over his bleeding mouth, head down, his brow is furrowed but his eyes sharp. With a tug and a shimmy he's back inside his jeans and storming away, deeper into the house without a word.

"You're welcome!" Trace calls sarcastically as he heads back outside.

Gabriel does not reply. He just turns the stereo up to ear-splitting volume and climbs under scalding-hot water in the shower, drowning everything out, washing it all away.

It plays out in his mind and then crumbles, breaking up into fragments and dispersing into the ether.

"The only thing..." Gabriel insists to the man in his arms, "the *only* thing that matters is how I feel about you. The past... well, the past is an evil bitch that doesn't want to die, but it *is* the past. What I want, Darrek, is a future. I want a *future,* you know? And when I look at you, I don't see the past, I see only what *could be*. And that? That's *everything*."

Darrek leans in just as Gabriel does and feels his soft, full lips close around his. As usual, the shocking sweetness evident in Gabriel—something that is not unleashed frequently, but when it is, is more powerful than anything else about him—nearly knocks Darrek right off of his feet. Whispering against those lips, Darrek tells him, "Love you... love you so much."

After a few minutes, lips kissed red, and breathless, Gabriel pulls away a fraction of an inch only to begin speaking, his tone serious and confessional.

"We never really talked about what's been happening between us. We seem to have just fallen into it naturally, this... lifestyle. But I think it's time we did talk about it. There's a lot of stuff we should talk about, actually. Like the fact that I want to pay my share of the rent if I'm going to be staying here."

Darrek smiles and says with a shrug, "Don't worry about it. I own the house."

"Oh, well, okay. Then I'll help you with the mortgage payment or whatever."

"No, you don't understand. I own the house. I paid for it and the land when I moved up here. I have the deed and everything."

"You paid for it? All at once?"

"Yeah, I did. See, I didn't go to college. I started working right away in construction the day after I graduated from high school. I apprenticed under another carpenter for a few years. I was living with my parents, so pretty much all of my income was getting saved. I was going to use it to fund my marriage, and buy me and Sara a house, but then... well, that whole fiasco happened. So, I bought this place instead. It wiped out my savings, but I feel like this place is a good investment. I'm still trying to build my savings up again, especially after buying the Tundra. I own that free and clear, too. Since I don't have a big mortgage payment or a vehicle loan to worry about, I don't need much money in order to live comfortably enough."

"That's... that's incredible."

"It was kind of comforting, having all that money saved up.

I felt like I could do anything, you know? It was a big confidence builder," he says. The profound sum of what he's lost—his fiancée, his family's support, his sense of self worth—appears to catch up with him, darkening his expression. "Possibly the only thing I *had* besides my friendship with Kyle to give me confidence. But it's just money. It didn't make me happy. It didn't make me any less lonely. I just decided what I wanted. I want to *belong* somewhere. That's all that matters. The money is gone now, but the work has been pretty steady, and I don't need much to get by."

"So, I guess that's why you weren't too broken up about being laid-off."

"Pretty much," Darrek agrees, "But, it's been a few days now. The gap between jobs is usually a week at most. I keep thinking I'm going to get the call to go back. I keep thinking...."

"That you're going to have to see Kyle again."

"Yeah. I don't even know how I would handle that."

"Okay, well, let's come back to that. Where the hell did you learn to manage money so well?"

"My mom is an accountant. She taught me a lot and then I just sort of ran with it. I wanted to be independent of my parents, and be able to live without crazy amounts of debt to anyone. I didn't want that hanging over my head. I wanted the place I live in and the truck I drive to be *mine*. My own little piece of the world. Does that make sense?"

"Yeah. That's a goal that I can identify with a lot, actually. And you did it. I'm proud of you for that."

"Gabe... I don't know how much you make at Diadem, but it has to be enough to afford your own place to live. Is there a reason you always stayed with Trace?"

"Yeah, that wasn't a money thing. I'm a saver too, I guess. We have that in common. It's always made me feel better to have a nice little nest egg ready if I need it. I've been paying Trace rent, or at least trying to, but most times he won't take it. Never cashed the checks, you see."

"Then why? If it wasn't a money thing?"

"Oh, come on. I'm sure you can figure it out."

"I don't want to assume anything...."

"I can't live on my own. I can't. I wouldn't sleep if I did. Even living with Trace, if he was out for the night, for whatever reason, I'd go stay at Ben's place."

"This is about Harry."

"When someone sneaks into your bedroom on a regular basis, and rapes you in the dead of night again and again and again... let's just say it gets really fucking hard to sleep soundly. Even when you know, logically, that they aren't around anymore."

"Have you been sleeping okay here?"

"Better than usual. I attribute that solely to you, by the way. And when I do wake up at night, and you're asleep, it's nice to come down here and have Sierra to keep me company. She makes me feel better, too."

"I'm glad. So, not that it matters to me, but how much do you have saved up?"

"Oh, I have no idea of the exact amount. I have a financial advisor and an account with an investment company. They take care of everything, and I get regular statements from them. I don't care how much money there is, as long as it's enough to keep me off the streets if anything ever happens. Homelessness is not something I want to ever have to live through again.

"But that's another way we're alike. I don't care if they reduce my pay at Diadem, or that I'm out of work for a little while. It doesn't really affect me. I just want to be happy and comfortable. The funny thing is, is that I thought I *was*. I really did think I was happy and had a good life. But now, being with you... I realize that I wasn't happy. *This* is happiness. That was just surviving."

Darrek presses his eyes closed and lays his head on Gabriel's lap. As Gabriel's fingers play in his hair, Darrek sighs, "I want you so bad right now. The fact that I have you with me, and that you're living here, it makes me so happy. To not have that loneliness inside me anymore, and to know I belong to you, it's everything. I just want you to let me make love to you and show you how beautiful you are. I want that so badly, and I'm just telling you that because I feel it too strongly to be able to hide it from you. It's just me being honest. I don't expect anything from you, but I need you to know how I feel."

Staring out through the room's picture window and stroking fingers through Darrek's hair, a battle rages inside Gabriel's mind at those words. He doesn't respond. He can't. But, as his hands move soothingly over Darrek's head, neck, and back, their touch conveys to Darrek his feelings more than any words ever could.

Gabriel is angry at himself, and at his past. He's hopeful that maybe, *possibly*, he can go through with this, and allow himself to have complete faith in the man he loves. He is certain that it will be the hardest thing he has ever had to do, the most seemingly impossible task he will ever have to face. Feeling Darrek embrace him, letting Darrek's confessed desires and affection wash over him and take away some of the fear, Gabriel searches his heart and decides what he needs to do.

Chapter 23
Angel With A Broken Wing

It's late. All of the lights in the house are off, except for the single bedside lamp in the master bedroom. The dog has been taken care of. The doors are locked. It's a hot night, so the window is open, and a soft breeze blows in, cooling Darrek's skin where it caresses over him and the light layer of sweat dampening his body.

Gabriel has just come back into the room after getting washed up in the bathroom. Darrek has been waiting for him, sorting some of his clothes, making more room for Gabriel's things in the closet and drawers.

He turns and grins at the sight of Gabriel's dark, stringy wet hair curling a little over his forehead, his jeans hastily tugged on, the button on the fly not even done up. His chest is bare, the skin flushed from the heat of the shower. Darrek is amazed at his tolerance for it, having personally witnessed the scalding temperatures Gabriel seems to prefer. As a stronger breeze whistles through the room, goose bumps raise on Gabriel's arms. Darrek licks his lips and averts his eyes when his gaze falls on Gabriel's hardened nipples. Wanting to touch, to kiss, Darrek busies himself instead with the clothes, and tries to stamp down the hard rush of need that swells in him.

Gabriel turns on the small stereo on the bureau, adjusting the dial until soft classical music, overlaid with the faintest hint of static, begins to play. Darrek feels a tug on his hand, and lets Gabriel pull him away from the closet and his busywork. He readies himself to go to his knees, prepares to obey and follow whatever orders his Master has for him.

But, when Gabriel rests a hand on Darrek's shoulder, guides Darrek's hand to his waist, and then takes Darrek's other hand in his own, he knows exactly what to do. Darrek begins to slowly lead them in a simple waltz, turning Gabriel around the open space in the bedroom, following the tempo of the music lilting from the small speakers nearby, accompanied now by chirping crickets and a few croaking frogs from outside.

"You're good at this," Gabriel smiles. "I didn't know you could dance."

"A hidden talent," he admits, moving Gabriel about, held carefully in his arms.

Seeing the sadness in Darrek's eyes, Gabriel says, "Sara made you take lessons, didn't she? For the wedding?"

Darrek nods.

The fact that Gabriel has arranged them so that Darrek is the one leading did not escape his notice. As they continue to waltz, Darrek somewhat bashfully, and with an ache in his heart, waits for Gabriel to tell him what is already so plain on his face.

"I'm giving you permission to do this," Gabriel says quietly. His gaze is lowered at first, but then it rises and locks onto Darrek's, searching his face for understanding. "But you have to know that I have these built-in defense mechanisms. Kind of a fight or flight deal. No one has ever... no one's even come *close* to...."

"It's okay," Darrek assures him. "I get it."

"Do you? Because I don't. I don't get it at all. Once I kicked Trace right in the balls for grabbing my ass when I wasn't expecting it."

Darrek chuckles and Gabriel laughs with him, but says, "It's not funny! I really hurt him. And he wasn't trying to be a dick or anything... I just don't want to hurt you, Dare. And I can't promise that my instincts won't take over when you start to... um... the point is, I might say or do things that I don't really mean...."

"That part, I do understand," Darrek cuts in.

Gabriel nods, "Of course. Of course you do.... Look, I've been thinking about this. I think about it a lot, actually. And I can't... *do* this. We've done some intense shit, but this is different. Even if I chained you to the bed and tried to just...." He sighs, "It's like a mental block. I wouldn't be able to do it. I need you to *take* this from me. It's not something I can be in control of. The best I can do is just to, like, *command you* to make love to me, despite everything else. Okay?"

"Yes, Master," Darrek says softly, then asks, "What's your safeword?"

"Discovery. Sticking with our theme and all... and um.... If you need to use the wrist shackles..." Gabriel says rapidly, a little breathlessly, "That's all right, but I want to try to do it without. I want to be able to touch you."

"I know," Darrek frowns, gently touching the swell of Gabriel's lip. "You scared?"

"Yeah," Gabriel laughs, but it's a desperate sound, and Darrek sees his body tense up, feels it happen under his hands.

They've stopped dancing and he doesn't even know if it was gradual or all at once.

Darrek pulls his shirt up and over his head. His hands go to the waistband of his pants, pushing them down. They puddle at his feet. He steps free of them and circles Gabriel with strong arms. Kissing him, Darrek guides him back to the bed.

Gabriel sits down then eases back, letting Darrek follow him by crawling up over his legs. Some of the apprehension melts from his face, and is steadily replaced by a growing, vibrant defiance. As Darrek straddles Gabriel, looming above him, he holds Gabriel's eyes as he takes hold of the sides of his jeans and starts to pull them off.

At first Gabriel is still as a statue, just watching Darrek's face, his jaw set. Then he moves, wriggling out of the pants and kicking them away.

His chest rising and falling, the war rages on in Gabriel's mind.

"Come on," he growls, wrapping his hand around Darrek's shaft and stroking him into full hardness as Darrek settles between his spread legs.

"Easy," Darrek says soothingly to him, pressing close between Gabriel's thighs, hooking the legs up and over his shoulders.

The position does something to Gabriel though, and his eyes squeeze shut tight, his lips close and small frown lines appearing in his brow. Leaning down, folding Gabriel in half, Darrek kisses him, coaxing him, until Gabriel is kissing him back. Feeling hands frame his face, Darrek exhales a breath as Gabriel opens wider. Gabriel lets himself be searched, licked into, and worshipped with every press of Darrek's lips, every dart and caress of Darrek's tongue.

It begins to become familiar, as Gabriel's fingers move and grip. His head even comes up off of the pillow a little, questing after Darrek's mouth. But, after Darrek coats his hand with lubricant and touches Gabriel experimentally with two fingers, just rubbing over his entrance, it all starts to change.

Head falling back, eyes shooting open, the dark coldness starts to come back into those gray-blue eyes.

"No. Stay with me. I'm just touching you."

"I know..." he sighs, "keep kissing me. Keep...."

Nodding, Darrek claims his lover's full lips once more and slowly presses two fingers inside his body. Hot, clenching inner muscles contract around them, and Darrek whispers soft words against Gabriel's lips. At first the words seem to work, and they continue to kiss. But when Darrek withdraws his fingers and pushes back in, twisting and scissoring his index and middle fingers, Gabriel begins to claw and push at Darrek's shoulders. Using his larger size and his full body weight, Darrek leans heavily down on the smaller man, thwarting his still-feeble efforts to push him away.

Running fingers back through Gabriel's hair, kissing over his jaw, Darrek uses his fingers to open him up. He can feel the fight in Gabriel's body, the tautness of his muscles, and hears the harshness of his breathing. Darrek is not sure whether Gabriel could push him off if he got worked up into a full-blown panic. Given proper motivation, it seems entirely possible. Luckily for him, the fact that Gabriel's legs are over his shoulders makes him at least feel confident that he's not going to get a knee to the balls, though he thinks perhaps Gabriel could figure out something else to get out of his current position on the bottom. Tasting the saltiness of Gabriel's perspiration, Darrek's lips skim over the side of his face.

Blinking up at the ceiling, Gabriel tries not to focus solely on the fingers buried and working inside his body. He tries to focus on the fact that it's *Darrek*. Inhaling his unique scent, savoring the feather-light tickle of the long hair at his skin, the mesmerizing sound of Darrek's low-pitched voice whispering near his ear, Gabriel repeats to himself, like a mantra, *'I'm okay. I'm okay. Darrek loves me. I'm okay.'*

Logically, he knows it's ridiculous, that he is being ridiculous. He is not afraid of Darrek, and he knows that Darrek would not hurt him. Gabriel knows this. But it doesn't matter. All that matters, is the feeling of his body being invaded, the loss of control.

A third finger presses inside and Gabriel bucks, pushing with almost his full strength at Darrek's shoulders. Darrek takes Gabriel's right hand, lacing their fingers together and holding it against the bed.

"Gabe... hey. Calm down, you have to calm down or I'm going to have to put the cuffs on you."

"No. No! I don't want you to. I don't want the cuffs on," he says gruffly, frantically.

"Then calm down."

"Okay. Yeah, okay," he nods, breathing deeply with effort, in through his nose and out through his mouth. He makes himself stop pushing Darrek away. Darrek leans close again and feels Gabriel tangle the fingers of his left hand in his hair.

Going almost entirely still, Gabriel is just breathing and staring. Darrek has hope that he's getting through it, that Gabriel is okay, until he hears him ask quietly, "You almost finished?"

He takes it right back though, hissing, "Shit. That's not... I didn't mean... I'm sorry, baby."

"Want me to make it better for you? I can do that. I was trying to just be fast, but..." Darrek says.

Angling his wrist, he finds the spot and fingers it. Gabriel arches up, actually moving up the bed a little, trying to get away. His hand leaves Darrek's hair and wraps around the headboard instead. He makes a grunting noise back in his throat, behind his pursed lips and turns his face away. Darrek feels Gabriel's body react every time he brushes over the bundle of nerves. Cock huge and full, hips coming up and rocking into Darrek's touch, Gabriel is clearly enjoying it. But it's just further evidence of the battle of wills and wants in him as Gabriel sniffs and wipes away a tear with the side of his arm.

"Can I let go of your hand?" Darrek asks, rubbing a little faster over the sweet spot.

Not looking at him, Gabriel nods. Darrek releases him and reaches down between them. Enclosing Gabriel's dick in his huge fist, he strokes him slow and steady, counter to the movements of his other hand.

Gasping, Gabriel undulates, grinding down into Darrek's hand then pushing up into his fist. The hand on the headboard grips tighter and his free arm gets slung over his eyes.

"Dare, stop... you've gotta stop! If you don't I'm gonna...."

"I know. That's the point. It's okay. Come on," he coaxes.

Gabriel groans, gritting his teeth, still covering his eyes. But his hips spasm, caught between sensations, dick oozing pre-come, balls drawn up, ready to unload. "Fuck!"

"Look at me, Gabe. It's just me."

The arm comes away, revealing damp eyes, but he takes a deep sudden breath and holds it with a grunt as he comes.

"Dare? Dare!" he cries out as the sensations explode through his body, pulsing outwards with his heartbeat, grabbing at Darrek, hooking his hand around the back of his neck. The words draw out and turn into a pleading, keening sound, before being cut off and swallowed down.

His stomach and chest now splattered with streaks of thick white drops, Gabriel's head spins, nerves still firing in his body, toes tingling. He loses track of what Darrek is doing. He doesn't hear him open the condom wrapper with his teeth, or see him roll it on.

Gabriel *does* feel it when the hand pulls out of his ass. He feels empty and open. It scares him intensely.

Darrek takes both of Gabriel's hands. His sheathed cock already aligned with its target, resting with gentle pressure at Gabriel's opening, Darrek knows all he needs to do is push. Gabriel reacts. He tries to fight off his hands, and says quickly, "Okay, I can't do this. I need you to stop. You've gotta *stop*, Dare!"

"Why? Why do I have to stop?" he asks soothingly, and Gabriel hears in his voice that he's not going to stop.

"Because!"

"It's all right to be afraid. But I love you. I love you so much, and you can trust me with this."

"I know!" he cries, and the words get stuck in his throat. Two fat tears leak from the corners of his squeezed-shut eyes. "All right, come on. Do it. Do it fast, before I chicken out."

"Not until you look at me," Darrek insists. "This isn't something to be afraid of, and I need you to see that. I want to make sure that you're *with me* right now. You with me?"

He opens his eyes, blinking rapidly as the tears keep coming, "Yeah, I'm fuckin' with you. I am. See?"

He finally meets Darrek's eyes, and it does seem to help him. Gabriel shifts a little, eases his painful grip on Darrek's hands and exhales.

Darrek pushes.

Groaning loudly at the perfect too-tight heat of Gabriel enclosing him, immediately certain that it's the best thing he has ever experienced in his life, Darrek gets lost in the need to get as deep inside that place as he can. He pushes and pushes, grunting and flexing, even as Gabriel yells and arches his back.

"*Fuck*!" Gabriel whines shrilly, suddenly too full, burning with the stretch, being split open by Darrek's dick.

And then he is fully sheathed and Darrek just breathes.

"You still with me?" he asks tentatively.

There's a pause then Gabriel wriggles like a fish snared on a hook, growling, "Get off of me! Get the *fuck* off of me!"

"Gabriel!"

"Get off of me!"

"No!"

"Fuck you! Fuck you! Fuck *you*!"

"Look at me! *Look at me*, goddamn it!" Darrek barks, frowning heavily.

Defiant and half-mad, Gabriel's eyes fly open. He goes still again, his face goes blank before he starts to fight again, but it's less panicked this time. Darrek leans down and kisses Gabriel's temple.

"I love you," he insists, emphasizing each word.

The reply is a whisper at his ear, a tickle of breath, a low vibration, full of honesty and pain, "Don't hurt me. Please? I'm so fucking scared."

"I know, baby. I know. I would *never* hurt you."

Darrek pulls back, tugging slowly out and thrusting steadily back in, and he whimpers freely at the indescribable sensation of finally being inside Gabriel, of having this with him.

On the second thrust, he says, it again, "I would never hurt you. Never."

"Okay," Gabriel says, and he has stopped fighting. His fingers return to Darrek's hair and his lips drag over Darrek's skin. "Okay."

On the fourth thrust, Gabriel moans. The sound of it shocks even him, as he becomes aware that he's actually enjoying the feeling of Darrek fucking him.

Wanting to see Gabriel, and wanting Gabriel to keep seeing him, to remember where he is and what is happening, Darrek leans back, gets a better angle and starts to set a faster pace. Hips slapping against Gabriel's ass, Darrek braces himself on the bed. Gabriel gazes up at him, and he looks so plainly confused, that Darrek smiles and chuckles a little.

The new angle has him dragging right over Gabriel's prostate. Hand going quickly to his re-hardened cock, Gabriel starts to jerk off as Darrek makes love to him, one hand curled around his arm, holding on.

"Good?" Darrek asks breathlessly.

"*Really* good," Gabriel agrees, still sounding bewildered.

"Surprised?"

"Actually, yeah. I am."

"I can tell," he smirks, and then curses, "*Oh shit,*" as he starts getting closer to release, but not wanting to yet. He wants to draw it out as much as possible, especially since Gabriel finally seems to be enjoying it as well.

Reaching down, he circles the base of his shaft and balls with his hand, squeezing as hard as he can to fend his orgasm off as he thrusts.

"Should have worn a cock ring," he pants, slowing his rhythm. "I knew you'd be tight, but *fuck*! Wanna just be inside you all night, but I'm... oh *shit*... I'm gonna come. *Shit*!"

"Don't worry about it. Just... mmm..." Gabriel groans, eyes rolling back. "Just... keep...."

Darrek lunges down, and takes Gabriel's mouth in a brutal, deep kiss. Gasping into him, Darrek moans down Gabriel's throat as he orgasms, filling the condom, riding his ass. Then, with a few more rapid squeezes up his shaft, Gabriel comes right along with him.

Shouting at the sudden contraction of muscles around his cock in mid-orgasm, Darrek claws at the bed, seeing stars, and his vision whiting out. He stops kissing Gabriel because he can't breathe, can't think, can only hold on, shuddering, as wave after wave of swelling, rolling heat and fire engulfs him.

It's long minutes later when Darrek can finally think, can finally move and speak again. Gabriel lies, doubly spent and exhausted, beneath him, wrung out physically and emotionally. In fact, he looks half-asleep as Darrek tugs free. In a swift movement, the condom is removed, tied off and tossed in the waste basket near the bed.

Shimmying down, Darrek takes Gabriel's softened cock between his lips and sucks him clean.

"Dare," he whines, "'M too fuckin' tired to get hard again!"

Darrek ignores him, moving lower and sucking on each of Gabriel's balls in turn.

"Dare! Evil fucker...."

Releasing him, he moves even lower, gripping Gabriel's legs and bending them sharply back and apart, licking once with the flat of his tongue over Gabriel's hole. Darrek moans with pleasure at the taste and feel of the heat under his mouth and thrusts his pointed tongue greedily inside.

"*Oh sweet fucking Jesus*!" Gabriel curses, unable to stop himself from pressing down into Darrek's mouth, inviting more.

Curling his tongue, stroking with it and licking over the inner walls, sucking at him, Darrek unabashedly and wantonly eats him out. Wrapping his large hands around Gabriel's thighs, Darrek just draws him in, holds him there as he plunders the cavity. Gradually, reluctantly, he pulls back, until his jaw isn't working quite as hard, teeth no longer dragging over puckered flesh, and he is giving Gabriel a very obscene type of French kiss. Then he kisses his way back up over damp thighs and lets Gabriel's legs fall back down to the bed.

"I need to do that some more later," Darrek confesses, breathlessly. "And I want us both to get tested so we can stop using condoms, though I'm pretty sure I've swallowed enough of your come anyway to make it a moot point."

"Agreed. Now fucking come over here and kiss me."

"Really?" Darrek squints.

"Shut the fuck up and kiss me, or I'll just chain your ass to the bed and *make you* kiss me."

"Are you sure?"

"I am NOT fucking kidding," Gabriel warns. Rolling his eyes when Darrek doesn't move, Gabriel grabs him, easily rolling them so that he is on top. Leaning down, he kisses Darrek, tasting himself, as well as the tang of the lube.

When he finally pulls back, Gabriel just sighs contentedly and collapses down next to him on the bed. Darrek curls around him, entangling their limbs, and says, "I swear I'm going to get up and get a washcloth in a second."

"Uh-huh," Gabriel hums, already mostly asleep.

"Thank you for letting me have you," he mumbles, succumbing to sleep as well.

Gabriel smiles and folds his arms over the one of Darrek's circling his chest, and falls into the best night of sleep he has ever had.

Chapter 24
Demonstrations of Control

Gabriel sniffs and wiggles his nose when he feels something tickle the end of it. It happens again, and this time he can smell the flower as well as feel it. Grinning, he peeks open sleep-heavy eyes.

"I tried to get out of bed to get something to wash you off last night, but you kind of had a death grip on my arm," Darrek explains, trailing the freshly-plucked purple flower over his lover's cheek. "So, now you have to wake up so that I can bathe you."

"Mmm... that sounds good," he admits.

"Plus, there's coffee."

"Even better."

When he rolls out of bed, he drowsily follows Darrek to the bathroom, but is awake enough to palm something from the bureau's surface on the way.

Noticing that Darrek's hair is damp, and that he smells like the lavender soap that's in the shower, Gabriel deduces that he has showered already without him. The quiet barking from outside and the scent of French roast brew from the kitchen are further proof of Darrek's early morning activities.

"You let me sleep in," Gabriel mutters, reaching out and wrapping his hands around Darrek's hips from behind once they are through the bathroom doorway. Darrek stops and lets Gabriel press their bodies together, smiling at the touch and the kiss Gabriel applies to his neck.

"You needed it... sir."

Heat swells low in Gabriel's belly at the honorific, his morning erection pressing at Darrek's ass.

"Bend over," he says into Darrek's ear.

"Yes, sir," Darrek replies. His eyes close and a flush colors his cheeks. A hand at the center of his back guides him forward, bending him in half over the sink. His pants are tugged down and he holds tight to the counter's edge as he hears the sound of foil ripping behind him.

Gabriel's fingers rub lubricant into his crack, over and into his hole, but don't breach him far. Moaning with anticipation at being entered with little prep, he feels the head of Gabriel's dick begin to press demandingly into his body.

A thunderous groan swells within him, rising from back in his throat, but Darrek bites off the sound, forcing himself to be quiet as the burning ache grows. It hurts, but Gabriel is going much slower than usual, and just gradually joining their bodies, pressing them closer and closer together.

"Okay?" Gabriel asks, his hands moving in a caressing massage over his hips and back, down his thighs, as he violates him deeper. The contrast of the pain against the tenderness makes it perfect for him.

"Yes, Master."

As Gabriel begins setting a smooth, slow rhythm, fucking Darrek and watching his face in the bathroom mirror, he says, "Today I'm going to make a call. All of our utility bills, any of our expenses, I'm going to have paid for directly from my account. You only have to work if you want to. If you want to just focus on your own carpentry business, then you can do that. No worrying about money. Just do what makes you happy."

Darrek cries out when Gabriel pushes in hard, not stopping until his pelvis is snug against Darrek's ass. Breathing heavily, lower lip quivering, eyes hidden by heavy lashes, Darrek is the picture of torturous bliss.

"And after we eat, we're going to head over to my doctor and get tested. The whole shebang. I'm fucking done with the condoms. No one else gets to fuck you, and you can bet your sweet ass that no one else is fucking me. I want to be able to come inside you. I want to feel your ass gripping tight around my cock with nothing in between. No more fucking condoms. I would have stopped using them anyway, but I didn't want to put you in any danger. You are the most valuable thing in the world to me."

Falling silent, he twists the fingers of his left hand into Darrek's hair, pulling on it hard enough to cause him to arch his back, head snapped back and gazing up into the mirror at Gabriel as he starts to pound hard into him.

Darrek gasps, bracing himself, absorbing the shock. The promises Gabriel is making to him, the particular way he's hammering right into Darrek's prostate on every push, has him right on the edge. One little touch and Darrek would be coming, so his hands squeeze at the counter and he pushes through the feeling, trying to control it. He doesn't want to let himself come unless Gabriel allows it.

"Oh shit..." Gabriel gasps, "*Ffffuck....*"

Panting, flushed pink, Gabriel doesn't stop long to enjoy his orgasm, but pulls Darrek upright. Still buried deep inside his ass, he cradles Darrek's balls, so full and heavy. He watches as Darrek swallows thickly, eyes shut as he struggles to master his urges, heat radiating off him, cock dripping wet.

Running his thumb gently up the underside of Darrek's shaft, Gabriel whispers, "Would you enjoy it more if I let you come right now, or if I forbade it?"

A low guttural noise slips from his lips, and Gabriel chuckles.

Rolling Darrek's balls, lightly touching the base of his reddened shaft, Gabriel watches Darrek's cock jump and twitch.

"Loved the feeling of your tongue in my ass last night," he says into Darrek's ear. "No one's ever done that to me before. I think you'll get to do that a *lot* from now on."

"Thank you, Master," Darrek blurts out, but it's strained and broken.

"See, you're getting better at this. At controlling yourself. Look how badly you need to come right now, but you're not. I'm proud of you."

Darrek smiles and laughs, but there's anguish in it and his face twists as he says urgently, "I love you."

"Love you too," Gabriel says against the heat of Darrek's neck, squeezing once up the length of Darrek's shaft, telling him demandingly, "Come for me, slave."

He erupts with a shuddering cry, splashing hot come all over his torso as his sphincter clamps down around Gabriel's dick. Gabriel's arm circles his chest, pinning their bodies together as he strokes him through it.

A couple minutes later, after Gabriel is sure Darrek is steady on his feet, they stand together under the steamy spray of water from the shower. Darrek, already scrubbed-clean, washes Gabriel down with the soapsuds-covered sponge, his eyes determined and focused. Gabriel watches him with a contented smile.

"Ben and Kyle are coming over tonight," Gabriel says to him.

Not even pausing his ministrations, washing down over Gabriel's left hip, Darrek nods, "Yes, sir."

Trepidation creeps into his eyes though, into the turn of his mouth.

"I know how much you care about him, Dare. Let me do this for you. I'll handle it, okay? I'll handle everything. You miss him, don't you?"

"Yeah, I do. And I've been worried about him. He was so upset the last time I spoke to him, and..." he says softly, trailing off, his brow furrowed with sorrow.

"Then this'll be a good thing," Gabriel assures him.

The sponge falls away from Gabriel's body and Darrek curls his arms around him instead, hugging him close.

"Thanks."

"You're welcome."

Rinsing them both off, Darrek shuts off the water. They exit the bathroom, and go to search out clothes. A minute later, they are dressed and their only thought is for the alluring scent of the large pot of coffee that is waiting and ready for them downstairs, any other concerns or fears now melted away, for the moment at least.

Perfect purple flower in hand, Gabriel leads the way, smiling.

They walk into the café and find a table near the window that overlooks the tree-lined downtown street just outside. It is still mostly empty of people due to the early hour. A waitress approaches and sets out two menus. She leaves the two men to look over the breakfast selections. Ben sighs, reclining into the padded back of the curved booth, reluctantly removing his dark sunglasses. Still waking up and trying to shake the heavy, sleepy feeling from his bones, Ben stretches out his arms and yawns. Craving his morning coffee and the full alertness that typically only comes once he has had it, he enjoys the alluring aroma of the brew that is wafting out from the kitchen. Ben glances over at Kyle beside him and smiles.

Letting one arm rest along the top of the booth, his fingers reach out and begin to play with the small padlock secured onto the back of the thick black leather collar wrapping Kyle's neck. It blends in well with the rest of his attire: black shirt, dark jeans, gleaming silver jewelry and black leather cuffs on his wrists. But even if onlookers happen to notice it, and know what the collar really *means*, neither of them cares or worries about their judgment.

Ben's other hand palms both menus and flips one open. After a quick scan of it, he folds it closed again. He lets his hand slip down under the table and into his pocket as they wait for the waitress to return and take their order.

When she strides back over to them, weaving between tables and chairs on the way, Ben presses the button on the small, black remote tucked away where no one can see it. He doesn't allow any reaction to show, no matter how pleased he is, when he hears Kyle make a low grunt from beside him. Instead, Ben says to the waitress, "Two large coffees. I'll have the waffle platter. He'll have... hmm... let's make it the scrambled eggs and toast."

"Sure thing," she smiles, jotting it all down on her pad. Giving Kyle a brief, curious glance, she turns and wanders back to the kitchen.

"Gotta keep your strength up, don't we?" Ben grins, still fingering the remote. "Protein and carbohydrates are essential."

Flushed and slightly dazed, Kyle replies, "Yes, sir," and then presses his lips together to keep in a deep groan as a faster burst of vibration rips through him, fire exploding up his spine and into his brain.

Slumping down in the seat, the position makes it a little easier on him, less intense as the plug buried in him shifts. But then he feels a tug at the collar, pulling him back upright so that his behind is firmly planted on the bench.

Ben's phone goes off in his pocket.

Cursing, he releases the remote, and Kyle sighs. Digging the cell phone out, Ben reads the text message from Gabriel.

Humming thoughtfully, he slips the phone back into his pocket. Seeing the wary darkness of Kyle's expression, Ben says to him, "Hey, don't worry about it. But it *is* gonna happen. We're having dinner there tonight."

"Okay," Kyle says quietly.

With his thumb brushing over the place where leather meets skin on Kyle's neck, Ben asks him, "I'm considering taking this off of you when we go. I want you to be as comfortable as possible. If you don't want to have to explain to Darrek... then, I get it. I won't make you wear it."

Instantly, Kyle's eyes snap up. His steely gaze locks onto Ben.

"I don't want you to take it off," Kyle says assertively. "I'm more comfortable when I'm wearing it, and when I know that you're...."

Taking care of me, he wants to finish, but doesn't. It doesn't need to be said for Ben to hear the words. "Can't we leave it on? Please?"

The waitress returns with their coffee and tells them that the food will be out in a moment.

Kyle wraps both of his hands around the steaming mug and a smile plays at his lips when Ben's hand goes back to the remote, slipping into the side pocket of his lightweight leather jacket.

"I don't want to make this harder for you than it already is, but if you say you want it, then it stays on."

"Thank you," Kyle smiles. A burst of vibration jolts him before he relaxes into it. His voice is only slightly unsteady he asks, "Do you need to go into work today?"

"No. I have other plans. Things to do. Busy, busy, busy," Ben says with a contented sigh. "Gonna pick up some steaks for dinner, do some paperwork, pay some bills, check my email... you know."

Kyle gives him a sideways glance. His face pink and need written plainly in his features, he takes a tentative sip at his coffee.

"I saw that," Ben laughs. "How long's it been now?"

"Three days. Seventy-four hours, twenty minutes. Approximately, sir."

"You've been keeping track?"

Kyle nods, sheepishly.

"It's actually seventy-four hours and *thirty-two* minutes," Ben tells him. Leaning in, he whispers against Kyle's ear, "Does kitty have an itch that needs scratching?"

He pushes the remote up to the highest setting and hears Kyle's gasp, sees him wriggle.

Kyle curses, and grunts out an affirmation, coffee shaking in his unsteady hands, his blue eyes closing as he blushes more deeply still.

"Okay then. Breakfast first."

It's Kyle's opinion that the best thing about Ben's house is his garage. Not the big-screen, high-definition TV with satellite hook-up, the designer furniture, the huge bed with the pillowtop mattress, or the glass-enclosed two-person shower. No, the best thing by far is the garage. He dreams about it almost every night, now that he has seen and experienced it for himself. Even when he is not inside it, he is wishing he were.

Ben's house sits on more land than Darrek's does. It's close to Diadem, out in farm country, and backs up to rolling fields and an expansive landscape. The driveway loops around the house and leads right up to the garage door, which faces the back of the property and the open acres upon acres of wheat. With not a neighbor in sight, it's exceptionally private.

The garage attached to Ben's house is not used for cars, or as a workshop, like Darrek's and Kyle's are. Instead it's well-equipped in a different way. Personalized and perfected over the years, it's even better than the dungeon at Diadem, fitted and ready with the latest and greatest in bondage gear, sex toys and torture devices. Kyle doesn't even know the name for some of the things in Ben's garage, can't even guess what their purpose is, not having encountered them himself in all of the time he has been Ben's submissive. But, now that he is officially Ben's slave, twenty-four hours a day and seven days a week, as well as a resident in his home, Kyle dreams of getting to try out each and every item inside that indescribably alluring space.

Once they get back to the house, they are fed, awake and happy, bearing frozen steaks fresh from the local butcher. Ben parks at the very bottom of the long, winding drive. He waits for Kyle to get out of the vehicle first, noting the sharp, pissed-off glance Kyle throws him as he goes.

"Go on. Say it," Ben coaxes.

After a pause in which he debates holding his tongue or not, Kyle gives in to the urge and says, "You *had* to park all the way down here, didn't you?"

"Of course!"

Ben fingers the remote as Kyle slams the door shut and starts to shuffle up the slight hill, taking small steps and dragging his feet.

"Come on, faster than that, ya slowpoke!"

He takes Kyle's hand, lacing their fingers together, and leads him at a vastly more rapid pace toward the house. Kyle begins to make a small whimpering sound after the first couple of wide steps.

"Hey, at least you're not worrying about tonight anymore, are ya," Ben winks.

"Yeah, I am. Of course I am. Hey, are you going to have me wear... this... tonight?" he asks, glancing down at his crotch. "I mean... I don't know if I could handle being this on-edge on top of everything else."

"Aw, don't worry, kitty. The whole on-edge thing I'll take care of, but yes, you'll be wearing it. It's yours now, just like the collar, and it only comes off when *I* say so and unlock it. But I promise that we're going to have an awesome time. Got it all under control, just like I always do. Gabey and I have an idea how to break the ice. He agrees that it's just what we need... but that's enough of that. Don't want to spoil the surprise, do I?"

They walk inside and Ben goes to put the steaks in the freezer. Stopping in the small office located off of the living room, he comes back with a stack of papers in hand and his briefcase slung over his shoulder.

"You're really going to do *paperwork*?" Kyle says with clear disappointment. "I thought you were just saying that to be a dick."

"Garage. Come on," is all the response he gets.

Ben takes Kyle's hand again and pulls him along.

A shiver of excitement races down Kyle's spine, shooting right down to his aching, tortured dick at the mention of the garage. His pout disappears and a wide smile takes its place.

Chapter 25
The Good Fight

Dragging a chair over to the narrow but sturdy wooden tabletop in the center of the room, Ben sets his briefcase and the papers down atop the makeshift desk. The garage door has been left open, allowing plenty of sunlight and fresh air to fill the room.

"C'mere," Ben murmurs, nodding to Kyle who suddenly looks like a deer in the headlights now that the moment he has been waiting for has actually arrived.

Eager hands tug off Kyle's shirt. Ben sees the rapid rise and fall of his chest, and enjoys how Kyle's lips fall softly open in the most sensual way. Ben quickly gets his own pants undone next, and that just sends Kyle even further into a bottled-up frenzy of desire. He stares at the exposed triangle of Ben's skin, at the glimpse of his muscular abdomen, not surprised at all that Ben is not wearing any underwear. But, before he can even push the pants down on his hips, Ben grabs Kyle's face, cupping it between his hands, and kisses him. Ben pours all of his affection for and devotion to him into it, letting its sweetness and tenderness show Kyle just how deeply he feels.

Holding on to the hands Ben has pressed to his face, Kyle gasps for air, but pushes for more, needing every moment of the kiss to soothe his still-growing apprehension.

"Love you, you know," Ben says against his lips.

"I know."

"Just relax."

Ben's hands skim down over heated skin of his lover's neck and chest. The backs of his fingers follow the line trailing down the center of his body, between his pecs, over his abs and back up, across his chest and to his shoulder before tickling down the flexed muscle of his arms. Goose bumps rise on Kyle's skin.

Their eyes lock in a wordless acknowledgment of what they know to be true, what they have both been thinking about for days.

Biting down on his bottom lip as desire surges through his veins, Ben's hand forces its way down into the back of Kyle's pants, palming his ass and squeezing the rounded flesh.

"Gonna be even better for waiting. Can't fuckin' wait to come inside you and mark my fuckin' territory... because your ass? It's *mine.*"

Kyle groans, lunging forward and tasting Ben again.

A fraction of a second passes where they are both still and calm, and simply looking into each other's eyes. There's a sedate readiness in Kyle, and, seeing it, unable to hold back any longer, Ben breaks the kiss. Spinning Kyle around, bending him sharply over the table, bare chest flush to the wood, Ben yanks down Kyle's pants. He tugs them all the way down and off before pressing a thigh between his legs and kicking his feet further apart. His fingers go to the base of the black plug nestled in him. As he pulls it quickly free, too impatient to be gentle, Kyle makes a soft cry. Ben gets his pants down low enough to free himself and proceeds to rub the dripping wet head of his cock against Kyle's backside, into and up the crevice. It nudges over the now empty ring of muscle and between his firm cheeks, smearing pre-come around as additional lube.

"Ben..." Kyle whimpers, and there's fear there in his voice as he extends an arm back and opens his hand, fingers splayed and grasping.

Taking Kyle's hand, clutching it gently, Ben pushes inside. There's a sharp cry from Kyle at the additional stretch and low burn, and Ben pauses for a second.

With his free hand, Ben grabs hard at Kyle's hip. Strong fingers dig into flesh deeply enough to bruise. Ben pins him against the edge of the wooden surface and pulls back out only to slowly reenter him, managing to get fully-seated with only a low groan from Kyle.

As he begins to ride the tightly clenched muscle, Ben thinks of how he has been fantasizing about doing exactly this for so long, having Kyle with no barriers, no protection, now that they both know they are clean and committed. Feeling everything that much more, especially the silky-softness of the hot inner walls gripped around him, every tremor and pulse from Kyle is felt keenly by Ben, tickling up his shaft. It's so much better than before, than it has *ever* been. No other man has ever given himself this completely and with as much love and trust to him, as Kyle has done.

With the building, tingling coil of heat that is curling deep down inside him, as the tension grows and grows until he is about to erupt, Ben loses track of everything but the feeling of Kyle clenched around his dick. The sight of the broad expanse of his lover's shoulders, his tan skin, muscle toned and lean from years of hard manual labor, and his pink, puckered, wet hole just taking him and swallowing him up with every digging push—it all makes Ben just pound harder, moan louder.

Kyle presses his face into the table and scratches at it with short nails, digging shallow grooves into the thick, worn surface. Since he was already stretched out by the plug, and lubed up from this morning when Ben had put it in place, it doesn't hurt much at all. It just feels *good*. Not too good, but just good enough.

Gripping Ben's hand, Kyle indulges in simply enjoying it. But when Ben pauses, stilling, and shifts the angle of his hips slightly, Kyle knows what he's doing and hears himself begging, "Ben, please don't... I can't take it... I can't... Not after three fucking days!"

"Sure you can," he pants, entering Kyle again with an unrelenting thrust of hips, nailing right into his prostate.

Ben watches the tension build in Kyle's back, in the clench of his ass and thighs. Ben releases Kyle's hand, so Kyle grips instead at the opposite edge of the table and tries to shift away.

Ben just grabs his hips and holds him in place, fucking him hard and triggering all of those nerves buried deep inside. When Kyle loses control, really, truly *loses it,* and starts crying out, every muscle tensed, sweating and shaking, Ben is right there. He speeds up his rhythm even more, then fills him up as he shoots his seed into Kyle's body with a prolonged moan of pleasure. His hips twitch against Kyle's ass as he slowly comes down.

He doesn't pull out. He just reaches into his bag on the table and pulls from it a large dildo with a multiple rings of textured nubs circling it above the flared base. Smearing it with plenty of lubricant, Ben tugs free of Kyle only to fill him up again with the huge toy, plugging him up and keeping every drop of his spunk inside.

"Oh fucking god!" Kyle cries brokenly, taking the thick, tapered object with only a little resistance.

Ben pushes at its base until it rests flush against Kyle's body and holds it there until he is sure it's not going to push back out.

"Got it?" Ben asks.

"Yeah," Kyle pants, nodding.

"Good. Stand up."

Kyle straightens and turns around—keyed-up, strands of blond hair stuck to his face with sweat, eyes dark, and lips kissed red. He doesn't even really see what's happening. He is much too far-gone for that. He just lets Ben move and guide him, so lost in the sensations that he doesn't even remotely care at this point.

Backing him up to the wall, Ben takes first one arm and then the other, shackling the cuffs on each of Kyle's wrists in turn to the hooks in the cement block. Arms spread wide and secured in place, Ben next binds Kyle's ankles with similar cuffs, making sure his feet are firmly planted but spread as well.

Next is the gag. Ben opts for the one in the form of a small dildo, easing the long, tapered, penis-shaped hard plastic between Kyle's lips, back along his tongue and into his mouth and throat, strapping it tight around the back of his head once it's in place.

Kyle's lips close on the base and he sighs around it, breathing through his nose, watching everything avidly. Ben looks down at where his slave's dick is straining against the confines of the padlocked, polycarbonate cock cage Kyle has been wearing for seventy-six hours and ten minutes now.

A hand moves to cradle Kyle's balls, letting the weight of them settle in his palm before he grips them, curling his fingers and squeezing gently. Kyle shakes his head frantically, grunting and begging around the gag.

"Jesus, your balls are full," Ben comments as Kyle continues to beg wordlessly.

Massaging and fondling them, he reaches out to the cart nearby with his free hand and picks up a small hood that he then secures around Kyle's cock cage, fitting it just above the ring circling the base. Then he hooks the first weight onto the hood's metal ring and watches as it pulls at Kyle's body, stretching him. Kyle's head falls back against the wall as Ben says, "Mmm... one more I think. For now."

The second weight goes on. Kyle shifts and moans.

Then Ben gets in his face, stepping close. His fingers close around Kyle's left nipple, rolling it and tugging gently on it. Kyle arches into the touch, especially when Ben's head lowers and he suckles it. Nipping at it gently with his teeth, he swipes his tongue over the hot, tender, peaked nub, tasting the saltiness of Kyle's sweat.

Ben releases him once Kyle is fully stimulated, and goes back to tugging at the nipple with his index finger and thumb. He stares at it then up at Kyle's wide blue eyes, the pupils blown.

"You know what I want to do, don't you?" Ben asks, voice low and intent.

Kyle nods, no hesitation, unable to speak around the gag.

"Want to watch?"

Kyle nods again.

Ben releases him and walks to the back of the garage, rummaging around in the stainless steel drawers where he keeps most of his supplies. He returns a minute later with a box of latex gloves, tugging a pair of them on. Kyle hears them snap against skin, the smell of them stinging at his nose. He follows Ben's movements when he picks up a bottle of disinfectant and wets a cotton-swab with it. The swab goes to Kyle's left nipple.

Covering the area with the cool fluid, circling the peaked sensitive flesh, Ben sees a shudder of anticipation shake Kyle in his bindings. Then he opens a sealed bag containing a single, very fine piercing needle.

Kyle doesn't see anything for a moment, as the reality of what Ben is about to do sinks in, as memories of the times they've done this before come flooding back. He does, however, come back to reality when he feels Ben's lips kiss his shoulder, neck and jaw, soothing him.

The glinting needle captures Kyle's attention. He watches it as Ben instructs him, talks him through it, like he always has done.

"Okay. Breathe in," Ben instructs, composed and speaking softly, "And out."

Kyle complies, trying to relax enough to stop shaking.

"Again. Breathe in... and hold it. Good. Now let it out."

The air rushes out through his nose, and Ben's fingers have closed around the nipple. He tugs it away from Kyle's body, stretching the skin as Kyle hears the blood beating in his ears, feels it pulsing in his veins all the way down to his fingertips. A rush of adrenaline surges through him as well and he almost begins to feel high from it all. He welcomes it and rides out the rush, every sense heightened and tuned-in to each little detail. Looking away from the point of the needle, he instead stares hard at Ben's lips as he says, "Breathe in... there ya go. Hold it... hold it...."

Kyle feels the prick of the needle pressing against his nipple.

"And let it out..." Ben says soothingly.

As he exhales, the needle goes through and out, and then it's done. Just like that.

Grunting sharply through the gag, he bites down on it at the sharp pain and pressure.

"Can you see it?" Ben asks with a grin.

Kyle looks down at his chest and sees the thin length of metal speared through his nipple. Fascinated, as he always is, he can't seem to pull his eyes away. Metal clinks as he shudders through the continued surge of blood and adrenaline, head buzzing with it.

"Good?"

"Mmm," Kyle nods, eyes rolling with pleasure and the hormones racing through his system.

Ben carefully takes hold of the pierced nub of flesh, slowly pushing on it, watching the needle shift inside the reddened tissue. Kyle moans and arches his back. Ben's thumb, encased in latex, brushes back and forth over the tip of the nipple and it's like he can see the pleasure and heat radiating off of Kyle's body. Reaching between his slave's spread legs, Ben flicks on the vibrator wedged deep inside his ass.

Kyle whimpers shrilly, wriggling against the wall.

"So good. Such a good kitty," Ben purrs, rubbing two fingers up against Kyle's taint, triggering more nerves in his prostate. He keeps doing it, watching Kyle's dick try to swell and strain against the cage, leaking milky-white drops even though he can't get hard. Undulating against the wall, he breathes harshly through his nose and shuts his eyes to focus on the sensations.

After long minutes, Ben stops rubbing at the sensitive, smooth patch of skin. He fits headphones onto Kyle's ears, setting the iPod to shuffle before placing it on the cart nearby. Next his fixes a blindfold over Kyle's eyes and checks the tightness of the gag.

Satisfied, leaving Kyle bound, blind, mute and deaf, his body wracked with many variations of pleasure, Ben goes to his briefcase and paperwork, ready to sit down to work, enjoying the gentle breeze and alluring sight before him as he does.

Darrek watches Gabriel talk on his cell phone, sitting at what had been Darrek's desk and is now, astonishingly, *their* desk, with a folder opened in front of him and some papers scattered around. He is in the process of setting up the bank account, and having their bills drawn directly from it. It's one of the biggest things anyone has ever done for Darrek, and it makes everything about the merging of his and Gabriel's lives that much more real and practical in the best kind of way. Darrek has never been so happy.

He lounges on the couch with his head resting on a throw pillow, watching Gabriel arrange everything.

That morning, as they cleaned up the breakfast dishes, Darrek had insisted on rinsing them and loading the dishwasher, not letting Gabriel anywhere near them, especially after what had happened the previous day and the revelations about Gabriel's home life when he was younger. Gabriel at first looked like he wanted to argue the matter, but when Darrek gently asked him, "Please let me do this for you. Let this be *my* job," Gabriel relented with unspoken gratitude.

As Darrek did the dishes, Gabriel had gotten the financial documents out, and had placed the call to the doctor's office to make their appointments.

When Darrek finished the dishes, he had watched Gabriel carefully from the kitchen for a few long minutes. Then he had gotten two Advil tablets out, and filled a glass of water. He had brought them over to his lover and Master, offering them to him.

Gabriel had stared at the things in Darrek's hands before looking up at his face with a question in his eyes. That's when realization set in and he looked quickly away, flushing with embarrassment.

"Thanks," he had said, quickly taking the painkillers.

"No problem. Are you all right?"

"Yeah. I didn't realize that it showed, though... you know. That I'm... sore."

"But you *are* sore?"

"Yeah. A little," he admitted shyly, head lowered.

Without hesitation, Darrek leaned down and caught his lips in a soft kiss, brushing a thumb over the hollow of his jaw.

"You were amazing," Darrek whispered to him. "Completely *amazing*. Do you regret it at all?"

Their lips were so close that Darrek could taste the coffee in Gabriel's breath. Gabriel frowned with seriousness and kissed Darrek's lips once more before answering him.

"No. Of course not. I just hope that... next time....it'll be easier for me. But I'm glad I waited... for you."

Then it was Darrek's turn to frown and pressed the issue by asking Gabriel again, "But are you all right?"

He tried to kiss away the wrinkles in Gabriel's brow.

"I'm trying to be all right. But the fact that you brought me Advil, and are asking about how I'm feeling... let's just say no one else ever did that for me. Every little bit helps. It all... it all helps."

"I want to just take it away. I want to take that whole part of your life away and make it so it never happened."

"But then I wouldn't be who I am. We might never have met. Gotta take the good with the bad and all that shit," Gabriel said to him, adding with a reassuring smile, "Let me make these calls and then we'll head out, okay?"

"I love you," Darrek whispered, kissing the middle of his

forehead.

"Me too," Gabriel smiled. He took Darrek's hand and squeezed it as he walked back to the couch. Hands clasped, their arms stretched out between their bodies as Darrek went, before their hands were forced to pull apart and fell reluctantly away.

Chapter 26
The Key to My Heart

A short time later, the phone calls are done. Gabriel finishes sending another text message to Ben, aware of Darrek's eyes on him.

Ben's brief descriptions of what is currently happening at his house highlight an issue that, for Gabriel, desperately needs to be addressed in his own relationship. Standing, he walks over and sits by Darrek's side as he shifts to make room on the couch.

"Uh-oh," Darrek says, "I know that look. What's wrong?"

"Nothing's wrong. But we need to talk about something."

"Okay," Darrek agrees, sitting up a little more.

"I want to talk about us... because, well, we've been living in what you would call a twenty-four/seven, Dominant/submissive relationship. Did you realize that?"

"Yeah, I mean, I don't know a lot about that sort of thing, not as much as you probably do, but... yeah. I realized that."

"But we've never really talked about it. We've never made it official."

"I feel like it's pretty official," Darrek says quietly.

"No, baby, that's not what I mean. Of course our relationship is official. I meant the fact that we're living together as a Master and slave, and that we've pretty much been making the rules up as we go along. That's the part we need to talk about. Um... okay. I have something for you. Uh... I'll be right back. Stay here."

He returns with a smallish, but long black box cradled in his hands.

"I debated this, and what to do, what to get you. There are different levels of commitment when it comes to this lifestyle. But see...

I wasn't even really sure that I wanted to define us in terms of our Master/slave dynamic. Sometimes I just want to be in love with you and have it begin and end there. So, I compromised."

He hands the box to Darrek.

"This is for you to wear, if you want to. It's symbolic of my commitment to take care of you in every imaginable way."

Darrek lifts the lid and sees a necklace. It's a heavy silver chain with a tiny lock connecting the ends. It gleams and catches the light. A small pendant hangs from the front, inscribed with a tiny G.

"It's platinum. I'm wearing the key already," Gabriel explains, pulling the necklace he's wearing out of his shirt, holding it up for Darrek to see. He gingerly lifts the chain from out of the box and uses the key on his necklace to unlock it. Holding the opened chain out to Darrek he asks, "Will you wear it? If you do, it means we belong to each other, that you're mine, my submissive, my lover, my partner—mine in every sense. And I'm yours. It's a big deal, so if you have any reservations...."

"Gabriel," Darrek hisses, biting his lip and clapping a hand over his mouth, "This *is* a *really* big deal!"

He feels the emotion threatening to choke him, memories of proposing to Sara really not so long ago in a similar manner.

"Are you sure you want me like this?" Darrek asks.

"I'm already wearing the key. I'm in this. I want this. I've never wanted anything more."

"But this is like... like we're getting... engaged."

"I know. Yes, it's just like that. And maybe, someday, we can do that too."

Gabriel grunts as Darrek lunges forward and nearly knocks him backward in a tight hug, pressing his tear-stained face into Gabriel's shoulder. Darrek feels Gabriel's fingers brush through his hair and he just cries harder.

When he's gotten it all out, he sits back and wipes the dampness off of his face with the back of his arm, sniffling.

"I'm such a sap. I didn't cry the first time I got engaged, though. I think it's your fault."

"So you'll wear it?"

"I'm never taking it off," Darrek grins, perfect teeth flashing white and eyes shining with pure happiness. "Can I wear it now?"

As Gabriel hooks it around his neck and secures the lock, both of them hear the small snick it makes. It is a delicate sound, but the weight of what it means enhances it in both their minds.

Darrek says, "This is like a collar, isn't it?"

"Yeah. It is. But it's more than that to me. Yes, this means that I am your Master. But it's also my proof to the world that I love you."

The chain is snug around Darrek's neck, fitting just like a collar, but in a more subtle way.

"Now, for some couples, when the collar is on, it means that the Master is in total control, but I don't want it to work that way with us. I want you to wear this as much as you want, without worrying about what the rules are at that moment. So, instead, I promise you that if we are in what's called a high protocol level, like when we're having a session, I will let you know verbally, okay?"

"Yeah. Okay."

"Those are the only times when you must obey the strictest, most formal rules that we establish together, like calling me by my title only and not my name. Any other time, as long as you show me respect, as I will show you the same respect, that's all you need to worry about. And if we get to the point where we want to move beyond the Master/slave arrangement, then I'm open to that possibility."

Darrek smiles widely, his eyes sparkling. Taking Gabriel's hand in his, he says, "Sometimes it feels like we were literally made for each other, like we were made so that neither of us could be happy until we had each other. I'm so happy. You make me so happy. I'm so lucky that I get to love you and have you in my life, taking care of me. And I promise to take care of you too. Thank you for the necklace, and for needing me."

"You're welcome, baby," Gabriel smiles, kissing him.

The trip to the physician's office is more intense than they had anticipated. More than just a couple of tests, for both of them it serves to emphasize the reality of what they are committing themselves to. They watch blood samples get drawn from each of their arms, and then they each in turn undergo a brief physical exam to look for any signs or symptoms of illness or venereal disease.

Not speaking much, the two lovers wait through it, holding hands. Darrek keeps playing absentmindedly with his collar and staring at the fine silver chain around Gabriel's neck holding the key.

The results of the tests are back in less than an hour, and they are each, happily, given a clean bill of health.

As they climb back into the SUV, the mood is tranquil, sedate, created by their shared fear of what the doctor might (but thankfully did not) find.

When Gabriel pulls into the parking lot of a sports supply store on the way home, Darrek is confused.

"I thought we had to pick up food for dinner? We're gonna barbeque, right?" Darrek asks, sitting in the passenger seat, the seat moved all the way back to accommodate his long legs.

"Yep. But Ben's got the steaks. We'll get the rest after we go in here. There's a few things we need."

"For tonight?" Darrek asks with only slight apprehension. "From *here*?"

"Yep."

"Do I even *want* to know what your kinky brain is plotting?"

"Maybe," Gabriel grins over at him, his eyes bright. "Maybe not. Anyway, you'll find out in a minute!"

"Look at you. You're glowing like a pregnant woman," Darrek laughs. "Tell me the truth, is that happiness *all* because of how hot my ass is, which, incidentally, now is now *officially* yours alone to play with, or just *mostly* because of it?"

"I can't believe you," Gabriel laughs, smacking Darrek's thigh playfully. "Get in the damn store."

"Yes, Master," Darrek grins mischievously.

"You're going to pay for that later, you know."

"Oh, I hope so."

An hour and a half after Ben had left Kyle bound to the wall he gets up from his workstation, abandoning his paperwork, and returns to him. Lowering the volume on the iPod, Ben goes silently to his knees and, trying not to disturb Kyle more than he needs to, he removes the weights and tiny leather hood from him. Next, he pulls two keys out from around his neck, and uses the smaller one to gently unlock the chastity device.

He removes the pins connecting the pieces together, sliding the cage off before unfastening the ring.

Kyle feels the relief immediately, and moans around the large gag stuffed down his throat as blood rushes to his cock, filling it more and more until he is ready to burst.

Ben stands, watching him.

"Do I need to empty your bladder?" he asks.

Kyle shakes his head and snaps his fingers.

Nodding, Ben unfastens the straps on the gag, and slowly pulls it from between Kyle's lips. The skin is cracked and dry where the base of the gag was resting and stretching his mouth open. Pulling a tube of lip balm from his pocket, Ben applies it to Kyle's lips, giving him a chance to flex his jaw muscles and clear his throat. Then, Ben grabs a bottle of water and feeds some to him using a straw.

"Better?"

"Yeah. Thanks," he nods. "And I can hold it. I don't want you to use the catheter. Please, sir."

"Okay, no catheter," Ben assures him since Kyle used their safe sign and snapped his fingers. "Do you need me to let you out or can I finish?"

"Finish. I want you to finish, sir."

"You're sure?"

"Yeah."

Curling a hand around Kyle's neck, feeling the thick collar under his palm, he brushes his fingers soothingly over the warm, soft skin of his nape, up into the short hair there and leans in to kiss him. Kyle exhales in a rush of air as he greedily kisses him back. Reaching down between his captive's spread legs, Ben's searching fingers find the base of the vibrating toy and start to slowly tug it free without turning it off first. The rows of nubs circling the base stimulate the over-excited nerves of Kyle's body on the way out and he moans down Ben's throat, sucking hard on his tongue as the large, tapered object gets pulled out more and more. Just before it comes free, Ben slowly pushes it right back in. Kyle's hips thrust forward, searching for contact, friction, *anything*, his cock dripping wet.

"Good?" Ben asks through a grin after pulling his lips away as Kyle whimpers.

"Uh-huh."

"I've got something that's even better," Ben whispers into his ear, the headphones still in place, but knowing Kyle can, obviously, hear him just fine over the music.

He tugs the dildo back out and sets it aside, taking up a hooked, black object instead. This particular instrument has always made Kyle a quivering mess and Ben cannot wait to see his reaction this time either.

He eases one end into Kyle's hole, pushing it until it's fully embedded then twists it, pressing the other curved end with its textured surface against his taint, both ends of the nearly U-shaped toy flush and pushing against his slave's most sensitive spot from inside *and* outside his body before switching it on. It starts vibrating, pressing right against Kyle's prostate.

Kyle's knees go weak and he momentarily hangs from his arms, pressing his lips closed to keep in a jagged scream of bliss.

Finding a feather, Ben laughs and tickles the edge of it up and down Kyle's throbbing, red shaft.

"Oh my guhh... *please*. Please, Master!"

"Should I leave you like this for another hour? Maybe pierce your other nipple? Or maybe you want me to pierce you somewhere *else*.... You liked that a hell of a fucking lot the last time Gabe and I did that to you."

"Please... *anything*...."

"You're so worked up right now, I could probably do just about anything to you and you'd get off on it, you little slut."

Setting the feather aside, Ben's hand reaches between Kyle's legs. While he starts moving the toy, pressing it harder into him before tugging it away, rocking it back and forth, he fondles Kyle's balls, careful not to touch his cock.

Kyle starts to purr, and it's just what Ben wanted to hear.

"Mmm.... Love when you purr for me, kitten. So fucking hot. You've been very obedient for me, so I think that you deserve a reward."

Kyle bucks and writhes, jerking in the chains when Ben starts rocking the toy faster. His cock is oozing, nearly jetting out thick fluid as Ben milks his prostate. It drips down Kyle's length and down onto his master's hand.

Kyle's lips part as Ben's hand comes up and gets licked slowly clean by his eager, pink tongue.

Unsure of what his reward could possibly be, the possibilities float through his lust-addled brain. Kyle is more than grateful but also incredibly shocked when soft, wet heat closes around the head of his dick and he feels gentle suction, pressure against the underside and circled fingers squeezing slowly up the still-exposed part of his shaft.

He could come right then, just at the thought of Ben sucking his cock, since he can count on one hand the number of times it has happened before. Trying to hold back, wanting the blissful feeling to go on and on, unfortunately it becomes more impossible to restrain the need to unload days of built-up tension the harder Ben sucks, the deeper he takes Kyle into his mouth and then his throat.

Wishing he could watch, but still blindfolded, Kyle is instead forced to endure the sensations and submit entirely to the pleasure he is being showered with.

Digging his fingernails into his palms, the back of his head thumping against the concrete wall, Kyle feels the vessel of Ben's throat squeeze and contract around his straining member as he swallows once, twice. Kyle hears the frantic pleading in the noises issuing from his own lips. It's almost like he's not even there anymore, reduced to impulses and reactions, sitting right on the knife edge of pure ecstasy and watching it all from above himself. His state could be called reverent and blessed if not for the vile curses and primal grunting, bucking and thrusting back into Ben's mouth.

His orgasm is like an explosion, sparks of light dancing in front of his darkened, blinded eyes starting as pinpricks before they slowly grow and merge into a wash of bright whiteness. His body strung tight as it convulses and unloads, it pushes out all it has with every beat of his heart. Ben's fingers dig into his hipbones, stilling him. Impossibly, he sucks harder, wrings out more pleasure, drawing it out until Kyle is crying real tears, hanging limp in the shackles.

Then, slowly, it is all stripped away. The toy is removed from his body. The ankles cuffs are unlocked. The blindfold pulled free. Everything is removed.

The wrist cuffs are last, and then he's standing before Ben, naked and bare of accoutrements, save only the collar and the needle. They look at one another for a second before Ben's arms shoot out and catch Kyle as he falls, legs suddenly boneless once more, unable to support him. Maneuvering him to a chair, Ben sets him down and cups his face, examining him.

He looks seriously concerned, so Kyle assures him, "Totally worth having to wear a motherfucking *cage* on my dick for more than three goddamned days. Let's do it again."

"You sick bastard," Ben sighs, shaking his head.

"Can I take it out? Please?"

"I don't think I want you to."

"*Pleeeease?* I'll beg. You know I will."

"All right," he sighs. Pulling two clean gloves from the box, he hands them carefully to Kyle.

"Do I really need those?"

"Yes! Don't make me change my mind."

"You sound like you trust yourself with my body more than you trust me with my body," Kyle accuses.

"That's because I do, dumbass. We've established this. Be careful. Slow and easy."

Kyle's gloved fingers close around the end of the needle and begin to tug it back out. Ben watches how focused his eyes are, the frown creasing his brow, the steadiness of his hands as the metal spear pulls out a millimeter at a time.

As soon as the point is free, Ben takes the needle out of his hand and disposes of it in a biohazard container sitting in the corner of the room, returning with a bandage and antiseptic ointment.

The wound is bleeding now. It had not been before. As Ben cleans off the blood and two small punctures, patching him up,

Kyle says thoughtfully, "I think I want to make it permanent next time. Just on the one side. Can I?"

Ben gives him a doubtful glance, taping down the bandage. "Maybe. How are you feeling? You look a little pale."

"I feel *incredible*. Gotta piss like a racehorse, but...."

Shaking his head in disbelief, Ben steps back to let Kyle get up. Checking his pulse and watching his eyes to check his alertness, Ben keeps fussing over him until Kyle rolls his eyes dramatically and smiles.

"You worry too fuckin' much. I'm fine!"

"No, you're just a cocky bastard. You collapsed in my arms a minute ago! Come on, I'll take you inside and then you're resting until we leave."

Circling Kyle and gripping him under his arms in case he falls again, Ben leads him slowly back to the house and the bathroom.

"Hey. Um... I was wondering...about my... uh... my... *you know*." Kyle mutters.

"You get your cage back after you pee and shower."

"Thanks," Kyle smiles shyly, leaning on Ben more than he really needs to, just to feel his arm tighten and hug him closer.

Chapter 27
Parley

"I can't. I can't. I can't," he repeats over and over again, panicked, "I can't do this."

"Hey! Look at me," Ben says. A few hours have passed. Grabbing Kyle's chin, Ben forces him to look away from the small house they have just pulled up in front of. The Zen-like calmness and serenity of the afternoon is suddenly shattered by Kyle's jittery apprehension in the face of having to see Gabriel and Darrek.

He loops a finger in one of the collar's rings and yanks on it.

"Feel that? That means you do what I say. *I'm* in charge. No one touches you or talks to you unless I allow it. Same goes for you—no touching, no talking. You just be my good little kitty and stay right by my side. I might tell you to interact with Darrek or Gabriel, but I will not have you do *anything* that will be traumatic for you. We clear?"

Ben means the words almost entirely, but also knows this is just about getting Kyle through the first minute or two until he gets past his initial reactions.

"Yeah," Kyle nods, looking calmer. "Yeah, we're clear, sir."

They approach the house, and Kyle frowns with confusion when Ben leads them around the side instead of ringing the doorbell. They follow the paved path that curves around the garage and toward the backyard, stepping through the fence's gate.

When they clear the back corner of the building, Kyle gets an eyeful of what Gabriel and Ben have concocted to break the ice.

Kyle snorts with sudden, hysterical giggles, nearly doubling over from them.

Ben smiles at the reaction and tugs on his hand, walking with him the rest of the way into the backyard.

Gabriel is busy manning the grill, adding lighter fluid to get the coals nice and hot. Seeing the black and red 'kiss the cook' apron tied around his waist, Ben barks with laughter and goes to give Gabriel a hug, puckering up his lips expectantly.

"Don't even think about it, you horny bastard" Gabriel warns. Nodding to Darrek out in the middle of the lawn with Sierra, "It was all his idea, not mine."

"It's good to see you," Ben tells him earnestly, looping an arm around Gabriel's neck and patting his back. "You look... happy."

"That's because I *am* happy. You're surprised?"

"A little. I've never really seen you *this* happy before. You're not *on* something are you?" Ben asks, sitting down on one of the lawn chairs arranged nearby.

"No, moron. When we were at the store, Darrek accused me of glowing like I was pregnant. I was probably not as offended by that as I should have been, now that I think about it."

When Kyle moves automatically to sit cross-legged at Ben's feet, Ben stops him with a hand on his arm and says quietly to him, but loud enough to carry, "Hey, I'd like you to shake Gabriel's hand."

Kyle nods, still smiling with amusement as he watches Darrek in the yard, and extends a hand to Gabriel, who takes it and smiles back at him.

"Wanna show Darrek what you've got?"

"Seriously?" Kyle asks, glancing down at Ben.

"Yeah."

"Yeah. Okay," Kyle agrees, shrugging.

Ben and Gabriel share a look as Gabriel hands Kyle a mouth-guard, which Kyle pops in, fitting it between his teeth. Taking the proffered headgear in Gabriel's other hand, Ben gets it snugly in place on Kyle's head. It is designed to wrap around most of the wearer's head, with padded cheeks, forehead, ears, and back. Next they strap onto him a pair of enormous, inflatable novelty boxing gloves that perfectly match the pair Darrek is already wearing. Darrek is also already wearing his own helmet-like headgear and, Kyle assumes, a mouthguard as well.

Kyle starts to giggle again, but when Ben asks him if he is ready, all he can give in return is an unintelligible mumble. Realizing he can't speak around the mouthguard, and can't even give a thumbs-up, he just nods with exaggeration from inside the padded headgear.

Sierra comes bounding over to Kyle, sniffing at him and barking excitedly when she recognizes his scent, if not his appearance.

Looking back at Ben, his eyes in shadow, Kyle gives his master an unmistakable look that Ben knows is a silent thank you before turning and jogging over to Darrek. Unable to worry about apologizing or speaking to each other with both of them adorned with the boxing gear, it takes any pressure off and allows them to laugh and begin to get past their issues. Apologies and formalities will come later, but first comes the ridiculousness of trying to whack each other around with giant-sized balloons on their hands.

Watching Kyle go, seeing Darrek try to dance around Sierra, who keeps snapping at his gloves, Ben hands over the package of steaks to Gabriel, saying, "People really do this for couples therapy?"

"So I heard. Looks like it's working so far. Is Kyle okay? He didn't seem too freaked out."

"Yeah, he was having a minor fit in the truck a minute ago, but... *OOH*!" Ben exclaims, seeing Kyle whack the side of Darrek's head with a left hook that Darrek simply returns in kind and Kyle goes tumbling backward over Sierra.

They can hear Darrek's belly laughs, even from almost thirty yards away, as Kyle struggles to his feet and goes charging at Darrek who flees in a panic.

"This is our most awesome idea ever," Gabriel gushes, watching Darrek and Kyle chase each other around the property, Sierra hot on their heels. "You seem more... sated... since the last time I saw you. Domestic bliss looks good on you, man."

"You have no idea."

"Aw, is Knox in *love*?" Gabriel teases, passing him a cold opened beer and tossing the steaks onto the grill.

"Best sub I've ever had, best *fuck* I've ever had, and the little bastard just *does* stuff to me."

"Oh, go on and say it. I promise not to revoke your man card."

"Fine. I love 'im. Satisfied?"

"Yes. Yes I am," Gabriel grins, a drink of his own in hand, as both of them settle into seats. The scent of grilling meat fills the air, making Sierra even crazier as she catches a whiff. He watches Darrek try to block a series of blows with his huge gloves, grumbling nonsense at Kyle all the while.

"Can I tell you something, without you giving me hell for it?" Gabriel asks quietly, not looking at Ben, knowing Ben is probably staring at him because of the seriousness of his tone.

"Oh, fuck you, Hunter. Come on, what is it?" Ben frowns, nudging Gabriel's shoulder.

Gabriel's response is to pull the chain around his neck, exposing the platinum key to Ben.

"No shit!?" Ben gasps.

"No shit. Did it today."

"Damn. That's a major thing, man. Didn't think you'd ever do that."

"Me neither. There's something else, though," he admits, still purposefully not meeting Ben's eyes, preferring instead to watch Darrek growl like a grizzly bear and storm after a fleeing Kyle.

"Why do I have a feeling that I'm not gonna like this news as much?" Ben asks.

"It's not something bad. I swear. And honestly, it's really none of your fucking business, but I need to tell someone, and I've always been able to talk to you about this stuff before, so...."

"Don't tell me you finally gave it up?" Ben squints, smile gone.

"Yeah. I did. But I wouldn't say it that way. More like I let Darrek have it," Gabriel confesses, drinking his beer. "No more virgin-Dom Gabey, though."

Finally daring to glance over at his friend, Gabriel practically sees the steam coming out of Ben's ears, sees the attack-mode switch in his brain get flipped on.

"Hey, he didn't do anything I didn't *tell him* to do. I needed him to do it. And you can't touch him or say *anything* to him about it. You know that," Gabriel scowls.

"I'll fuckin' kill him for touching you. Snap his goddamned neck," Ben spits, sitting forward now, eyes burning as he glares at

Darrek on the other side of the property.

"Hey! Wha'd I just say?" Gabriel reprimands. "I love him! I need to get past this shit! You know how I get when shit starts to happen. It's not right. I'm over *thirty-fucking-years-old,* man! I want to be able to have sex without panicking! And I trust Dare more than anyone. So what if he helped me get through it?"

"That's fuckin' hilarious, Gabriel. I love how you say that, 'helped me get through it.' What'd he do? Hold you down? Chain you to the bed while you screamed for help? Yeah, he must love you a *lot.*"

"Fuck you, Knox. It wasn't like that. The reason why I *trust* Dare is because he's *not* a Dom. He's not a tough guy like that or out to *prove* shit. He just wants to make me happy, and be a good person. My issues are *my* issues. And I feel... I don't know. Lighter? You said yourself that I looked happy. I am happy. Do you think I'd look *happy* if Darrek raped me?"

Gabriel sees the retort on the tip of Ben's tongue, sees the inner battle as he fights not to say it.

"Don't," Gabriel warns. "I'll kick your ass all the way back to your goddamned truck if you do."

Fists clenched, Ben stands and starts to pace, chugging his beer and then tossing the empty bottle into the bin by the house's rear door.

"I'm *sorry,* okay? I'm sorry for even thinking it," he growls out, long minutes after the impulse has passed.

Gabriel stands as well and lets Ben hug him.

"Please just be happy for me," Gabriel asks him.

"I'm trying to be. Oh hell. Fuck it. Okay. I am. I'm happy for you. See this?" he asks, pointing to his forced smile, "This is me happy for you."

"Yeah, and I'm the motherfuckin' tooth fairy."

"I'm always going to be on your side, Gabe. Just like Kyle's always going to be on Darrek's side. It's just the way it is."

"I know. I get it. Help me with the food, okay? Go wash some potatoes and wrap 'em in foil so we can throw 'em on here too."

"Sure thing," Ben nods, heading inside the house's rear door. Pausing once to glance over his shoulder at Darrek's giant, imposing figure in the distance as he goes, he forces away the unwelcome images that threaten to come.

With all of the food finally on the grill—five steaks (four for the men and one for Sierra, too) and ears of corn—and Darrek and Kyle collapsed in exhaustion on the grass, a decision is made for them to switch places with Gabriel and Ben. Gear is handed over as Gabriel begins to look way too excited at the prospect of beating the piss out of his best friend.

Ben grumbles warnings at Gabriel around the mouthguard as Gabriel taps his gloves together and waves him on. Laughing, Darrek and Kyle go to sit and keep an eye on the grill.

"So, can we not?" Darrek asks once they're relaxed and the silence has stretched out between them too long. "Can we just say sorry and not get into it?"

"Yeah," Kyle nods. But when he glances over, Darrek can see the emotion in Kyle's eyes as he says urgently and thickly, "I'm *so fuckin' sorry,* Darrek."

"Shit, don't make me cry!" Darrek complains with a pained laugh, blinking rapidly, rubbing his eyes with the back of his arm, and nudging Kyle's shoulder. "I'm sorry, too. For all of it."

"I'd do *anything* to not lose your friendship," Kyle tells him. "It means too damn much to me."

He looks levelly at Darrek, saying with his eyes what he can't speak aloud. Darrek sees that the love is still there, that it always will be, no matter what.

"I feel the same way," Darrek assures him.

"I'm glad. Thanks."

They both start to laugh as they see Gabriel and Ben wailing on each other, faces turned away and sending punch after clumsy, air-filled punch at each other, neither backing down.

"They're so fucking stubborn!" Kyle says in amazement. "Food smells awesome though. I didn't really get to have lunch, so I'm pretty much literally starving right now."

"I'm not even gonna ask why you didn't have lunch. I can tell it's probably something I'm better off not knowing. When'd you get your collar, by the way?"

"I was chained up and tortured in the garage for a few hours until I came so hard I think I went blind for a couple of minutes before I passed out in exhaustion on the couch," Kyle tells him, answering the unasked question with a grin anyway, before saying, "Got the collar the day after Ben saved my life. I'm the luckiest son of a bitch on the planet. Best thing that's ever happened to me."

"I know what you mean. And seriously? You over-share. Often."

"Yeah. Well, now that the big, gay, submissive cat is out of the bag, I figure why the hell not? Oh! You ever try temporary piercing? *Really* fucking awesome. Such a rush. I recommend it highly. I see you have a collar, too, by the way."

"Yep. As of today. But it's not... well, it means something else. It's not as... literal. Just means he loves me."

"Of course he *loves* you. How could he not?" Kyle says, only half-teasing, knowing Darrek knows it.

"Well, I *am* pretty incredible," Darrek admits as Kyle rolls his eyes. "I'm glad you have Ben to keep you out of trouble. Seems like you need it. Troublemaker."

"Oh, so *I'm* the troublemaker, but you just get to be irresistible?" Kyle frowns, punching Darrek's shoulder.

"Ouch!" he says with exaggeration. "No punching without the nice squishy gloves, you bully! I don't think I'm *completely* irresistible. Ben is resisting my charms just fine. Looked like he wanted to head butt me or rip my nuts off a minute ago. And *not* in a sexy way."

"The hell did you do?"

Darrek shrugs, "Maybe he still hates me for what happened between us."

"Could be. Dude is protective as fuck."

"Seriously, did you ever think we'd be here, both of us full-time slaves for two *men*?"

"Whatever would Sara say?" Kyle grins wickedly at him, like he is already mentally planning the phone call to her, sharing the good news.

"Forget that, what would our *moms* say?"

"Jesus, I hope Mom never finds out. That's a scary thought."

"I think it'd be kind of funny, actually."

Kyle shudders and goes for a beer as Darrek laughs at him.

"Beer me!" Darrek calls, catching the bottle Kyle tosses over.

Gabriel waves to Darrek from across the yard, checking on how he's doing. Ben tries to use the distraction to his advantage and sneak up on him. Sierra gets in his way though, and barks wildly, chasing Ben back and away.

"Good girl!" Darrek calls. "See Gabe? She loves you too! Good girl, Sierra!"

Laughing, Gabriel watches Sierra go after Ben, who is still retreating, trying to hide behind a tree. Making his way slowly back to the house, Gabriel removes the gloves and then the other gear.

"Who's ready to eat?" he grins, seeing the easiness of Darrek's smile, the laughter in Kyle's face as he watches Ben.

"Steak!!" Kyle howls with eagerness.

"I'll help," Darrek says, going with Gabriel to the grill and gathering plates and utensils.

"So?" Gabriel asks Darrek subtly, nodding back at Kyle, who is now walking over to Ben to help him get away from Sierra.

"We're cool. I'm... relieved," Darrek tells him.

"I'm glad to hear it," Gabriel grins, kissing him once.

"Thanks for doing this. I guess you know me pretty well. It was a great idea."

"You're welcome," he nods.

Snaking an arm around Gabriel's waist, kissing his cheek, Darrek tells him, "And thanks for being civil with Kyle. I can tell that Ben isn't too thrilled with me right now, and I'm not exactly sure why, but I think Kyle's hard enough on himself for all of us. Right now, I'm just glad we can all be in the same place without throwing real punches. I just wanna eat some of this steak that smells so damn good and then see our guests on their way so I can have you all to myself again."

"Hell yes to that. Don't worry about Ben. He gets protective of me when he has no right to. I told him what happened last night in a *very* non-specific way. Told him I trusted you enough, *loved you* enough, to be with you like that. He *is* my best friend and it meant a lot to me to be able to tell him that, and kind of show him how much I trust you. But, I also want him to see, somehow, *why* I love you so much. Plus, the fact that my best friend is in a relationship with your best friend... it means we *have to* all get along somehow."

"Well, progress has been made. I can see why Ben hates me if you told him that, though. I think I'd hate me too."

"He doesn't hate you," Gabriel assures him, secretly amazed that he manages to sound so convinced of the fact when he says the words aloud, handing over a plate full of potatoes and another loaded with ears of roasted corn. "He just needs to get to know you. Come on. Let's eat."

They set the food out and the four of them sit down at the picnic table on the back patio, in the shade. The conversation is stilted at first, but once Darrek begins to tell embarrassing stories about his and Kyle's adolescence, with Kyle jumping in to supply further gory details and cringe-inducing anecdotes, the ice begins to break and they all dissolve into laughter as they enjoy the barbequed feast.

A few hours later, Gabriel and Darrek are watching Ben and Kyle drive off, and waving goodbye to them from the yard before heading inside to escape the gathering mosquitoes. They content themselves with the knowledge that even if Gabriel and Kyle, and Darrek and Ben cannot yet be called the best of friends, they at least know that they all have enough in common, and enough motivation, to put forth the effort to try to get along.

Chapter 28
Being the Bad Guy

"You're not really going to quit, are you?"

"Well, I was thinking about it. I'd almost completely decided to do it, and just go independent. I mean, it's not like we need the money, but...."

"But what?" Kyle prods.

Darrek sighs, the phone pressed against his ear, sitting back in the lawn chair and watching Sierra chew frantically on a steak bone. It was one of the remnants of dinner, which he had made for two, in the hopes that Gabriel would be home in time to eat. He wasn't, and had called to say he would be home late. Again. So, Darrek had eaten alone for the fourth time that week.

"I'm waiting...."

"I know. Okay, well, Gabriel's been working really hard this week, training the new Dom, and he says he's backlogged with video work too, and he's still hoping to have time to start a video production business once the training settles down, so...."

"Dude. Finish a sentence."

"I'm sorry," Darrek sighs, "I just...."

I'm lonely, he thinks, but doesn't say.

"So you're bored?"

"Yeah. I'm bored. It's not fun to sit around at home alone all day. Even when I have projects going, I need something to break the monotony. I want to see other people."

Kyle laughs, saying with a sarcastic, scandalized tone, "Does Gabriel know?!"

"Oh, you know what I mean. So, I'm not quitting. I need to have something to do."

"Build a dungeon."

"That'd be a little... self-serving, wouldn't it?"

"So?"

"Haven't *you* been bored?"

"Not really. Ben keeps me occupied, and I've been doing some video shoots here and there at Diadem, doing some repairs around Ben's place, too. He's not really motivated to do carpentry projects himself. Says he'd rather watch me do it."

"You're still doing those submissive videos?" Darrek asks, trying to make the question sound as easy as his others, and not entirely succeeding.

"Of course. They pay well, and they don't exactly feel like work. I'd rather do that than be sweaty and sore on a job site. Still sweaty and sore, but...you know...in a *good* way."

"Should we be...should we be talking about this stuff? Is it weird?"

"Not weird for me."

Darrek rolls his eyes.

"That's because you over-share. On all fronts."

Kyle asks, "Hey, did you ever... um... look at the site? At the videos?"

Darrek hears the change in Kyle's tone, the sudden meekness in it. At the same time that it makes Darrek uncomfortable to catch a glimpse of his friend's submissive side, it excites him as well, so, therefore, he feels guilty about it.

"Honestly? Almost. But I stopped myself, because it felt like if I did look at it, I wouldn't be able to un-see it, if you know what I mean. Plus, I need to...."

He pauses, unsure whether to continue speaking. But then he does, because it's *Kyle*, and he's always been able to tell Kyle everything.

"...I need to obey Gabriel. I belong to him now, so it would be a... a break of trust to look without his permission."

"Don't worry, Dare. I get it. I don't know if Ben would be thrilled about me looking at videos of you and Gabriel. He has let me watch videos of other people, but he wouldn't like it if it was you."

"Just me?"

"Yeah. Just you."

"Um, I have to ask, man. You don't have to say anything, because I know your situation with Ben is a little more hardcore than me and Gabe, but... does Ben seriously hate me? Has he said anything to you?"

"Dare...."

"I'm sorry. Forget I asked, okay?"

"No... it's just... look, if I tell you this, then I have to tell him that I told you."

"I don't want to get you in trouble. Don't tell me then."

"I want to. You deserve to know. Hell, I think he'd want you to know so that he doesn't have to worry so damn much. And he wouldn't talk about this stuff to me at first, but, thankfully, he trusts me now, so.... Okay. He thinks you forced yourself on Gabriel. He's worried that you're hurting him, and that Gabriel is letting you hurt him. Gabriel has stopped telling Ben anything about your relationship and it's making Ben go bat-shit crazy. You're not... you know... to Gabriel, are you?"

"No! We haven't even had sex all week. Gabe gets home and he wants to just sleep 'Cause he's so tired. It was only the one time anyway, and he wanted me to. It's hard to explain. But I would never hurt Gabriel. I love him! I know the shit he's been through and I would never hurt him like that or make him relive it. Ever."

"What happened to him?"

"You don't know?"

"Not really. Ben never told me, and...."

"I'm sorry. I can't tell you anymore. It would be a betrayal of Gabriel."

"I know. All I know is it's about some guy named Harry. Was he raped? Is that why Ben acts that way? It would make sense. But it seems like this has been going on for years. Gabriel's always been this, like, *treasure* of Ben and Trace's. They won't let anyone near him. Did it happen when he was a kid? Jesus, was it... it wasn't a *family member*, was it?"

"I can't."

"I know. I know. I'm sorry. God. Poor Gabe. No wonder he was always so defensive and shit."

"I've gotta get going, man. But I'll call you tomorrow. And then I guess I'll see you Monday at work."

"Yeah. Back to the grind. Take it easy, Dare."

"You too," Darrek responds softly before closing the phone and tucking it away.

Gabriel shuffles through the door and drops his keys, cell phone, iPod, wallet, sunglasses, and some change on the kitchen table before somehow making his way over to Darrek on the couch and pretty much falling onto him, straddling his lap, arms limp by his side. Darrek's big hands go to his back, feeling the heat bake off of Gabriel through his thin shirt.

"You smell like mangoes," Darrek murmurs, sniffing at Gabriel's hair.

Grinning, Gabriel admits, "Yeah. Took a shower at work before I left. Hot as balls in that damn place sometimes. They always have the fruitiest soap there."

"Appropriate."

"Hey!"

Gabriel sits back on Darrek's thighs, squinting down his nose at him. Then he finally catches the mouth-watering scent of cooked meat, and his eyes scan the scrubbed-clean dishes drying in the rack.

"Oh fuck. You... you made dinner, didn't you? I missed it. God, I'm *sorry*, Dare!"

"It's okay. Saved you leftovers, but you probably ate already, right? And you look tired as hell. Let's go up to bed," Darrek coaxes, but doesn't move since he's enjoying having Gabriel sit on him way too much. His fingers curl around the sides of Gabriel's hips over to the roundness of his behind, thumbs hooking in the waist of his jeans and brushing over the soft skin under his clothes.

"I'm such an ass," Gabriel groans. "You made dinner, which you had to eat alone, cleaned up, and now you're watching the game but because of me and my stupid insomnia you have to go to bed early. And we haven't even gotten to fuck for *days* because I've been working so damn much!"

"Gabe..." Darrek tries to interrupt, and fails.

"No. I don't care how tired I am. I'm making this up to you. Now. What do you want? Name it."

"Gabriel..." Darrek sighs, frowning and turning off the television with a click of the remote.

"I'm serious."

"I know you are. But, you've been working all day! It's okay to need to rest. I don't only love you for the sex, you know. Tell me about the new Dom. What's his name?"

"You really want to hear about this stuff?" Gabriel asks doubtfully.

"Yeah. This is what you do. This is important to you. So, tell me."

"Okay, well, his name is Micah. He used to be a client of Ben's, but he expressed an interest in learning to dominate, so I'm training him. Today he was with a client and I just kind of instructed without getting involved. Gradually I'll become less and less involved until he's all on his own."

"How does that make sense for him to go from being a sub to a Dom?"

"Well, it's actually pretty handy, because he's familiar with a lot of the techniques already, and knows how everything feels. Makes him a better Dom if he knows exactly what he's doing to people."

"Did you ever... um, *assist* with him, when he was a submissive? You said Ben was his Dom, but did you...?"

"Yeah. I've assisted a bunch of times. Just a few weeks ago I did some stuff with him – watersports, actually. Ben bound him to a table with a vibrating toy up his ass and his jeans still on. I straddled him and peed on him," he admits.

"Damn," Darrek murmurs, his face unreadable.

"Does it make you uncomfortable that I've done stuff with him? You can be honest."

"A little. I guess I just don't like that it seems as if everyone has had a piece of you. I want you all for myself," Darrek confesses, brushing his fingers over Gabriel's lower back, not meeting his eyes.

"Well, no one gets a piece of me anymore. Now I'm yours. Only yours," Gabriel promises, grinding purposefully forwards on Darrek's lap.

"Don't," Darrek gasps. "It's hard enough with you sitting on me like this, without you doing that too...."

"Hard enough?" Gabriel smiles, teasing, grinding forward again. The pronounced bulge in his pants squeezes up against Darrek's groin, rubbing at the sensitive, swollen flesh through their pants. "Show me. Show me how hard it is."

"*Don't...*" Darrek whines.

"Why not?"

"Because I'm just *barely* holding myself back from yanking these goddamned jeans off of you and fucking you right now."

"Who said you couldn't fuck me?" Gabriel asks softly, enticingly. Too much so.

"I did."

"Well, I disagree," Gabriel says simply.

"Gabriel, I can't do that again. I refuse to be the bad guy and hurt you. I won't do it. I can't. Please don't ask me to."

"Where did this come from?" Gabriel frowns, searching Darrek's face, his movements stilling. "I thought last time went fine. A hell of a lot better than I hoped for, honestly."

Turning his face away, Darrek admits, "Your friends think I'm *hurting* you."

Gabriel knows he can't deny it, knows it's the truth. He's seen it in Ben and Trace's eyes, heard it in their accusations. He can't deny it, so instead, he becomes infuriated.

"No. No! You know what? Fuck what they think! Fuck it! It's none of their damn business," Gabriel yells gesturing at the window and the entire world waiting outside of it. "I'm in love with you, Darrek! We're in a relationship. You and me. Not them. And I want to get to be with you like a normal person! What happens in our bedroom is none of their business!"

Darrek grabs him and pulls them chest-to-chest, wrapping Gabriel in muscular, powerful arms.

"It's okay," he whispers to Gabriel, feeling his lover's anger, frustration and sadness shake him.

"I want you," Gabriel whispers back fervently. "I want you to be touching me and kissing me. I want to feel your mouth on me. I want to *be with you*. At least that much."

"I can do that," he agrees, glad that Gabriel is beginning to calm down.

With a grunt and one swift motion, Darrek sits up and then stands with Gabriel wrapped around his waist. Gabriel grabs on tighter to him with surprise, locking his legs around the larger man.

"Goddamn, you're strong," Gabriel breathes. "You can put me down now."

Smiling wickedly, hands cupped under Gabriel's upper thighs, fingers pressing dents in the muscle there through his jeans, Darrek teases his bottom lip between his teeth and pretends to think about it for a second first.

"Is that an order?" he asks. "Because I kind of like you like this...."

"Dude, put me down."

Chuckling, Darrek releases him, and Gabriel's legs uncurl from around him.

"Um..." Gabriel hums, glancing at the floor and then up at Darrek, like he's being shy, "Help me get ready? I want to be... clean... for you, and it's easier if you help."

"Is *that* an order?" Darrek asks quietly with a dark, lustful gleam in his eyes.

"It can be."

"Okay. Let's go," he nods, adding a second later, "Master."

Darrek wastes no time once they're both naked and entangled on the bed. He climbs on top of Gabriel and kisses him dizzy, gripping his legs and guiding them up so they are wrapped around his waist like they were downstairs for that brief moment. Pulling Darrek down by digging his heels into his lower back, Gabriel grinds up against him, letting their cocks squeeze and drag between their bellies as they tongue-fuck each other's mouths.

"Okay, I can't fucking wait anymore," Darrek breathes, pulling back a little. "Flip over. On your knees. It'll be easier."

There's a moment of hesitancy that Darrek is too feverish to notice where a small and bright spark of apprehension flashes behind Gabriel's eyes. Gabriel forces away the reasons why it causes that reaction in him, the associations that have been burned into his soul from being pinned under someone like that, knowing he won't be able to see Darrek in that position to pacify his nerves. Gabriel rolls onto his stomach. All at once, Darrek is low on the bed, between his lover's legs, bending Gabriel's knees up under his body and apart. Cupping his ass with both hands, he dives in, trailing his tongue over the warm skin, teeth grazing over smooth flesh and biting gently at the thick rounded curve of his cheeks. He licks and kisses closer and closer to his target before focusing only on that spot.

The intensity with which Darrek eats out his ass leaves Gabriel gasping and moaning with blissful pleasure. He enjoys it almost as much as Darrek does, which says a lot. He's right there, tugging slowly at his dick as Darrek licks him open, sucks at the rim, jabs the thickness of his tongue into his heat. Darrek grips hard enough to leave bruises on Gabriel's hips, bringing his body back into his face, needing more, like he could never possibly get close enough and far enough inside.

Gabriel loses track of time, it's all a wash of delirious sensation.

Then he hears Darrek growl from behind him while he fingers his opening, loosening the muscle and getting it wider, "God, I don't even know what it is about your ass. I just want to be *in* it. Just how fucking good you taste, the way you tense up and squeeze around my tongue, so tight with these little flutters, how fucking *hot* and sexy you are. Jesus fucking Christ. Just wanna be *in* you. Lick you open, finger you, fuck you, and just fucking ride you, show you how crazy I am for you...."

"Do it," Gabriel sputters, "Go on."

"Gabe... don't tempt me right now. I'm hard as fuck and I have, like, *zero* willpower."

"Do it!"

"Mmm..." Darrek moans, getting up on his knees behind Gabriel. Lifting his dick, he forces it inside, thrusting his hips and sliding home in a smooth movement, his saliva there more than slicking the way.

He only pauses long enough to let out a thunderous groan of relief, hands caressing Gabriel's back and sides as the inner muscles clench up and clamp down around him. It's perfect but he tries to get a handle on the need to go too hard and too rough on Gabriel.

But, just as he pulls back until the head of his dick catches and he begins to press back inside, Gabriel, who has been utterly silent and still since Darrek entered him—holding him in position on his belly, ass in the air—bucks forward. Breathing harshly through his nose, he grabs the headboard, pulling away from Darrek, who instinctively grabs on to Gabriel's hips and holds him still.

"Get off! Get off! Dis-discovery!"

"Oh god," Darrek groans with horror, releasing him.

Gabriel scrambles away, off the bed.

He goes to the corner of the room and backs up against it, sinking to the floor and covering his face with his hands.

"I'm sorry. I'm sorry," Gabriel gasps.

Darrek hurries over to him, hand over his mouth, feeling like he's just been punched in the gut.

"Gabriel, I'm so fucking *sorry*," he hisses.

"Just... gimme a second. It's not your fault. My fault. Should have said something," he murmurs, curled up in a ball with his head between his knees.

"Stand up," Darrek urges. "C'mere."

Slowly, he struggles up and lets Darrek wrap him in a hug.

Kissing Gabriel's head, rubbing small circles on his back, Darrek whispers, "I feel like a horrible person."

"Dare, I told you, it's *my* fault."

"Are you okay?"

"Yeah, I'm fine. I just... panicked. Bad memories."

"I'm sorry," Darrek whispers, hugging him tighter.

"Stop apologizing. That *is* an order. God! I ruined it. It felt so good. You make me feel so damn good, and then I *ruin* it."

"You're too hard on yourself. You're allowed to be sensitive about this. Come back to bed, and we'll just sleep, okay?"

"That's not fair to you, though."

Rolling his eyes and quirking an eyebrow, Darrek looks down

at him and says again, "Gabriel, come back to bed."

They climb under the covers and Darrek lays on his side, watching Gabriel's face beside him as he gazes up at the ceiling.

"I'm gonna make it up to you. Tomorrow."

"You're being ridiculous," Darrek tells him. "You don't owe me anything. I just want you to be okay. Are you okay?"

Gabriel nods, frowning.

"Love you," Darrek whispers.

"I love you too."

They soon both drift off without realizing it. But, in the middle of the night, tangled up in the blankets, Gabriel starts thrashing as a familiar nightmare overtakes him. Darrek is jolted from sleep by the movement and the sound of sharp cries for help.

At first he doesn't know what in the world is going on, whether he imagined it or is still dreaming. Then he feels Gabriel's struggles beside him and sits up, grabbing his shoulders.

"Wake up! Gabe, wake up!"

"Dad, stop! *Help*! Somebody help me!" Gabriel begs weakly.

"Gabe, *please* wake up!"

An elbow connects painfully with Darrek's arm as Gabriel tries to knock him away, his eyes still closed, still lost in terrible dreams.

Turning on the lamp by the bed and calling his name loudly again, Darrek finally succeeds in waking him.

Gabriel blinks at the brightness, breathless and confused.

"What... Dare...?"

"You were having a nightmare," he explains.

"Yeah?" Gabriel asks groggily.

Turning the light back off and taking a deep breath to calm his racing heart, Darrek flops back down onto his pillow. His stomach churns with nausea at the thought of what Gabriel must have been dreaming about, but grateful that he seems to not remember it.

"Sorry for waking you," Gabriel grumbles, turning onto his side and looping an arm around Darrek.

"S'alright. Go back to sleep."

"Mm-hmm," Gabriel nods, tucked into Darrek's arms. He's out in seconds, but Darrek isn't as lucky.

Chapter 29
Interrupted Indulgence

The alarm goes off at quarter after eight. Gabriel shuts it off with a smack of his hand and swings his legs over the side of the bed. Darrek yawns and stretches beside him, climbing out of bed before Gabriel is even on his feet.

"What are you doing?" he blinks, "Keep sleeping. You don't have to get up just because I do."

"I know," Darrek yawns again. "Want some pancakes for breakfast? I'll make 'em while you get ready."

"Yeah, that sounds great," he agrees, looking up at Darrek with a telling expression laced with guilt. "Look...."

"Gabe," Darrek says, cutting him off and pointing a finger, "if you say it, I'll spank your little ass raw."

"How do you know what I was gonna say?" Gabriel asks.

"Because you look miserable and pouty. Go on. Get ready. I'll be downstairs," Darrek tells him, kissing his forehead before he goes.

When Gabriel makes it downstairs, dressed and washed up, he slaps a piece of paper covered in sketches, notes and measurements down onto the counter next to where Darrek is stacking the pancakes.

"I need you to build this for me," he says.

"Is it kinky? It's kinky, isn't it?" Darrek grins eagerly.

He sets aside the ladle and turns down the burner, picking up the sketch and laughing with amusement at what it shows.

"What's the hole for?"

"Guess," Gabriel grins. "I need it to be sturdy, so use some sort of hardwood, but don't make it too thick. Is it okay with you if we bolt it to the floor in the extra bedroom upstairs?"

"Yeah, we can do that," he nods. Then, waving the paper, his tanned skin mildly flushed and voice an octave lower all of a sudden, Darrek says, "This is pretty fucking kinky, you know."

"You don't even know what I'm gonna do to you once I get you on it. This is *nothing* compared to what I have planned for you. This is just to get you where I want you."

Darrek smiles wider, tucking a rogue piece of hair back over an ear and out of his eyes, "And where do you want me?"

"Spread out, bound and helpless, begging me to fuck you, making you hurt in all the right ways, teasing you 'til you scream...."

They lock eyes, smiles gone, breath caught. And then they're kissing. Darrek curls his arms around Gabriel and leans him back against the kitchen wall, sucking at his lips.

Gabriel's hands lower, going to his fly, opening it up and pushing the pants down along with his boxers. When Darrek feels Gabriel opening his pants as well, he tries to break the kiss. Not letting him, Gabriel chases his mouth, tugging Darrek's dick free and coaxing him into hardness with a few tugs.

"Pick me up," Gabriel instructs breathlessly.

When Darrek hesitates, Gabriel wraps a leg up around him, drawing him in.

"I don't have any lube down here," Darrek confesses.

"Already prepped myself upstairs. I'm wet and open and ready. Told you I wanted to make it up to you, didn't I? Come on, Dare. Fuck me."

Bending a little, curling his large hands around the backs of Gabriel's upper thighs, Darrek lifts him, pinning him against the wall. Gabriel clenches his inner thighs, hooks his legs tightly around Darrek's back and circles his neck with his arms, keeping himself up.

Picturing Gabriel upstairs, fingering his ass loose, slicking himself with lubricant, Darrek moans. Kissing at Gabriel's neck, he angles his hips and guides his cock to his lover's entrance.

His weight and gravity pull Gabriel right down onto it, making a surprised grunt and exhaling the air in his lungs in a rush.

"Goddamn," Gabriel curses, head falling back, eyes closing.

"You okay?"

"Mmm," he moans, nodding, squeezing his thighs and rearing up a little, just enough to get Darrek's dick to begin to slide out. Then he presses himself back down on it. Smiling, he coaxes Darrek with, "Come on... fuck me... wanna fuck me?"

"Hell yes, I wanna fuck you," Darrek groans. Adjusting his hold, arms straining, Darrek holds Gabriel in place as he starts to move inside him.

Too turned on to be able to last long, after a few minutes of kissing and rocking against him at a steadily increasing pace, Darrek comes, shuddering and clasping onto Gabriel, supporting his weight. Once he's convinced he's not going to drop him, Darrek retightens his grip and carries Gabriel over to the sink.

"What in the great hell are you doing?" Gabriel asks.

"Cleaning up," Darrek says matter-of-factly.

Setting Gabriel down on the edge of the sink, Darrek braces him one-armed and turns on the water, splashing it up against Gabriel's ass and washing him off.

"Can't fucking believe you," Gabriel chuckles. He gasps a little in surprise when Darrek's fingers push inside his ass. Prying him open, Darrek gets some more of the warm water up inside him to wash off the leaking come.

"What? It's efficient, and this way your pancakes won't get cold, and you won't be late for work, Mr. Fuck-Me-Now."

"Please don't use that as my new nickname," Gabriel mumbles against Darrek's neck, repressing a grin.

Darrek snickers and kisses at Gabriel's reluctant smile.

Then he asks, "Want a blowjob?"

"Mm-mm, I wanna wait until I have you on the new piece of *furniture* you're gonna make for us. I don't wanna come until then, after I've played with you for *hours*. It'll be better if I have to wait."

Darrek dries him off, happy to see the contented grin Gabriel is wearing.

"You know, people are gonna be awfully suspicious if you walk around with that big goofy smile all day, seeing as how you're usually such a scowly bastard when you're at work," he teases.

"Eh, let 'em," Gabriel replies.

Sitting at the dining table, Gabriel hurries through breakfast, not speaking in order to savor every bite. Once finished, he gathers his things and prepares to leave.

Before he does, he asks, "Um, so I wanted to see if you had any interest in seeing some of my videos, and watching them with me? I wanted to maybe get some ready to show you, in case you are able to finish that bench sometime this weekend."

"What do the videos have to do with the bench?"

Gabriel only grins wickedly in response.

"Uh... well, yeah. I do want to see them, if you want to show them to me. I didn't know if you wanted me to see that stuff."

"Of course I do. I want you to know everything about me. No secrets. And this way, I get to see how you... *respond*... to things."

Darrek blinks at him and Gabriel laughs. Standing on his toes, he kisses Darrek goodbye and heads out the door.

The following day, Saturday, Gabriel finally has a break from work, and basks in anticipation of the long weekend, knowing he isn't needed back until Tuesday. Darrek spends the morning finishing up the bench and polishing the edges, wanting to have it done as soon as possible so that they can try it out. He's also in a hurry to do everything he can to be productive before going back to work on Monday.

Once he gets to the point where his muscles are aching and the garage has gotten too stifling, Darrek heads out into the fresh air with Sierra to stretch his legs.

It's late afternoon, and, turning on the radio to listen to the local baseball game, Gabriel busies himself in the kitchen while Darrek is out.

Certainly not expecting any company, he's confused when the doorbell rings, and he notices an unfamiliar silver Lincoln Towncar in the driveway.

Opening the door while wiping his hands on a dishrag, he

squints out at the sixtyish man on the front stoop, asking, "Yeah, can I help you?"

"Who are you?" is the abrupt response.

"Gabriel Hunter. I live here. Who are you?"

"Jerry Grealey." The man frowns in displeasure, arms crossed over his perfectly starched, canary yellow polo shirt, not a hair of his short, gray, impeccably styled hair moving out of place, even in the strong, warm breeze. He's at least as tall as Gabriel, at six-foot-one.

"Darrek's father."

"Yes," Jerry nods. He takes Gabriel's outstretched hand and gives it a firm shake.

"Come in," Gabriel says to him, nodding inside. "Darrek's out on a jog with the dog. He should be back any minute. Can I get you something? A drink?"

Jerry follows Gabriel into the living room. He looks around the place, surveying the furniture, the few photographs and possessions scattered about.

"No, thank you," he replies, adding, "I wasn't aware that Darrek had a tenant."

"He doesn't," Gabriel replies shortly, returning to the stove.

That's the end of the conversation as the older man sits perched stiffly on the edge of the couch to wait. As expected, only a few minutes later they hear barking and then a rattle at the door as Darrek returns. He's breathless, covered in a thick layer of shining, dripping sweat, and overheated from the exercise in the warm weather. Sierra bounds inside first, having sensed an unfamiliar presence and, straining at the end of her leash, barks at Jerry. Darrek walks in behind her, holding tightly to the leash and reining Sierra back.

Having instantly recognized his father's car in the driveway, Darrek doesn't hurry to look up at him or say hello, choosing instead to smile at Gabriel who meets him at the door.

Gabriel unhooks the leash from Sierra's collar after giving her a treat and letting her lick happily over his hand. She runs, sniffing and curious, over to Jerry. Well-trained enough to know not to jump up, she smells him out as he backs up a step or two in apprehension. The dog's sniffing does distract him, but not enough to not see his younger son grip the back of Gabriel's neck, drawing him close and planting a soft kiss directly on his mouth.

"Smells incredible," Darrek says to Gabriel, "Makin' lasagna?"

"Yeah," Gabriel nods, licking his lips wet. Noting the significance of the gesture, he decides to simply follow Darrek's lead. "I was just checking on it. Needs five more minutes."

Finally, Darrek turns to their guest and says, "Daddy. Guess you've already met Gabriel. What are you doing here?"

More than a little taken aback at his son's cool directness, Jerry sputters, "We... we haven't heard from you in months, Darrek. Your mother is worried and we don't have your new phone number. I was in the area on business, so...."

"Tell Mom I'm fine. I appreciate the concern, but I'm fine. Work is fine. My health is fine. Now, if you'll excuse us, we're about to sit down to dinner."

He had crossed the distance between them while speaking and leads his father back to the door with a hand on his shoulder. They step outside as the screen door closes behind them with a thwack.

"Darrek," his father insists, gesturing toward the house, "who is this Gabriel person? What exactly is going on here?"

"Daddy, what's going on here is absolutely none of your business. Gabriel is my partner. I don't care if you don't approve, and I can tell you don't. I'm happy and I will not allow you to try to ruin that."

"You're screwing around with a *man?* Son, just because Sara didn't want to marry you, that's no reason to write off women altogether."

Laughing maliciously, hands planted on his hips and wiping the sweat off his brow onto the sleeve of his t-shirt, Darrek points at the car in the driveway and says, "Leave. We're done here."

"Yes, I suppose we are," his father agrees, turning away. "Please call your mother, Darrek."

"Right. Fine."

Once sure that Jerry is, indeed, returning to the car, Darrek turns to go inside, and almost runs right into Gabriel.

"What are you doing?" Darrek asks, confusedly.

"Gonna go kick him in the balls for what he just said to you," Gabriel says simply, with the fire of rage burning behind his cool blue eyes.

"No. Just let him go. He's just an insensitive prick and I don't want to deal with this right now. I want to go sit in our home with you and have a nice meal together. I know how hard you worked on making dinner for us. I just want to enjoy that and, temporarily, forget about this. I'll deal with it tomorrow, but I am *NOT* letting him ruin our night. Please?"

"But tomorrow I won't be able to kick him in the balls," Gabriel replies, not backing down.

"Gabe," Darrek implores, pressing his hands together like he's praying. "Let it go this time? For me?"

"I only let this go once," Gabriel warns. "No one gets to talk to you like that. I don't care if he is your father."

"He's always been like that. But he has *no say* over what I do with my life anymore. He knows it and it pisses him off. That's all. Come on. Let's go eat."

After supper and washing up, Darrek discovers that Gabriel has bolted the new bench in place, and that it's ready to be tried out. Standing in the spare bedroom's doorway and grinning happily, he admires the sight of it and says, "I can't believe you set this up already."

"Of course I did," Gabriel says, "You up for it? Not too tired from the jog are you?"

"Are you kidding? Yes. I'm up for it. In fact, I think I need it. I have all of this fidgety, bottled-up energy, and I know how good I'll feel if we do this."

His hand plays at the chain around his neck and he gazes down at the key glinting on Gabriel's collarbone.

"Okay," Gabriel nods. "Clothes off *now,* slave. And from this point on, you will obey me completely, understood?"

"Yes, sir," Darrek answers readily, shrugging out of his clothes.

Chapter 30
Measured Reactions

Darrek lays facedown on the bench, his face turned to the side and right cheek resting on its surface. As Gabriel shackles his wrists together under the board, Darrek focuses on calming himself, using deep, even breaths to push past his anxiety. It only partially works, and a grimace curls his lips.

Gabriel glances up at his face, saying, "I haven't even started yet. Relax."

"I'm trying, sir," he grunts, and starts to turn his face away as he whines.

"No. Look at me."

Darrek stops himself and faces Gabriel once more. Under the bench, Darrek's cock and balls have been fed through a hole drilled out of the wood specifically for this purpose. Gabriel cradles him in his right hand, examining the heavy metal circle resting snug under the ridge of his cock head. The thick, sharp points circling the inside of the ring are nipping at the skin covering Darrek's shaft as he continues to swell and harden under Gabriel's feather-light touch.

The jewelry had been well-sterilized, as had Darrek's dick, before Gabriel fastened it on. He'd had Darrek close his eyes and had locked it in place before he could see what it was, after first ensuring that Darrek was ready to feel pain and wear a chastity device of Gabriel's choosing. Darrek had also previously confessed to Gabriel that his interest in temporary piercing was piqued after the conversation he had with Kyle about his experiences with it. Gabriel sees the weighted, spiked ring as a trial run before going through with a true piercing. If Darrek can manage to control himself, he won't even need to feel the spikes, which are far too widely-tapered, short and thick to do much more than break the surface of Darrek's skin.

The heavy, solid weight of the silver ring pulls against Darrek's penis, another form of gentle torture, as he struggles to not become erect, but does anyway. What his body *wants*—to curve up—and what the heavy metal *does*—pull him down with gravity—fight for dominance.

Gabriel sees the strain already on Darrek's face, but there's that old defiance in his eyes.

"Please give me more, Master," he asks at Gabriel's hesitation.

"Okay," Gabriel nods.

Testing the leather cuffs, making sure they are tight, Gabriel next secures Darrek's ankles together.

The bench's long board, about two feet wide and five feet long, supports Darrek's body. His arms are bound beneath it. His legs straddle it as the end runs out past his backside, and his ankles are cuffed snugly together. With this done, Gabriel ties and then wraps a very thin, strong rope around the base of Darrek's testicles. Winding it around and around, the end of the rope is tied off on the ankle cuffs, keeping Darrek's legs drawn up and still. If he moves them backward at all, it will pull on the rope and yank on his balls.

Grunting throughout this process, Darrek wills the pain he already feels to wilt his growing hard-on, but of course it doesn't. He has always enjoyed the pain.

Gabriel had assured him that it was okay if he became fully erect and the spikes wounded him, leaving the antiseptic and bandages in his view. The spikes on the ring are incapable of severely injuring him. They are designed to maximize the pain, the sensation, without causing much harm.

Arms tensed, fighting his instincts, lost in trying to breathe through it, trying not to move, and murmuring quietly to himself, Darrek ignores Gabriel moving around the room, expecting him to leave him to stew for a while like he is.

But then Gabriel places a small, portable DVD player on a table by Darrek's face, turning the glowing screen toward him with the sound turned up loud enough to clearly hear everything through the tiny speakers.

Darrek sees on the screen two hooded men, two *Doms*, one of whom he recognizes instantly as Gabriel, and another person, also masked, a tan and toned young man strapped to a table, the sub.

"Do you know what this is?" Gabriel asks.

"Yes, sir. They're your videos."

They watch the playback as a long metal needle, almost too thin to see on the small screen, is pushed through the submissive's penis, spearing the soft spongy head from left to right. The Doms praise him for his quietness and obedience. One of them runs his hand over the sub's chest to soothe him. His rough breathing can be heard through the playback, but he does not even so much as cry out.

"Add another," they hear Ben's voice say.

Kyle nods in permission.

Darrek looks away from the screen and up at Gabriel. His master's fingers brush through his hair, pushing it tenderly out of his eyes. Darrek quickly angles his head, turning it as far as he can to press a kiss to the inside of Gabriel's wrist before it can draw away.

"Watch," Gabriel urges him gently.

Darrek shifts his eyes back to the screen.

Sitting at the end of the bench, right behind Darrek and straddling it as well, Gabriel watches him watch the videos as they play. Once in a while he reaches under the wood plank, playing his fingers over Darrek's bound sac, fondling him. It causes Darrek to breathe in raspy tears, growling through the pain as his pleasure makes the spikes pierce his dick. When Gabriel finds one of the small clips he likes so well, the ones he used on Darrek before, he attaches one to Darrek's balls. It actually calms him down. He breathes more evenly and savors the pain as it shifts and grows into something familiar.

The video changes. Next is Micah, whom Darrek has not yet met in person. Ben supervises as Gabriel stuffs the olive-skinned, dark-haired man's cock with a thick metal rod, similar to what Trace had done to Darrek on their first encounter.

Measuring Darrek's reactions to each sight he sees, Gabriel slowly decides that it's not the submissives themselves that affect Darrek the most; it's seeing *Gabriel* do things to people that gets Darrek arching his back, writhing and gasping with pain as his dick swells.

He had been idly rubbing back and forth with the pad of his thumb over Darrek's asshole, teasing him open, watching the muscle twitch, clench and pucker. Taking a piece of ice from a cooler at his feet, Gabriel touches the tip to the opening in his slave's body. Darrek squeezes his eyes shut and groans through pursed lips as Gabriel feeds it inside. The ring of muscle presses around the ice as it slowly breaches him. Then Gabriel leaves it there, working it in and out as Darrek's heat melts it. Water trickles down his taint, down through the hole in the wood and over his balls encased in rope.

He holds the stream of words inside as long as he can manage, but eventually, the burning discomfort wins out over control.

"Goddamn it! God, it's too cold. It hurts, it really, really, oh fucking *GOD*. I- it's too cold! Shit! *Shit!*"

When it's nothing more than a sliver, Gabriel pulls it free and leans down. He licks over the chilled rim of Darrek's opening then presses his lips there, thrusting his tongue inside just enough to warm him back up.

"*Ffffuck!* Ow! Ow, fuck!"

Gabriel keeps kissing him warm, brushing his hands over the backs of Darrek's thighs. Darrek's whole body seizes up and a small whine of hurt leaves him before he falls quiet. Pulling away from Darrek's body, wiping his mouth dry with a hand, Gabriel leans to the side and glances under the bench, seeing the size of Darrek's erection, the metal piercing him, denting the flesh. He rubs a hand up Darrek's back, feeling his ribs expand and contract with each breath.

Lost in a daze, Darrek becomes overwhelmed with everything, and it actually mellows him. He goes back to gazing at the video, detaching a little from his own body. The screen is back to showing Kyle and Ben, and Darrek watches with fascination.

Meanwhile, Gabriel begins feeding small anal beads into his captive.

He plays them in and out of the orifice before nudging them all the way in with a fingertip, one by one. When he has the beads completely inside Darrek, their string with its looped end trailing out, Gabriel picks up a second string of them, and feeds them inside as well.

Darrek's cock is fully erect, and he comforts himself with the knowledge that at least it can't hurt any more than it does. He becomes acclimated to it, leaving him able to focus more on the images flashing before him, the very welcome feeling of Gabriel teasing him and filling him up.

When the second string of beads has also been swallowed up by Darrek's hungry hole, Gabriel tugs gently on the two strings. Not enough to pull them free, just putting pressure on the ring of muscle from inside. With the beads as small as they are, Darrek is not even stretched out much at this point.

Halfway through feeding the third string of beads into Darrek, Gabriel's gaze snaps up when Darrek gasps with shock and exclaims with his eyes locked to the video, "Hey! That's you!"

Repressing a smile, Gabriel quickly pops the last three beads through, and goes back to playing with the strings, tugging on them, using a finger to push the beads farther up inside Darrek's body and then tugging more. Darrek moans. He pulls a little harder and one of the beads oh-so-slowly forces Darrek's hole open wider as it pops back out. The strands have gotten tangled up in Darrek's body, like Gabriel knew they would, and a group of at least three more wedge in his entrance as Gabriel pulls on them.

Moaning loudly, Darrek's arms tense. Gabriel can see his back muscles flex, hears a deep grunt as Darrek forgets about his feet and jerks them hard, pulling the rope around his balls.

"Keep watching," Gabriel instructs without passion. He tugs hard at the strings, and a knot of four beads expels from Darrek's body.

Bucking his hips, and gasping, Darrek curses but does as told. He watches as Trace feeds a sliver of ginger root into Gabriel's cock. The pain is only reflected in the deep flush on his fair cheeks, the redness of his tearing eyes and the small convulsions wracking his body. With a hand clapped to Gabriel's shoulder, Trace speaks softly to him, but doesn't stop tormenting him.

Catching a glimpse of the playback, Gabriel explains, "You know how I told you Micah's experience as a sub was valuable? Well, I asked to experience some of the techniques too, before I did them to other people. We videotaped it since I was under contract with Diadem anyway, and they could use it on the website without having to deal with a lot of paperwork and shit."

"Mm... *uh*... I didn't... didn't know you did that," Darrek manages in response as Gabriel alternately yanks the beads free and then pushes them slowly right back in.

"Of course I did."

Approximately an hour after that, the beads have all been extracted. Using an extra-long, well-lubricated dildo, Gabriel fucks Darrek with it, pushing it in until the base is flush to his ass, and then pulling it free, doing it repeatedly. With his free hand, he carefully squeezes up and down the base of Darrek's dick, rubs fingertips over the seeping crown, mostly avoiding touching the spiked ring, but not *always* avoiding it.

Darrek is shaking uncontrollably and completely face-down, trying to swallow-back the rough yells that keep getting out anyway. It goes on for longer than Darrek expects it to. He's forgotten about the videos. All that matters is the torment radiating through his body from the focal point between his legs.

When Gabriel stops touching his dick, Darrek breathes out sharply and loudly, and feels his Master begin to untie the rope, unshackle the bindings while still slowly working the dildo in and out of him. Minutes later, he's free. The dildo slides free of his body as well, leaving him empty and gaping.

"Get up," Gabriel tells him.

With intense care, Darrek lifts his dick out of the bench's hole, making sure not to catch the metal on the wood as he does. Legs shaky and almost unable to support him, he stands before Gabriel.

With swift, skilled fingers, before Darrek can blink, the ring is unlocked and pulled-off. As blood bubbles to the surface at each dented pinprick mark on his shaft, Gabriel covers the small wounds with gauze soaked in cooling antiseptic. Gabriel grabs hold of Darrek's shoulder just to be sure he doesn't collapse. The bleeding stops in mere seconds.

"Okay, go get on the bed. Get in position. I want your ass pulled open and ready for me to fuck it when I get in there," Gabriel commands him with only the briefest glance up.

"Yessir," he slurs in response.

After turning off the DVD player and the lights, collecting his supplies to be cleaned and disinfected, Gabriel goes to the bedroom. He finds Darrek on his knees, ass in the air, and, as instructed, holding himself opened wide with both hands pulling his cheeks apart.

Not even breaking his stride, Gabriel gets his pants down, climbs on the bed and enters Darrek with a snap of his hips, bottoming out with a deep moan.

Frantic and as desperate to relieve the ache in his over-hard cock as Darrek is after hours of play, Gabriel fucks him quick and rough. With only three squeezing pulls from his Master's talented hand—exceedingly grateful for merciful release—Darrek orgasms with a cry that goes on and on as he unloads on the bed, soiling the sheets. Going limp and boneless, the firm plant of his knees in the soft bedding and Gabriel's hold on him are the only things keeping his ass up. Exhausted and spent as he is, he almost falls asleep before Gabriel finishes and comes inside him.

Letting Darrek collapse down completely, Gabriel crawls over his body, kissing him everywhere and murmuring, "So amazing, Dare. You're just totally fucking *amazing*. Thank you. Thank you, baby. I love you. Love you so much."

"Mmm..." Darrek smiles drowsily. "Yeah, what you said. Me too. Love your kinky ass too."

"How do you feel?" Gabriel frowns down at him.

"Better than fuckin' ever. Sore in all the right places, just how I like it. Now come on and snuggle with me."

Laughing, Gabriel goes to get something with which to clean Darrek and then does just that, falling into his arms right where he belongs.

Chapter 31
Trust Issues

"Slow down," is the raspy, aching and breathless, but perfectly controlled command. The strain of keeping himself that controlled is beginning to show on Gabriel's face, which is all the proof Darrek needs of how much he is enjoying this.

Gabriel can feel Darrek's thigh muscles quiver as he decreases his pace, using his grip on the back of Gabriel's chair to brace himself. Gabriel glances down between their bodies to Darrek's reddened cock where it is sliding slickly against Gabriel's abs. Circling it loosely with a hand, Gabriel feels the leather and metal encasing it. The smooth, cool metal rings bite into Darrek's hot flesh, blood is pulsing hard and fast under the skin, the bindings preventing him from getting fully erect.

Rubbing a thumb over the weeping crown, he says directly into the shell of Darrek's ear, "Does it hurt?"

Exhaling out the word with an evident, pleasure-filled tenseness to his voice, Darrek says, "Yeah."

He keeps riding Gabriel, focusing on regulating his movements.

"Slow down. More than that."

"I *can't*," Darrek whines.

"Sure you can," Gabriel grins, wrapping his hands under the backs of Darrek's thighs to help support him. "I'm not letting you take it off, you know. Not until I get home tonight. And even though your leg muscles will be sore and burning, I'm gonna make you ride my cock again, nice and slow, just like this, before you get to go to sleep."

Darrek whimpers and lets his lips press against Gabriel's skin.

"And then...maybe I'll let you take it off and come all over my face."

"*Shit,*" Darrek curses, falling heavily down onto Gabriel's dick as his legs give out, forcing him to take all of the thick length at once. His voice reverberates in a loan moan.

"Get up. Pull off, but don't go anywhere," Gabriel instructs.

Straightening his legs completely but with effort since his thighs are knotted up painfully, Darrek feels the friction of Gabriel's cock expelling from his body. Taking one step back when Gabriel's hands guide him, Darrek whines loudly as Gabriel bends forward, dipping his head to lick the come-slicked head of Darrek's cock. His eyes peering up curiously at Darrek's face, Gabriel purses his lips and blows across the tip, chuckling darkly when Darrek's eyes roll back and slip shut. Then Gabriel straightens up, scraping his teeth over the taut skin of Darrek's belly while reaching behind him and fingering the puffy tissue of the swollen, stretched opening between the muscular columns of his legs.

"*Please!*" he wails, begging without even knowing what he's begging *for*.

"Please what?"

Four fingers jab up into him and he shouts hoarsely.

"P-please, *sir*."

"That's better. Manners count," Gabriel smiles up at him. He hears Darrek murmur something insulting under his breath. Laughing, but pulling his fingers free, Gabriel says, "Turn around and sit the fuck down on my dick, slave. We're not done yet."

Darrek pivots, straddling his Master with his back to him.

Gripping the base of his shaft to steady it, Gabriel guides Darrek down slowly. When they are fitted snugly together once more in the new position, Darrek tries to start moving again, but Gabriel forbids it, holds him down with hands clawing Darrek's upper thighs.

"Nope. Just sit there. Wanna feel you."

Gabriel guides Darrek's thighs even farther apart. He slides his right hand upward, toward Darrek's crotch, over the soft hair covering the inside of Darrek's right leg until it cups his balls. At first, he fondles them gently, listening to Darrek grunt and fight not to move. But as the hand squeezes tighter and tighter around him, it gets painful, moves *beyond* painful, and Darrek's feet slide out from under him. He curls forward, chin tucked to his chest, stomach muscles contracted, and hard as steel. He succeeds at first at not making a sound of protest, and breathes in hisses through clenched teeth. Gabriel twists his hand and a sharp cry rips from Darrek's chest, but he stays still, shaking and sweating.

"Good," Gabriel whispers, "Very good. You're so good for me."

He kisses the side of Darrek's neck and tugs at the soft flesh enclosed in his fist.

"*Ahhh!* Ah-ha-ah..." Darrek cries, mouth wide, fallen open.

Releasing him finally, Gabriel strokes the pad of his thumb up the ridges of the cock cage and says, "Fuck me. Hard as you want."

Darrek groans, his back, dripping with sweat, slides up against Gabriel's bare chest as he pulls up and then eases back down. He speeds up, legs still aching terribly, feeling Gabriel's hands on his ass, guiding him faster, thrusting up into him, skin slapping against skin with almost brutal force every time Darrek brings his weight down.

Gabriel comes with a jagged moan and a shudder, pinning Darrek down hard to his lap with an arm slung tightly around his pelvis.

"Damn," he hisses, "I enjoyed the hell out of that."

"Mnnn," is the dizzy response from the man on his dick.

Stroking his hand up and down ridged abdominal muscles, over Darrek's sweat-slicked skin, listening to him catch his breath, Gabriel tells him, "I'll let you get a shower, but I have to tell you something first. Wanna make sure you're okay with it."

The serious, marginally less confident tone in Gabriel's voice prompts Darrek to attempt to focus his thoughts more on what he's saying, sensing that it's important.

"Yeah. Okay, what is it?" he grunts.

"We're training Micah today since we have a light schedule, only one client coming in for Trace."

"Well, you've been training him for a while now, right?"

"Yeah. But we've been having him practice on Kyle. It's been convenient, for obvious reasons. He drives in with Ben and knows his stuff well enough that we don't have to worry about him. But..." Gabriel says, trailing off, letting Darrek finish the thought.

"But Kyle's going to be busy working today, with me and our crew downtown."

"Give the man a prize," Gabriel grins. He takes a long pause before saying, "So, I'm going to let Micah practice on me instead."

Darrek tenses noticeably and actually stops breathing for a second or two.

"But look, it's just technique and positioning. He's not going to be touching me in a sexual way or stimulating me. It's a class. And if it'll make you feel better, I'll set up one of the cameras and send you the link to the feed. I won't broadcast it to the website. I'll keep it on the secure server and give you the access code. Okay? So you can watch the whole thing if you want to. But if you aren't okay with it, I'll call it off. We'll reschedule for a time when Kyle can be there."

"Why can't someone else do it?" Darrek asks quietly.

"Ben was his Dom," Gabriel explains. "We can't expect him to be able to do this stuff to Ben. And Trace will be with a client. No one else is working today."

"I don't like it. I don't like it at all."

"Okay then. I'll give the office a call and...."

"But I trust you, Gabe," Darrek interrupts. "I trust you completely. If you need to do this for work, then do it. I know it's for your job, and not for... whatever. Pleasure, I guess. So do it. I'm okay with it."

"Thank you," Gabriel says, kissing Darrek's shoulder. "Hey, Ben was going to give me a ride in to the office, but I'll probably be there later than him. Could you pick me up after work?"

"I would love to pick you up after work," Darrek grins, weaving their fingers together and kissing the side of Gabriel's hand.

When Gabriel and Ben arrive at the office together an hour or so later, Ben goes to finish some work on billing, and make some calls before he has to assist in Trace's session. He disappears into the file and records room with a mug of coffee brought from home. The beverage, Ben told Gabriel very reluctantly during their drive, was made for Ben by Kyle, which of course brings much amusement to Gabriel who goes on to praise Ben's thoughtful, culinary-gifted domestic partner. This leaves Gabriel to go in search of his own coffee, walking through the hallways to the rooms in the rear of the building, one of which is the kitchenette, home of the coffee pot. Discovering once he gets there that a pot has conveniently been brewed and is still hot, he pours a cup, adds some creamer and sits at the table to skim the morning paper.

A loud smack and a thump from one of the recovery rooms in his line of sight causes him to look up. Through the doorway he sees Micah, who is both shorter and slighter than Gabriel, being manhandled against a far wall. The lamps in the room are turned off but a shaft of morning sun lights the contours of his face, highlighting his exotic eyes, and shining on his raven-black hair. Trace is at Micah's back, holding him to the wall with a forearm braced cross-wise against his shoulder blades and a hand twisting one of Micah's arms behind him. Gabriel can barely make out the gruff murmuring of Trace's voice as he speaks quietly but forcefully to the other man.

Body tensing momentarily, Gabriel wonders if he needs to intervene and tries to figure out what in the world is going on, especially at the pained expression seen on Micah's face when he turns to glance over his shoulder. Gabriel stands and steps forward, coffee forgotten.

Trace releases Micah, growling out something that sounds like an order he would give one of his submissives. Astonished, Gabriel watches as Micah bends himself over a table, holding on to it, and Trace, behind him, pulls out his dick.

Gabriel watches avidly as Trace proceeds to force down Micah's pants and fucks him. The scene doesn't shock him. It does *surprise* him, only because he has never seen Trace and Micah do more than interact professionally together, with no prior hints that there was anything sexual between them. The commonness of seeing people fooling around or being dominated at Diadem—employees, clients, or otherwise—is the reason why Gabriel does not avert his eyes, or go back to his coffee. Instead, he keeps walking forward until he's standing in the doorway to the room with Micah's green eyes staring daggers into him.

Gabriel folds his arms over his chest and watches, impassive.

"Gabey," Trace croons, "see how good this little bitch is for me? Just bends his ass right over for fuckin'."

The room smells of sex. Their bodies slap together. Micah, his teeth bared in a grimace of discomfort, grunts roughly at the force of Trace's ruts into him.

Gabriel wonders whether this is all Trace, if it's just him being the way he is, finding a pretty young man to screw around with, mentally and physically. His question is answered when Micah grips the edge of the wooden table for leverage, locks eyes with Gabriel and starts to push back onto Trace. Stilling, Trace lets Micah fuck himself back on his cock, laughing merrily through his moans as Micah stares at Gabriel in a way that somehow manages to get *Gabriel* blushing.

"Come suck on me with those pretty lips," Micah says, low and demanding, to Gabriel.

Trace laughs with renewed vigor and slams Micah against the table, pinning him to it, wrenching both arms behind his back and taking back control as he pounds into the captive man.

"He won't do it," Trace whispers loudly in Micah's ear, both of them looking at Gabriel now. "The husband wouldn't like it, you see. Heard Darrek's *real* possessive of him. So, you?" Trace pulls out and holds his dick by the root before plunging it completely into Micah, getting a soft, startled whimper from him. "You get to play with *me*. Ain't you lucky?"

"You guys are twisted fucks," Gabriel laughs.

He turns and leaves them, Trace's gravelly laugh ringing in his ears. Grabbing up his coffee, he heads outside to finish it in the fresh air. He wants to enjoy the gorgeous morning while he can before hiding himself away in the office to dive into his work on the company's website.

Gabriel spends a few hours in the office, editing and then posting two new videos. When lunchtime rolls around, he orders a steak sandwich from the closest deli. The food is delivered shortly thereafter, and Gabriel returns to his outside seat at the picnic table to eat. Checking his phone messages, and sending one to Darrek, he doesn't hear Micah approach until he sits down across from Gabriel with a can of soda.

"Hey," he grins over at Gabriel. "Mind if I join you?"

"Not at all."

Tucking his phone away, Gabriel goes back to his sandwich.

"Texting the husband?" Micah asks.

"Hmm? Oh, we're not really married. Trace is just a dick. As you've discovered."

"Indeed. But it's serious, right? With Darrek?" he asks over his drink with keen, sincere eyes.

"Yeah. It's pretty serious. Who knows, maybe one day we'll get hitched in a big gay ceremony," Gabriel grins. Then he chuckles to himself with amusement at the thought and the images it stirs in his mind. "How about you? Guess you're unattached, since...."

"Oh, I'm attached. Married for going on ten years now," Micah says easily, taking a drink.

Gabriel blinks at him.

"I'm not kidding," Micah assures him.

"Damn. Okay. Well... congratulations?" he says uncertainly.

"We have an open marriage," he explains, helpfully. "My wife likes to watch or get involved when I take a lover. She hasn't met Trace yet, but she's okay with it since we work together and I know him pretty well by now."

Gabriel sets down his sandwich and simply squints over at Micah with utter befuddlement.

"Dude... I don't even know what to say to that. You have a *wife*?"

"Mm-hmm," Micah nods. "I'll have to introduce you. Her name's Lily."

Quirking his head to the side, Gabriel shrugs and drinks some of his own soda.

"Takes all kinds I guess," he allows. "Not like I'm really one to judge. It's cool that you've worked it out with her. Must be an amazing woman."

"She is. I'm a lucky man."

Ben appears and sits down heavily on the bench beside Micah saying, "What are we discussing?"

"He's *married,*" Gabriel says, pointing helpfully to his lunch companion.

"Mm-hmm," Ben nods, unsurprised.

"To a *woman*."

Micah smiles behind his soda, eyes bright with delight.

"And this shocks you?" Ben frowns, with mock-concern.

"Yes! Have you *met* Micah?"

"Only *here*, at our superbly unique place of employment, would someone be shocked by a heterosexual marriage. We live in strange, sad times," Ben sighs, shaking his head and playing with the keys to Kyle's collar and cock cage strung around his neck.

Gabriel frowns, throwing a piece of his sandwich at Ben.

"He's shocked because this morning he watched Trace fuck me in the south-facing recovery room. The one with the blue flowers on the wallpaper?"

"Oh," Ben nods, wagging a finger at the south side of the building, "I enjoy that wallpaper. Tell me, do you think those are pansies or violets?"

"Blue bells," Micah replies, thinking it over. "Gives the room a quaint, country charm, don't you think?"

"I hate you guys," Gabriel complains half-heartedly.

"Trace fucked me in that room once," Ben says, recalling the memory fondly with a sigh and a small smile. "He's a vigorous lover, isn't he, our Trace? Bet your asshole is plenty sore right about now."

"And how," Micah agrees.

"Sitting on wooden benches doesn't help much, either. Want me to get you a cushion?" Ben offers.

"Wait," Gabriel interrupts, "Trace fucked you? In the ass?"

"Well, I don't have a pussy, so yes. In the ass. Shall I describe it for you? The fucking, not my ass. You've seen my ass. Obviously."

"*'Obviously'...?*" Gabriel squints before waving a hand in annoyance, moving on and asking, "When did Trace fuck you?"

"It was just the once. What can I say? I was curious about his man-meat and legendary sexual prowess. It was a tranquil but bitterly cold fall day in October of the year two thousand and five, I believe. I caught him leering at me from across the dungeon, the wooden spanking paddle in his hand gave me lewd ideas and I felt myself blushing like a schoolgirl...."

"Ben!" Gabriel shouts, interrupting and covering his ears with his palms. "For the love of *God*, dude!"

Ben beams at Gabriel's discomfort.

"I like you," Micah grins over at Ben.

"Thank you, Micah!" Ben gushes happily, "I like you too. What do you say, shall we go fuck in the recovery room with the quaint, country charm? Who's gonna take it up the pooper? Flip a coin?"

"Jesus Christ," Gabriel moans, though laughing. He stands, taking the remains of his lunch with him. He tosses it into a trashcan. "I'm going back to work. Enjoy your lovefest. You two deserve each other."

Chapter 32
Back to the Beginning

The sheer ridiculousness of the entire morning and then lunch puts Gabriel at ease for his turn as symbolic sub to Micah's Dom that afternoon. But, when they find themselves all alone in the dungeon, knowing that Trace, Ben, and the client are in a session in Diadem's outdoor setup located in an old barn to the back of the property, his ease falters.

Gabriel gets to the bottom of the dungeon's stairs and sees Micah standing in the relative darkness, candlelight and shafts of daylight from the stairwell the only brightness in the huge space. He has removed his shirt, as the Doms of Diadem are wont to do, and his black trousers hang almost obscenely low on his hips, the belt barely catching on the rounded swell of his backside to keep them aloft. Gabriel is forced to admit to himself that he looks much more attractive that way—half-dressed—especially with a determined fire burning in his eyes; clearer and more intense now than that morning when he had first seen it. Micah's slightly off-kilter personality and bizarreness was funny and entertaining at lunch and when Trace was there to control it. It only seems dangerous now that it's just him and Gabriel with no one else even in the *building*, let alone in the room to mediate.

Micah shakes his hair back out of his eyes and measures out lengths of rope.

"You don't mind the lighting, do you?" Micah asks, noticing how Gabriel is standing immobile and hesitant by the exit to the upper floors. "I wanted it to be as real as possible to see if I can tie these knots in the dark."

After a delay, he answers, "No," rousing himself. He starts to unbutton his shirt. "That's fine. Makes sense."

It occurs to Gabriel that this is the first time he's been alone with Micah for an extended span of time. In a flash he remembers how Ben always used to tease him that Micah had a crush on him, and always specifically requested to have Gabriel assist in his sessions.

Getting his shirt off, and hanging it from an arm of the Saint Andrew's cross nearby, Gabriel walks around Micah to where the cameras have been stashed against a far wall. Sliding one of the tripods over, he positions the digital camera in front of the padded tabletop they will be using for their practice session.

"Is it all right with you if I turn this on? I gave Darrek the access code so that he could watch if he wanted to," Gabriel says without turning around.

"Of course. Having an audience always makes things more interesting."

Gabriel glances back over his shoulder and sees Micah winding the thin, strong, hemp rope around and around his fists, testing the give and feeling the texture of it against his skin. Brow lowered, and eyes in shadow, he looks rather menacing. Gabriel wonders that he ever questioned Micah's ability to switch to the Dominant role, as he's clearly able to make even Gabriel, a larger man and more experienced Dom, feel anxious with only a look.

Spread out on a counter are printouts—diagrams of a handful of positions that Gabriel had emailed earlier for Micah to review. Micah studies them thoughtfully and Gabriel's stomach flips at the thought of Micah putting him in those specific positions, one after another until they finish. Gabriel's fingers hesitate only a moment before they begin undoing his fly.

"Are you okay with this?" Micah asks seriously. "Tell me now if you aren't. You seem... unsure."

"I'll be fine. I'm just not used to being on this side of things."

Pushing his jeans down and stepping out of them, leaving himself in his boxer briefs, Gabriel thinks of something to say or ask to relieve the suffocating tension.

"Um... I, uh... always wanted to ask. What's your day job? So to speak."

"I started a tech firm. Web hosting. Really boring stuff, but I sold it last year for a big profit. Since then, I haven't exactly needed to work, so I've been... bored. Sometimes I write or act as a consultant to my former colleagues, but mostly I've been doing this."

Gabriel boosts himself up onto the tabletop and sits on the edge with his legs dangling over the side. The response and the relative normalcy of Micah's previous occupation both calms and concerns him. The concern stems mainly from the knowledge that, yes, Micah really is that smart, and yes, Gabriel thinks Micah is probably cleverer than him, by a great deal.

Walking over to the table, and Gabriel, bringing with him the cart laden with his supplies and instructions, Micah nods, indicating wordlessly that Gabriel should lie down.

"You know what we're reviewing then?" Gabriel asks, easing back onto the padded vinyl and stretching out his legs, resting his hands on his chest.

"Yes. I think I have the knots down; I've been practicing those. But I want to make sure I get the correct tension and body positioning for best effect. Plus, I'm still working on my... technique... so I'll be treating you as my sub."

"Understood."

Taking one length of rope, Micah slips a hand under Gabriel's wrist, lifting it off of his chest. He begins to wind it around repeatedly and knots it. As he secures it to the other wrist, binding them together, Gabriel watches. Micah asks, with a flash of green irises beneath dark lashes, "What's your safeword?"

"Discovery," Gabriel says, staring up at the ceiling and trying not to recall in detail the last time he needed to use his safeword.

Guiding the bound wrists up above Gabriel's head, Micah pulls the other man's arms until they are straight and fully elongated. He ties off the ends of the rope to a metal hook at the head of the very long tabletop. Taking his time, he tests his handiwork, wanting to get it tight, but not too tight. Gabriel tries to be patient, all too aware of his near nakedness and the way the figurative helplessness of his situation is beginning to arouse him in the sickest of ways.

He's all too familiar with being made to do sexual acts, acts that the person with him is enjoying much more than *he*. His cooperation is borne out of misguided duty or expectation. Offering himself up as a plaything, something to be toyed with and used, triggers intense negative reactions, but those emotions tend to get buried under conditioned responses honed over years and years of abuse. This is how Gabriel begins to feel himself mentally submitting to Micah even before they really start, and without fully understanding why.

Staring at the camera, Gabriel knows that the glowing red light on the side means that Darrek could be watching, that Darrek is there with him in one sense at least. Gabriel feels Micah's hands skim down the underside of his taut arms, over his armpits and it tickles but he can only twist a little, unable to get away or cover up. Seeing Gabriel's response to the tickling, the instantaneous reaction in his body which twitches away, wriggling, he does it again, getting Gabriel to squirm even more. He shoots Micah an angry glare and ignores how good it feels. Fingertips of both of Micah's hands brush down his sides, and that tickles too, so he curses under his breath, closing his eyes to calm down. But then the fingers hook in the waist of his snug-fitting boxers, easing them slowly, steadily down.

A war of reactions and thoughts buffet him as Micah pulls the underwear down and off his legs. Staring away from Micah, and over at one of the flickering candles instead, Gabriel licks over his suddenly dry lips, half hard. He hates himself for it. This is even though he knows he needs to be naked for this, and that he also needs to be fully erect so that Micah can practice binding his genitals with the rope, this being the area of the body that needs the most care and skill when it comes to this sort of binding. They certainly don't want to injure a client, so practice is a must.

Micah takes in the sight of Gabriel's complete and utter nakedness, reluctantly looking away to glance over at the printed diagrams before he goes on with the next step. His hands skim over Gabriel's bare hip and right thigh lightly enough to drive Gabriel insane. The backs of fingers brush back and forth over his navel, tracing circles around and dipping into his belly button and down to his pelvis, closer and closer to where his twitching cock lays up against his belly. Deciding on which pose to do first, Micah says, "Bend your legs sharply, calves flush to your thighs, with your knees back to your chest."

Biting his tongue and breathing through his nose, Gabriel does as told, knowing, dreading the position Micah has chosen. He doesn't watch when Micah ties a rope end to his left ankle and then winds it around his leg, binding his calf to his thigh, keeping his knee sharply bent, doubled up with his heel near his ass.

"Arch your back up as high as you can."

The rope snakes under the middle of his back and through to the other side where it is all repeated, binding his right leg in the same way. Unsatisfied with the rope tension in his first attempt, Micah undoes his work and tries again, getting the rope under Gabriel's back tighter to keep his legs yanked farther apart, and unable to move.

It's a long process, but Gabriel knows that speed comes with practice too. He is almost able to relax and detach from what's happening as the minutes tick by. But then, the position is nearly complete, his legs are bound, and he feels incredibly exposed.

As he works, Micah rests his right hand every so often just below Gabriel's navel, his pinky finger only a hair's breadth away from grazing the tip of Gabriel's cock. It makes Gabriel nervous. With his other hand, Micah winds the longest length of rope on the cart around and around Gabriel's torso and under the table as well. Soon he is tied flush to it, tightly enough to keep him from taking too deep a breath.

With the pose finished, Gabriel waits to see what will happen next. Micah steps to his right and turns slightly, putting his back to the camera, blocking the shot.

"You're in a twenty-four/seven, Dominant/submissive relationship with Darrek, I hear," he says conversationally, with a slightly brittle edge that Gabriel doesn't miss.

Micah's hand slides over the ropes that are beginning to really bite into the flesh of Gabriel's left leg. It glides along the inside of his thigh, over the soft, sensitive skin at his hip, the junction of his thigh and torso. Then the hand moves lower, tickling over his ass cheeks.

"Control and power must be very important to you," Micah says.

Fingers find the crease of his ass, trailing through it, avoiding the one spot Gabriel is most conscious of. He thinks Micah is just fucking with his head, testing him. He thinks he's not going to go through with it. But then, the pad of one finger circles the rim of his opening lazily before coming to rest right on it, not pushing, just touching. Gabriel squeezes his eyes shut and counts backward from ten in his mind.

"Don't," he spits out. He opens his eyes with effort, staring up at Micah, and warns, "Don't fucking do this. This isn't supposed to be...."

The dry finger pushes, the tip breaching him.

Gabriel makes a small noise and tries to move, to escape, and can't. He can't move. He's bound too tightly for that. The finger stays there, inside him. And impossibly, Micah ignores him; keeps talking as if Gabriel did not say a word.

"But I get the sense that you need to give up that control once in a while. You like to pretend that you are this powerful, impenetrable Dominant...."

The finger presses deeper, up to the second knuckle before pulling out and free. Gabriel whines.

"...but I think you get off even more on being dominated, and having the control taken away from you."

"No. You don't know me. You don't...."

He doesn't finish the thought because what happens next wipes all thought from his mind.

The fingertip forces back into his rectum to the first knuckle. Gabriel tenses every muscle in his body at the same time, not thinking, just spasming, pushing and fighting with every primal response in him. At the same time, the fingers of Micah's left hand close gently around his dick, tickling up and down it once. Then, with light pressure, he pinches them around the shaft, down by the root. They shift slowly upward, squeezing, pinching as they go, applying pressure to his shaft and moving the flesh so that it is perfectly centered where it lies against Gabriel's stomach.

When they get to the smooth skin of the head, they squeeze firmly around the spongy ridge. Micah traces his index finger back and forth over the dip on the underside, rubbing and pressing at the bundle of nerves. All of the specific, focused attention works. Gabriel's cock swells even more, until it strains against Micah's hand, completely full and wanting to arc up. But Micah restrains him there as well, and keeps it pushed down flat against his belly. It's uncomfortable, but the point is to make him aware of how aroused he is, and it works.

"You enjoy having Darrek fuck you, maybe even more than you want to admit, don't you?"

Gabriel tells himself that Micah is only trying to get in his head and exploit his perceived weaknesses, that his uncanny ability to pick out the very things that bother Gabriel the most is disturbing, but simply him doing his job as Dom. It's the same thing Gabriel would be doing in his place, finding the triggers, the sub's vulnerable spots to manipulate and take advantage of.

Eyes closed, Gabriel tries to detach from his body and go to another place, a safer, better place, like he used to as a teenager. As Micah extracts his finger from his body, Gabriel blocks it all out with resolute determination. He doesn't see Micah slip on the glove or hear the snap of the latex against skin. He also doesn't see Micah get a good dollop of lubricant on his fingers from the dispenser on the cart.

Gabriel *does* feel it when two fingers are inserted precisely into his rectum. Digging deep, they curl up with a sharp, corkscrewing twist of Micah's wrist and pull a strangled gasp from Gabriel's softly opened mouth. Unable to move, *trying* to move, being touched intimately by someone he does *not* want touching him—Gabriel's mind snaps. He bucks harder against the ties, but the knots hold and his dick does not lose interest as Micah finger-fucks his asshole.

"Don't hurt me," Gabriel asks softly as the ropes strain against his tensed body, his eyes going dull and vacant.

"Does it hurt? What you feel right now?" Micah asks, frowning. He prods Gabriel's prostate. It makes his cock jump. Micah's left hand closes around his dick, and he pulls on it rhythmically. Gabriel's body clenches up around the invading fingers working in and out. "Answer me, slave, or you get another finger."

"No."

"No, what?"

'I've played this game,' Gabriel muses silently to himself in a broken way. He falls farther back into his mind, moving through space and time until he is back in his childhood bedroom with his old posters covering the walls. Someone is holding him down, touching him.

"Daddy...."

The word slips out, and it's curious, simple and questioning.

'What's the magic word? The word that makes it all stop?' Gabriel wonders from far away.

"Please... *please*, Daddy."

A third finger penetrates him, forcing him open even more, and the hand jacking his cock speeds up as his balls draw up, preparing to unload. Tears fall down the sides of Gabriel's face, joining others he did not even know he's been crying. He makes no more sounds, just a single grunt as his body empties itself, contracting and sending jets of semen splattering over the ties across his chest and belly.

The hemp ropes get untied from his torso and then his legs. Micah helps Gabriel straighten out, and he doesn't say anything, doesn't open his eyes.

Gabriel is lying there, prone, mostly untied, all except for his wrists, as Micah walks away, over to the cart, leaving him there for the moment.

"Discovery."

Micah turns to Gabriel. He doesn't ask him to repeat himself. He just picks up a knife and cuts the rope in one swift movement.

Gabriel struggles up to a seated position and then hops down. Unseeing and silent, he wrestles out of the rope and walks in the direction of the showers.

Chapter 33
Head Games

When Gabriel does not emerge from the showers, even after Micah waits a full forty-five minutes for him, Micah decides to go and check on him. He finds Gabriel under the spray of water from the farthest showerhead on the wall, and from the way he's shivering Micah determines that the water must have gone cold.

"Gabriel?" he asks tentatively, walking up to him. "Hey. Gabriel?"

There is no response, Gabriel just closes his eyes tighter, and leans against the wall with his flat palms braced on the tile. When Micah gets closer, only two steps away and just out of range of the water, Gabriel flinches away.

"Gabriel? Are you all right? What can I do?"

He looks so on edge and mentally absent that Micah's concern grows dramatically, and he moves to step even closer, intending to grab the knob that turns the water off.

The movement startles Gabriel terribly, and he goes right into attack-mode, trying to defend himself from whatever he thinks is going to happen, from whatever he believes Micah's intentions to be. Gabriel can still feel the other man's fingers invading him, and bruises are beginning to come out, coloring his body on his wrists, torso and all down his legs. The ropes had held, but Gabriel had fought them the whole time, whether he realized it or not. It has taken its toll.

Gabriel kicks Micah squarely in the shin with his right foot. Micah hisses with pain but lunges to grab hold of Gabriel's arms as he draws them back to deliver more blows. They struggle but

Micah's determination and calm wins out over Gabriel's weak-kneed panic. Holding him still against the tile, getting drenched by the water spraying both of them, Micah holds Gabriel's stare and says, "Calm down! I'm not going to hurt you."

"Get off of me! Don't touch me! Don't fucking touch me!" His voice cracks on some of the words. "Help! Somebody help!"

"Gabriel!" Micah snaps, "What's going on with you? I'm not letting you go until you calm the hell down."

"Don't..." Gabriel gulps, eyes darting away. He looks paler than is healthy, dehydrated from being in the water so long. He tries to shake Micah off whilst also trying to keep their bodies from touching. Overly aware of his nakedness, Gabriel knows how easy it would be for Micah to shift their stances slightly and proceed to fuck him, especially with lubricant already in his well-stretched-open body. He becomes convinced that it's about to happen. It's happened to him so often before that it seems unavoidable, no matter what he does or says. He can't help the desperate frailness of his voice as he begs, "*Please* don't do this...."

"Do what? I'm trying to help you. You've been in here for almost an hour! You don't look well."

"Just get off! I need to... I need...."

"If you weren't okay with what happened in there, why didn't you use the safeword?" Micah asks, confused.

"I did! I said it..." Gabriel whines. Then he appears to realize *when* he said it, that he said it after the fact, and that what happened was not Micah's fault at all. He realizes that he wasn't forced into anything, and that Micah had no intention to molest him. Gabriel moans, "Oh *Christ*! What the fuck is wrong with me?!"

"Can I let you go? Get you a towel?" Micah offers.

"Yeah. Yeah, okay."

They hear muffled noises from the upper floor, a bang and heavy, running footsteps. The noise gets louder, a deep voice that Gabriel instantly recognizes. He hears someone pounding down the steps and shouting his name.

Gabriel sighs, and feels new tears stinging his eyes. His knees start to give out, and Micah feels him start to collapse, so he tries to hold him up.

Then Darrek appears in the doorway, seething like an angry bull. Teeth bared, nostrils flared and red-faced, he's across the room in a flash, yanking soaking wet and half-dressed Micah off a naked and bruised Gabriel, sending Micah stumbling backward against the rack of folded linens stacked neatly behind them.

"Darrek..." Gabriel moans just before Darrek spits out at Micah, *"You son of a bitch!!"*

His fist connects with Micah's jaw, splitting his lip open, smearing bright blood over his chin and Darrek's fist. Then Darrek's knee comes up, connecting hard with Micah's balls, doubling him over and sending him collapsing to the floor, curling up in a ball to avoid further assault.

"Darrek!" Gabriel rasps louder, pulling at his arm, tugging him back and away from Micah. "Stop! It's not his fault. I forgot the safeword. I...."

Darrek gets an eyeful of Gabriel's eyes, red, puffy from crying, his unhealthy pallor and his shivering beneath evident bruises. Grabbing one of the towels, he hastily wraps Gabriel in it and encircles him in a hug, letting out the breath he had been holding all the way over from his work site.

"Did he rape you?" Darrek manages, somehow, to ask in a fearful whisper. "I couldn't see. Micah was blocking the camera angle. I just heard your voice, heard *him*, and...."

"No, he didn't. Not really. It's my fault. I should have used the safeword, but it felt like... like before, with Harry, and I forgot where I was, and I forgot...."

"It's okay. You don't have to explain. Come on, I'm taking you out of here. Let's get you dressed and in the truck, okay? *Are you okay??* I was *so fucking scared,* Gabe! I drove as fast as I could."

"Wait. Is Micah all right? You shouldn't have hit him. He was trying to help. He wasn't...." The words trail off as Gabriel's knees give out again. This time Darrek catches him.

Giving Micah, who is still crumpled on the floor, an unforgiving glare, Darrek notices that the other man is beginning to recover.

Darrek growls, "Should fucking call the cops on you, you sick fuck! But I won't, for Gabriel's sake. Where the fuck is everyone anyway? No one's upstairs!"

"The other building. The barn. Sam's not in today. Don't call the cops. The company might get in trouble. Micah, are you okay, man?" Gabriel croaks, biting his lip and pulling the towel closer around himself.

"Don't worry about him," Darrek grunts, guiding Gabriel away.

"I'm good. Don't worry about me. Let Darrek help you," Micah nods. "I am sorry, for what it's worth."

He wipes blood off of his face with another towel, dabbing at the spot and wincing as he shifts his legs. That's as much as Gabriel sees as Darrek gathers his clothes, gets Gabriel into his pants before he even realizes Darrek is dressing him, and then they are headed upstairs.

They do not encounter anyone as they walk over to Darrek's truck. After helping Gabriel get seated on the passenger side, Darrek jumps in and guns the engine. He puts his hand on the stick shift and pauses.

"Gabe, look at me. I don't know the whole story here. What do you need me to do?" Darrek asks worriedly. "Are you injured? You look like hell. Should I take you to the hospital?"

"Let's just get home. I don't wanna talk about it. Not here," Gabriel mumbles, folding his arms across his chest, clutching his crumpled shirt and underwear. "I don't need a hospital."

"Are you *sure*?"

"Yeah."

When Darrek still does not move to shift into reverse, because he is too busy staring at Gabriel's many bruises, Gabriel pleads, "Dare, come *on*."

"Sorry. Yeah. We're gone."

The truck peels off down the road, stirring up thick clouds of dust and dirt as it goes.

They get home. Once through the door, Gabriel goes right to the steps and climbs them, heading to the bedroom. On the way, he undoes his pants and peels them open. Darrek is right behind him, and frowns as Gabriel digs in a drawer for clean clothes. Then Gabriel heads to the bathroom with shaking limbs, his hand fumbling at the doorknob.

"What are you doing?" Darrek asks, worried.

"Taking a shower."

Darrek stares at the pruned and wrinkled skin of Gabriel's hands, and shakes his head, "You're too dehydrated. Let me get you a drink. Come and sit first."

Gabriel sets his jaw and clenches his fists at his sides after setting the clothes on the counter.

"No, I need a shower. Now. Right now."

"Then let me help you. Just to make sure you don't collapse or something," Darrek offers, brow still furrowed as he pleads with his lover.

"I can't..." Gabriel sputters. "I can't have anyone *touching* me right now. I just... need to be alone."

"Tough shit. I'm not leaving you alone."

Gabriel looks pointedly away from him and turns on the hot water, jeans opened but he does not move to pull them down.

"Gabe, look at me. Please?"

"No. If I look at you I'm gonna lose it, and I can't lose it. I need to think. I need to figure this out. But... I'd like you to stay and wait here while I get clean."

"All right. I can do that," Darrek nods, biting his thumbnail with anxiousness.

"Um... can you turn around while I...?"

Just for a second, Darrek's face twists with pain at the stark contrast of the self-assured man that Gabriel had displayed just that morning, compared to the broken and terrified trembling man before him now, afraid to be naked in his presence.

Chewing at the inside of his cheek, Darrek does as requested and turns to give his Master privacy.

The next twenty minutes pass slowly as the room fills with steam, and Darrek listens to Gabriel scrub frantically at his skin with soap and a washcloth, breathing raggedly and roughly. When the water is shut off, Darrek hands Gabriel a towel and goes to the doorway, turning his back again while he gets dressed.

"Okay," Gabriel says from behind him.

Darrek lets him pass. Gabriel goes to the closet, pulls out one of Darrek's extra large hooded sweatshirts, and slips it on. Swimming in its bulkiness, he stuffs his hands in the pockets in front and goes downstairs. Sitting curled up on the couch, he pulls out his phone while Darrek goes to let Sierra in from the backyard and get Gabriel a glass of orange juice.

Handing over the beverage, Darrek sees the phone.

"What are you doing?"

"Calling Micah. I have to talk to him before he talks to Trace or Ben. They should still be in session with the client, so hopefully I'm not too late."

"Wait, what?" Darrek squints, sitting next to Gabriel but giving him space.

"I need to tell him not to say anything to the others," Gabriel says, dialing.

Darrek reaches over and closes the phone with a scowl.

"What the hell are you doing? Why would you tell him that?"

"Because if Trace or Ben thinks Micah hurt me, it'll fuck everything up. They'd overreact and bad, bad stuff would happen. Micah doesn't deserve that. He was just doing his job and being a good Dom. He shouldn't be punished for that. Not when it's me being so fucked up that's the real problem. Look," he says when it seems like Darrek is going to interject his opinion again, "let me do this and then I'll explain everything. Promise. You trust me?"

"Of course I trust you! I *love* you," Darrek insists, laying one of his hands on one of Gabriel's.

Sierra, who has been busy first sniffing them, then going to her water dish, before returning to the couch, sits curled up near Gabriel. She rests her chin on his knee and whines. Pulling his hand away from Darrek, Gabriel reaches to scratch behind her ears, murmuring lovingly to her. The tenderness in Gabriel, and Sierra's evident concern for her new master, breaks Darrek's heart.

A few clicks of the phone buttons later, Gabriel says into the cell phone, "It's Gabriel. Look, I have a history that I should have made you aware of. I was abused for a long time, and it fucks with my head. The reason I'm calling, though, is because I need to ask you to not tell anyone else—Trace, Ben, Sam, *anyone*—what happened between us today. Let me handle it."

There's a pause as Micah responds, and Darrek watches Gabriel's face, unable to hear the other side of the conversation.

"Yeah. And I don't blame you. You did your job. You're going to be an awesome Dom, and I don't want to screw things up for you with Diadem, or with Trace and Ben."

Licking his lips, and scratching at his chin absently, Gabriel mutters, "Okay. Thanks. Later."

He hangs up the phone only to dial it again immediately, holding a finger up to Darrek and asking him silently to wait just a little longer.

"Hey Sam, it's Gabriel. I know you're not in right now but I'm calling to let you know that I quit. As of today, I won't be coming in anymore, and I won't be able to help you with the video or online facets of the company. I'm sorry for leaving you without any notice. You've always been a good friend to me. Give me a call when you get this. Bye."

Hanging up, he turns the phone off and tosses it away.

There had been a hold up after their lunch break. A plumbing issue had to be resolved before Darrek, Kyle and another of their buddies could go back to work on laying the trim and framing out a half-wall in the restaurant downtown. That left Darrek time to find a quiet corner of the room to check in on Gabriel. Wincing at the grip of the metal of the cock cage he has been wearing since the morning, Darrek pulls out the iPhone Gabriel had given him the previous week. Darrek popped in his earbuds and tried to see if he could figure out how to access the secure server per Gabriel's instructions. He had almost accomplished it when Kyle appeared at his side.

Darrek had noticed over the course of the day that Kyle had been hanging back from the other men on their crew in favor of sticking with him when possible. Still wearing the leather collar that marks him as Ben's submissive, just as Darrek was still wearing his chain, it could possibly have been chalked up to self-consciousness.

Darrek, however, tended to think it was Kyle realizing how different his life was to most of the other people around them. He was finding comfort in the company of another submissive, specifically *Darrek*, instead.

Kyle observes Darrek's efforts with the phone, and doesn't say anything, at first.

Once he sees the web address, he makes a curious grunt and asks only, "Training? Or the archives?"

"Hmm? Oh. Well, training, I guess. 'Cause, you know, since you're back to work here, and can't help with Micah..." Darrek says, letting the suggestion hang in the air between them.

"Oh damn. Gabe's subbing, isn't he? 'Cause I know Ben said that him and Trace were out in the barn today, and Gabe and Micah were gonna be at the main building."

He can see from the look on Darrek's face that he's right, but holds his tongue, not saying more.

"Um... might as well ask, since you figured it out," Darrek says. "What's Micah like? As a Dom? Gabe will be okay, right? He said it was just positioning and technique but I'm not really sure what that means."

When Kyle lowers his eyes and considers his response, Darrek adds, "Gabe is going to set up a camera feed for me to watch the whole thing, so I feel more comfortable with it."

"Dare, the thing about Micah is that he kind of gets in your head, and I've never had him *not* do that to me when I've helped him in training. It's not *what* he does to you specifically, as much as what he figures out about what really *gets* to you. And it's unnerving because, though I do trust Micah in the sense that I allow him to Dominate me with Ben present, I don't trust him like I trust Ben. Or you. Or even Gabriel, for that matter."

"Should I be worried?" Darrek frowns. He finally gets hooked into the feed, and he sees Gabriel sitting on a table in his underwear. Micah moves into frame with a rope and Darrek feels a chill race up his spine.

"Tell you what, I'll try to reach Ben on his cell and see if he can check on Gabe. Sometimes he forgets to turn the volume off and he knows I'd only call if it was an emergency."

"Thanks," he says with quiet distraction, watching the tiny screen in his hands.

Sitting in their living room in the dying light of the day, Gabriel describes for Darrek what happened in the dungeon, not omitting any detail. When he finishes, and Gabriel is quiet, Darrek moves to kneel at Gabriel's feet in front of the couch. They sit like that for a long while.

"I didn't expect him to go there, and turn it into... what it was," Gabriel says vaguely. "I thought we'd just practice the binding techniques, but I guess that was naïve of me. It's his *job* to go there. It's what we pay him to do. But, truthfully, that isn't what freaked me out."

"I know," Darrek assures him. "You don't need to explain that to me."

"No, I do. I need to say it out loud. He didn't rape me or do anything against my will. That's the real reason why I didn't say the safeword. I just didn't want to think about it until now. I fucking *enjoyed it*. It felt like when Harry used to rape me. It felt exactly like that, and I *liked* it, and I felt so... *disgusting*. I couldn't move. He had all of the power over me. He knew I was getting off on it, and he showed me that. Micah made me recognize that, and see myself as I am. And I'm fucked up."

"Gabe, we're all fucked up. But at least you're able to look at your issues and work through them. That means you're strong. You're *so strong*, Gabe. You'll be okay. But I think it's good for you to take a break from Diadem."

"It's not a break. I'm done. Completely."

"Okay," Darrek nods, "But... there's something you need to know."

Gabriel's head snaps up, eyes wide and nervous. "What?"

"Kyle knows. And Ben knows too. Or at least he will once he gets his voicemail or talks to Kyle." He adds, "I'm sorry."

Darrek explains what happened with Kyle while they were at work. Darrek explains how Kyle tried to call Ben. And, once Darrek saw the tears on Gabriel's face, with the view of what was happening mostly blocked, he asked Kyle to cover for him and took off, driving over to Diadem. The iPhone continued to play on the passenger seat, with the audio playing through the speakers. Darrek heard everything.

"And Kyle kind of figured out on his own about Harry from what he's overheard from all of us. I swear I didn't tell him about that," Darrek says.

His phone rings on the table behind him.

They both see Ben's name on the caller ID. Darrek answers it as Gabriel groans, slumping back against the couch with tired dread.

"Let me talk to Gabriel," Ben demands before Darrek can even say a word.

"I don't want to talk to you!" Gabriel yells at the phone.

"Ben, he's fine, he's just freaked."

"Why did you hit Micah then, if Gabe is 'fine'?"

"Because I overreacted. I didn't know what happened and I overreacted. That's all."

"Gimme the phone," Gabriel says, grabbing for it. He says into it, "They shouldn't have called you. I'm fine. See? Fine. Don't worry about it."

"What did Micah do to you, Gabriel?" Ben demands. "What did he do?!"

He opens his mouth to reply, but then he remembers. He feels the ropes biting into his skin, feels fingers inside him and on his body. He remembers what he said, the dark place in his head it sent him to, and sputters.

Dropping the phone, he pulls his knees up to his chin with a vacant stare.

Darrek picks the phone up and tells Ben, "Look, this really isn't a good time. He'll call you later."

Hanging up and turning the phone off, Darrek sits beside Gabriel, wanting to hold and comfort him, frozen by uncertainty, afraid of making things worse. Gabriel hugs his legs to his chest more tightly. Sierra whines and lays her head on her paws at Gabriel's feet.

Over at Diadem, Ben stares off at a spot on the wall, hearing the phone click off as Darrek hangs up on him.

"Oh fuck *that*," he says, quickly dialing Kyle's number.

"Hey, you almost done over there? Yeah? Good. I'm picking you up. We're going over to Gabe and Dare's place. Be ready in fifteen."

Tucking the phone away, he glances around, wanting to get his hands on Micah, and ask him more questions. Micah has gone, though, along with his car. Ben storms out of the main building, cursing colorfully. He leaves Trace, who is still back at the barn finishing up, without warning or an explanation.

Gunning the engine, he tears out of the lot, onto the road. Confused, with only the vaguest of ideas of what could have occurred, Ben runs things through his head. He is glad that Darrek stood up for Gabriel to Micah, even if it was uncalled for, and especially if it *was* called for. Ben also knows that the details of Gabriel's sexual life are not technically his or Kyle's business, but the fact that something clearly happened *at work*, during the training of an employee, makes it his business. He knows Gabriel well enough to know that he will not get the police involved, no matter what. So, if something needs to be done, even something as trivial as a verbal reprimand, Ben needs to be aware of it. Considering Trace's current sexual involvement with Micah, and Sam's absence, he puts himself in charge of handling it.

Ben's personal history of talking Gabriel down from panic attacks compels him to get over there and assist Darrek in any way that he can. Darrek might be Gabriel's partner, but he *is* still new to the psychodrama that has filled their lives for years.

Acres upon acres of fields fly past in a blur, and all Ben can think about is the blood on Micah's face, the way he was limping, the indescribably scary that way Gabriel sounded, and the fierce protectiveness he heard in Darrek. Simultaneously ready to inflict serious bodily harm on Micah, glad for Darrek's response and care of Gabriel, and anxious for Gabriel himself, Ben tries to keep a level head as the road unwinds before him.

Chapter 34
Confession

A sudden chill sends a shiver racing up Gabriel's spine. It creeps outward, past his shoulders and down each arm. He tugs his sleeves down to cover his hands, tucks his fingers under his arms to warm them. Glancing sideways at where Darrek is sitting on the opposite end of the couch, Gabriel is keenly aware that his lover is not touching him in any way. In fact, Darrek seems to be specifically trying *not* to touch him.

Gabriel asks him, "Hey, pass me that blanket?"

Darrek doesn't move to get it. Frowning slightly, he replies, "It's almost eighty degrees outside. It's nearly that warm in here, and you're already wearing a sweatshirt. You'll get heatstroke."

"Thanks, *Dad*, but I'd still like the blanket," Gabriel snaps, hearing that somehow the ice in his veins has reached his voice as well.

Darrek recoils visibly at the words as a pang of guilt hits Gabriel.

"Shit," he groans. "I'm sorry. I didn't mean to compare you to...."

"It's all right," Darrek interrupts. "You don't have to apologize."

Gabriel's forehead creases with worry lines and deep discomfort twists his mouth. He shifts on the cushion, folding his arms tighter across his chest.

"Well, could'ya come over here then? I don't have the plague or something, you know."

Darrek just stares at him warily for a second before sliding sideways. As he lifts an arm to rest behind Gabriel on the couch, he is surprised when Gabriel moves closer to him and tucks himself under Darrek's arm, leaning against his chest.

Wrapping his arms around Gabriel, Darrek doesn't pretend to understand what's going on in his lover's head. He simply holds him close, rubbing some warmth into his arms when another shiver shakes him to the bones.

"I didn't want to make you feel worse," Darrek says. "I figured you wanted some space."

"I don't want space from you. I feel better when you're holding me," Gabriel confesses, moving his knees so that they lean against Darrek's legs. He flips through a few stations on the television and settles on a special on preparing barbeque on the Food Network.

"Hungry? I think we have some chicken cutlets we can throw on the grill."

"Hmm. Maybe," Gabriel grunts. After a loud sigh, he mutes the volume on the program and lets the hand holding the remote fall to his lap. "Listen to me for a second, okay?"

"I've *been* listening to you," Darrek says with a measure of frustration and intense concern.

"I feel like I cheated on you today with Micah."

"Okay, now you're being *ridiculous,*" Darrek sighs. "He took advantage of you! That's not your fault!"

"No!" Gabriel argues, sitting up and facing Darrek directly. "I told you! I fucking *liked* it! He jerked me off and I came all over myself like a goddamned...."

"That's biology!" Darrek tells him insistently. He takes hold of Gabriel's gesturing hands in both of his and tries to catch his gaze as well as it flies around the room. "You *know* that! Someone touches you the right way, of course you're going to orgasm. It has nothing to do with anything! It doesn't mean you're responsible for what happened, with Micah *or* with Harry!"

"But it... it felt good. It felt really good. Well parts of it, at least," Gabriel sputters, curling back up into himself.

Leaning forward, Darrek places a kiss on Gabriel's forehead and says, "Hey. I love you. It's gonna be okay. I promise."

"Love you, too," Gabriel murmurs as a knock sounds at the door.

They both turn, startled, but it's Gabriel who sees the truck in the driveway.

"Ben...."

Darrek is instantly furious. Lips pursed, he gets up off the couch without a word. Catching his arm, Gabriel says gently, "It's okay. Let him in. He's probably here because he's worried about me."

"No Gabe, you're in no kind of shape right now for this shit!"

"Dare, baby, *please*. Let me show him I'm okay," Gabriel pleads.

Wincing at Gabriel's meekness, a clear sign that he is *not* okay, Darrek nods. He squeezes Gabriel's hand once as the knock comes again. It is followed by a shout and then arguing voices.

Walking over to the door and pulling it open, Darrek takes in the sight of Ben and Kyle on the front stoop.

"Dare, I'm so sorry. I tried to convince him to leave you guys alone," Kyle says quickly before Ben can speak.

Ben is mildly taken aback at Kyle's words and the impertinent tone in his voice, but then says to Darrek, "I just want to get the story of what happened directly from Gabriel so that I know how to handle the repercussions for Micah. It'll just take a second."

"Fine. Come in," Darrek says shortly, stepping aside to let them through.

Ben moves past Darrek, going directly over to Gabriel's huddled form on the couch. Kyle hangs back and takes a closer look at Darrek.

"I'm sorry this happened," Kyle says quietly. "If I'd been there, than this wouldn't have..." he stops himself there, changing tactics, and picks up with, "It looks like you're doing a good job helping Gabriel deal with this. He's lucky to have you. How are *you* doing?"

"I'm fine."

Watching Ben talk to Gabriel, catching a word here and there, Darrek feels Kyle looking at him.

"What?" Darrek grunts, shifting uncomfortably, shoving his hands deeply into his pockets and adjusting himself discreetly.

"I know that look," Kyle says.

When Darrek gives him an intentionally confused glare in response, Kyle tugs him toward the kitchen, so that they can talk more privately. He doesn't stop until he's sure Gabriel and Ben can no longer see them.

"What?" Darrek says in annoyance.

"It must be bad if I can see it in your face even with all this other shit going on right now," Kyle says, nodding back to the living room.

"I have *no* idea what you're talking about."

Rolling his eyes, Kyle says quietly, "Ben makes me wear the damn thing almost every day. Believe me, man, I know a look of... discomfort... really fucking well by now."

Darrek blinks at him, frowning more.

"Stubborn ass," he sighs. "Chastity device, am I right? How long you been wearing it?"

"Fuck!" Darrek curses, and then groans into his hands after he covers his face with them. Leaving his features hidden, he mumbles, "Since this morning. I think Gabe forgot about it, since, well, obvious reasons. But it's too tight and it's, like, *chafing* me. A lot. And it sucks *major* ass."

He turns away from the living room, and Gabriel. Putting his back to it and the wall that separates them, he confesses, "I feel like the biggest jerk on the planet right now. Gabe's been traumatized. He's in this really dark, vulnerable place and all I can think about is how horny I've been all day and this *thing* on me. It's really distracting."

"He's got the key, doesn't he?"

"Yeah. And I tried to pick the lock in the bathroom when Gabe wasn't looking, but I can't get it, and I don't know what to do. If I tell him it's bothering me, then he might feel bad for forgetting I had it on in the first place. Plus, I don't want him to think I'm turned on at all by seeing him in pain, and I don't want him to feel obligated to... assist me."

Fidgeting and restless, he turns and walks to the fridge to get a beer.

"Want one?" he asks Kyle, pulling three more out with his own.

"Thanks," Kyle nods. "I'll bring these out to Ben and Gabe. Stay here, I'm not done talking to you yet."

"Tell me what I need to do here," are the first words out of Ben's mouth as he sits next to Gabriel, hunched forward with his hands clasped between his knees. "Do I fire him? Reprimand him? Cut his balls off and stuff 'em down his throat? 'Cause I'd do it."

"Yeah," Gabriel mutters. "Whatever. Look. We should've... talked more... beforehand. We should have set parameters and boundaries, but we didn't, and that's partially my fault. He just went with it, you know? And he went...." The words lodge in his throat. He swallows hard and tries again. "He went too far, and I mean, yeah, he should have seen that I wasn't...."

Gabriel fidgets, and pulls at his sleeves because he is just purely *sick* of talking about all of this. The rest of the words come out without inflection, which only serves to disturb Ben more. "I wasn't okay. I wasn't. At all. And he didn't stop. He saw I was panicking and the fucker used it against me, pushed me further into that place in my head, and...."

"Okay. Plan C it is then," Ben nods, his face drawn.

"No, I mean, maybe I wanted him to. Maybe that's why I didn't remind him about setting up boundaries or why I forgot the safeword. I don't know. But it doesn't matter. I'm done. I'm not—I'm not doing it anymore. Even the video part of it. I'll find something else. But I can't. I can't be there, in that place. Even as a Dominant. Even as a videographer. I quit. I told Sam that I quit."

Ben doesn't respond. He stares out into thin air instead.

"Don't do something stupid, man. Just, um, talk to him. See what he says. I think he got it, that it was fucked up. It might teach him to be a better Dom. It might be good for him, that he experienced this. He's good at it. At Dominating. This isn't... it can't be about Harry. It has to be about what happened between me and Micah, and that's all. Got it?"

Ben is still staring with unfocused eyes and begins restlessly bouncing his knees.

"Say something, you asshole."

"It's a really good thing that Darrek is the one that found you," he says to Gabriel's surprise. "It was good that he got you out of there and.... If I'd been there, Gabe? I would have hurt the son of a bitch a lot worse than a kick in the balls and a split lip. And I know that I need to handle this better than that. I can't get angrier just because it was you. Because he *didn't* know about Harry and all of that. Fuck. *Fuck*!"

Gabriel reaches down and pets Sierra, curled up and dozing at his feet.

"Have you talked to Trace?"

"His phone is off. Went right to voicemail. Told him to call me."

They both turn and see Kyle approaching with two cold beers.

"Hey, can I talk to you for a second?" Kyle says to Ben with a nod to the stairwell, handing Gabriel his beer.

Gabriel nods to Ben and pops off the cap on a side table before taking a drink.

When they've moved slightly out of earshot, Kyle says as quietly as he can to Ben, "Dare needs your help. He's, uh, wearing a locked chastity device, and not one designed for long-term wear. He needs to get it off. But with Gabriel all..." he splays his fingers and quirks an eyebrow to imply the rest.

"He doesn't want to tell Gabriel."

"Yeah," Kyle nods, happy that Ben gets it. "Feels like it's inappropriate, and all. He wouldn't have even said anything to *me*, but I kind of, um, guessed. Do you think you could get the key from Gabe? Or get the cage off yourself? You're good with those little padlocks."

"Darrek needs to grow some balls and tell Gabriel himself. This has nothing to do with us."

"But," Kyle says in exasperation, "He *won't*. He'll take it as some sort of twisted penance for letting this happen to Gabriel and stay in the damn thing night and day until Gabriel remembers and by then his dick might have fallen off!"

"Drama queen."

"Please?" Kyle begs in a whine, scrunching his face up with concern.

"No!"

"*Please?*"

"Still no."

Ben takes his beer from Kyle and heads back into the kitchen with it, leaving Kyle to squint testily after him as he goes.

"Hey," Ben says, pulling Darrek aside. They go through the back door and wind up standing on the back patio on the other side of the closed door. Darrek hears Sierra's nails clicking on the kitchen floor, so he re-opens the door to let her out to run in the yard.

Getting directly to the point, Ben asks, "Okay. I need you to be straight with me. Was Gabriel anally raped? It's not something I would ask him, and I wouldn't ask at all, but if it went that far, Micah is going to suffer more... let's say, *extreme* consequences."

Darrek is taken aback by the query but answers with a curt, "No." When it appears that Ben isn't going to let it go at that, Darrek adds, "It was more... molestation... with a heavy dose of psychological trauma involving his abuse issues."

"Thank you," Ben mutters, biting his thumbnail and thinking. After he seems to have processed it, and made a decision, he says to Darrek, "You handled that well. With Micah. Better than I would have, anyway."

"Thanks," Darrek nods.

"I'm going to talk to Micah, and if he doesn't seem to get what went wrong today, he's gone. But if he's sincerely remorseful and willing to learn from this, I'm just going to suspend him. Sound fair to you?"

He's got his arms crossed over his chest, and though his tone is clipped, it's the warmest Ben has ever been to Darrek. He's treating him as an equal instead of Gabriel's plaything, and Darrek notices the difference.

"I... yeah. That sounds fair. But I don't think it even matters. Gabriel's made up his mind. He's not coming back to work. He's reached his limit. He, he was doing better. You know? He was working through this stuff with Harry and these issues he has, and now.... Now this has all set him back so far. And it makes me so *mad*, I can't even..." Darrek growls, and unconsciously clenches his fists and grinds his teeth. The anger he expresses is tainted by an evident twinge of something else as he shifts his stance and shoves his hands back into his jeans pockets.

Ben sighs, seeing the discomfort immediately, "Let me tell you something, as someone who's known Gabriel for a long time, and has seen him go through bad shit before. He's good. Considering what I'm assuming happened in the dungeon today, before he met you, Darrek, if something like this had happened to him, he would have gone off the deep end. I'm talking no speaking to anyone, and hiding away in that room in Trace's place for fucking weeks at a time. You're good for him. He's a lot more stable than I even hoped for. That's all you, man. So whatever you're doing, keep doing it. You're right, he's getting better. And Micah picked the wrong guy to screw with today, but... I know him, too. In fact, I've known Micah for a few years now. Professionally. He's not an evil guy. He just gets intense. Gabriel doesn't do intense very well. Now Kyle, *Kyle* does intense. Kyle can out-manipulate even a scary guy like Micah."

Darrek feels his lips tease up at the ends in a smile. "Is that why you were okay with him submitting to Micah for training?"

"Yeah. I don't think I need to tell you this, since I'm pretty sure you know this better than anyone, but Kyle's vulnerable spots are nowhere someone like Micah would ever think to look. And the rest of him? Tough as nails."

"But you... it's not weird for you to let him be with someone else? To see him being touched like that? Or even just know that he was getting off with some other guy?"

Ben locks eyes with Darrek, and understands why he's asking. It's a hard question to answer.

"Hmm. Well, I see it this way. If I know about it beforehand and give my permission, then no. It doesn't bother me. Because I know it's just stimulation. It doesn't mean anything. It doesn't change how we feel about each other. But even if it does bother me a little, I remind myself that I trust him, and if something that stupid can mess things up between us, then it wasn't meant to be in the first place."

"Okay," Darrek nods, thinking it through. "Yeah. Yeah, okay. I see what you're sayin'."

"The way Gabriel looks at you, I've never seen that in him. He's happy; even on days like today, when he's freaking out, he's happy because he's got you here with him. If he got off on submitting to Micah... so what? It happens. Doesn't change anything unless you let it."

Sierra comes running up to them with a stick in her mouth. She looks excitedly between them before Darrek wrestles the stick from her, throws it, and sends her running back into the yard to fetch it.

"She's not trying to chase you off anymore," Darrek smiles. "Guess she's startin' to like you."

"Guess so," Ben nods, fishing in his own pocket for something he knows is there. He finds it, closing his fingers around the thin metal of the paperclip. After exhaling a long breath filled with resignation, Ben turns to Darrek. Stepping up to him so that he's facing him and they are shoulder to shoulder, he says quietly near Darrek's ear, "I can pick a lock pretty quickly. And those tiny padlocks are the easiest to pop."

Darrek goes still, and blinks out at the yard.

"I agree that Gabe's in a weird frame of mind at the moment. You wanna wait 'til he's sleeping and get the key from him then, or do you want me to get this thing off of you now? Count to five and it'll be done."

His face turned away, toward Sierra, Darrek's throat works as he lets his body make the choice for him. With a curt nod, it's decided.

Ben goes to his knees in front of him, pulling the short wire from his pocket and undoing Darrek's pants before he's even aware of Ben touching him. Then he feels pressure as Ben lifts the contraption closed around his genitals and fiddles with the lock.

One.

Two.

Three.

Four.

It pops open and Ben frees him of the cage. The metal rings have left angry, dark red abrasions along the length of Darrek's penis. Ben stands as Darrek carefully tucks himself away and zips back up. Handing over the cage, Ben sees Darrek puff out a breath and close his eyes in relief.

"Oh my god," he moans. "I *hate* that thing. I owe you, man."

"If he asks, you picked the lock on your own," Ben tells him.

"Yeah. Thank you."

"Don't mention it. Consider it repayment for what you did for Gabe today."

"I'm gonna... um..." Darrek mutters, nodding to the garage.

Ben smirks knowingly at him, and heads back inside alone.

Chapter 35
What Goes Around Comes Around

Later that night, Darrek and Gabriel are curled up in bed together. Weariness and alcohol are taking effect, but Darrek struggles to stay awake as he senses Gabriel's wakefulness. They'd changed into pajamas after ordering in some Japanese food for dinner and seeing Kyle and Ben off. Gabriel has not mentioned the cock cage, and seeing Darrek naked without it before he'd slipped on loose boxers apparently wasn't enough to spark the memory that he'd been wearing it all day long.

The wind buffets the house as a small storm passes overhead. The timbers of the roof creak, and the windowpane rattles. Gabriel pulls Darrek's thickly muscled forearm against his chest and stares wide-eyed into the dark.

"So, I have to ask," Darrek whispers gruffly.

"Mmm?"

"What in the world did you and Kyle talk about while Ben grilled me for all of your secrets?"

"Oh, um. He was kind of great, actually. Was telling me about how letting people call you on your weak spots, even if they aren't right, lets you confront things and makes you a stronger person. Looking the devil in the eye. And he... he gave me a card. He's got this friend who's a shrink. Thinks she could help me. She specializes in child abuse cases. He said she's easy to talk to."

"Wow," Darrek says in surprise. "That's great. Are you gonna do it? You gonna talk to this woman?"

"Sophia," Gabriel supplies. "Yeah. I think I am."

He leaves it there, and for a long time Darrek just listens to

Gabriel's breathing underlain with the crickets' song from outside, audible under the occasional whistling gusts. Once in awhile, Gabriel will clutch Darrek's arm and trail his fingers up to Darrek's shoulder and then back down again. He is almost lulled to sleep by it when Gabriel says, low and gravelly, like his voice is strained, "I saw you, you know. I saw you with Ben."

Darrek's heart sinks like a stone into his belly and he winces. Trying to adjust their positions so that he can see Gabriel's face, he says, "Let me explain...."

"No."

"Gabriel, please," he asks, saying the words as quickly as he can.

"No!"

Darrek's breath puffs out through his nose in quick little exhales of air as he tries to will his racing heart to calm down.

Gabriel tells him, "I was taking my empty over to the sink, and I put that card from Kyle by the phone so that I wouldn't lose it. I saw him taking the cage off of you. And I saw that you were *hurt*."

His voice cracks on the last word, and Gabriel sucks in a breath, holding it until he's more in control of his emotions. Then, though he had been purposefully preventing Darrek from turning and looking at him by clutching at his arms, Gabriel lets go. He sits up and pulls away despite Darrek's futile efforts to stop him.

"Let me see! I need to see what I did to you."

His face is wrecked; his eyes red and tired. While he pulls at the elastic of Darrek's pants, Darrek grabs hold of his hands and tries to tug him back down into his arms.

"Dare! No, I need to... I need to *SEE*! I forgot about you! And you were hurting and you couldn't even tell me because I'm so fucked up in the head. I don't blame you for not telling me, because I probably would have gotten weird about it anyway, and felt guilty for forgetting. But you had to ask Ben! *Ben* of all people! To get you out of the stupid contraption that *I* put you in and *locked*...."

"Gabriel. STOP," Darrek growls, holding his lover's hands tightly. He feels bad about having to practically yell at him, but with how far gone Gabriel is, Darrek sees it as his only option.

Gabriel's face twists with anguish and he asks softly, "Let me see?"

Turning his face away, Darrek rolls onto his back and tugs the underwear down. Gabriel reaches out and lets his fingertips hover over bright red slashes where the skin is nearly rubbed entirely away. He doesn't touch, though, since Darrek flinches violently away the first time Gabriel gets close. The boxers get tugged back up and Darrek looks Gabriel in the eye.

"Don't you dare feel bad about this, Gabriel! There's a *reason* I didn't tell you. I would never lie to you unless I felt like the alternative would hurt you even more and be counterproductive to everything."

"But I hurt you."

"No! You didn't! And *stop it*! You've done things to me during our sessions that hurt way more than that, and I get off on pain. You know that. It's not a big deal. You had a good reason to forget. And all I... all I want, is for you to stop feeling bad about yourself. I love you... so much, and I... I want you to be okay. You don't seem okay, and it's killing me. So please. Please just lay with me and try to sleep."

Gabriel is curled up on the edge of the bed, away from Darrek, but he relents and lays back down, this time facing him chest to chest. At first he lays there, with closed eyes, intentionally not touching Darrek. But, gradually, he softens. His fingers begin to play over Darrek's chest, tracing the swell of each muscle.

"Good things happened too, today, you know," Darrek says encouragingly. "This morning, you were amazing. That's one of the reasons that damn cage wore on me so bad. I couldn't stop thinking about you and how you made me feel."

"I'm gonna bash that thing with a sledgehammer first thing in the morning and turn it into scrap metal. I swear to you, Darrek, that I will *never* put you in one of those again."

Sighing at that, Darrek wants to argue with him, and to remind him about the spankings that left him unable to sit for the welts on his ass and thighs, the gingerroot that left him burning and in excruciating pain, the tiny clips that sometimes left small tears in his skin, and hell, the time Gabriel fisted him didn't exactly tickle. But then, Darrek figures that it may be best to not remind Gabriel of all the varied ways he's caused Darrek pain in their time together. He knows that Gabriel's guilt is transference of his own reactions to the ways *he's* been hurt. Gabriel is feeling like he's turning into the monster that used to torment *him*.

So, Darrek doesn't argue. He says, "Okay."

"And it was... shocking, actually. Almost as shocking as how stupid I was to forget about you, to see Ben looking at you like that, and talking to you like that. He looked... like he *wanted* you, like he respected you, beyond the sub thing, beyond what you mean to me. And that's a big deal."

"Because Ben hated my guts, and wanted to rip off my dick and nail it to the wall," Darrek supplies.

"Yeah!" Gabriel exclaims, and they laugh.

"Kyle likes you too. He was really worried about you today. He was doing everything he could to help. I think he feels guilty about his part in the whole thing, like if he'd been there and not you, Micah wouldn't have... you know."

They sigh together and Gabriel tucks his head to rest on Darrek's upper arm, against his chest. Each breath is felt by Darrek as Gabriel's exhales heat the patch of skin underneath his thin t-shirt.

"Did you go and jerk off after you were out of the cage?"

"Yeah. In the garage. Wasn't as comfortable as I would have liked, but..." he shrugs.

"I bet Ben wanted to do it for you. Bet he wanted to touch you. Taste you. Suck your aching cock until your knees gave out and you begged for him to stop."

"Um, I'm a little doubtful of that," Darrek says with a lopsided smile.

"No, trust me. I totally could see it in his face when he came back inside," he says. "It's okay. I don't blame him. He can dream, but only *I* get to have you."

"Mm. I like the sound of that," he hums, kissing Gabriel's temple.

"'Night, Dare," he mutters, fingers tangling in his shirt.

"Night," he whispers in response, adding a hopeful, "Sweet dreams."

Meanwhile, back in their own home, Kyle loads the dishwasher and gets the trash ready to be taken outside, emptying the bins from various rooms in the house. He overhears Ben on the phone with Trace when he gets to Ben's office. Kyle sees him pacing, his jaw set and eyes mean.

"We'll handle it! In the morning. Sleep it off. Trace?! Sleep it off! I'll swing by your place. Nine A.M."

Ben looks up at Kyle and shakes his head once, rolling his eyes.

"If I get a call from Lily or the cops saying that you went over there, I am *not* bailing your ass out of jail. And don't fucking laugh. I'm serious, you sick fuck. Okay? ...Yeah."

He hangs up and groans, walking over to Kyle. Ben collapses into him, circling his neck with his arms. After a long exhale, he says, "This sucks."

"Trace knows, I guess?"

"Yeah, Trace knows. This afternoon he was straightening up after we'd all taken off and left him there alone. He was putting away the video equipment and found the tape. Don't know why Micah didn't trash it. Maybe he knew better. But anyway... the dumbass is drunk and angry right now. He's not thinking straight."

He releases Kyle and grabs the trashcan from him.

"I'll do this. I need some air," Ben says tiredly.

Kyle heads upstairs to bed, hearing the back door open and close as Ben goes outside with the bags. Then he's back inside, footsteps creak on the steps and the bathroom door clicks shut. Twenty minutes after that, Ben appears by the bed, and slides under the sheet next to Kyle.

Unsure of what to expect, but assuming that Ben's too worn out to fool around, Kyle decides to ask about what's been at the back of his mind since he saw Ben reenter Gabriel and Darrek's house alone after speaking with Darrek.

"Hey, um..." Kyle says meekly, "I was just wondering.... With you and Darrek, today.... You took him out to talk...?"

Ben sighs and rolls over on top of Kyle who's lying on his back naked, without even the collar on. The circle of leather sits, instead, on top of his bureau, unlocked and ready. Shifting and sliding a knee between Kyle's thighs, Ben drags it up. He feels that Kyle is soft and asking out of curiosity alone.

"I picked the lock. It wasn't my place to do it, and Gabe's probably gonna be pissed if he finds out, but... I did it."

"Good," Kyle says in a relieved breath of air over Ben's shoulder.

"Know what I think?" Ben asks as he rolls his hips, rutting down against Kyle's upper thigh, dragging his very interested cock over tight muscle to ease the ache.

"Mmm. No, sir," he replies, using the honorific out of habit alone.

"I think you just wanted me to get my hands on Darrek's cock."

Kyle freezes, his eyes widening. He sees in Ben's eyes that it's true, and that it also appears to be part of the reason for Ben's present mood. It's astonishing—touching Darrek's dick made Ben hard.

A hand closes around Kyle's slowly swelling cock and Ben sucks at the sensitive spot behind his ear as he continues to push his own hardness in a slow, constant grind against Kyle's thigh.

"Did you?" Kyle asks.

Practically able to hear the thoughts and fantasies churning around in Kyle's brain, Ben chuckles and squeezes his hand tighter around throbbing flesh.

"Come on," he pleads in a whine when Ben holds out on him, "Tell me."

A pause and then an amused, "Yeah."

The admission gets Kyle to moan thickly and it only makes Ben smile wider.

"Got on my knees in front of his bound cock and..."

"*Fuck...*" Kyle gasps, pushing up into Ben's tugging hand.

He can see it happening, can see the look that must have been on Darrek's face: fear, need, resignation. He asks Ben a vague, "When you touched him, did you want to...?"

"Play with his dick like I'm doing to you right now?"

"Yeah."

"Maybe suck him, see what's got Gabe all hot and bothered. Or maybe order *you* to suck him off instead and watch how crazy it makes you. Blindfold you, cuff your wrists. Make you suck Darrek's dick while me and Gabe watch. Get your mouth all stuffed full of him while I fuck your tight little hole."

Kyle whimpers. Ben can feel that he's close, so he shifts. Straddling both of Kyle's thighs, he takes both their cocks tightly in hand, pumping his fist in a blur of motion up and down shafts well-slicked with pre-come. Kyle arches up off the bed and makes his plaintive, low kitten-like purrs and mewls that go right to Ben's dick.

"You, you wouldn't," Kyle gasps. "You're just... fucking with me."

"Am I?" Ben teases. "Or, am I being serious?"

Kyle stares up at him, lust-addled and pupils blown. His stomach muscles are rock hard, knotted up as he gets ready to shoot. Unable to maintain eye contact, he writhes on the bed under Ben, his head snapping back into the pillow.

"Uuh! *Mmm....* Ga-Gabe would never go for it," Kyle mumbles in delirious argument.

"I think he'd want to lick Darrek's come out of your mouth while I rode your pretty ass. Suck the salty taste of him off of your pink tongue. And Darrek would watch. Watch you take it from both ends, impaled on my dick while Gabe tongue-fucked his spunk out of your mouth."

Then he's seizing up, slamming his hips up, spasming beneath Ben's hand. Grabbing at Ben's neck, Kyle pulls him down into a rough kiss, as he cries out and unloads onto his chest. Ben is quick to follow.

"You evil fucking bastard," Kyle pants as he wraps his legs around his lover to keep him there. "God, I love you."

Ben laughs, kissing over Kyle's bare neck.

The next morning, a truck pulls up in front of a nice little house two towns over from Diadem. There's only one car in the driveway, as hoped.

"We clear?" asks the driver.

"Yep," grunts Trace, taking the proffered switchblade and slipping it under the cuff of his shirtsleeve.

The front door is ajar, letting some of the morning breeze filter through the screen door and into the house. Trace has been here before, knows the layout inside. He gets silently up onto the front porch and waits by the side of the door until he sees Micah's figure in the kitchen, down the short hallway that leads back from the foyer. Then Trace is moving. He gets inside, eases the screen door shut without letting it bang and then is back through the house to Micah in only a handful of rapid steps.

With a sweep of his foot, Trace gets Micah's feet out from under him, sending him falling to his knees. Trace pins him there by planting his knees on the backs of Micah's calves, yanking Micah's arms behind his back.

"Trace, give me a chance to..." Micah growls defiantly, recovering quickly from the initial jolt of shock.

"Shut up," Trace hisses with a snarl curling his lips, his eyes blank and dead.

Micah hears the metallic snick of the blade popping open, feels a hand push down the front of his drawstring pants. As a cold, sharp edge is pressed underneath his balls, Micah makes a sick grunt and gets very still.

"That's right. Don't move. It'd be *really* bad if you moved so much as a hair right now, so act like a statue and listen to me. Now, see, Benny wanted to get to do this, but then I figured you might not take him *seriously*. 'Cause Benny's done something like this to you before, hasn't he? 'Cause sometimes you *like* to be afraid. So, he'd tickle your nuts with a knife. Huh?"

Trace angles his wrist slightly, pushing the well-sharpened edge against the skin. A small, warm trickle of thick fluid slides over Trace's fingers.

"Don't!" Micah cries, trying to draw his hips backward and get away from the blade. Trace simply uses his body to prevent escape, pressing closer to Micah's back.

"But, you know me," Trace croons darkly. "Don't you? I don't fuck around. Not when it comes to this shit. You know I'd do it. Slice 'em right off, right here. Wouldn't I?"

"I didn't mean to hurt Gabriel!" Micah yells, breathing roughly, his face tight with anger.

"You *did* hurt him, though. And do you know why? *Because you didn't respect his boundaries.* You saw it was messing with his head, and you didn't stop. So this is your punishment. Now I'm not gonna respect *your* boundaries. Tit for tat."

Trace slides his thumb above Micah's sac, pressing down while pushing the blade up from beneath. It's gentle pressure, feather-light, and Micah knows that if Trace pushes any harder the blade will cut right through.

"Do I have your attention now?"

"Yes!!"

"What we do with our clients is a very intimate thing. The most important thing to remember is that there are some places it is *not okay to go.* And when you go there, *that* is when it goes from dominating to barbarism and rape. Understand?"

"Yes," Micah grunts, his rebelliousness growing less vigorous by the second as Trace's words pierce his fog of fear and sink in.

"Gabriel's stepdaddy started fucking him when he was just a boy. You know that?"

"Oh, *Jesus,*" Micah groans, and Trace is pleased to see his face twist with nausea.

"And he never stopped. Gabriel was his *son* and Harry raped him over and over again. For *years.* And Gabriel didn't have anywhere to go, no one to help him, so he ran away. Started staying with me when he wasn't yet eighteen. So, Gabriel is *my* responsibility. I take care of him when no one else is around to do it. I was here before his little boyfriend showed up, and I'll be here long after he's gone. If you mess up my boy? You will fucking *pay for it.*"

"I don't think I'm the one you want to be talking to," Micah retorts.

"You think I haven't tried to get my hands on that piece of filth? Gabriel won't even tell us the guy's last name, won't even say aloud the name of the town he grew up in. Because he *knows* what we'd do if we ever got that information."

"But Gabriel's social security number is on his employment papers, right? It'd be nothing to go online and pull up his info using that."

Micah hears Trace take a slow, deep breath before answering. "There's two problems with that. First is that I'm not a motherfucking computer wiz. Second, Gabriel is family. You don't betray family by hiring a private detective to investigate them behind their backs, especially when they have pretty profound trust issues."

"But you have thought about it."

The knife twists and Micah cries out, in fear more than pain.

"Drop it," Trace growls.

"Okay! Okay! Well, if you ever find out where the kiddie-fucker is, count me in on the payback."

Trace sighs and carefully extracts his hand without doing further damage. He eases back and stands up, letting Micah go.

He struggles to his feet and turns so that he's face-to-face with Trace.

"It was a bad judgment call with Gabriel, and I know that now. I understand completely."

Micah's eyes burn with visible hurt that it was Trace that had to do this, but he accepts the reasons why. He also sees the roiling emotions in Trace, and feels marginally better when he recognizes regret for his actions hidden in Trace's eyes. Part of Trace didn't want to ever have to hurt Micah like this, but his loyalties to Gabriel easily won out.

"Take a couple of weeks off. If you're still interested in the job after that, give us a call."

His gaze falls to the smattering of blood drops soaking into Micah's cotton pants.

"Get yourself cleaned up. This is settled now. It's done."

Micah nods, crossing his arms over his chest.

Trace wipes the blade off on his shirt before snapping it shut. "But if I get wind of you saying *a word* to Gabriel, or if you even *look* at him funny.... And the same goes for what I told you. That was in confidence. Keep your mouth shut about it. Even with Lily. *Comprende*?"

"Yeah," he says shortly.

A few heavy footsteps and a slam of a screen door later, Trace is gone. Micah walks to the front of the house to lock up. When he gets there, he watches from the shadows as Ben, Micah's Dom, revs the truck's engine and takes off down the road with Trace, Micah's lover, riding shotgun. Pain, heavy and creeping, threatens to swallow Micah whole, and only some of it is from the wound between his legs.

There isn't a doubt in his mind what he needs to do. Trace had left the door open for him. All that's left is for Micah to walk through it. It doesn't matter that Trace told him to drop it. It's Trace's job to say that. It's part of the act. That's how Trace's conscience stays clear. Micah, on the other hand, has no misgivings whatsoever about doing a search on Gabriel Hunter's past. Trace's revelations regarding said past make Micah certain that he's already violated the man in much worse ways than a simple background search would. And if all goes as Micah plans, Gabriel never has to know about any of it. Vengeance can finally be had, Micah can find a way to live with the way he's betrayed a friend, and he can get back in Trace and Ben's good graces.

Micah glances at the clock on the wall. It's early. Sam is gone. Trace and Ben are accounted for. It's hours before they're due at the office. Micah would bet money that the last place on Earth Gabriel would be is at Diadem. The building is most likely vacant, and one peek at the parking lot in front would tell him so anyway once he gets there.

Groaning, Micah cups himself, feeling a small amount of wet, warm blood seeping through the fabric under his crotch. Twenty minutes, he tells himself. Twenty minutes to patch up his wound, get a change of clothes and he can set out to do what no one else will. For Gabriel's sake most of all, Micah knows he has no choice.

Chapter 36
Sharks in the Water

Darrek calls Gabriel from work at every available chance he gets. Sneaking off to hidden alcoves and wandering off-site to seek out privacy, he calls again and again, finding each time that Gabriel is fine, and relaxing with Sierra in the house or backyard. And each time, Gabriel doesn't want to talk. He cuts the conversation short whenever it drifts into serious territory, finding excuses to go, whether it is Sierra misbehaving or a call on the other line. Of course, this only worries Darrek more, and provokes further calls.

Somehow, he makes it through the workday, and is happy to be driving home for a face-to-face talk with Gabriel. Darrek firmly believes that avoiding help and conversation will only make things worse.

Pulling into the driveway, Darrek can hear a reverberating, constant noise coming from their house, even from inside his truck with the windows rolled up and the house shut-up tightly. He leaps from the vehicle and hurries up to the front door to find out what's going on.

Unlocking the front door, it slams it open. Darrek calls Gabriel's name. It gets lost in the din of music, though. The lights in the house are all out except for a dim glow from the upper floor. Darrek follows it, finding that the pounding, bass-heavy electronica is coming from the bedroom as well as the warm, orangey light.

Darrek becomes less worried when he sees the light is from candles lit and placed carefully around the room, and sees new, black silk sheets on the bed. Stupidly he calls out again, knowing he can't be heard over the noise. But just as he's ready to search every shadowy corner and closet for Gabriel, he gets distracted by a note on the bed, the white paper stark against the inky black.

Picking it up and glancing around, Darrek reads the looping script upon it: *"Get undressed. Put on the hood. Lay stomach down and spread-eagle on the bed. Wait for me."*

He can't help it when he rolls his eyes and debates following the instructions. This isn't the time for this. Gabriel should be healing, not thinking about sex and falling back into his role as Darrek's Master. Darrek doesn't move and waves the paper around as he makes up his mind. Then his eye catches what's written on the back of the paper. One word, underlined.

Please.

It helps Darrek do it, seeing that it's not an order, that it's a *request*. He gets undressed, feeling the weight of Gabriel's stare on him from wherever he may be hiding, wondering if Gabriel is seeing him with his own eyes or has rigged up a video camera to do it for him. There are only so many places he could be in the small space and he appears to be in none of them.

Once naked, Darrek marvels at the hood for a minute, feeling its thick, leather texture, fingering over the breathing holes for his nose and the zipper in the back. They have never used anything like it yet in their sessions and it fascinates Darrek. He can see that it'll blindfold him as well as keep his mouth closed tight.

Fitting it over his face, his hair cascading out the back from inside, he slowly zips it up and lies down on the cool, buttery-smooth sheets. Once his hands and ankles are spread, it's only a second later before he feels the bed dip, smells the scent of Gabriel's cucumber soap as Gabriel climbs on. Darrek wants to ask what's going on, if Gabriel is all right. He would say a million things, and even the hood wouldn't stop him from trying if it wasn't for the godforsaken music rattling his brain and drowning everything else out.

Darrek is unsurprised to feel cloth tied around his wrists and ankles, keeping them in position. What happens next also doesn't surprise him. Fingers rubbing lubricant into and around his hole accompany the warmth of Gabriel's mouth, kissing over the dip of his lower back. Once he's well-slicked, the narrow end of something hard and cool is pushed gently through the outer ring of muscle.

Gabriel keeps pressing it inside a few inches before tugging it to the side as the wet trickle of more lubricant is dripped into the cavity. Then the toy is inserted with easy, rocking movements, a little at a time, until all eight, tapered inches are seated deeply inside his ass. Aching from the plug's size alone, Darrek's body adjusts to the intrusion, but Gabriel was too thorough with the prep and pace for it to hurt.

And then, Darrek waits. He waits to see what Gabriel might torment him with – what sort of beautiful pain or anguish will be his fate this night.

That's when Darrek is surprised. He hums with sudden delight and content as the solid warmth of Gabriel's body settles on him, and hands begin to knead at his tired muscles, working the tension out with careful attention. Starting up at the back of his neck, Gabriel works steadily outwards, massaging across the wide span of his shoulders, down his arms, and then over his entire back before going to his lower body. And every touch is punctuated by gentle kisses, presses of Gabriel's full lips to Darrek's rapidly overheating skin, and trailing licks from the point of his tongue.

Darrek's full-body massage isn't completed until even the ends of his fingers and each toe on his feet have been touched, shown love and care.

Relaxed from head to toe, Darrek's moans sharpen behind the leather hood when the toy embedded in his ass is slowly pulled out. Gabriel plays with it, watching Darrek's wet, pink opening swallow it up on each push. He watches as the ring of muscle catches, clenching around it, and tugging against the plastic each time it's gradually extracted.

Then it's gone, and Darrek feels loose. His muscles are soothed but there's a tight, burning pit of need as Gabriel positions himself atop Darrek. Fingers dip inside his now empty and stretched-out orifice, touching him on the inside, stroking over the velvety-soft inner walls in the same careful way for a few precious moments.

Gabriel's mouth seals around the junction of his shoulder and neck. Biting and sucking hard, he enters Darrek in an easy push of his hips, sheathing the length of his fattened cock. Darrek moans at the too-full feeling of Gabriel inside him, and savors the soreness radiating from the spot on his neck that Gabriel continues to worry. Biting gently and licking over the indents from his teeth and the hot, reddened skin, Gabriel deepens the mark. Every feeling is intensified by Darrek's blindness, deafness, muteness, and immobility, as Gabriel wordlessly makes love to him. Each pistoning thrust of Gabriel's cock pounds against his prostate in the most perfect way as he drowns in pleasure.

That's when Darrek figures it out.

Sometimes there are no words, no explanations needed. Sometimes the best thank you is done through actions, not spoken in promises or pleas. Gabriel needed to thank him for being there when he was most needed, and he needed to do it in his own way, with control and a display of power.

Each time a small drop falls onto his shoulders, Darrek feels it, knows them to be Gabriel's tears. He wants to be able to assure his lover about so many things or maybe just touch Gabriel and tell him again how much he is loved. But that's not what Gabriel needs. He needs Darrek to do nothing but let him do this. So, he makes love to Darrek, with the bed vibrating under them with bass, teardrops peppering Darrek's flushed skin. Darrek climaxes even before Gabriel does, the steady, unrelenting rhythm of Gabriel fucking him is more than enough to get Darrek off against the bed.

When Gabriel gets close, Darrek feels fingers clutching the nape of his neck, scratching over the leather covering his scalp. A tingle shoots down Darrek's spine as Gabriel cries out in a jagged scream near his ear. Hips slap and stutter against the swell of his ass as Gabriel unloads, filling him up.

They lay there until Gabriel recovers. Then, before he moves to release Darrek, the music gets turned down enough that Gabriel's words can be heard.

"I want to go to sleep. I'm not talking about anything. Not tonight. I need to just be with you right now. There'll be time for talk later. Okay?"

Darrek nods, grunting his assent and shifts his arms in the bonds.

"That means no talking. Not even a word. Perfect silence. Can you do that? Or do I need to keep the hood on you while I get us cleaned up, and prepare dinner?"

He reluctantly nods again.

"If you can't do it, the hood goes back on. We're doing this at *my* pace, okay? I get that you're worried about me, and that you love me, but this is an order."

With a third nod, the hood comes off. The bonds are untied. He's released. Darrek sits up on the edge of the bed, with Gabriel kneeling between his feet.

There is sadness but deep love in Darrek when he sees Gabriel and his red, puffy eyes. He places a gentle kiss on Gabriel's lips then bows his head, waiting.

But there are no more orders. Gabriel hugs him and says, "Thank you."

It's a difficult night for Darrek to endure, but when he sees how the silence comforts his Master, how Darrek's compliance eases frayed nerves, he is merely happy to give Gabriel what little peace he can as the battle against his ghostly demons wages on.

Trace is exactly where Micah expects him to be—bent over the engine of the classic Chevy parked in his garage. Parking on the street, Micah crosses the lawn in a straight line. The whole way he feels Trace's attention zero in on him, knowing that just because Trace isn't looking at him doesn't mean he isn't calculating the distance between them and planning the best ways to forcefully incapacitate Micah should Trace deem it necessary to do so, or hell, should the mood strike. It's not like Micah is Trace's favorite person in the world at the moment.

Trace doesn't move. Micah gets as close as he needs to, inwardly giving thanks that Trace doesn't lay a finger on him or knock him down to the concrete in a fit of uncorked rage in the name of Gabriel's honor. Staying a foot or two away, Micah holds out a slip of paper, folded once.

"This is for you. Call it an act of contrition if you want."

Trace favors it with the barest of glances before going back to scanning the fan belt for signs of wear. "What the hell is it? Your resignation?"

"Nothing so trite as that. It's a gift, unasked for, but given freely."

"Get the fuck out of here," Trace sighs tiredly. "I'm busy."

Unwilling to turn back, even though Trace might never forgive him for what he's about to do, Micah says bravely, "He's a defense lawyer, specializing in child advocacy cases. Did you know that? I'm guessing you didn't. I'm guessing even Gabriel doesn't know that."

The change these words cause in Trace happens so quickly, but so subtly and profoundly, that Micah has to make a conscious effort not to void his bladder in sheer fright of the man and what Micah knows him to be capable of. Like a starving tiger catching the scent of fresh meat, Trace turns on his prey. Pulling up to his full height and holding Micah with an unwavering, unblinking, predatory stare, Trace whispers, "What did you just say to me?"

"Harry Branden. His address, telephone number, email address, the name of his secretary, it's all here." Trace doesn't move a muscle. The folded paper remains held out between them, untouched. "I already told you the name. Even if you don't take the paper, you could still find him using that alone. It's not a betrayal of Gabriel, it's just happenstance overhearing of pertinent information regarding the true identity of his stepfather."

Fluidly and without hurry, Trace reaches out to his left and wraps his fingers around a heavy, dirty wrench, gripping it like a weapon. Micah starts to tremble visibly. His testicles draw up. He thinks of his wife's smile, the way she appears to glow with inner light when she's truly happy, and prays that these moments aren't his last in the world.

His voice is much less steady than it had been when he says, "He works with *children*. He's been utterly unpunished for his actions. There was one charge, years ago, but it was settled out of court."

Trace surges toward him, and Micah shuts his eyes with dread, trying to breathe though his throat has closed up. A hand grips his wrist painfully and he moans.

"*Please,*" he begs. "We could stop this. We could *end* this, once and for all."

"You had *no right,*" Trace sneers viciously. "You went in his files. You...."

"It was easy. And I'm good at this, you know that. You knew that when you told me how you would never do it yourself. Now it's done and all you have to do is decide whether Gabriel's rapist deserves to be out there destroying the lives of who knows how many other helpless children."

The fear for his life begins to dissipate, but it's still a huge relief when the wrench clatters loudly to the ground and Trace uses the freed hand to take the slip of paper from Micah.

"Oh thank god," Micah groans, willing his racing heartbeat to a slower pace.

A few minutes later, after staring avidly at the information neatly printed out, given over by Micah with all the deadly potential of a live grenade, Trace tells him quietly, "You follow my lead on this from here on out, understand?"

"Yes, sir."

"And you keep your fucking mouth shut, like I assume you have so far."

"Of course. Yes, sir. Are you going to tell Ben?"

They lock eyes, and Trace debates it, the consequences of involving him, and those of not involving him.

With a sharp, angry exhale, Trace nods, "Yeah. You, me and Ben. That's as far as it goes."

"Ben will be able to keep this from Kyle?"

Trace growls his frustration, squeezing Micah's arm until Micah is simply waiting to feel the bones snap. "*Ahh,* s-sorry."

"No," Trace eases up. Micah is grateful. "You're right. Kyle might be able to help in his own way. I'll discuss it with Ben."

"Okay."

Trace releases him.

"We're in this shit now, you know that, right?"

"Yes. I know. Whatever it takes."

Slipping the paper into his pocket and turning toward the house, Trace recedes into the gloom, muttering only a gruff, anxious but resolute, "Goddamn it," before he disappears entirely from sight.

Gabriel is bored. And not the normal kind of pleasant, lazy bored, but a niggling, pestering, restless sort of bored. There are only so many distractions he can indulge in at home, only so many power tools to explore and projects to tinker with, only so many times he can take Sierra for a walk, or go online to check the status of his and Darrek's various accounts before he starts getting stir crazy.

Or at least, that's what he tells himself.

He's stir crazy. That's all.

Putting the computer to sleep without remembering to close the browser window – which is currently displaying the results of his search for a *particular* person's information – he gets Sierra into her collar and leash, and takes her outside, loading her into the back seat of his SUV.

He feels terrible about the current impasse in communication between himself and Darrek. They haven't had a real conversation for over a week. What happened with Micah at Diadem is still something Gabriel just cannot bring himself to open the floodgates on. Soon he'll open up, and 'talk,' but not yet.

Meanwhile, there's a lot he wants to talk to Darrek about regarding *his* issues. They'd never discussed the visit from Darrek's father, or the reality that his family might know all about his status as a gay man now. And the worst part is that Gabriel can *see* how much it's fucking Darrek up to keep that stuff bottled up inside. Darrek's issues are right there like an elephant in the room, rubbing its big, wrinkled, pink shoulders with Gabriel's elephant. No wonder he feels suffocated in the house – it's stuffed full of huge, pink elephants. Also, the fact that Gabriel can't help Darrek and get him to start venting about *his* fears and worries without sounding like a complete and utter hypocrite is very, very plain to him.

Gabriel asks himself if he is actually taking the first steps toward destroying his relationship with Darrek. Is he sabotaging his happiness just so that he can keep his demons under lock and key? Is it really worth losing Darrek over?

He knows it's not worth it. He *knows* that and feels it in the ache of his heart.

But still, Gabriel isn't the type of guy to only go part of the way. He needs to dive right in to murky, churning, shark-infested waters until he's buried up to the tippy-top of his skull in them. And truth be told, his feet have already left the diving board. It's too late to turn back now.

So, he goes to talk with the shrink that Kyle recommended—Sophia O'Malley. He brings the dog with him, because Sierra is tangible, panting, slobbering, smelly, beauteous, incredibly reassuring proof that his life is not what it used to be. He's not just a scared kid on the run anymore. He loves Darrek, and even when he messes everything up, Darrek loves him back. So, Gabriel takes the hot seat in Sophia's office, holds on to Sierra, and starts talking.

It's a nightmarish hour.

It's only an hour, though. That's all. Sixty minutes. And when every single question takes a good five minutes just for Gabriel to figure out what to say in response, the time passes rather quickly.

Feeling only the slightest bit more purged, but purged nonetheless, Gabriel leaves the psychiatrist's office, and plans out his next move.

Chapter 37
From Acceptance of Weakness Is Strength Born

"Damn. That's... weird."

The two-story office building in front of him, sandwiched between a long row of other buildings on the opposite side of town from his shrink's place, looks perfectly normal from the outside. The brickwork is completed, the windows installed, the roof tarred and the sidewalk fully paved. But the inside of the structure is nothing but a shell. There are no floors, no walls are framed out, nothing. You open the front door and there's a sheer, nine-foot drop to the loose gravel ground of the basement level below. It gives Gabriel vertigo and an insane fear that he might walk right off the edge, falling far enough to break an ankle or two just because he knows, logically, that he *shouldn't* do something that crazy.

He's so transfixed by it, that he doesn't see *or* hear Kyle mosey over to him until his voice sounds from Gabriel's right side in a chuckle, "Cheap bastards."

"*Shit!*" Gabriel yelps, jumping a few inches right out of his skin.

"Scared ya?"

"No," Gabriel scoffs. "Absolutely not."

"Yeah, I did," Kyle grins proudly, with something thin jutting out between his teeth.

Gabriel squints at it, so Kyle digs in his pocket, holding out a small plastic container and offering, "Toothpick? I've got some gum, too."

"Dude, oral fixation much?"

"Heh. 'Oral.' Yeah. Totally," he nods. "Well?"

"Eh, sure. Thanks."

He takes one of the toothpicks and bites down on it.

"What're you doing here?" Kyle asks, "Checking up on the wife?"

It's said with affection, but Gabriel can hear the protectiveness in it. He wonders, fleetingly, if Darrek has been complaining at all about the recent tension at home with his best friend.

"Dare's the wife now?" Gabriel retorts.

"Well, *he* doesn't think so, but I keep telling him it ain't so bad. He should just give up fightin' it and embrace it. I know I have."

"Have you?"

"Oh sure. I know I'm the wife. But it all works out. I get what I want. And Ben still has 'issues' with bottoming, so...."

"Still?" Gabriel squints over at Kyle. They've walked a little closer to the building's entrance and are peering down at the workers below. Spotting Darrek immediately, Gabriel watches him work at framing out the sections in to which concrete will be poured.

"Yep. Can you believe it?"

"And I thought *I* was bad," Gabriel says. "I'm, uh... just stopping by. I was in the neighborhood. What's the deal with this place, by the way? Why isn't there anything inside?"

"Plumbing contract hit a snag, as did the electrical. So, they finished the exterior work while negotiations went on. Plus they're still trying to lease the place to someone, and once they do that they'll know more about what they want the inside to be, the layout and all. Detail work."

"Oh. Makes sense."

The silence draws out, punctuated by low banging from the pit in front of them. Darrek hasn't looked up, too focused on what he's doing to notice that he's being watched.

Sensing eyes upon *him*, though, Gabriel glances over at Kyle who's watching him closely.

"Okay, so I went to see Sophia today. Er, well, Dr. O'Malley, I guess. Whatever."

"How'd it go?" Kyle asks, and it's the gentle easiness of his tone that gets Gabriel to answer.

"Good. Better than I thought it would."

Kyle lowers his voice and tugs Gabriel away from the doorway and the tall step-ladder set up for the workers to use to climb down into the basement level. "Look, I know it's none of my business, and Dare hasn't told me much, but I can see it in his face that stuff ain't right between you. He's acting like a kicked puppy. And I *get* how it'd be easy for you to use the whole Dominant thing to keep stuff balanced how you want it to be, but it's *not fair* to him to do that. Because he won't fight you on it. He'll just get more and more unhappy. With me and Ben, it's... different. I don't need to talk about my feelings and shit like Dare does. I hate talking about emotional crap. That's why I appreciate that Ben doesn't need me to do that. But Darrek has this need to make people happy. He's gonna do whatever it takes to make the people he loves feel better, even if he fucks himself over in the process."

Gabriel sighs and turns fully away from the building. He walks a few feet away to a short wall and sits on it. Kyle hesitates, but when Gabriel motions him over, he follows and sits next to him.

"You're right," Gabriel sighs tiredly.

"Gabe, man, I admit that I didn't like you for a long time. But maybe that was because I didn't understand where you were coming from. Obviously Dare loves the hell out of you though. And he would never *hurt* you. You know that, don't you?"

Gabriel doesn't respond, only staring out into the sunshine, chewing his toothpick to splinters.

"Are you just being a dick to make yourself feel better? I mean, I don't see what the problem is."

"*I* do. *I* see it," Gabriel murmurs, almost too low to hear.

But he can't say any more. It won't come out.

Kyle's talent, however, is reading people. He reads people better than anybody. It happens naturally, with little effort. And Kyle loves Darrek in a way entirely different from the way he loves Ben, but it's still real love, and he still would do anything for Darrek.

So, he calls Gabriel on his problem. Because otherwise, everything might just go to hell and hurt the man he loves so very much.

Leaning in close, so that the warm puff of his breath slides over the back of Gabriel's neck, making his skin pebble as much from the tickle of air as much as Kyle's words, he says, "Darrek's easy to hurt. He's *easy* to break apart and I bet he's real fuckin' pretty when he breaks, isn't he? I won't deny I haven't thought about it, what it'd be like to be in your place. I bet he lets you push him really fuckin' far before he says stop, and that it makes you feel better when you do it. But *hurting Darrek* is not going to ever make you feel better, Gabriel. It just makes shit worse. Because what you are doing to Darrek is like what happened to you. You are taking advantage of him, and Darrek's fear of making you unhappy. Why didn't you collar Darrek? Hmm? What stopped you?"

"I don't know."

"*Bullshit,*" Kyle hisses almost angrily.

"Fine," Gabriel relents. "Fine. I didn't want to."

"Why not?"

Because that's not what I want. That's not what Darrek wants, either. Not at all.

"You should know better than *anybody* that it's all right to get off on weird shit. What makes *you* so special? Huh?"

Gabriel pulls away an inch or two, just enough to let him get a better look at Kyle's face.

"I don't even know why I'm talking to you about this."

"That's a good point, Gabe. Why talk to me about the stuff you're afraid to confront when you've got Ben and Trace waiting to take care of you? Matter of fact, why are your best friends a couple of *Dominants?* And why did you start screwing around with them? What were you hoping for? Maybe you wanted a little taste. Maybe you wanted them to keep going and treat you like a client instead of an equal."

"No," Gabriel says, but it's a whisper, faltering and hushed.

"Maybe that's why you never got emotionally attached to your clients before. Your heart wasn't in it. Because *you* wanted to be in the restraints, to take their place."

Gabriel stands up and walks away, down the alley next to the building, but he's not walking quickly and Kyle catches up easily. Even *Gabriel* isn't aware when his footsteps slow more and more the closer Kyle gets. Gabriel is almost at a full stop when he feels the presence of the other man behind him.

It's for Darrek when Kyle pushes Gabriel. Grabbing his wrists hard enough to feel the flutter of his pulse in the thick veins there, he shoves him up against the brick, hidden in shadows. Pressing bodily up against his back, slipping a knee easily between his thighs, Kyle says into Gabriel's ear, "See? See how easy it is? Comes naturally to you, doesn't it?"

His knee pulls up snugly into Gabriel's crotch, his hands tighten on his wrists, pinning them to the wall on either side of Gabriel's shoulders.

Eyes closed and cheeks pink with a mixture of heat and shame, Gabriel tries to bottle up his soft sigh. It comes out anyway as a grunt. There's plenty of nausea and self-hatred behind it though, rising up in his gut.

"What do you *really* want to know, Gabriel? What do you want to ask me?"

"How do you do it? How do you let Ben do *all this shit* to you and still seem so...."

Strong? Capable? Sane?

"'Cause it feels really fuckin' good to let go, and give in, and see what he's gonna do to me. But just because I'm the sub doesn't mean there aren't ways to get my Dom to do what I need him to do. It's all mind games. But he loves me and knows me well enough to *get that* about me. Sometimes he wins the game, sometimes I win. But I trust him and love him enough to let him win sometimes. It's not so scary, you know. Not when you're with someone who would sooner throw himself in front of a bus than cause you real harm."

He lets Gabriel go, but Gabriel doesn't move. Not right away. He stays there, hands planted on the brick, eyes lowered.

"That's what makes it different than being raped or assaulted. You give your *permission*, and it's all done with *love*."

Gabriel stays there, hearing Kyle recede another step.

"Look, I've gotta get back. Do you want me to tell Dare you stopped by?"

Nodding, Gabriel finally turns around. His head is bowed, and he looks more wrecked than Kyle's ever seen him, even more so than that day after the incident with Micah.

Kyle is shocked silent when Gabriel cups his jaw with one hand and kisses him once, softly on the lips before turning and hurrying away down the alley.

"Hey."

"Um, hey. What's up?"

"Can I borrow something?"

"Like what?"

"Your vacuum bed."

"Kinky."

"Shut up, dude. Can I?"

"I guess. Should I bring it over, or do you want to use it here so that we can watch?"

"I'm gonna pretend that you're joking."

"Whatever gets you through the day, Gabe."

"Yes, bring it over."

"You know, they're not that expensive, only about five hundred bucks. Or you can make your own. It's not that hard. Even *I* could do it if I wanted to, so I know *you'd* be perfectly capable of...."

"It's not something I think I'll need to use more than once," he interrupts.

"Whatever. Give me an hour. I'll be there."

"Thanks."

Darrek is glad to be home. It's only four o'clock in the afternoon, but the day had seemed long after getting word from Kyle that Gabriel had been by but hadn't waited around for him to go on break. He wonders about the reason for the spontaneous visit and the odd look on Kyle's face when he'd shared the news. All Darrek wants to do is throw open the truck's driver's side door and run into the house to seek Gabriel out, and ask him what's up. He wants to feel him in his arms and pretend everything is okay. He wants to get a beer and relax, maybe out back while Sierra sniffs out the gopher holes in the yard.

Darrek is glad to be home, but he doesn't do what he wants to do. He doesn't get out of the truck and go inside. He just sits there, in the driveway, and waits for his enthusiasm to die down. Slowly, the urge to take Gabriel, hold him close, and kiss a smile onto his lips, fades back.

Getting himself under control, Darrek finally exits the vehicle and goes up to the front door. Putting himself in a submissive mind-set before he's even inside, Darrek zips his lips and bows his head, ready to be silent and obedient for his Master.

It didn't used to be like this, he thinks. It used to be about letting Gabriel make Darrek feel things he was too afraid to feel. It used to be about release. But now, all it feels like is tension and pain.

He shuts the door quietly behind him and sets down his bag, hangs up his keys.

"I'm home," he calls out, leaving the formality of 'sir' or 'Master' implied but unspoken. The resignation is audible in his voice, however. Darrek wants Gabriel to hear that he's not going to argue with him. Not tonight.

He hears footsteps on the stairs, descending them and approaching him where he stands. Automatically, Darrek's hands link behind his back and he keeps his gaze fixed to the floor beneath his feet as he senses Gabriel getting nearer, smells his cologne faintly in the air.

Gabriel's hand reaches up toward his face and Darrek closes his eyes. Fingers skim over his cheekbone, circle down around his chin, tilting it up.

"Do you know what a vacuum bed is? What it's for?"

"No, sir."

"It's complete sensory deprivation. You lay flat inside an envelope of fourteen gauge latex rubber and get zipped inside. When the motor is switched on, it sucks all of the air out, pulling the latex tightly to your skin from head to toe like shrink wrap. You are blind and mute and all you can hear is the whir of the motor. You can't move, can't do anything. Your only connection with the world is the breathing tube in your mouth.

"Now, the one I have upstairs, and all set up, ready to go, is unique. There have been... *modifications*... to it. Because it's more fun if *something* is left exposed to be played with."

A hand cups Darrek's cock inside his jeans, squeezing around it.

Sighing unevenly, imagining what it will be like to be inside such a device, the helplessness and vulnerability of being immobilized and desensitized while his master torments his genitals, Darrek struggles to find his voice again.

"Y-yes, sir. Whatever you'd like."

Gabriel's hands fall away, and Darrek feels him pull back, putting space between them.

There are a few moments when nothing happens, and because Darrek's eyes are still closed, he doesn't see the wide, glassy look to Gabriel's darkly framed light gray eyes, or the way his whole body begins to tremble in something close to panic.

Then it's Gabriel who can't find his voice. He waits until he's fairly sure it won't break before speaking, saying, "Come up to the bedroom."

Nodding, Darrek's eyes peek open and he follows Gabriel's turned back as they walk upstairs.

As he passes through the doorway, he catches a glimpse of the black framed structure on the bed's mattress. What appears to be PVC is stretched in a rectangle within the latex bag, approximately the size of a twin bed.

His first thought is that he should get undressed and maybe take a shower before they get started, but he's distracted by the realness and intimidating appearance of the device.

Gabriel's voice startles him from his musings, and at first Darrek doesn't notice the shift in his tone, the way his voice raises an octave and quivers on every other word.

"I thought it might be more comfortable on the bed instead of the floor. Not that I'd know how much of a comfort that'll be. I've never been inside one of these before. They're a really effective way to take all power away from someone, though. Really... uh... effective."

Darrek ignores the dull ache in his heart and opens his mouth to ask if he should get undressed when he sees that Gabriel is shirtless and now undoing his pants as well.

"What are you... um... what would you like me to do?"

"Take a look at the motor. See if you understand how the controls work."

Struck dumb, Darrek simply stares at Gabriel and sputters, "Um, why?"

"'Cause I won't be able to answer any questions with the breathing tube down my throat, will I?"

Darrek literally recoils like he's been slapped. Then Gabriel is stepping out of his pants and sliding his boxers down as well.

"No! Gabriel, *no*. I'm not gonna let you do this."

He finds his feet and is next to Gabriel in a flash, holding his arms still and pulling his underwear back up.

"Dare, I *really* didn't want to have a big talk about this beforehand, 'Cause I'll probably chicken the hell out if I do. *Listen to me*. I trust you and I love you, *so much* sometimes that I feel like it's tearing me in half...."

His voice breaks on the last few words and now Darrek can feel him shaking, can see the helpless look in his eyes.

"I need this from you. I need it, and I want to feel you, just you. Show me how good it can be. Show me, and hurt me, and torture me, and make me feel so fucking good like I know that you can until I can't even take it anymore."

"I will *never* hurt you, Gabriel," Darrek hisses, wiping a stray tear away from his cheek as Gabriel kisses the side of his clenched jaw.

"I know, baby," Gabriel says gently. "But you know there's a difference between good pain and bad pain. I'm not afraid of good pain."

Seeing Darrek's gaze drifting over to the black latex again as he envisions having Gabriel under his power like that, Gabriel pulls off his boxers and kicks them away.

"Can't I just hold you? I just want to hold you, Gabe. Let me make love to you and take some of this horrible shit away."

"I can't give you that yet," he confesses. "My head is still so fucked up, and I'm done taking things out on you. This scares the hell out of me, but I can't move forward without conquering that fear. If you do this for me, and show me that it's not something to be afraid of, then maybe I won't be so scared all the time. Please, Darrek? Do you want me to beg? Because I will, if that's what it takes."

No longer able to bear the wide-eyed, innocent terror in the face of someone usually so very strong and capable, Darrek folds Gabriel into his arms. Breathing him in and kissing his temple, Darrek murmurs, "Okay. I'll do it. But this is going to change *everything*. You know that, right?"

"Yeah. Yeah, I know."

"If you need me to stop, hum three times fast and then two times slow. Gabriel?"

Gabriel doesn't respond, nor peel his eyes away from the ceiling. He doesn't look down when he feels Darrek tug his dick and balls through the reinforced hole in the rubber sheet. He just hums once around the breathing tube already in place and waits to be zipped up.

Darrek frowns at the minimal response and leans down over him, getting in Gabriel's face and kissing the bridge of his nose once. It gets him to meet Darrek's eyes, and when Darrek says, "I promise you a *really* strong drink after this. Okay?" Gabriel laughs around the rubber tube.

It makes Darrek feel more confident. It's time to get started.

And then Gabriel is being zipped up. The world is blacked out. The end of the tube is threaded through the small hole made for it, and he's sealed inside. The motor begins to whir loudly, and the latex gets tighter and tighter around him, front and back. He tries to stay still, but his hands twitch and toes curl all on their own and his nervousness intensifies. But then it gets harder to move. Gabriel can't even twitch.

He's stuck. Hugging his eyelids, the arc of his nose, his nostrils, the necklace against his throat, in between each of his toes, the material feels poured onto him, more liquid than fabric. That's when the wave of panic grips him, and his breathing comes fast and harsh through the rubber tube pursed between his lips. His heartbeat pounding under every inch of his skin, he focuses on trying to calm down and relax. It helps when he feels hands—Darrek's big hands—stroking down his body, tracing every line and curve.

When those hands fondle his exposed flesh, Gabriel knows instantly how hard he already is, and fights not to be embarrassed by that.

The touches are gentle at first. What feels like the edge of Darrek's thumbnail traces down the center of the underside of his dick, scratching lightly over skin and the pulsing vein. It traces back up to the crown and scratches over the head, wriggling into the wet slit until Gabriel feels his dick jump in Darrek's hand and *god* he's so close already and they've only just started.

He can't help it though. Darrek could do anything to him right now, with all of Gabriel's supplies and toys at hand to choose from, all of the techniques that Gabriel has performed on him in mind to be inspired by.

Something—probably Darrek's hand—swats his dick, left to right then right to left. There's a pause and then it happens again. Then his balls get smacked, lightly, but repeatedly and Gabriel bites down on the breathing tube. Humming, Gabriel's eyes roll back under his eyelids as the teasing smacks come every few seconds, faster, harder.

Then it stops. And he waits. He can only wait.

Both hands close around him then, swallowing him up almost completely simply because of the monstrous size of Darrek's hands. One is vice-tight around his shaft and the other completely encloses his sac. Gabriel waits, not sure whether to be grateful that he can't hear Darrek's voice or not. The deafness saves him from the teasing mindfuckery that Doms, like himself and Micah, tend to use against their submissives, but it also means he has no clue at all about what's to come.

Both hands start to squeeze him at the same time. Gabriel's body tries to pull away and arc up simultaneously, reflexively, but he doesn't move a hair. He can't twist or draw his legs up. He's as trapped as he was inside the rope with Micah at Diadem, but somehow even more trapped than that. He can't blink, can't move his jaw, inhale through his nose or claw at the bed.

Darrek squeezes Gabriel tighter, hearing his captive moan through the tube. The hot, silky smooth flesh of Gabriel's rock hard cock throbs in his hand. He releases only Gabriel's shaft, staring at how red and thick it is. Again he wonders at how beautiful Gabriel's lean, toned body looks like this, encased in black rubber. He's a statue of himself made of glistening, wet obsidian.

Using his free right hand, his left still clamped around Gabriel's balls, Darrek caresses lightly up and down the latex over Gabriel's body, tracing his thighs, calves and feet, his stomach, chest, arms, and fingers. Everything. He fingers lightly over Gabriel's face, and drags his lips and teeth over the edge of his jaw.

The black marble figure of Gabriel, too perfect to possibly be real, doesn't react other than with small sounds and the twitch of his dick.

Meanwhile, Darrek contracts his other fist in small pulses, softly then firmly, alternating the intensity of his grip. Pressing his ear to Gabriel's cheek, he hears and *feels* his small mewls through the barrier, beneath the steady hum of the motor. Darrek relaxes his hand for five seconds, cradling Gabriel in his fist and rubbing his thumb over the velvety, wrinkled skin.

It doesn't relax Gabriel, though, to have a reprieve, and the hiss of air through the tube as he inhales and exhales gets rougher, more frantic.

Sucking kisses at Gabriel's jaw, Darrek tightens his fist around Gabriel's balls all at once, as hard as he dares. Gabriel cries out through the tube and it's a sharp, keening sound.

Snaking lower, Darrek quickly takes the head of Gabriel's twitching cock between his lips.

He gives the damp, salty-tasting, heated flesh one concentrated *suck.*

That's all it takes.

Gabriel comes like a shotgun going off, jetting into Darrek's mouth, spurting over his tongue and down his throat. Humming with pleased amusement, Darrek sucks Gabriel's pulsing, oozing cock back into his mouth, taking him as far as he can. He doesn't stop until his nose presses at the black rubber and he feels his lips brush the reinforced ring where the latex squeezes around the base of the shaft.

Enclosed in the wet sucking heat of Darrek's mouth, and feeling Darrek's fingers stroking gently over his balls, Gabriel moans loud and long. His brain is as fried as much as his nerve endings, his whole body tingles and shudders with aftershocks, and he gives into the hug of the latex. He's beginning to love the way it forces him to feel every little thing. A prisoner. A mummy. Darrek's captive. Darrek's submissive. Darrek's slave.

Gabriel keeps moaning, because he knows that Darrek's not done with him yet. Not by a long shot.

Chapter 38
Trapped in Free Fall

Darrek debates whether to use a cock ring on Gabriel. Clearly the ring of rubber isn't enough to keep him from ejaculating. But, he decides that he wants to *see* how much this is affecting Gabriel, and if Gabriel needs to climax, Darrek is going to let him.

So, after going to rifle through the drawers in which Gabriel keeps his supplies, Darrek pulls out a few things and brings them back to the bed. Figuring that if Gabriel had decided to keep such things in the house, he was open to using them on Darrek whenever the mood struck, he doesn't feel guilty about using them on Gabriel.

The first thing he uses is a piece of penis jewelry that he's never seen or felt Gabriel use before. It is a small plug connected to two rings that fit around and beneath the ridge of the head. Each of the rings is encircled on the inner edge with rows of small, sharp spikes. Seeing that Gabriel is beginning to harden again just in anticipation, having been laying on the bed and untouched for almost ten minutes, Darrek sits next to him and coats the plug with plenty of thick, gooey lube.

Taking Gabriel's dick between his fingers, Darrek rubs more lube into the already-wet-with-come slit. Under the latex, Gabriel hums twice as he figures out what's going on, and what the prep must mean. The hums turn to whimpers of anticipation and more frantic breathing as Darrek lines up the plug and lets it oh-so-slowly ease its way in, letting gravity do the work. Gabriel's noises grow sharper, and Darrek can *see* his muscles bunching up under the second-skin of the black material.

Gabriel feels the cool metal embedding itself into his urethra, and it feels like he's being pulled apart. It hurts a lot, but in the sickest of ways it's turning him on so *intensely* that heat surges to his groin, pooling there and making him harder. Then the ache grows no deeper. The plug must be in place, but it's not more than a few inches deep, which tells Gabriel that it's not a sound but something else. He figures out *exactly* what it is when the rings snap into place and the points kiss the sensitive skin of his penis, making themselves known and threatening to push deeper if his erection grows thicker.

And he loves Darrek for deciding to use it. His cheeks twitch in what wants to be a smile.

The next thing is ties being wound around and around his balls—the right side then the left—and then Gabriel feels a tug as the first parachute weights are attached. Groaning, the sound of his pleasure twists into a yelp as the metal spikes bite into him deeper.

Pressure builds as the ties cut off blood flow, making his balls feel over-full and ready to burst, even as they're pulled harder and harder as more weight is slowly added. He drinks in the pain, lets it keep his pleasure at bay and ease up the sting from the metal rings around the head of his dick. Remembering advice he'd gotten earlier that day, he tries to take back control, even if it's only control over his own body's reactions.

And it works. At first.

Because then, after Darrek has three one-pound weights attached to each side of Gabriel's sack, and the spikes have pierced the surface of his skin, reddening it in tiny pricks, Darrek dips his head and licks at Gabriel's skin.

He licks up and down and around, along his shaft, teasing the point of his tongue around the end of the silver plug. Then he licks down, sucking kisses down the shaft until he reaches the reddish-purple orbs held in bondage by the thin, silken black cord. Closing his lips around the tight, hot skin, Darrek sucks and flicks his tongue, darting it out in jabs and strokes, at Gabriel's balls, one at a time.

Gabriel's sounds grow wild, almost feverish, and Darrek hears another yelp as Gabriel's dick jumps, suddenly achingly hard, *hugely* hard, and the spikes are sticking him.

But Darrek doesn't have as much willpower as Gabriel. Not by a long shot, not when he sees Gabriel being hurt. He unfastens the metal rings, and gently, carefully, pulls the plug out. It leaves Gabriel's flesh peppered with red marks, his urethra stretched open wide, and Darrek can't help himself when he decides he *needs* to taste and feel that under his tongue. Swiping the flat of his tongue over the hole, pushing the point of the muscle into the new, widened gap, he strokes a hand up and down the shaft. He knows Gabriel can't unload and climax, not with the cord binding him cruelly the way that it is, but Darrek can get him close, can bring him right up to the edge.

Then Darrek's willpower caves a little more because he wants to see Gabriel come again, wants to see it paint over the latex—pearly white on tar black.

His fingers work quickly, clumsily to get the cord off. Every loop he undoes gets another moan of relief from Gabriel's mouth, and encourages Darrek on. Opening his throat, he swallows Gabriel down whole. The muscles in his throat contract and constrict around the organ as he keeps swallowing. Dimly aware that the breathing sounds have cut off sharply, Darrek finally gets the ties off. Sucking as he pulls his mouth off then dives back down on the shaft, his lips sealed up around the thick column, Darrek works quickly, bringing Gabriel to a frenzy.

Strangled sounds are followed by the feeling of flesh turning to unyielding iron on Darrek's tongue. He hurriedly releases Gabriel with a wet pop. Gabriel unloads in a flood for the second time, spurting in long streaks over the rubber. Darrek pumps him through it, fast and hard.

Whining now, Gabriel tries to push up into the rough, tight tugs of Darrek's large, strong hand. When he can't, he feels a second wave of tingling, heated bliss rippling out through his body. Fearful that it's just going to keep going on like this, endlessly, that Darrek's just going to keep him coming and drive him crazy with it, Gabriel makes a decision.

Finding his breath again, and inwardly steadying himself as he feels simultaneously like he's spinning wildly, turning to a boneless heap of mush, and vibrating with increasing claustrophobia,

Gabriel makes the safe sign.

He hums three times quickly and then two times more slowly.

It takes a matter of seconds. The motor gets shut off and the all-consuming pressure eases up. The sweltering, unforgiving heat of his body inside the non-breathing fabric, making sweat course in rivers from every pore, is broken. The zipper gives, and a shaft of light splits the darkness.

"Gabe? What's wrong?" Darrek says with almost suffocating concern as he peels the latex back to see Gabriel's face. He feeds the breathing tube out so that Gabriel can speak.

"I wanna try it without the latex," he croaks.

"What?" Darrek asks, confused. "You wanna keep *going*?"

"Yeah. I want to try it with fewer restraints. I wanna see you, and hear you."

"Okay," Darrek nods, running his fingers over Gabriel's dry lips and sweat-slick skin.

He helps Gabriel get out of the contraption, and gets him settled in a chair while he moves the vacuum bed, setting it aside in the second bedroom. When he returns, biting uncertainly at his lips and hooking his hands on his hips, Darrek looks to Gabriel and wonders how he's going to proceed.

"Um... so.... on the bed?"

"Yeah," Gabriel nods.

Darrek steadies him by grabbing his elbow as Gabriel stands and walks to the bed, sitting and shifting back to the pillows. Covered from head to toe with sweat, his hair stringy with it, skin shiny and face flushed from overstimulation, Gabriel looks absolutely gorgeous and sexy as sin, but also near exhaustion.

"C'mon, Dare," he urges when Darrek hesitates.

"Gabe, you're *so bad* at this," Darrek sighs with a frown, shaking his head. "You need to give me *boundaries!* I don't know what's okay, and what's gonna freak you out."

Averting his eyes, Gabriel laughs with self-deprecation and nods.

"You're right. Did the same damn thing at work, didn't I? Okay. No boundaries. Well, maybe no serious bloodplay or branding, but I don't think you'd do that stuff anyway."

"What about penetration?"

"That's fine."

"You *sure*?" Darrek presses.

"Yes."

"Any requests?"

"Surprise me."

"No, I want you to give me *one* request," Darrek insists with darkened eyes.

Gabriel gazes down and sees how Darrek's jeans are tented in the front around the bulge of his cock, and he warms at the sight, happy that Darrek is at least enjoying this too.

"You know, you're kinda hot when you're bossing me around."

"I think you're avoiding my question."

Gabriel sighs, "Okay. Flogger. The small leather one that's made for CBT."

"Yeah?"

"Yeah," he nods.

"Okay, well I think I have an idea for the restraints. Give me a second to get the cuffs."

Gabriel's lips curl in the smallest of amused smiles as Darrek guides his hands up, getting his arms straight and tight, before handcuffing him snugly, without any give, in soft but thick leather. If Gabriel tries to sit up or arches his back, he's able to bend his arms slightly, but he's got to work to do it. Then he watches with interest while Darrek wraps his ankles in matching cuffs but doesn't chain him to anything. He simply guides Gabriel legs apart and into a sharply bent position with his feet planted flat on the bed. Then he begins to retie the cord around Gabriel's balls, wrapping the loops of silk-lined but strong cord around the base of his sack, right up against his body.

"*Oh shit,*" Gabriel curses as he realizes what Darrek is doing.

Eyes half-lidded, he peers down through his lashes at Darrek as he ties the ends of each of the cords to one of his ankle cuffs. The cord winding around his left testicle gets tied to his left ankle and his right to his right. But they are tied tightly, without give, and Gabriel has to keep his heels almost up against his ass in order to keep from pulling on himself.

Darrek smiles, and it's the most wicked thing Gabriel has ever seen. His splayed, huge hand caresses up through the soft curls of dark hair on Gabriel's leg, up his calf, down his inner thigh. Reaching the junction of his legs, he circles his fingers around Gabriel's dick and slowly strokes it. It's already hard for a third time, and, careful not to give Gabriel any relief, Darrek teases him. He picks up the flogger with his free hand.

"You looked so goddamned beautiful in that latex, Gabe," he says softly. "Like a work of art. Made me want to lick you from head to toe."

Releasing Gabriel, he stops stroking him, and watches his cock arc back up toward his belly. Darrek tickles the ends of the flogger's tails over Gabriel's red shaft and then down to the exposed, over-sensitive red orbs of his balls inside the cord.

"I think I'll warm you up a little first. Then I'm gonna get my fingers stuffed up inside your pretty pink hole, see you squirm on my hand and make all those sweet sounds for me."

Gabriel curses again and tenses his muscles in anticipation of the first lash from the tiny whip.

Snapping his wrist, and flicking the leather tails over his hand, they spin and strike squarely between Gabriel's legs, hitting the underside of his shaft.

He moans, clenching his hands into fists and reminding himself not to move his legs.

Darrek doesn't pause. He circles the whip over and over again in a circle as Gabriel's dick jumps and leaks, smearing wet trails over his belly. It goes on and on, and Gabriel counts ten strikes before Darrek shifts his target, aiming lower. The first slap of the whip to his balls makes his feet shoot out even as he instinctively tries to close his knees.

Of course, this makes him yank hard on his ball sac while Darrek just keeps spinning the whip the other way, coming up between his legs instead of down.

"Mmmm... *fuck... FUCK,*" Gabriel groans, his arms tensing up, face scrunching into a grimace.

"You can use your safeword. It's 'Discovery' in case you've

forgotten."

"*Ass*hole," Gabriel grunts, hissing sharply between his teeth.

"Nope, that's not it. I just thought I should remind you. Just in case, you know. 'Cause I know sometimes you forget these things."

"You... are *SO*... gonna pay for this...."

"Oh, I *hope* so," Darrek grins. "What're you gonna do to me, Gabe?"

"Rattan cane. Five lashes right to your taint. You'll be bleeding and crying like a baby."

"Ouch," Darrek teases. He's stopped whipping Gabriel and goes back to rubbing the flogger over his balls, squirting lube onto his fingers out of Gabriel's line of sight.

As soon as he pulls the flogger away, he gets on his knees between Gabriel's legs and leans over him, putting them eye to eye as his fingers find Gabriel's opening and rub gently over it.

"I'm gonna do it. Last chance," he warns.

"*Mmm,*" Gabriel hums, shutting his eyes and frowning.

Darrek's index and middle fingers push inside and Darrek sighs at the tight squeeze of Gabriel's ring of muscle around them. Slowly and shallowly working them in and out, he leans down and licks some of the sweat off of Gabriel's neck, nuzzles his nose into the skin as Gabriel shudders and tenses up.

"You're... n-not a very... scary... Dom..." he sputters with a wavering voice.

"S'okay, Gabe," he hushes as Gabriel keens. "It's okay. You don't have to be brave, you know. You're allowed to be freaked."

"I'm not... f-freaked," he argues weakly.

"Yeah you are."

The fingers pull out with a squelch and Darrek reaches for something, lunging away. He returns with a medium-sized plug that he quickly coats with a thick layer of lubricant.

"Okay. 'Mokay. 'Mokay," Gabriel murmurs to himself, arching up off the bed when it starts to get pressed into him.

But then Darrek kisses him, swallowing his scared words. With a snap of Darrek's wrist it plunges deep, sitting flush against his ass.

"*Mmm*!" Gabriel cries out into Darrek's opened mouth before relaxing a little and kissing him back.

"Good, Gabe. You've got it. You've got it. Gonna leave it there for now."

The next fifteen minutes pass slowly, as Darrek alternately uses the flogger roughly, leaving Gabriel with red marks where the tails bite him, and then gently, tickling him, pebbling his skin and making him shiver. All the while, Darrek plays every now and then with the plug, pushing at it or tugging it out a few inches. Soon Gabriel is a wreck, pupils blown black and delirious with sensation.

Untying his legs, Darrek asks, "You with me? Hey...."

"Mmm," Gabriel hums straining against the chains holding his arms.

"That's not an answer," Darrek frowns, "You wanna be unshackled for this part?"

"Yeah," he sighs. "Yeah, get me out of these so I can touch you."

The leather cuffs come off. Gabriel rotates his shoulders and rubs at the muscles to unknot them. Sliding off the bed, Darrek undresses completely, aware of how Gabriel's lust has somehow replaced the anxiety he has always had when it comes to submitting or bottoming. Unsure if mentioning it will destroy the effect, Darrek keeps his observations to himself and settles between Gabriel's spread legs, hooking them up over each of his shoulders.

"Face-to-face. Like before. That okay?"

"Mm-hmm," Gabriel nods, still sounding woozy. "Do me a favor, though? I'm gonna fuckin' blow if you so much as *look* at my dick right now, and I wanna have a chance to get inside you tonight. Wanna get my turn, so don't... you know... touch it."

Darrek's lips purse sternly, so Gabriel whines, "*C'mon,* Dare! I'm really goddamned horny right now, and all I want is to get fucked and then feel your ass squeezing up around me when I come. That's all I want."

"Maybe a little nap first...."

"Darrek, don' make me hurt you. You jus' whipped my balls for twenty minutes, and I will do *whatever it takes* to fuck yer ass right now. You get me?"

"You know, even when you're drunk you don't sound this wasted," Darrek grins.

"Shut up and *fuck me*, bitch!" Gabriel demands impatiently.

Snorting with laughter, Darrek captures Gabriel's lips in a kiss that quickly deepens.

It's time to see how 'okay' Gabriel really is.

Twenty minutes later finds Gabriel draped over and leaning heavily on Darrek's back. Darrek is on his hands and knees on the bed with four fingers completely buried inside him. He muffles his deep moans in the pillow under his face, riding Gabriel's hand unashamedly. He's pushing back onto it with quick thrusts as fingers stroke and rub up over his inner walls, filling him up so full and splitting him open so far that he suspects that Gabriel might have somehow got that last digit in there and is fisting him instead of fingering him.

He wants to complain, to ask if this is payback, but he already knows it is. It feels awesome but he wants to get fucked. He wants it as bad as Gabriel did a few minutes ago, but the words won't form in his brain. He's on autopilot, humping his lover's hand and chasing his second orgasm.

So worked up over the sight of Gabriel's pleasure, Darrek hadn't lasted long once he was snugly nestled in the throbbing heat of Gabriel's body. It had been rather embarrassing for him, orgasming with a startled shout after four pumps of his hips, but Gabriel had secretly been relieved.

Gabriel had gotten through it by holding on tightly to Darrek and biting down almost hard enough to draw blood on his shoulder. But he hadn't panicked, or gotten afraid. He'd moaned at the too-full feeling and friction of Darrek's dick rubbing inside him, and pushed down into every thrust.

"*Ga*-aaehbbe..." Darrek finally manages to complain, drawing out the name into at least four syllables.

"Maybe I should make you come like this first. God, Dare, you look so goddamned hot fucking yourself on my fingers. I wanna tape this so I can watch it all day when you're away at work. But I'd probably be jerking off so much my dick would get blisters."

A wet squelch and a startling emptiness between his legs is all the warning Darrek gets as Gabriel's hand is removed and instantly replaced by the full length of his tortured dick.

"Ohhhh*fuck* yes..." Gabriel moans wantonly, pulling Darrek back by his hipbones so that their bodies are literally squeezed together. "There's nothing better than this. Nothing."

He draws it out as much as he can, pinching his fingers around himself in a makeshift cock ring to stave off completion. But after everything, Darrek's dominance of him and the near-perfect love making afterwards, Gabriel can't last long either.

Crying out into the sandy curls of Darrek's hair spilling over the back of his tan neck, the smell of their sweat and sex filling his nose and lungs, Gabriel releases everything, emptying himself utterly.

They both collapse down onto the bed, with Gabriel still impaling Darrek's body, and they lay there, trying to recover.

"We need to talk," Darrek whispers eventually.

"Yeah, we do," Gabriel agrees. "And we will. But first I want that strong drink you promised me. And a long, long shower."

Earlier that day

Ben gets the vacuum bed upstairs with minimal assistance from Gabriel. It's lightweight and the size is the biggest challenge. Twisting it to get it over the railing at the top of the stairs and angling in to the left to turn the corner into the bedroom, they manage to get it in place.

"How's it going at work, then?" Gabriel asks, broaching the subject since it looks like Ben's not in a very forthcoming mood. Or maybe he's just trying to protect Gabriel again by keeping him in the dark. Either way, Gabriel would rather know what's going on than be babied.

"Fine," Ben says shortly before removing his head from his ass and realizing he shouldn't be acting so suspiciously reserved if he doesn't want Gabriel to suspect anything. Ben had had a long, involved, complex conversation with Trace shortly after Gabriel had called Ben to ask to borrow the vacuum bed. Now, faced with interacting with his best friend while planning to secretly and thoroughly undo a former member of his family, Ben tries to bury it all and play his part. "Yeah, it's crazy and busy and we, uh, need another guy in there, but we're managing. Micah comes back next week on a trial basis."

"How about the site?" Gabriel asks as they head downstairs.

"Trace and I are splitting duties on that, but we're looking to hire a programmer to manage that stuff long-term," Ben says, looking down when his phone goes off in his jeans pocket. "Shit. Um, give me one second to take this?"

"Sure," Gabriel nods, "Go ahead. I'm gonna go test out the vacuum motor and make sure it's working."

He disappears upstairs.

Ben answers the phone on the fourth ring, once Gabriel has gone through the bedroom doorway.

"Yeah."

"Hey Benny," Trace purrs, his words laced with menace. "You really think this is a good idea, goin' over there when you had murder in your eyes not twenty minutes ago? You think Gabriel's not going to pick up on that? You wanna fuck this whole thing up before we even get started?"

"I got this," Ben says with a confident lilt in his voice. "The bed was a lot lighter than I thought it'd be. Glad you have such confidence in me though, man. I'm done here if you need me to swing by."

"I have confidence in you, kid. We just have to be extra careful, especially around Gabe."

"I know. Catch you later?"

"Sure thing, sweetie pie."

Ben snaps the phone shut, the need to inflict violent revenge long years in the making is threatening to overwhelm him. He beats down his boiling emotions, until once more all he exudes is calm and control. "Hey, Gabe?! I'm gonna take off. You got everything you need up there?"

Gabriel appears at the top of the stairs.

"Yeah. Thanks. I owe you one."

Ben nods then pivots a quarter of a turn back toward the steps. "Oh, speaking of.... Next time I see Darrek, he owes me one, too. An eye for an eye or a kiss for a kiss, eh?"

"Oh..." Gabriel says, eyes suddenly wide, realizing why Ben seemed so off. "I'm sorry about that, Knox. Really. It was just...."

"No, I get it. I do. Kyle's kissable. I'm just giving you fair warning. Darrek's got his coming. Later Gabe. I'll tell Trace that you send your love."

And with that, he's gone with a swing of the screen door and hurried steps down the path.

Chapter 39

Taking Aim

Two rounds of Jack and Coke, two showers, and two reheated burgers later, Gabriel and Darrek sit facing each other at the kitchen table. They are slouched low in their chairs, and looking sleepier by the minute.

"Can we have this talk in bed?" Gabriel asks hopefully.

"Nope. I need you conscious for this. I've been waiting a full week for this talk, ya know. But we can make it fast."

"Okay," Gabriel sighs, swirling the dregs of his alcohol inside the short glass. "You go first."

"What does that mean?"

Rolling his eyes, he says, "Ask me something. What do you want to know?"

"Um... okay, uh.... What just happened upstairs... with me dominating you and you asking me to have sex? What does that *mean* exactly? 'Cause I'm a little confused. Well-fucked, sore and happy, but confused."

"Fair enough," Gabriel nods, tapping the bottom rim of his glass on the tabletop. "It means no more rules. I don't want any more rules between us. You do what *you* want to do, and I do what *I* want to do. If I want you to fuck me raw up against the dishwasher, or you want to tie me up and spank me, you can do that. If I want to shackle you to our bench upstairs and dominate you for hours until you pass right the hell out, I can do that too. I don't want you to be afraid of me, or treat me like I'm fragile, or treat me like all I am is your Master. I want more than that. I want to just be in love with you. Like a normal person."

"Wow," Darrek says, reaching across the table for Gabriel's hand. "All right. No rules then. I can do that. You get what you want and I get what I want? Which is you, by the way."

"Yep," Gabriel nods. "Okay, my turn. I want to take you to see your family. Like a visit. They deserve to know you're doing fine."

"Whoa... what? Gabe...."

"No. No arguing about this. Your mom is worried about you, Dare. Your dad said so, and I don't think it's completely healthy the way that you've cut your whole family out of your life. And before you say anything, because I can see your lips moving like they're revving up for a doozy of a comeback, I realize that saying that makes me sound like a major hypocrite. Which is why I've been thinking about going to Texas to face my mom and Harry, too, just to show them that I'm alive and that no matter what my stepfather did, he didn't keep me from living my life."

"Are you sure? That's... a really big deal."

"No, honestly. I'm not sure. At all. But I looked him up today online."

"Harry?"

"Yep. Still a big shot at his stupid firm, but apparently he divorced my mom a few years ago. But let's come back to that one. Your turn again."

"I think we should talk about the whole visiting-our-fucked-up-families thing a little more."

"It's not something we have to do if you're really against it, but I *will* insist that you at least call your mom. Just that."

"A call. One call. I think I can do that. Okay, hmm.... Oh. Um, where'd that vacuum bed come from? Did you buy it today? Did you have it at Trace's?"

"I borrowed it. From Ben. It's his."

Darrek's eyes pop, and his eyebrows jump in surprise.

"Don't... imagine it," Gabriel says, holding up a hand. "Just... don't. But that leads me to my next confession. I kind of kissed Kyle today. And Ben told me that the next time he sees you that he's going to kiss you as, like, payback. Or something. It's ridiculous, but I'm pretty sure he meant it."

Darrek simply stares blankly at him for a second. Then he

gets up out of his seat and slides it around the table so that he sits right next to Gabriel, knee to knee. "Okay. Um, *WHY* did you kiss Kyle?"

"Huh, uh. It's kind of complicated. Well, first off, I went to see Dr. O'Malley today. The head shrinker. And then after that appointment I had to see you, so I went to your work. But Kyle was there and it was like he saw right into my head and figured out how freaked I was about wanting to submit to you. And he pretty much talked me into doing it. There might have been a little bit of literal pushing me up against the wall and kneeing of my crotch but he was just trying to make a point. Anyway, um. He told me that I owed it to you to trust you that much, that anything you would do with me would be done with love, and not to control me. And I felt so much better. He really, really helped me, and I was grateful, so I kissed him. Like a thank you. Plus, I kind of wanted to see what all the fuss was about."

Darrek doesn't say anything. His brain is pretty much incapable of processing that amount of startling information quickly enough to have any sort of reaction to it.

"So I fully give you permission to kiss Ben," Gabriel tells him. When Darrek still doesn't respond, Gabriel says, "You're picturing it, aren't you?"

"Uhh...."

"It was amazing how much Kyle was standing up for you. He's really on your side, you know. He's a good friend. I despise him less now."

"You kissed Kyle. I'm ignoring the whole wall part, though, because... yeah. Brain-melting and, um...."

"Are you mad at me?"

"Um...."

"Darrek?"

"Oh god. Ben's gonna kiss me."

"Yeah. He's good on the follow-through with this sort of thing. You *can* say no. You're bigger than him anyway... could probably snap him in half if you wanted, but..."

"Gabe?"

"Yeah?"

"Are you okay? I mean really, really okay? Did the doctor help at all? I'm just... all this stuff with Kyle and Ben... I'm worried about *you*," Darrek sighs. "The rest of it..." he shrugs, "Doesn't matter to me."

"I'm just trying to get my head on straight. I think I've been only half-living my life for a long time. I'm done with that though. I need to be who I am, flaws, scars and all. So, are we good? Can I go collapse in bed now?" he asks hopefully as he stands and brings his empty glass to the sink.

"Yeah. C'mon," Darrek grins, taking his hand. "Sleep sounds good to me too."

Ben sits restlessly on the edge of the bed as, in the next room, he hears the water in the shower turn off. His mind and body are on fire with excitement and an overload of energy, which he absolutely intends to use to full advantage on Kyle.

There's movement and rustling as Kyle dries off. Water runs in the sink as he brushes his teeth. When he finally emerges into the bedroom, his steps falter once he sees the dark intent in Ben's eyes.

A shiver races down his spine and he only has time to mumble, "*Fuck*ing hell," before Ben is on him.

Kyle gets manhandled forward and slammed up against the bench in the room's corner. Pushed down into position on the kneeler, Ben bends him sharply in half to lay facedown against the top.

"Hands," Ben growls, and Kyle quickly plants them with his fingers spread loosely by his shoulders. Then he feels the small plug inside him get tugged out once, pushed downward firmly and painfully at his rim as it's removed. He grunts quietly at the ache it causes. Expecting Ben to get rid of it, it just pushes back inside, along with something else, something much thicker and bigger than itself.

Kyle sputters, "S-sir?"

"Silence!"

The command is punctuated by a hard slap to the dark bruise he already carries on his backside.

The toy and Ben's dick ease slowly, carefully inside and Kyle remains quiet, straining, breathing roughly through his nose as he grits his teeth to hold any sound in. All his fingers tense, the joints locking and splayed out in a wide fan on the bench's top as he's otherwise pinned down, unable to escape the two things stuffing him gradually full.

He doesn't know if what Ben is doing has anything to do with what happened with Kyle and Gabriel earlier, if Ben is still wound-up over that or if it's something else entirely. The most difficult part for Kyle is staying quiet. Small sounds slip out despite his best efforts, mixed with the rasping of his breathing as he drinks in every exquisite ounce of the pain.

"What do you think, kitty? Is this punishment?" Ben asks as he pushes his hips hard, watching the rest of his shaft get engulfed in the stretched-wide hole, all the way to the root. Pulling back just far enough to grab the plug and twist it, he pushes it farther in as well.

"*Ahh!*" Kyle gasps, trying to writhe away. He gets another hard slap to the side of his ass, and when *that* doesn't have enough effect, Ben reaches under between Kyle's spread thighs and pinches tightly at the sensitive flesh near the base of his sac.

Whining sharply, Kyle stills and quiets down.

"As I was saying.... Is this punishment for being such a dirty fucking *whore?* Or is this *prep*?" Ben asks him low and intently. "Just how many cocks do you think we can fit in you at the same time? Should we find out? I think I want to find out...."

Kyle knows better than to answer, but his eyes go wide at the implication.

An hour later, they've moved to the bed. Ass throbbing but sated, Kyle finishes Ben off with a thorough blowjob. He's surprised when Ben spreads out his legs as he approaches his climax, getting them parted enough for Kyle to get a single finger inside Ben as he comes hard into Kyle's mouth.

Kyle's cheek rests softly in the slight concave dip of Ben's pelvis as he recovers, and he runs a hand up and down Ben's thigh to soothe him.

"Thank you, sir," he whispers, wondering if Ben is going to fall asleep before he can glean what's on his mind. He's now very certain indeed that something is on his Master's mind.

"I want to ask you something," Ben murmurs, the hard edge gone from his voice for the moment. "Theoretically, in your opinion, should a dangerous person be held accountable for their crimes?"

Kyle frowns, propping himself up on his elbows to better see Ben's face.

"Of course. Yeah," he answers.

"What if there's no chance that the law will do it, and the only way to stop them is to take matters into your own hands?"

"Hey, what's this about?"

"Just answer," Ben prods.

"Well, it depends on how dangerous they are, and who's going to be hurt and how badly. You can't just make a blanket statement...."

"What if the person rapes kids?" Ben says quickly. "And they're out there, *free*, and no one knows what they've done... or knows what they're probably still doing? The recidivism rate on that type of thing is through the damn roof. Guaran-fucking-teed they'll do it again and again and again."

Kyle locks eyes with him, then slowly nods. Aware that Ben knows he's not dumb, this is the closest he's going to ever come to telling Kyle flat out what's going on here.

"The fuck are you gonna do to him, Ben?" he asks quietly. "You think Gabriel would really want you to do this?"

"I'm only talking about *justice*. Nothing extreme or unwarranted. Only justice, and only enough of it to keep more people from getting hurt. Just that. And look... you *cannot* tell Gabriel *anything*. Or Darrek. That's a motherfucking order."

Kyle doesn't say anything, but keeps watching his eyes.

"We'll be careful. You know that," Ben assures him gently.

"You better be."

"I'm doing this *with* you," is the low purr of words by Trace's ear. When Trace tightens his grip, however, the words break off and turn into a yelp. Micah had been there during Trace's conversation with Ben. Trace has been keeping Micah on a very short leash, sometimes literally, since becoming aware of Harry's whereabouts.

"No, you're not. You're staying here. Ben and I will handle the rest."

"No. I'm coming," he insists.

Trace rotates his wrist in a slow clockwise motion and Micah screams sharply.

"Not if I forbid it. You have no idea what you're getting your delicate little ass into."

Exhaling in gruff pants, he chokes out, "Fucking Harry up? Getting blood on our hands? I got it."

Trace laughs darkly and *pulls,* hard. Moved beyond the ability to yell, Micah simply gapes soundlessly, his mouth working.

"Shhhh... good. *Good* boy," Trace croons.

The next morning, Darrek and Kyle are seated on the same low wall that Gabriel had rested on when coming to visit the job site the day before. Darrek catches himself staring down the alleyway and imagining what had reportedly happened between his lover and his best friend. A few feet away in the basement level of the building they're working on, the concrete has been poured and they are waiting for it to set while they have their lunch.

He had told Kyle about his plan to call home, but has yet to hear his response to the idea. Darrek thinks Kyle has been exceedingly quiet the whole morning though, and wonders if that may be guilt or confusion over his encounter with Gabriel.

"Maybe I'll just call right now," Darrek thinks aloud to himself. "Get it over with. We aren't going anywhere anytime soon and she might be home. Dad would be over at the church so there'd be less of a chance of getting him instead."

"What if you get Steven? Or Sara? They could be visiting the house. It could happen. That asshole brother of yours could pick up the phone and you'd have to talk to him. You might call to talk to your mom with perfectly good intentions of pretending like you give a shit whether she knows you're alive or not, which you shouldn't by the way, and wind up getting a lecture from Steven on how pathetic you are for letting a heartless skank like Sara slip through your fingers," Kyle sneers, picking at the skin of his shiny red apple.

"Ohhhkay. Sure. It's possible. I guess. I take it you don't want me callin'?"

"They don't deserve the courtesy. Any of them. Your mentally and physically abusive, religious freak of a father; your mom who couldn't be bothered to pry her nose out of a bible long enough to stand up for you, like, *ever*; your rotten brother; they all treated you like shit. You've moved on, Dare. You have a good life now, without them, and calling isn't going to change anything. It's not going to make you happier. It just gives them more opportunity to make your life miserable. Forget them, dude. They aren't worth it."

"Hmm," Darrek ponders, "I see where you're coming from. Solid arguments, I can't deny it. You may be biased, though."

"Fuck yeah, I'm biased. You used to be biased too!" Kyle huffs in astonishment. "What's up with this change of heart? You never showed any interest in forgiving those bastards before."

"Yeah, well, if Gabe can try to move on, and heal old wounds that are much worse than mine, who am I to stay bitter and immature? Forgiving them doesn't change the fact that they have to live with the choices they've made. They'll never have a close relationship with me again, because they don't deserve the privilege. But forgiveness does help me let go of any lingering resentment and shut the door on the past."

"Dammit! I hate when you're logical."

"Heh," Darrek grins. "He's talking about going down there, you know. Gabe. And standing up for the man he's become, chasing those old ghosts away and telling that prick he can go burn in hell. I think it'd be really good for him, you know? He could show himself how strong he is. And I'd be with him. Keep him safe."

Kyle bites his tongue and squints sideways up at him.

"You're fucking insane. Both of you."

"Maybe. Maybe we're saner than ever."

"Huh... Doubtful. So he's going to go see Harry? Like, soon?" Kyle mumbles and shifts uncomfortably.

"Yeah, seems like it. We'll see."

A few minutes later, Darrek manages to find the courage to dial the number to his childhood home with shaky hands and a pounding heartbeat. It's picked up on the fourth ring, just when hope begins to bloom that no one will be home and he can just leave a message on the answering machine.

"Hello?" a woman's lilting voice asks.

"Mama? It's Darrek."

There's a pause and Darrek braces himself, biting his thumbnail nervously.

"It can't be. Darrek?? That's really you? Oh *sweetheart*! I've been so worried about you! How are you? Are you okay? You haven't called and what's a mother to do but fret and pray that God's keeping you safe."

"I'm fine, Mama. Just fine. I'm... at work right now, so I can't talk long. But I promised Dad I'd call you and I'm sorry I didn't do it sooner, but I needed to figure stuff out for myself. There's no need to worry about me anymore. I've got a good life up here."

The weight clenching his heart had caused his shoulders to sag, too—a weight built up with anxiety and from the beginnings of a regression into the wound-up, repressed man he used to be. But the longer the call goes on, the more Darrek realizes how much things have changed for him. He is a different person now—stronger, and more able to withstand fear and looming threats, real or imagined. Darrek feels much better for it, and begins to smile with relief.

"I will *always* worry about you, Darrek, if only because you've given me so many reasons to. I'm just so happy to hear your voice. When you left, I never thought you'd be gone for good. I thought it was just you acting out after the business with your brother. I knew you were upset but if I'd have known I was really losing you... I am so sorry for what happened, Darrek. It was all a big misunderstanding. But it's done and over now. I love you. We *all* love you and miss you...s o, so much."

"I'm with someone," he says, feeling brave. "I'm in love. Real, true love. So much more than with Sara. She never understood me. Actually, no one's ever understood me like this before. Not even you, Mama."

There's a pause where she doesn't make a sound. It makes him wonder in a distant way if the accusation hurt her, and how deeply. "I'm glad. You deserve love like that. What's his name again?"

Darrek smiles, "Gabriel."

"What a lovely name. An angel's name."

"You don't have to pretend you approve, Mama. I'd rather you be honest about your feelings. I know Daddy thinks I'm goin' to hell for all I've done."

"Your Daddy is full of horse pucky sometimes, and that's God's honest truth. It's just who he is, and he'll never be any different. Is he good to you? This Gabriel?"

"He is. He's a good person. With him... my whole life is better. So uh, how's Steven?"

His mother sighs, and says with forced enthusiasm, "He's gonna be a daddy himself soon! Sara's about six months along, and it's a blessing. Steven doesn't always see it that way, but I know it is. They're living in a little house nearby, getting the nursery ready. It's stressful for them, but, you know... that's how these things go sometimes."

"Huh, wow. Um... tell him I said congratulations?"

"I will. I certainly will. He'll be pleased we've heard from you at last."

Rolling his eyes in disbelief at this, Darrek says, "Look, I've gotta go and get back to work, but I'll be in touch. I promise."

"Okay, darlin'. *Please* do."

He closes the phone and groans. Kyle's hand rubs over his shoulders.

"Okay?" Kyle asks.

"Yeah," he grins with a quirk of his lips. "It went better than I expected, though I didn't expect much. But I'm gonna need a strong drink or three after we're off."

"I think that can be arranged," Kyle assures him.

Chapter 40
Three's a Crowd, Four's a Party

With a light schedule that day, Ben is able to agree to Kyle's request that they all go out for happy hour after work. Swinging by Gabriel's place on his way back from Diadem, Ben picks him up and drives him to Darrek and Kyle's job site in town.

"What are you so giddy about?" Gabriel asks with a smile at the evident delight on Ben's face. He watches him drum his fingers on the wheel and sing tunelessly along with the radio.

"The thought of getting a taste of your boy. Seeing the jealously on Kyle's face, and yours too. It's gonna be so sweet."

"Not if Darrek kicks you in the balls before you can get close enough to try," Gabriel warns.

Ben's smile falters for a second and he shoots Gabriel an uncertain glance. "You're kidding. Right?"

Gabriel laughs and doesn't say a word. The road gets eaten up by their tires. Buildings, trees and strangers blur by their windows. The sun gets low on the horizon.

"How are you doing, Gabe? You seem good."

"I am," he nods. "I'm starting to realize some things. And I feel pretty lucky. Got love, got freedom, got perspective, and a future. What more could I want?"

Ben laughs, and Gabriel doesn't catch the dark note to his chuckles nor does he have access to the sinister images flashing through his mind.

"Not much, I guess. I'll have to thank Darrek for making you so happy."

"Yeah, right. Just don't overdo it, or I'll kick your balls

myself."

"Ooh... I'm terrified," Ben says solemnly, seeing it for the empty threat it is, and also catching the glimmer of desire in Gabriel's bright eyes. Licking his lips wet in anticipation, Ben adds, "*Kyle* overpowered you yesterday, you know. That's kind of sad."

"Dude, you just burned your own boyfriend."

"Hey, I'm allowed. He knows I love 'im."

The drive continues with contented silence for a few blocks, until they get to a red light and Gabriel speaks up again, still with a grin, but earnestly admitting in a softer tone, "There is one other thing I want."

His ears perking up, and his own grin slipping away, Ben says, "And what's that?"

"Closure. I'm done being afraid. Of anything."

"And what does that mean?" Ben asks with curiosity and an intent darkness that Gabriel doesn't notice.

Gabriel shrugs as he catches sight of Darrek through the windshield.

"Hey! There they are," he says happily.

Parking in a spot across the street, Gabriel and Ben wait for Darrek and Kyle to walk across to them and away from the prying eyes of the other workers. Standing in the shade of a long line of tall trees beside the sidewalk, they're well-hidden behind Ben's truck. When Darrek finally sees Gabriel, everything else fades back, and he smiles hugely at him with laughing eyes and dimpled cheeks. He tucks a lock of stray hair behind his ear, and jogs up to Gabriel, giving him a tight squeeze and a peck on the cheek.

"Wow, you look happy," Gabriel says with amusement.

"I am! I called home on my lunch break and talked to my mom for a minute. It went really well. A lot better than I thought it would," he confesses shyly, his lips still curled up on the ends, skin glowing with relief.

"That's awesome," Gabriel tells him. "I'm so proud of you for doing that. See? I knew it'd be good for you."

"Yeah, it really was. I was resistant, but now that it's done... yeah. It was good," Darrek nods, finally looking around to Ben and Kyle who are watching them. Ben is leaning back against the truck's side panel and grinning slyly at Darrek.

Darrek's giddy mood is spilling out and infecting everything and everyone around him. The sun shines brighter, the birds sing louder, the breeze feels cooler, and nothing in the world seems impossible or daunting—even kissing Ben Knox. Darrek bites at the tip of his finger, hesitating, debating and moving restlessly. When Ben starts to straighten up, Darrek decides and moves, with a brief glance over at Kyle as he goes.

Stepping into Ben's space and planting his hands on the cool metal on either side of Ben's body, Darrek presses close. Their hips press snugly together as Darrek tilts his head and leans in. Ben cups Darrek's jaw in one hand and meets him, leaning forward.

The kiss is brief, a slipping and curling, hot slide of tongues hidden behind the fallen curtain of Darrek's hair.

Darrek tosses his hair back out of the way when they part and grins over his shoulder at Gabriel.

"You guys up for grabbing some drinks?" Gabriel asks.

"Sounds great," Ben agrees, sucking the taste of Darrek from his bottom lip and moving to pull Kyle into an even deeper, longer kiss. Darrek and Gabriel go to find Darrek's truck, agreeing to meet them at the bar around the corner.

Two hours later, they all pull up at Gabriel and Darrek's house—Ben in his truck, Kyle in his car, and Gabriel and Darrek in Darrek's truck. Intending to run in to get the vacuum bed, Ben and Kyle climb out of their vehicles and follow them inside the darkened home.

"It's up in the second bedroom," Darrek tells Ben. "C'mon, I'll show you."

They go upstairs together while Gabriel and Kyle crash on two of the seats in the living room, flopping down and sprawling out. Gabriel turns on the baseball game and settles back only to quickly change his mind and struggle back to his feet. Going to the kitchen, he comes back a second later with shot glasses and a bottle of Sailor Jerry rum.

"Um, I'm driving," Kyle says, "I really shouldn't...."

"It's not like we're kicking you out right this second, you know."

"Oh. Okay. Thanks then," he says, taking the shot. "Cheers."

They clink glasses and down the burning liquid, listening to the low conversation and soft thumping from upstairs as the other two men get the large contraption down the stairwell.

Once the bed has been carried outside and set in the back of Ben's truck, Darrek and Ben join them for drinks. At Gabriel's urging, Darrek sits in front of Gabriel on the oversized leather chair in the corner, settling between Gabriel's legs, with Gabriel's arm draped possessively over his chest. Ben sits beside Kyle on the couch and pulls him back to lean against his chest as well, drinking down his rum in one swallow before reaching to refill his glass.

The bluish glow from the TV and the golden, upstairs hall light filtering down the steps are the only sources of illumination in the dark space. Already slightly buzzed from the beer, after a few more shots of rum, they all begin to feel the effects—all of them but Kyle, that is, who stops drinking after his first shot. They watch the game, but as the fourth inning becomes the sixth, the television is less and less the focus of their attentions.

It all starts with Gabriel simply dragging the backs of his curled fingers over the soft t-shirt covering the hard planes of Darrek's stomach. Ben watches the arching movement of the touch, and then catches Gabriel's eye when Darrek tilts his head back, nuzzling into the warmth of Gabriel's neck.

Darrek knows Ben is staring at them, sees Kyle pretending he's not watching as well. Even though all Gabriel is doing is caressing his midsection over his clothes, the act feels much more intimate. Blood heats Darrek's skin, making his whole body begin to vibrate from the increasing pressure and warmth. The feeling only gets worse when Gabriel's fingertips catch in the hem of his shirt, dragging it up to reveal a wide swath of skin. His stomach muscles contract at the next pass of Gabriel's fingertips, and the feel of skin on skin, knowing they're being observed. Back and forth over his navel and up almost to his sternum the warm, softly caressing touch of Gabriel's hand goes. Darrek loops his right arm back around Gabriel's neck, the move exposing even more of his chest as his shirt rucks up. He fingers through the soft hair at the nape of Gabriel's neck as Gabriel's fingers dip under the waistband of his jeans, pushing inside over the velvety smooth skin.

His soft exhale sounds louder than it should, especially with the blare from the TV. It gets lost in the tinny crowd noise and endless rise and fall of the announcer's baritone voice. But when Gabriel's hand slips out of Darrek's pants only to rub firmly down the junction of his right thigh with his pelvis and downward along his inner thigh, Darrek's small breathy grunt is clearly audible—especially when Ben reaches for the remote on the coffee table and mutes the sound on the television.

That's when it really hits Darrek what's happening. He starts to get self-conscious, seeing Kyle draw one of his legs up, pressing back into Ben as a wide hand strokes down the front of Kyle's body. It reaches Kyle's crotch and closes around it, gripping tightly there around the bulge between Kyle's legs as Ben stares across at Darrek.

"Kiss me," Gabriel whispers in Darrek's ear, letting his thumb skitter over the head of Darrek's cock through the rough denim. He sees the moment of reluctance in Darrek's eyes, and says again, louder and with evident want, "*Kiss* me, Dare."

His head fuzzy and a smile on his lips, Darrek leans farther back and catches Gabriel's mouth in an open, hungry kiss.

Kyle watches Gabriel's thumb drag up and down along the hard line of flesh encased in Darrek's pants, and hears the soft, wet sounds of their kiss and low moans, even as Ben's hand kneads him purposefully through his blue jeans. He wishes fleetingly that he were wearing the cock cage, unable to get so achingly erect. The thought makes him smile in delirious anxiousness. His heart rate speeds up as the reality of touching like this in front of each other sinks in. His breathing quickens.

Admittedly, Kyle has been in intimate situations with Gabriel and Ben countless times before for work, but this is different—*so much* different. And it's not just because of Darrek's presence. It's because Kyle feels Ben's love in every touch, sees Gabriel and Darrek's love in their touches as well. *That's* the difference. There was never love in it before in the dungeon. It was sex. Basic and primal and uncomplicated. This is so much more complicated.

But he trusts Gabriel, and he trusts Darrek even more. As he does with Ben, Kyle even trusts Darrek with his life. That's not the issue. The issue is, without a doubt, *control*. It all feels too much out of control.

"Ben?" he whispers nervously, his voice lilting a little on the word.

"Shh..." he hushes, bringing his left hand up, closing it once around Kyle's neck and the leather collar there. "I've got ya, kitty. Relax."

The hand releases his throat and slides higher, over his opened, gasping mouth and even higher until it reaches his eyes, covering them tightly and sealing out all of the dim light, folding him in blackness. Kyle sighs and relaxes the tiniest bit.

"Better?"

"Yeah. Thank you, sir."

That hand stays there while Ben's other hand unzips Kyle's pants.

Gabriel watches from the corner of his eye as Ben keeps Kyle blinded and tugs free his swollen cock. Communicating wordlessly with their eyes, as they did so often, for years, in the dungeons of Diadem, the two Dominants agree at once and proceed.

Stroking Kyle slowly, Ben watches Gabriel begin to work open Darrek's jeans too. He does it carefully and gently. Darrek isn't even fully aware that he's doing it until he feels the sudden release of pressure as his cock springs free of its prison. Then he breaks the kiss and glances around. Darrek moans thickly, seeing Kyle, how his eyes are deliberately covered, and what Ben is doing to him, the way that Kyle's hands curl tightly around Ben's arm and leg as Ben slowly squeezes up and down his exposed, reddened dick. The sound of his voice causes Kyle's cock to twitch in Ben's hand. But then Gabriel starts stroking Darrek too and Ben is watching closely, staring at the growing length and thickness of Darrek's cock in Gabriel's hand.

"Do you trust me?" Gabriel asks his lover gently.

"You know I do," is the equally hushed reply.

"Do you trust *Kyle?* Enough to let him touch you?"

Darrek stares up into Gabriel's eyes, questioningly.

"I'd... I... want to be restrained for this," he says in a quiet burst of words, confessing into Gabriel's neck as he turns his face farther into the comforting heat of him. "Please."

"Okay. Sit up a little."

Gabriel lunges sideways and digs quickly in the side table's drawer beside the chair. He knows they have a small supply of toys and S&M gear down here, and he finds what he's looking for in only a moment. Pulling the leather ties from the drawer, Gabriel also pulls out a blindfold, tossing it one-handed to Ben who catches it out of the air and fits it snugly on Kyle's face.

Gabriel guides both of Darrek's arms behind his back, and has him brace his forearms together, hugging his elbows with his hands. Tying his arms together like that, Gabriel winds the leather strap around and around the length of Darrek's forearms until they're secured. Then he pulls Darrek back against his chest once more and goes back to stroking his cock to full hardness, corkscrewing his hand tightly along the shaft.

Running his free hand through Darrek's hair, with his head leaned back on Gabriel's left shoulder, Gabriel says gruffly to Ben, "Okay," and beckons him over with a nod.

Glancing down his body, Darrek sees Ben get Kyle down on his knees making him crawl forward, over to their chair. Kyle stops a foot or two away when Ben places a hand on his shoulder, halting him. Then Ben moves around his kneeling, waiting submissive, and tugs Darrek's jeans and underwear off of him.

"Oh, *shit...*" Darrek pants, suddenly unable to breathe properly as Kyle shifts closer at Ben's urging.

Rubbing a thumb over and under the ridge of the leaking crown of Darrek's dick, smearing the dripping wetness around and watching every fat drop that oozes free, Gabriel whispers to him, "I'm going to tell Kyle to suck you. Okay?"

"*Gabe,*" Darrek whines.

"Is that *okay*?" Gabriel presses.

Darrek nods. He stares down through lowered eyelashes as Kyle tentatively raises his hands and rests them on Darrek's thighs, sliding even closer between Darrek's legs. Ben kneels down behind Kyle, pulling Kyle's pants farther down his body so that they puddle around his knees and guiding his legs as far apart as they'll go. Darrek sees Ben's right hand disappear behind Kyle, and hears the surprised gasp that parts Kyle's lips wide, making his lips tremble. Kyle's hands tighten momentarily around Darrek's legs and then Darrek sees Ben's arm flexing, pumping rhythmically in and out behind Kyle's ass.

Fixated on the sight of Kyle getting fingered right in front of him, Darrek forgets himself until Gabriel wraps him in his hand and guides the head of his cock closer to Kyle's lips. Ben closes his left hand around the back of Kyle's neck and guides his head forward. Darrek's wet cockhead rubs over the seam of Kyle's lips at the urging of Gabriel's hand. It's too good, too obscene to watch, so Darrek closes his eyes.

"Go ahead, kitty. Use that pretty mouth for me," Ben says.

Kyle whimpers as his tongue darts out and licks for the first time over Darrek's flesh. After that small taste and too afraid it won't be permitted to last, Kyle stops holding back and darts forward. He closes his lips just behind and around the head, taking Darrek in.

"Fuck!" Darrek rasps, bucking up. But then Gabriel's hands brace his hips, holding him down.

Close, wet heat swallows him right down too fast and it feels so different than when Gabriel does it. But as incredibly hot as it is to have Kyle actually *sucking his dick*, it's really Ben and Gabriel's presence, encouraging this to happen, that drives Darrek into a frenzy. When he can't shift his hips an inch due to the bruising hold Gabriel has on him, Darrek's thighs and belly contract. He curls forward, gasping, as Kyle deep throats him.

"Oh *fffuck*!" he cries out, shuddering, pulsing thickly on Kyle's soft, curling, suckling tongue.

Ben shifts behind Kyle, pushing a third finger into him, causing him to groan long and low around his mouthful of Darrek's cock, and Kyle almost comes spontaneously right there, without anyone touching his dick. It's just the sudden realization that Ben's really going to fuck him while Gabriel and Darrek watch. He's not just teasing him. He's really going to do it, Kyle knows, from the way in which Ben's fingers move rapidly and efficiently inside him, getting him ready.

Arching his back, he meets each thrust of Ben's hand, fucking himself on it. He hears the others' reactions as Darrek groans above him and Gabriel hums in pleasure.

"I'm gonna let go with my right hand, now," Gabriel tells Darrek, "But I need you to stay still."

"Okay," Darrek whines. Then he feels Gabriel's hand slide around the back of his leg, cupping under it.

"Spread your legs wide," Gabriel says near his ear.

"W-why?"

"Gonna finger you while Kyle sucks you off."

"*Shit!* Shit, *shit*," Darrek whimpers, spreading out as requested. Each moan Kyle makes vibrates up his shaft and it's too good, Darrek's afraid he's going to come any second. Trying to fight back the urge and control his breathing, he finds his throat suddenly locked up when Gabriel's hand snakes around his opened legs and fingertips rub over his hole.

Watching Kyle take long sucking pulls of him, sucking up to the tip and licking out over the head each time before plunging back down to the root and swallowing around the fatness of his dick, Darrek also sees Ben's eyes on them both. Darrek remembers, then, the feel and taste of Ben's mouth, the easy way he'd kissed Darrek back and used his tongue. Darrek bites his lips closed as Ben intently watches Gabriel push two slicked fingers into him inches from Kyle's mouth.

"G-gabe? Gabe, I'm gonna come..." he rasps weakly as the fingers fuck into him quick and deep. Kyle's hands slide higher up his thighs and stroke gently over his skin while his stretched lips suckle at his dick. "Gabe!!"

"Not yet," Gabriel commands, locking his left hand around Darrek's pelvis when he starts to buck up into Kyle's mouth again.

"I'm trying! But I... I... *fuck*!"

"Kyle," Gabriel says in a husky purr, "You wanna touch him? C'mon. It's okay."

Kyle moans thickly around Darrek who hisses between clenched teeth. Darrek's whole body goes tight as a rubber band when Kyle's finger eases into him between Gabriel's two that are already inside. Gabriel's fingers scissor wide open, keeping Darrek's hole stretched out while Kyle's finger rubs through the ring of muscle and farther in, stroking up against his inner walls.

"Pull off," Ben commands Kyle when he sees Darrek about to blow.

With a wet slurp, Kyle lets Darrek's cock pop out from between his lips. It strains up into the air as Gabriel and Kyle finger him to orgasm. Darrek's hips buck counter to the thrusts and then he's coming. The white ropes of semen jet from the slit in the reddened wet tip, landing in splatters on his belly. That's when Kyle circles the base of Darrek's shaft with a hand and guides him lower. Still coming, some of the milky white drops land on Kyle's tongue, which darts out of his opened mouth to catch what he can.

Darrek cries out in a wrenching whine. He shudders through his climax, riding the hands buried inside his tight hole.

Even before he's fully spent, though, Gabriel's fingers tug free and he moves away, getting up off of the chair and going to Kyle instead. He cradles Kyle's face in his hands and licks into his mouth, chasing the hot taste of Darrek there, and sucking Kyle's tongue clean of it.

If the sight of *that* wasn't bad enough for Darrek, Kyle's finger is still in him, pushing deeper as a second is added a moment later. Darrek keeps shuddering, tingling from head to toe, awash in blissful sensation, and he can feel his softened cock trying, already, somehow, to re-harden, twitching against his belly.

Ben shifts behind Kyle as Gabriel keeps kissing him. Pulling Kyle's hips back, Ben thrusts his own forward. A small grunt forces out of Kyle's mouth and into Gabriel as Ben fills him up in one push with his cock and begins to fuck him with tight slaps of his hips.

"Oh my god... oh my god..." Darrek gasps, urging Kyle's hand on with small rolls of his hips, fisting his own dick now as horrible, welling, surging need floods his drained body, demanding *more, now*.

With his left hand still curled around Darrek's leg, Kyle feels his tension and kisses Gabriel with need as Ben moves inside him. Kyle wants to feel it all, and savor every part of this, which is exactly why he didn't drink enough to dull his senses or cloud his memory. Grateful affection and a strangely jagged undercurrent of anxiety colors the way he kisses at Gabriel's full lips and sweet tongue. Every press and suck of lips is a wordless thank you for his own happiness, as well as Darrek's, which Kyle knows is due in large part to Gabriel.

Temporary confusion causes him to pause when he feels Ben tug free of him and press a too-loving trail of kisses to the back of his neck, around the collar.

"Climb up on the chair," Ben tells him after a glance and a nod from Gabriel. "Straddle Darrek."

A shudder of want and apprehension races up Kyle's spine and he swoons a little on his knees.

This is crazy, he thinks even as he feels his body moving of its own accord. He stands, pulling his fingers free of Darrek's body. Using his hands to find his way, Kyle gets up on his knees, settling them beside each of Darrek's hips on the edge of the cushion, and braces his hands on either side of Darrek's head.

Fully convinced he wouldn't be able to do this if he wasn't blindfolded, and if Darrek was touching him, Kyle feels Ben penetrate him again. Fucked into roughly until he's panting and trembling above Darrek, Kyle feels a hand circle his cock, bringing him off with a few expert tugs. But it's not Ben. He knows instantly that it must be Gabriel fisting his cock and it causes Kyle to make a small sobbing sound, even though he's smiling a little.

"Hey," Darrek hushes to him, seeing the emotion twist Kyle's flushed-red face.

But then Kyle is coming, bucking into Gabriel's fist and coating Darrek with hot, pulsing jets of fluid.

"Hey, Kyle. C'mere," Darrek says gently, struggling in his bonds.

His arms giving out, Kyle's body complies before his mind can catch up, and he finds himself nuzzling into Darrek's neck as Ben finishes himself off, knocking Kyle forward into Darrek with each push.

Kyle tries to catch his breath, inhaling Darrek's musky scent and reaching a hand behind himself to find Ben. Ben folds their hands together, holding on to Kyle as he recovers.

"You okay?" Darrek asks.

Kyle nods and laughs brokenly, thinking that he wishes Ben wasn't so good on the follow-through sometimes. Everything spins in his head. Everything Ben ever threatened or promised, it could all come true—every sinful act, of sex or of violence. Ben told him it would happen, just like this—with his mouth stuffed full of Darrek, his ass stuffed full of Ben, and sweetly kissed by Gabriel, taken and used by them all—and it did. It happened perfectly—perfectly heartbreaking, but perfect nonetheless.

"Wow," Darrek sighs. "Um... I guess you can have the first shower, if you want."

"Huh... I don't know if I can stand up right now, honestly," Kyle admits hoarsely.

"I'd uh... take your blindfold off for you, but my arms are kind of... trapped."

"Nah, I don't want to take it off yet. I'm afraid it'll get all weird if I can see you."

Kyle feels hands manhandling him, pulling him back and up off of Darrek. He tries to bat them away, because he knows what's coming, but Ben gets the blindfold off before he can do anything about it.

"So? Is it weird?" Ben chuckles, looping an arm around Kyle's waist and resting his chin on his shoulder.

"Yes. It is. Happy? Now you've ruined it," Kyle sighs dramatically.

Gabriel laughs and pulls Darrek up from his seat, getting the ties on his arms unwound. When Darrek is free, and grinning at Kyle's exaggerated pout, he lets Gabriel pull him over toward the stairs.

"C'mon stud. The shower is calling," Gabriel says as they go. "Ben? You get jizz on my furniture, I'll paddle your ass red and raw. You hear me?"

"Yes, Master!" he calls with a laugh and a salute.

Chapter 41
Voyeur's Plaything

The hot water slicks over Darrek's body like liquid fingers touching him everywhere. The spray beats against his face, and he pushes his fingers back through his hair as the dampening strands mold to his skull and neck. He opens his mouth and lets it fill up before spitting it all back out against the tile wall. When he's thoroughly wet, and the grimy feeling he's been carrying around after another long, sweaty day on a job site begins to wash away, he soaps up his hands with a thick coating of bubbles. Shifting his legs apart he rubs around, under and between the firm globes of his cheeks before working his fingers over the rim of his hole. Then he's fingering the soap inside, making sure he's thoroughly cleaned for Gabriel.

Before he'd gotten into the shower, Darrek had flushed his ass out with anal douche. It was part of Gabriel's instructions to him, delivered as soon as he was through the front door of their house. After he'd dropped his keys in the foyer, Darrek had seen the video equipment Gabriel was in the process of setting up in the living room.

Gabriel had grinned slyly over at him, and said, "So? You tired or can we play for a while?"

"*Play*?" Darrek smiled back, pulling his sweat-stained tank top over his head. It had been a week since their surreal episode with Kyle and Ben, and his and Gabriel's love making had been rather tame after that. It had been almost like after doing something so extreme they needed to find balance by having really vanilla sex for a while—mostly lazy blowjobs and manual stimulation. But it appeared in that moment as if Gabriel had had enough vanilla. His skilled hands angled the digital camera secured to the tripod and checked the view screen.

"Yeah. *Play,*" he emphasized somewhat impatiently.

"All right. Do I get any hints?" He watched Gabriel perfect the shot of the lens aimed at the large armchair and ottoman that had been the site of their foursome the previous week. A tilt here and tweak there—Gabriel's face was set and focused as he worked. Darrek could see it was important to him to have everything exactly as he wanted it to be. "I don't see any gear laid out or hardware...."

"No hints. Go get cleaned up. There's some cold beer in the fridge if you want to have a few while you're up there," Gabriel said, flicking his eyes in the direction of the upstairs bathroom.

"Drink in the shower?"

"Sure. Why not?" He smirked with a sideways glance at the hard expanse of Darrek's thickly muscled, dirt-streaked, bare chest, gleaming with perspiration.

"Yer just trying to liquor me up, aren'tcha?"

"Maybe...."

Gabriel watched Darrek walk into the kitchen, grab two bottles from the refrigerator and take them both back to the steps as he went upstairs.

That had been about ten minutes earlier

. One of the beers is now empty, the bottle sitting on a small shelf in the shower stall. As Darrek washes the rest of his body with the sponge in his hand, he ponders what Gabriel could possibly be planning for him. The more he thinks about it, the faster his hands move, impatience kicking in. The slight burn of the soap that he had rubbed into himself over the sensitive tissues of his anus gets stronger the longer he waits to rinse it out. Even that small bit of discomfort, mixed with his growing desire to be at Gabriel's mercy, perks up his cock. It fattens and fills with blood where it hangs between his legs. He tries to will the erection away and is slightly successful.

There are other things on his mind—worries and distractions. Some worries have to do with Gabriel, and some don't. Darrek tries to refocus on those, but nothing can blot out the thrumming of blood and heat growing more powerful within his body with every beat of his heart. Need for Gabriel—Gabriel's love and attention, his gorgeous, perfect body, his hands and lips, the feel of his rock-hard dick forcing its way deeply into him, filling him up so much that he aches from it—overpowers everything else. But it's also the curiosity as to what Gabriel's keen mind, filled with a rich wealth of knowledge of all the ways to make a man hurt and feel pleasure, has in store for him once he gets downstairs. No matter how many times Darrek endures this sort of moment of physical and mental preparation, readying himself inside and out for his Master, it never gets easier, because Gabriel never stops surprising him.

Nervousness and anticipation knot Darrek's insides. The second beer cools him in the steamy humidity of the bathroom, and he finishes it quickly. Getting a quick buzz off of it, since he still doesn't have much of a tolerance for any sort of alcohol, Darrek dries his hair enough that it's not dripping everywhere, and heads downstairs in a snugly-fitting pair of gray briefs. Half-hard, the fabric contains him, but just barely.

Gabriel is still in the living room, and though the light outside is dimming as the sun sinks lower in the sky, inside it's as bright as ever. All of the lights are on in the front room, with the rest of the house dark. Walking to the window, Gabriel tugs the curtains closed for privacy, and Darrek stares at the small floodlight pointed at the chair from behind the camera. It's all set up for them, the oasis of light in an otherwise shadowy space. But just as it was when Darrek first walked in the door, there are no toys set out or restraints ready to bind him. The only thing on the side table is a large bottle of lubricant and two shot glasses filled with a dark, amber liquid.

"Are these for us?" Darrek asks, running a finger around the rim of one of the tiny glasses and shooting Gabriel a questioning glance.

"Those are for you. I want you relaxed and loose. I know we

don't use cameras that often when we do this, so I figured you might feel a little self-conscious about it."

Darrek gives him a lopsided grin and bites at his lip. "You might say that."

"I want to make a video of you, for me. There's two smaller cameras wired up to the ceiling for other angles I can splice together when I edit the footage later. I was going to put on some music to make you more comfortable, but it'd affect the playback if the background sounds were choppy. Plus, this way, I'll really be able to hear you. There's a mic clipped to the bottom of the chair, just out of shot."

Looking around the space, Darrek sees he's right. He hadn't even seen the cameras before, but now he does. They're hooked to the ceiling with wires running down the wall. He can't see the microphone, but has no doubt that it's where Gabriel said it is too.

"So, is this practice for you, with the whole videography thing, or is it to fuck with my head?" When a wicked smirk is the only response, Darrek answers his own question with, "Okay. Got it. It's both."

"It's a*lways* both," Gabriel teases.

Gabriel steps close to him now that he's sure no one can see in through the windows. The doors are locked, the dog is outside with a new bone to chew on, and the phones are all turned off. Standing chest to chest with his lover, Gabriel stares down his body, and hooks his index finger in the front of the waistband of Darrek's gray briefs. The sight of the bulge inside them makes his mouth water. Pulling with his finger, the material stretches outward, easing the pressure on Darrek's swollen flesh. He tugs the underwear down in the front, and Darrek's cock springs free, twitching and curving upward as he gets harder from the attention.

"Drink the shots," Gabriel rasps. "I want you to leave these briefs on while I stretch you out, okay? You look so fucking hot. I love how huge your dick looks in these."

He pulls the gray cotton back up, getting it stretched over the lengthening erection, and stuffing Darrek back inside it. The elastic strains away from his belly. Darrek picks up the first shot glass as Gabriel runs his fingers along the underside of Darrek's shaft through the fabric. Sniffing once at the mysterious liquid, Darrek swirls it around and gives it a doubtful pout.

"Just down it as fast as you can. It'll burn, but it's good stuff," Gabriel tells him.

"What is it?"

"Straight bourbon."

"Fuck me," Darrek groans. "Okay. Cheers."

He swallows it in one gulp, and feels Gabriel's eyes on his throat as it works to get the searing liquid down his gullet.

He grimaces, coughing as his face scrunches up.

Gabriel hands him the second shot. The one inside him radiates heat through his throat and stomach as the fire spreads instead of dampening. Swallowing the second shot, Darrek's eyes water a little as Gabriel takes the glass from his hand.

"Okay, baby. Over to the chair for me. Don't pay any attention to the cameras, all right? It's just you and me. No one's gonna see this but us. And no rules just yet."

"Yet? So there will be rules later?"

"Yeah. I wanna see how obedient you can be for me. That's why I didn't plan on using any restraints on you. Is that okay?"

"Yeah. I'm ready," Darrek nods. "Wow... I'm... kinda dizzy. That's strong stuff."

"Come on over here. Get on your knees facing the back of the chair. Hold on to that so you don't lose your balance. Put your head down if it's more comfortable for you."

Darrek climbs onto the ottoman and gets into position. The chair is soft and warm, the lights shining on him heat his skin, and he notices vaguely the overall mugginess of the room.

"Did you turn the air conditioning off?"

"Yeah. And I turned the furnace on just while we're doing this."

Gabriel's hands begin to rub over Darrek's back and legs. He arches into the gentle touch, and shivers when Gabriel combs his fingernails though his stringy wet hair, scratching over his scalp and down the back of his neck.

"Good. Just relax... good...."

It's so quiet in the room that every sound seems amplified, echoing loudly in Darrek's ears. The snap of his underwear against his thighs when Gabriel pulls them down in the back is like a gunshot. The briefs hug around his legs just under the curve of his ass, and his balls and cock are still encased uncomfortably in them in the front, but he knows better than to free himself if Gabriel hasn't already done it for him. They may not be following formal rules at the moment, but Darrek's too well-trained at this point to do anything but submit to Gabriel's will.

He's hot and flushed from the oppressive heat of the room, but his newly bared ass seems strangely cool. Then he hears the snap of the lubricant's cap and wet squirting as Gabriel squeezes some of it out.

The chilliness intensifies when he feels dripping fingertips rub over his hole, circling the rim and spreading the lube up through his ass crack.

Gabriel says in a low purr, "Now, I want you to reach back and spread yourself open for me. Let's get a good look at your pretty pink hole. Gonna make it nice and wet and get you stretched out so I can fuck it, all right?"

"'Kay..." He shifts, bracing his body with his shoulders planted on the chair's cushion, his hips high and arms reaching back. Grabbing on to his ass cheeks with each hand, he pulls. He knows it's only Gabriel, and that he has no good reason to be nervous, but butterflies flutter in his stomach as his head spins and tilts from the booze. A tidal wave of self-consciousness buffets him, and he feels his opening wink shut against a soft puff of Gabriel's breath across it. "Um... Gabe...."

A single finger presses at the ring of muscle that keeps alternately relaxing then clenching shut. A tight knot of dusky pink in the center of Darrek's pale backside, Gabriel's tan finger eases through it to the first knuckle, pushing a dollop of lubricant inside the cavity. It makes a too-loud squelch as Gabriel pushes the gel in only to pop his finger back out and do it again, rubbing the shiny liquid into the wrinkled skin of his rim and then inside again, pushing farther this time.

Gabriel rubs three fingers over the twitching orifice, feeling the muscles clench and release under him, getting pinker for all the attention.

"I'm so fucking hard right now," Gabriel says to Darrek. He thrusts hard with his middle finger, getting it inside Darrek's body up to the last knuckle then twisting and pulling down with it. It stretches the opening, and it gapes open slightly as Gabriel applies pressure to the inner wall. Positioning the tip of the bottle of lube at the gap, Gabriel squirts some more up Darrek's hole and hears his hiss at the sudden coldness. "Can't wait to see this little pucker of yours take my fat cock, get you all stretched out around me. You want it?"

"Yeah, I want it," he moans.

"No one else gets to fuck this but me," Gabriel growls. "*No one.*"

Adding his ring finger beside his middle finger, Gabriel spreads them apart and holds Darrek open. When Gabriel doesn't move, doesn't do anything but keep him pried apart like that, Darrek moans again and tries to push back on Gabriel's hand which is already buried up the hilt inside him.

"God, look how hungry you are for it. You like the feel of my fingers stuffed up your ass? Mmm, maybe I need to get a better look at you..."

Darrek glances back and sees Gabriel reach for a small, handheld camera with a light secured to the top.

Pointing it at Darrek's opening, Gabriel lets the light shine into his body and films a close-up of his fingers pulling at the dark-pink tissue of the inner walls of Darrek's rectum.

"You're so fucking tight in here, Dare...."

Darrek feels himself clench up reflexively around Gabriel's fingers, knowing that the camera's recording all of it. He whines and tries to muffle the sound in the chair. He can feel his dick pulsing, pre-come seeping out, in the sheath of his too-tight underwear as a wet spot darkens the fabric around the head. The fingers inside him twist around and bend. Gabriel strokes once over the bundle of nerves of his prostate. Darrek makes a choked whimper and his hips buck.

"Making your little panties nice and wet for me, aren't you?" Gabriel chuckles, rubbing the spot a second and third time. "Maybe when I fuck this little hole I should stuff those panties in your mouth and make you suck on 'em."

The handheld gets shut off and put aside. With his hand now free, Gabriel closes it around Darrek's cock through the soaked underwear and squeezes.

Manipulating Darrek, tugging on him and rubbing a finger over the still-oozing slit in his cockhead, Gabriel digs in his pocket and pulls from it a small but thickly tapered butt plug. Drizzling lube over it, Gabriel smears the liquid around and gets it as wet as he can before placing the tip at Darrek's entrance. Applying downward pressure as he pushes it at a sharp angle through the outer ring, Gabriel hears Darrek's deep moan and feels his cock go rock hard inside his fist.

"Mmm..." Darrek pants.

Gabriel pushes at the base until it's flush with Darrek's body at then uses his fingertips to nudge it even deeper.

"Don't you dare come yet, you hear me?" Gabriel warns.

"'M sorry," Darrek whines, "It just... *ahhh...* it hurts so fucking good."

Grabbing the base with his fingers, Gabriel pulls it back out an inch or two, watching Darrek's reddened rim hug the black plastic. Angling his wrist, he jabs it violently into Darrek's hole. It causes him to yelp and buck forward on the chair, pulling himself mostly free of the toy in the process.

"That hurt?" Gabriel grins.

Darrek doesn't answer, panting roughly into the chair.

"Look at me."

Almost reluctantly, he complies, turning to face Gabriel.

"Don't fucking move," he warns. "You want hurt, I can give you hurt. So stay still, or you get shackled and then I'll *really* make it hurt."

Darrek nods, his nose crinkling up in anticipation.

Then Gabriel starts ramming him with the plug, impaling him on the hard plastic at a brutal angle, twisting the point inside his ass in a swiveling motion as he yanks it slowly out to do it again. Darrek does as he's told and stays as still as possible. His fingers dig in so hard to the flesh of his ass, which he's still holding on to, that it leaves little crescent moons where his fingernails bite the skin.

And it still hurts, but he rocks back on each rough push of Gabriel's hand, and he knows that if Gabriel moved just a little faster, he'd be able to come. So he starts rocking back onto the wriggling point of the plug at an increased pace, his breathing coming quicker and more shallowly.

"You're gonna come, aren't you?" Gabriel asks, in a quietly threatening voice.

Darrek whimpers and pushes his hips back in an even harder thrust.

"Darrek, I *order you* not to come. You hear me?" he warns, turning the plug and slamming it right into Darrek's sweet spot on the next penetration. Darrek shudders and rasps a low noise.

"Oh fuck..." he manages.

"Darrek...."

Releasing his hold on himself, he reaches between his legs instead, knowing that with one tug at his dick he'll be able to release all of the torturous pressure swelling up in his balls.

"*No,*" Gabriel insists.

With a fluid movement, he removes the toy, pulls Darrek upright on his knees, and gets his arms pinned behind his back. Darrek curses wildly and fights the hold, writhing. The front of his briefs are almost black in spots they're so wet with his pre-come, and the purple-red head of his dick is peeking out the top of the waistband.

Gabriel laughs cruelly in his ear and says calmly, "I said, *no*."

"You said no rules," Darrek complains. "I wanna fucking *come*."

"Okay. Fair enough. You go ahead and do that then, but if you come, we stop playing. Right now. So it's your choice. I can give you even more of what I know you want, and then when I let you come, you'll climax so hard your head'll fucking explode from it, or you can do it now and go upstairs and watch TV or go to bed."

"God damn it, Gabriel!" Darrek rasps. "Fine. But I get payback for this shit."

Gabriel chuckles again and kisses his neck. "All right. It's a deal." As he manhandles Darrek around so that he's facing the camera, and gets his own pants off, he asks, "Why are you so riled up over this, anyway? You usually have better self-control. Is it the cameras? You get off on having an audience?"

"Umm... yeah," Darrek admits shyly.

"Take your underwear off," Gabriel says softly to him as he throws his jeans and boxers aside and sits on the chair, leaning back.

Darrek shoves the clothing down and somehow gets them off. They cling to him though, and it takes an effort to get free. But then he's out of them and there's nothing to conceal him from the all-seeing eye of the lenses aimed his way.

"You're not really going to make me suck on 'em, are you?"

Laughing, Gabriel retorts, "Why? You want to?" He pulls Darrek's hips back, getting him straddled over his legs, and decides, "Nah. Toss 'em. I want to hear every pretty little sound that fuckable mouth of yours makes."

"So... now what?" he asks, all too aware of how he must look. "How do you want me?"

He hears Gabriel open the lube again, and out of the corner of his eye sees him slicking himself with it.

"I want you just like this," Gabriel tells him. "Don't overthink it, just close your eyes. The only rule right now is that you can't touch yourself. That's all."

"I can handle that. I think."

Eyes shut tight, Darrek feels Gabriel caress the sides of his upper thighs and guide him back and down. It comes naturally. Darrek reaches behind his body and guides Gabriel into his well-prepared opening. The biggest part, the silky-smooth, spongy, rounded head, forces its way through with all of Darrek's weight behind the movement as he sinks down onto it.

Breathing through the burn, Darrek keeps lowering himself on the shaft, taking it in inch by inch. Gabriel's a lot bigger than the plug was, so he feels the stretch.

Gabriel's arms circle his chest, and pull Darrek's back flush to his chest. Every expansion and contraction of Darrek's ribcage is felt, every deep inhale of air. Gabriel closes his lips around Darrek's earlobe, nipping at it and sucking hard. Using the muscles in his thighs, Darrek rears up then rocks back down. He feels the friction of Gabriel's stiff cock rubbing along the inside of his body. The intensity of being so intimately connected to him continues to affect Darrek like nothing else. Every time, it's like coming home again. He breathes easier, and relaxes even more. Everything else dissipates and all that matters is the sharp inhale Gabriel makes, the small pain of his teeth biting Darrek's ear and then his neck as he moves a little faster, fucking himself down onto him.

He builds a steady rhythm, slapping his ass down against Gabriel's pelvis a little harder each time, a little faster too. Soon he's bouncing on Gabriel's lap, dimly aware of his dick bouncing as well, but counter to his movements and smearing wet over his belly. He lets his head fall back on his shoulders and spreads his legs a little wider. Gabriel begins to push up when Darrek thrusts down. His fingers rub the crease of Darrek's ass and down around the delicate, silken, stretched skin of Darrek's rim. The touch causes Darrek's movements to falter.

"You like that?" Gabriel croons, rubbing harder at the ring of muscle, working his finger at the junction of his body and Darrek's, he presses at the spot to try to get inside. With his thumb he rubs hard over the smooth patch of skin behind Darrek's balls, stimulating his prostate.

Darrek's face scrunches up and his lips part in a soft gasp. He's completely still now, unable to do anything but feel Gabriel touching him and penetrating him.

"Gonna stick my finger in here, too," he warns. "So relax your sphincter as much as you can."

He pushes at Darrek's lower back with his left hand, guiding him forward. Darrek braces his hands on Gabriel's legs and leans in that direction. Concentrating on regulating his breathing, he unclenches and lets the digit slip in beside the pulsing length of Gabriel's dick.

"*Mmm...*" he hums unevenly at the extra stretch.

Circling his shaft, and fitting it within the junction of his thumb and index finger, Gabriel watches Darrek push back down onto him, swallowing up the exposed length of his flushed cock as well as Gabriel's thumb.

"Good... *ahhh...* feel so good, Dare... okay. Go. Hard as you want."

Darrek rides Gabriel, slowly at first, because every time he happens to pull up more than a few inches, Gabriel's thumb pops out and then catches at his rim on the thrust back inside. Each time that happens Darrek gasps harshly and blinks wide-eyed at the cameras. He builds speed and force as he controls his movements, making them shorter and quicker. Then Gabriel is thrusting up frantically into him, his hips twitching in violent bursts. He removes his thumb and pins Darrek down flush to him, just pushing, and pushing, and *pushing* as he orgasms and unloads up Darrek's hole. Sinking back against Gabriel's chest again, Darrek is pleased to hear Gabriel's gruff little moans and mewls as he comes down. He strokes his fingers along Gabriel's body, caressing his arms and legs. Reaching behind his shoulder, he combs through Gabriel's short hair and cranes his neck to catch Gabriel's mouth in a soft kiss.

"Do you know how gorgeous you are right now?" Gabriel says against Darrek's lips before licking between them and sucking Darrek's tongue.

"Yeah, sweaty and hard and sticky... real 'gorgeous'," Darrek huffs.

"You are. I'm obsessed with having you like this. You're not worrying about anything. You're just here, with me, letting me turn you inside out and loving you through it," he whispers, eyes wide and dark with promise and devotion. "Thank you for giving me this. It's the most anyone's ever given me."

"You're welcome," Darrek smiles, sweeping his tongue deeply into Gabriel's mouth to lick there while letting Gabriel move him to a new position.

He knows they're not done yet. They're far from it.

Chapter 42

Obedience Warrants Reward

All Darrek knows is the taste of Gabriel's mouth, the soft, wet warmth of his sweet-tasting tongue as his body gets tilted back. Gabriel bends his knees, spreading them out. They nudge Darrek's legs apart. He'd been straddling Gabriel, but now Gabriel grabs Darrek's thighs and guides them as far apart as they'll go, hooking them over the arms of the chair with Darrek's knees back toward his chest. Gabriel keeps them there by locking his knees in under them, forcing Darrek wide. The downward angle of the camera on the tripod should be perfectly angled to catch the spectacular view of Darrek's parted thighs—his used and filled hole, hugged tightly around Gabriel's cock, his swollen dick and drawn-up-tight balls. Gabriel fondles him as they kiss, urging on each little jump of Darrek's flesh.

"This is when the rules kick in," Gabriel tells him. "Right now, I'm your Master, and you are my slave. You will address me as such, and the only way you get out of obeying my orders is by using the safeword. Say your safeword for me, slave."

"Tundra," Darrek murmurs, adding, "Master."

"Very good. Do you understand my rules? Will you obey me?"

"Yes, Master."

"Now, I want you to stay perfectly still. Hook your arms around and behind my upper arms. I need your hands out of the way."

Darrek fits his hands into the narrow space available between Gabriel and the sides of the chair. His heartbeat is starting to race wildly in anxiety and it's causing him to breathe in shallow, audible gasps.

Chuckling, Gabriel rubs the pad of a thumb firmly around the root of Darrek's shaft and down over his balls, teasing, "I love when you get nervous like this. Why are you nervous, slave?"

"'Cause I know it's gonna hurt, but I don't know what you're gonna *do*. There aren't any... toys."

"That's right. No toys, just my hands. My hands make you nervous?"

"Yes, sir," Darrek groans as Gabriel scratches a fingernail up the full, pulsing vein on the underside of his shaft. The scratch is deeper than is comfortable and Darrek wants to writhe or twist away, but he'd be disobeying. Plus there's nowhere for him to go anyway. Then the nail scratches up to the ridge and through the divot to the tip. It catches in the slit and tugs at it as it digs across.

Sealing his lips together, Darrek tries to swallow back a deeper groan and fights to stay still. When Gabriel simply reverses course and scratches his way back down, Darrek hears his pleased hum and feels the vibrations of it tickle his ear. The fingernail scrapes down over his balls to his taint. It causes Darrek to make a broken keening sound. Then the scratching stops and the hand instead tugs the flesh of Gabriel's cock that's stuffed up his asshole. It frees Gabriel from him, leaving him gaping. He can feel how loose he is, how stretched out and wet. And the cameras are seeing all of it.

Gabriel purrs in his ear, "Gonna leave you like this for a good long time. I wanna see my come drip out of you."

The words go straight to Darrek's dick and it pulses out a thick dribble of clear fluid, which oozes down the crown and drips down his length. Gabriel inserts the thumb of his right hand into Darrek's hole then sticks his left index finger in as well. Pulling with both, but in opposite directions, he widens Darrek even more and rubs a third finger inside through the fluid that begins to seep out of his rectum.

"Maybe I should try to fist you right now," Gabriel murmurs. "You're so fucked out from my cock... nice and sloppy wet. I could do it. I've done it before...."

Darrek doesn't say a thing, but he stops watching Gabriel's hands and relaxes back against him and the chair. Four fingers get pushed into his ass, and he rocks down onto them, seeking contact with his sweet spot in order to help himself find release. But Gabriel purposefully avoids the sensitive area, while getting his hand in until the base of his thumb catches on Darrek's rim. Then he simply strokes the fingers along the come-slicked inner walls and simultaneously draws his unoccupied left hand up Darrek's pelvis.

He gives Darrek's achingly full hard-on a slap. It causes Darrek to clench up around his hand and twitch away.

"No moving," Gabriel tsks, giving the bobbing purplish thickness an even harder slap using the back of his knuckles. He does it again and then a fourth time.

Darrek whines and fights to stay still. His reward is a gentle stroking of Gabriel's fingertips around his cockhead.

When Darrek relaxes again, Gabriel curls his index finger and uses it to flick the dripping member, catching his fingernail right on the spongy ridge. Darrek moans and arches his back. The hand up his ass pushes farther and the flicking continues in uneven bursts. There are two, then one, then four quicker ones. Darrek's hands curl into fists as the small, sharp pain builds. But Gabriel doesn't stop, he just shifts his target, flicking right down on the slit from above, on the back of the head, on the front, and then slowly down the underside of the shaft. The closer Gabriel gets to Darrek's testicles, the louder the gruff keening low in Darrek's throat gets.

"Shh..." Gabriel purrs just as he begins to repeatedly flick the orb of his left testicle and then the right. Corkscrewing the hand nestled within Darrek, Gabriel taps his prostate in an equally unsteady rhythm, causing him to yell roughly.

Gabriel closes Darrek's balls in his fist, tugging hard on them as he corkscrews his right hand around in the velvety glove of slick muscle.

"Wanna come, slave?" he asks, as he begins to rub over the small bundle of nerves of his prostate from inside Darrek's abused orifice and from outside as well, pressing his thumb firmly to Darrek's taint and drawing circles with it. Trapping the nerves between a barrage of stimulation, he doesn't let up for a second, just fingering and squeezing and rubbing the spot.

Darrek arches up violently, all of the muscles in his body drawing up tight from the curl of his toes to the cords popping in his neck. A sobbing, yelling sound rips from him as he shudders and thick jets of semen spurt from his untouched cock. Tears leak from his eyes and he writhes, trying to bring his knees together and twist away. Gabriel just chases him and keeps fingering the too-sensitive spot. Darrek convulses and keeps shooting the milky fluid. Gabriel's left hand rolls his balls, but doesn't touch Darrek's dick once as he continues to milk him. Darrek comes and comes and *comes* some more. He comes until he's pulsing dry and his body is empty with nothing more to give, but the nerves somehow don't know that and they still fire and fry his brain. Gabriel's hand works in him furiously, working at the spot even when Darrek is obviously spent.

"AHHH! Ahhhuhhhuughhh...stop! Stop! It hurts!"

"That's not the magic word," Gabriel says to him. "Gonna safeword out on me? Hmm?"

The hand closed around Darrek's balls yanks on them, pulling them away from his body. The sounds his right hand makes as it rubs away in the fluttering muscles are wet and loud in the room. Gabriel eases up with his left hand and the taut tension being applied to Darrek's sack. He makes a circle with his thumb and index finger, using them like a vice that closes up on Darrek's sac and squeezes the orbs of his balls until the wrinkled skin is tight and smooth and red.

Finally Gabriel pulls his right hand free of Darrek's asshole, and Darrek lets out a grateful huff of air, hisses roughly through clenched teeth. His body is tingling from head to toe. His hands are going numb, as well as his toes, everything between his legs is tender and too-sensitive and part of him wants nothing more than for Gabriel to stop touching him so he can recover. Aware that saying the safeword will get him what he wants, the part of Darrek's psyche that enjoys the fuck out of the torment keeps the word unsaid.

At least Gabriel's not hammering his prostate anymore, he figures. But the way Gabriel is squeezing his balls makes Darrek want to scream too. His hips come up, trying to relieve the pressure.

Gabriel's hand drags through the thick fluid that's leaked out of Darrek's opening, smearing it around the hole, making him feel what a sloppy mess he is. Then it drags up to his softened member, stroking it, pumping him back to stiffness.

"*Fuck*... please don't. I can't... I can't get hard again right now," Darrek complains.

"Sure you can. You either get hard, or I slap your balls around until you do."

Darrek's cock jumps inside Gabriel's hand and he laughs into the shell of Darrek's ear.

"Mmm... so that sounds good to you, does it?" Gabriel taunts. His hand blurs, jacking Darrek roughly and when he lets go, Darrek is more than half-hard again. "Good boy. So *obedient*...."

Drawing back an open palm, Gabriel slaps Darrek's dick left to right, then right to left. Then he smacks the underside, watching it jump and slap back against his belly.

Darrek groans. His rectum clenches up, and the wet sound embarrasses him into another groan.

The dreaded opened hand moves, aiming for another target entirely.

"Don't. Gabe, *don't*," he begs.

It smacks the tight, red orbs enclosed in the vice of Gabriel's fingers. *Smack, smack smack, smack.*

Darrek's mouth works soundlessly, his head rolling back on Gabriel's shoulder as his hips come up again. The knees holding his thighs open pull wider, keeping him from shutting his legs.

"Why do you lie to me like that?" Gabriel muses. Flattening his hand he rubs the center of the palm in wide circles over the imprisoned organ. Each circle brings a slightly harder press than the one before it to Darrek's testicles. "Obviously you're getting off on this. Your prick is completely hard again. You're making these adorable little puppy whimpers for me. So why are you *lying?* Why do you ask me to stop and then use my name in a way that you KNOW will earn you more punishment? Tell me. Tell me the truth. Now."

Gabriel's flattened hand curls around both Darrek and the hand that's squeezing and yanking on the base of his sack, trapping his balls between his fists and it *squeezes*.

"*Now*," he repeats.

"Oh FUCK! Uhhh, okay. Okay. *Mmm*... OW. Ow, ow... *fuck*.... Um...."

"Say you like it," Gabriel coaches.

"Mmmnnn," Darrek hums, straightening his hands out and pushing them down to grab and squeeze around Gabriel's waist. His hips chase up until his ass is completely off the chair. Gabriel stops squeezing and instead closes his fingertips around the abused orbs and pinches them in small pulses. "Oh god *yeah...* h-harder. Harder! Mmmm, th-thank you... M-master."

"What do you want?" Gabriel whispers into his hair.

"Sl-slap my hole and rub my balls..." he pants.

Gabriel grins, "Mm, okay. Good plan, slave."

His right hand gets drawn back and hovers in mid-air over his target as the thumb of his other hand rubs around and around the darkened tissue of Darrek's entrapped balls.

"Yeah... do it," Darrek urges, "Please, Master."

Slap. He strikes the come-smeared hole squarely and Darrek moans, pulling his legs wider still to invite more. *Slap, slap... slap, slap, slap, SLAP*. Darrek shudders and moans even deeper. *Slap, SLAP*. The next couple strikes fall on Darrek's taint and prompt a loud gasping from Darrek's parted lips.

"Nnuhh...so good. So fucking good. Thank you. Thuhhh..."

SLAP, SLAP, SLAP, SLAP.

Darrek's cheeks and inner thighs get the same treatment, as Gabriel smacks them as well, the skin pinking up. But after every few blows, Gabriel returns to the twitching ring of muscle, hot and swollen and flushed a bright red now. Each slap brings a deeper groan and sharper flinch from Darrek.

SLAP, SLAP, SLAP, SLAP. Slapslapslapslapslapslapslapslap.

Head lolled back, Darrek pants and gasps when Gabriel eases up. Gabriel soothes the inflamed skin with gentle caresses of his hands over his balls and opening.

"So beautiful. Such a good slave for me.... Think you could come again? Should we try?"

"Yes please, sir," he gulps, swallowing down lungfuls of air as he catches his breath.

"Okay," Gabriel tells him softly, still rubbing between his legs, massaging the soft flesh of his sac and well-spanked hole. "Free your hands. Let's get the blood flowing back into those."

Gabriel slides his legs out, straightening them and letting

Darrek's legs slide off the arms of the chair. Darrek's feet come to rest on the ottoman, and he flexes them. Stretching, he shakes his hands around, which have been pulled out from behind Gabriel. Pins and needles sting him in places, but all the soreness and throbbing is beyond perfect and exactly what he craves. He loves feeling Gabriel's effect on him in the form of aching tenderness that will last for hours if not days.

Gabriel is sucking a mark on his neck and fondling his balls. Hard enough to cut steel, Darrek fantasizes about what way he'll be permitted his release.

What he least expects is what happens. Gabriel licks over the dark bruise his mouth has left on Darrek's skin and tells him, "All right, Dare. When you're steady enough to manage it, I need you to stand up for me for a second."

Flexing his legs and back, Darrek grunts as he gets to his feet, keeping one hand on the chair for balance.

He pivots to find Gabriel turning on the seat, bracing his hands on the back and planting his knees wide on either side of the seat in exactly the same way Darrek had been positioned when Gabriel was stretching him out. Gabriel's back is bowed, with his ass sticking out toward Darrek and the cameras. That's when he sees the flared, bright red base of whatever Gabriel has lodged up his ass.

"You've had that in you this whole time?" he gasps.

"Mm-hmm," he nods, rocking a little as he fists his erection and clenches his ass around the toy. "Take it out really slow, okay? Then I'm yours."

"Fuck, I love you," Darrek moans.

"Hey, I said I'd let you have payback, didn't I?"

Getting a good grip around the red plastic circle, Darrek pulls gently. At first it doesn't want to come, though, so he pulls even harder to get it moving. Gabriel's hand goes white-knuckle tight where it is curled around the seat back. Gabriel's other hand, still slick with his own spend, works on his cock as a large rounded shape tugs out of his pink hole. When the widest part is free, Gabriel makes a thick, low sound and arches his back more, because although the toy tapers to a narrower diameter, it immediately begins to flare out again. The more Darrek pulls, the wider it gets and he stares as the delicate, flushed tissue hugs, stretched around the hard red globes. The second ripple tugs free, and for a second Gabriel's opening is loose until he clenches up, squeezing the toy inside him.

Darrek pulls even slower as the last ripple stretches Gabriel wide again, and Gabriel's knees tremble under him. Releasing his dick, Gabriel grabs the chair with both hands instead. Leaning forward, he rests his forehead on his forearms. Darrek finds the widest spot on the last globe of the rippled plug and works it in and out, in and out, in and out, teasing it back and forth inside the tight ring of Gabriel's sphincter.

He gasps in what sounds like relief when Darrek oh-so-slowly guides the tip of the plug all the way out and then rubs it up the crack of Gabriel's ass, then down between his legs and over his balls.

"*Shit...*" Gabriel hisses.

Pulling Gabriel's opening apart with fingers prying at the puckered, slightly swollen rim, he rubs over the spot as he nudges the gap with the tip of the huge plug.

"Oh fuck, Dare.... *Fuck...*" he whines.

With steady pressure, Darrek pushes the toy's base, watching the orifice widen again until the wrinkled skin is stretched smooth. With a hard twist of his wrist, he pops the first globe through, and then angles it sharply as he keeps pushing.

He can hear how rough Gabriel's breathing is, sees how flushed his skin has gotten already. Alternately letting his head hang and rest on his arms, and then tensing his whole body and straining his neck with an undulating curve of his spine, Gabriel fights to endure the teasing way Darrek plays with him.

After everything Darrek just gave him, though, and how obedient he was, Gabriel has no choice but to let Darrek have his fun in return.

Darrek shifts to the side, bracing a knee on the ottoman, but otherwise getting out of the way so that the closest camera gets a clear shot of him forcing the thickness of the second ripple into the abused hole. Once through, Darrek twists and rotates the toy, tilting it up then down, grinding the half of the toy buried in Gabriel against his inner walls. Gabriel rasps out rough breaths and widens his stance.

Pushing harder still, Darrek quickly pops the last swell through Gabriel's throbbing and now deeply red pucker, getting the base flush to his body once more. Keeping it in place with two fingers pressing hard on the bottom, Darrek slaps Gabriel's cheeks, the left and then the right. It makes Gabriel gasp and clench. Peppering the thick muscle of Gabriel's backside with strikes of his open palm, Darrek pushes hard in pulses at the red base.

"C'mon, Dare... want you in me, baby..." Gabriel whines.

"Soon," Darrek assures him. "Get up on your knees. Straighten up for me."

Gabriel's brow creases as he gets upright. Darrek dips his head in front of Gabriel and closes his lips around the pink head of Gabriel's cock, licking repeatedly over it. Then he kisses down the shaft until he reaches his balls, which he sucks into his mouth one at a time, rolling his tongue around them and giving as intense pressure as he dares before allowing them to slip free with a wet *plop*.

Then he straightens up too and hugs Gabriel close, guiding Gabriel's arms up to hook behind his neck. Gabriel holds on to Darrek just like that as Darrek bites at Gabriel's lips, sinking his teeth in and tugging while his right hand begins to extract the toy once more. Fingernails scratch along Darrek's spine and Gabriel mewls softly as inch-by-inch, the violating object is tugged back out.

Dropping the rippled plug, Darrek nuzzles into Gabriel's neck and kisses there, dancing his fingertips down along Gabriel's spine. When they get to the curve of his pert little ass, Darrek kneads the muscle—gently at first and then roughly. Heat bakes off of the smooth, flawless skin. Rubbing his palm over the right cheek, Darrek draws his hand back and spanks it soundly.

Gabriel cries out and presses his lips to Darrek's neck. He begins to grind his erection against Darrek's hip in little drags and presses as the next strike of Darrek's palm falls, stinging him, and then the next. A few thick drops of pre-come pulse out over his lover's hipbone and Gabriel ruts against him harder. Threading the fingers of his left hand through the back of Gabriel's hair, Darrek kisses over Gabriel's temple and cheekbone and hits him yet again. His ass jiggles after each hard slap, and Darrek rubs some of the sting away before applying more blows.

Then he simply disentangles himself from Gabriel's embrace and moves to the side. Sliding off of where he'd been kneeling on the chair, Darrek guides Gabriel with a hand gripping around the back of his neck. He gets him bent over more sharply, still kneeling on the seat cushion. Circling the base of his cock, Darrek squirts on a dribble of lube, slicking it quickly over his length. Then, without further warning, he lines up and enters Gabriel in one smooth push, not stopping until his pelvis is snug to the slapped-red curve of Gabriel's ass, covered now with his handprints. Keeping Gabriel steady with a hand wrapping his neck and one bracing his hip, Darrek doesn't ease up and fucks him with deep, long strokes. He moans at the fluttering squeezes of Gabriel around his shaft, at the drag of his head over the velvety soft, but tight cavity. Hearing the slick, fleshy sound of Gabriel jacking himself with brutal force and keening low in his throat, Darrek works his length to full advantage, skittering over Gabriel's prostate again and again.

He knows when Gabriel is about to orgasm. Gabriel's already jagged breathing chokes off completely, and his hand blurs with speed. He fucks himself back onto Darrek and cries out brokenly when Darrek slaps his ass as hard as he can over and over again until ropes of pearly white fluid erupt from him, along with his shuddering cry.

Darrek can feel how close he is too, holding Gabriel's hips with both hands and jackhammering into him with bruising force until he's yelling through his dry orgasm. He fucks into Gabriel as wave after wave of nerve-shattering sensation tears through his body, spiraling out from his balls. He blacks out for a second to find himself draped over Gabriel's back when he awakens a moment later.

Somehow, Gabriel manages to find his feet and Darrek collapses down onto the soiled chair as his Master and lover goes from camera to camera, turning each one off. Gabriel then waddles, bowlegged, to the kitchen, and returns from it with tall bottles of fresh spring water for each of them.

They curl up together on the chair, and try to recover.

"This is my new favorite chair," Darrek grins. "It's ours, now."

"It's *been* ours," Gabriel mocks.

"You know what I mean," he retorts.

Gabriel fingers through Darrek's hair and sips his water. "Do you regret it?" he asks, knowing Darrek will understand.

"No. Do you?"

"Sometimes. But mostly no."

"I wouldn't do it again, I don't think. It was something I think I needed to try, but it's not what I want. I get that now. All I want is you. Because *you* are all I know how to handle."

"Mmm," he hums. "Likewise. But we *will* need to have the chair cleaned."

"Do we have to?" Darrek complains. "I like that it smells like sex and *you.*"

"We'll see. Oh. Hey, I um... booked a flight today. Two round trip tickets to sunny Texas. There and back the same day. We don't even need to pack."

"Wow, really? Gabriel... you don't have to do that you know."

"Yeah, but I need to say goodbye to all of that. I need to show my mom I'm alive, and that I survived without her, and I need to show Harry that he didn't win. We leave this Saturday morning."

Gabriel presses a kiss to each of Darrek's eyelids, wanting to soothe away the concern there.

"You make me so happy, Dare. That's why I can do this now. All my dreams have come true. It's incredible. I'm finally free of the nightmare."

"Whatever you need," Darrek agrees. "If you need this, we'll do it together. If it means you'll be able to let it go—let *them* go."

"That's what I'm hoping. Out with the old, in with the new," Gabriel declares.

"Mmm...."

"My ass is stinging like a bitch, by the way."

"Aw, want me to rub some ointment on your tushie?" Darrek offers with a waggle of his eyebrows.

Gabriel grins and says, "Okay. Want me to get some ice for your nuts? I smacked 'em pretty fucking hard."

"Yeah, but wrap the ice in a towel or something. The last thing I need is more ball torture from you right now."

"Oh, you can take it. Don't be a pussy."

"I think I've soundly proved tonight that I am not in any way, shape or form, a *pussy*, thank you very much."

Grinning hugely, Gabriel leans in and cups Darrek's face in his hands. Kissing Darrek tenderly, sweetly and repeatedly on the mouth, he breaks away after long moments. Licking his kiss-swollen lips, Gabriel gets to his feet to fetch the ointment and ice.

"Okay. You can have a towel," he relents.

"Oh, look at how much you love me," Darrek gushes. "It's adorable."

Gabriel shoots him a happy, supremely contented glance and shakes his head, chuckling, as he goes.

Chapter 43
Please Allow Me to Introduce Myself

There are plans being made by Gabriel and Darrek's friends to confront Harry behind their backs. The only clear sign of this that Gabriel and Darrek ever receive is Kyle and Ben's extreme quietness in the days leading up to their one-day trip to Texas and back. Ben's quietness is less noticeable than Kyle's, though, since all he has to do is avoid Gabriel's phone calls and maybe send a short text in reply, using a heavy workload as an excuse.

Kyle, however, is forced to be with Darrek all day, every day during that week at work. And as the one of their foursome with the most guilt-stricken conscience over what they are planning to do, it's hardest for him to act like everything is normal. It's not that he doesn't want to do it, or doesn't think Harry deserves it, it simply is doubtful to Kyle that it's their responsibility to dole out this man's punishment, especially if they do it without Gabriel's knowledge or consent. Ben and Trace will not be dissuaded, though. After so many years with having to live with the graphic, nightmarish knowledge of what that man did to Gabriel, and not being able to do a damn thing about it, this is their one glorious chance to set things right.

Meanwhile, Darrek is distracted by the looming emotional turmoil that the trip will undoubtedly cause Gabriel, so at first he doesn't notice the oddness of Kyle's behavior. But, after a while, when no snarky comments have been made, no corny jokes told or any off-color references to Kyle and Ben's sex life alluded to, Darrek starts to catch on.

Friday, the day before the trip, he pulls Kyle out of earshot of the other guys they work with before they both leave for home after a long day slaving away in the hot, blistering sun. There is a bench in the shade, and they sit on it.

Kyle's lowered gaze drifts up and over Darrek's legs to his thighs where his hands are resting, his fingers woven loosely together. He can't help thinking about that night—that *one night* he was permitted to be with Darrek; the taste of his dick sliding on his tongue, trapped between his lips, the tight, silken feel of his ass when Gabriel let Kyle finger Darrek as he sucked him off. Kyle savors the memory, locked away like a priceless jewel in the vault of his mind, of what he was given permission to experience with a man he will always love in some sense or other. Darrek will always be in his heart.

Kyle's hand creeps over to Darrek's and overlays it. The fingertips tuck under the side of Darrek's hand and Darrek gently closes up his grip, holding on to Kyle. The softness and warmth of Kyle's hand is a contrast to the cold tension and warring emotions in his face.

"What's up?" Darrek asks.

"So you guys are really going down there tomorrow?"

"Yeah."

Kyle bites his lip and drags a thumb over the back of Darrek's hand. He wants to get down on his knees for Darrek again, and give whatever Darrek wants to take from him. He wants to submit to him and use sex and pleasure to distract them both from their worries. It's not going to happen. Kyle gets that. But it doesn't mean he can't still want it.

"What are you gonna do when you see those people? How are you going to keep from just wringing their necks?"

"I have to do what Gabriel needs me to do. I'm there as a support system for him, and hell, I know what it's like to have parents fail you. If *he* can be strong, and mature, and rise above all this bullshit, with everything he went through, then I have no choice, do I? Plus, I fully believe in karma. They'll all get what's coming to 'em. I have no doubt in my mind."

Kyle laughs nervously, and shakes his head as if to clear it. "Me too, man. Me too."

Darrek smiles and looks down at their joined hands. It occurs to him the intimate places where Kyle's hands have been, and the recent sexual encounter they have shared. Butterflies knock around in his stomach at the dim certainty that one day, it will happen again. The circumstances will be just right, there'll be temptation, and then... then it'll go even farther than it did the first time.

Shifting a little in his seat, Darrek hopes that Kyle doesn't see that his jeans are getting pulled a little snug in the front. But when he tugs down the front of his t-shirt, he's pretty sure Kyle is staring right at his crotch anyway. It only gets worse when Kyle slides closer on the bench and asks right by Darrek's ear, really soft and light, a purr of sounds that make goosebumps rise over the skin of Darrek's neck, "You really love him, don't you? You really want to do right by him."

"Yeah, I do," Darrek nods, clearing his throat. "He's a part of me now. Always will be. I just want to see him happy. He's had too many demons to put up with for too long. Maybe tomorrow will be the thing that sets it all right. Then we can move on and just live, you know?"

Kyle makes a small sound and turns his face away. He's crying, Darrek sees in a flash. Just a little, just some redness and dampness around his eyes, but it's enough for Darrek to notice.

"Hey, what's going on with you? You've been weird all week. Maybe longer actually, now that I think about it... Why are you upset?"

"Just ignore me," Kyle grins, wiping at his eyes. "Must be my time of the month and hearing your awesome love story."

"Bullshit," Darrek frowns. "You're freaking me out now. Is this... is this about us? You and me? About what happened? 'Cause I thought we were cool...."

"We are. And it's not. I'm just... reevaluating things for myself." He flicks a glance up at Darrek's eyes and looks instantly away in case he's able to read what's there. "I do think about it. About being with you and kissing Gabe. I won't lie. And you know how I feel about you. That hasn't changed. This is about something else entirely, though. I swear. But I can't talk about it, okay? Can we leave it at that?"

"Of course," Darrek says. Kyle stands and Darrek doesn't quite understand why but he doesn't want to let go of Kyle's hand. He grips it tighter and holds him there.

"Good luck. Tell me how it goes," Kyle says in goodbye, deflecting the daggers of concern shooting from Darrek's eyes.

"Do I need to be worried about you?"

Kyle lifts their joined hands and kisses the back of Darrek's. He tastes of salty sweat and something familiar when he licks over his lips, tries to pull away and fails. "Let me go. Please? I'm fine."

He doesn't bother to try to disguise the flush of heat coloring his face at being trapped there by Darrek, at being made to beg for his freedom. Kyle pulls harder at the vice of Darrek's fist clamped down over his hand and Darrek simply shifts his grip higher, holding Kyle's wrist instead.

"Then why don't I believe you? You're not fine. And you're lying to me."

It feels important. It feels like the universe trying to tell him something. Like fate whispering in his ear if only he could make out the words. Kyle is staring at Darrek's hand clutching to him, and says Darrek's name in a barely audible, hopeless supplication.

Darrek misinterprets.

"If he's hurting you, Kyle, and I mean really *hurting* you, I swear to *God*..."

"Nah... nothin' like that," Kyle assures him with a too-easy grin and lies hiding in his eyes. "No worries. Have a great trip, okay?"

And with that, Kyle turns his back, sets a quick pace and is lost from sight as he disappears around the corner.

"You're sure this is it?" Darrek asks, sitting on another, different bench less than twelve hours later, but this bench is in Texas, two car rides and a short flight away. It's in front of a towering office building. Floor after floor of shining glass windows reach up to the sky. The downtown traffic bustles just behind them, with the raised, paved courtyard in front of the building's main entrance providing a small barrier to keep milling pedestrians away. They are seated on the far side of the courtyard, eying the doors across from them. So far only two young women have emerged as lunchtime nears.

"This is it," Gabriel nods. "I called his Executive Assistant, Cherri, when we got off the plane and you were in the bathroom. She confirmed he was in today. I said I was a relative with a surprise for him. She said he leaves by this door to go get lunch at the café across the street there every day, and that was our best chance to catch him."

Darrek's knees bounce restlessly. He feels cold though the day is a humid one. Skin clammy and stomach sick, he would rather be anywhere else. He's already asked what Gabriel's planning to do. Each time he asks, the response is always the same: *'I'll know what to do when I see him. I just need to see him with my own eyes, one more time.'*

While Darrek is visibly a nervous wreck, Gabriel, as usual, is calm and collected. Not a hair out of place, dressed in a dark gray suit minus the tie, he looks as intimidating and determined as he did when Darrek first saw him—catching a fleeting glimpse in Diadem's dungeon of the eerily beautiful man that knew just how to sweep him off his feet and take him apart piece by piece. Gabriel's hands are folded loosely between his knees, and he stares, predatory, at the double glass doors. He doesn't move, doesn't blink. He barely breathes.

Time draws out. And then....

"That's him." It comes out quiet, a confiding whisper from the side of his mouth. Darrek's eyes shoot open wide and his head snaps up to stare at the nondescript, gray-haired man with briefcase in hand striding on a diagonal path to the steps leading to the crosswalk near where their bench is positioned. When he has scanned the trim figure of the fifty- or sixtyish guy that Gabriel has identified as his stepfather, Darrek looks back to Gabriel with concern.

"Okay, let's go," Gabriel says quickly, ducking his head down and nearly bolting from the bench toward the stairs in the opposite direction of Harry.

"Uh... sure," Darrek manages, jogging a little to catch up.

But the sudden movement attracts the attention of their prey.

Gabriel gets not twenty feet when he hears, "*Gabriel?* Gabey is that you? I can't believe it. Is it really you...?"

It freezes Gabriel to the spot, mid-stride with his back to the others. Darrek positions himself between Gabriel and the man addressing him, but keeps his eyes locked to Gabriel, waiting for the word, the sign, to act, to do *something*.

Eyes focused on nothing, Gabriel calls out, "No. No, it's not."

"Yes it is. It's you. Come here. Let me see you. My eyes aren't what they were...."

"No! Don't you talk to me like you *know* me!" Gabriel barks viciously, finally turning in place, facing the greatest monster he has ever been haunted by. "You don't *know me*! You are *nothing* to me."

Darrek watches out of the corner of his eye as Harry gets closer, walking slowly their way. He can almost feel him looking at Gabriel, trying to get a full, vivid image of his face, his body.

"Gabe, let's go," Darrek says quietly, taking Gabriel's arm.

"Son, wait!" Harry calls when he sees the gesture.

"You are *nothing* to me!" Gabriel repeats, not shaking Darrek off but not leaving either. He has a few things to say first after all it seems. "I see that now. You're pathetic. Just a pathetic, perverted, disturbed old man."

"Son!!"

Harry is closer now. Darrek's skin begins to itch. His hand clenches into a fist at his side.

"My father is *dead*," Gabriel spits. "You aren't my goddamned *father*. You? You're just a sick piece of shit who can't hurt me or tell me what to do anymore. Goodbye, Harry."

Gabriel takes hold of the hand Darrek has been using to grip his elbow and they start walking without looking back. They descend a small flight of steps and take off down the block. Crossing a crosswalk with the stream of humanity flowing around them, they round a corner and see the rental car waiting.

"Get in," Gabriel grunts, hitting the button on the keys to unlock the doors.

"Are you okay??" Darrek asks with raw and almost frantic worry in his voice. He gets in and sits in the passenger seat, scanning Gabriel for signs of an impending breakdown.

"We should get going. My mom lives about a hundred miles from here and it's gonna take a while to get free of the city traffic. It isn't noon yet, so we might be lucky and miss the rush if we go now. Then we might get back to the airport in time to have a nice dinner somewhere—"

"Gabriel!" Darrek interrupts. He reaches over the armrest and takes Gabriel's hand in his again. It had been gripped to him tightly enough to bruise on the way back to the car—strong as steel and twice as unyielding. Now, it lays timid as a butterfly in Darrek's palm, fluttering with tremors that start to wrack his body. Closing his other hand over the hand to still it, Darrek presses Gabriel with audible love, "You okay?"

"No," Gabriel gasps, shaking his head as wetness gathers on his eyelashes. He sniffs loudly and fiddles with the keys in his left hand. "No, I'm not *okay*."

"Maybe this was a bad idea. Maybe a letter would have been better...."

"No. I needed to see him. He... I don't know. He got bigger in my head after all the years with only memories to go on. I didn't take any pictures of my family with me when I ran away. I didn't want to remember them, so things got distorted I guess. He was huge, but... he's just an *old man*. I'm *bigger* than him. A *lot* bigger. And that voice... it's the same voice I hear in my head all the time, but... I don't know."

"Not so scary?"

"Mm-mm," Gabriel grunts, stabbing mindlessly at the dashboard's plastic with the point of the thick metal ignition key. "This was good. It was good. Wasn't a bad idea. It was good. Stupid, but good. Really good. Really..." he mumbles dazedly.

"Hey..." Darrek hushes. "Want me to drive?"

"Um. Yeah. Yeah. Here," he says, handing over the keys. Gabriel doesn't reach for the door handle to get out, though. He keeps staring at the steering wheel.

"Gabe?"

"Mm?"

"I'm proud of you," Darrek smiles hopefully.

"Me too," Gabriel grins shyly back.

Chapter 44
Wicked Lies

The three men wait until Gabriel is walking away and almost out of sight. The side basement door they have been waiting behind opens out on the busy sidewalk, and the lock had been easy enough to jimmy and crack open.

Hundreds, if not thousands, of pedestrians flood by, thinking only of themselves and clutching their handbags and cases as they shuffle toward their destinations. They don't see the three uniformed men in dark glasses and hats hook an arm around the elderly businessman and pull him in through the darkened doorway, closing the door swiftly behind. It happens in not even a second. One moment they're there, the next they're not.

Micah had scouted out the pattern Harry took on his lunch breaks over the past week. It had been the most consistent part of his day. Never failing, he would go to the same corner café, taking the same route each time. They'd found out through Kyle's texts with Darrek that morning that Gabriel was planning on confronting Harry near the same time, for the same reasons—it was the best chance to pin Harry down.

Kyle has been left back at home, his phone calls to Darrek their only link to Darrek and Gabriel's actions and whereabouts. In case they should ever be suspected for what they are about to do, however, they need Kyle's calls to originate from home, and not Texas. It's instrumental to the plan, but a source of much anxiety for Kyle, who is therefore able to do nothing but imagine what is happening with his Master, his lovers, his friends.

With the single, ancient security camera easily dismantled, it is safer to act in the basement than to try to take Harry away by car, or try to grab him in the parking garage. Latching the metal door, they each pull black hoods down over their faces and turn on the flood-light in Ben's hand, shining it at Harry's face to blind him.

Trace has him down on the ground with an arm pulled up tight under his jaw, pressing gently on his windpipe. Micah swiftly gets the metal cuffs on Harry's wrists and ankles, chaining them together with as little slack as possible. It leaves Harry with his arms pulled awkwardly down between sharply bent knees, his spine digging painfully into the concrete. Kneeling on the length of chain strung between his ankles, Micah keeps him from twisting away.

For a long minute he looks like nothing but a grandfatherly, harmless old man. But they all know better than to be fooled by appearances.

"Who was that pretty little thing you were just talking to? That your boyfriend? He's awfully pretty..." Trace coos, bile dripping from the words, as he slides the long, well-sharpened blade from its sheath on his thigh.

"You the assholes that broke into my apartment?" Harry growls. Fighting against Micah and Trace, he blinks at the blinding light.

"Did you like our present?" Trace grins. "Notice you didn't call the cops or anything, so you couldn't have been *too* upset with us."

"If you're trying to blackmail me with those files... well... they aren't mine. You can't prove they're mine. I'm with one of the best law firms in the state. You... you...."

With a jerk of his arm, Trace cuts off Harry's air, silencing him. As Harry chokes, Trace says, "That's enough from you. You talk when we allow you to talk. You know those files are yours. We can prove it. Let's leave it at that. We're not here to blackmail you. We don't want your filthy money."

By now Harry is bucking and pulling at Trace's arm in a feeble attempt to get a breath of air.

"Understand?" he asks sweetly.

Harry makes a strangled sound and nods, his face beet red and lips beginning to turn blue.

Trace lets up, and Harry gulps down a lungful of air.

"Now, here's the game we're going to play," Trace instructs.

"Those pictures we found? One of those little boys is a member of my family. You raped him. Repeatedly. What you did scarred him for life and hurt him in ways you can't even begin to imagine. So I want to hear you say his name. That's all. I want to hear you say his name and admit what you did to him."

Lifting the knife, he drags it feather-light over Harry's throat. Micah reaches up and, using huge, equally sharp scissors, starts to quickly cut his suit away. The edge of Trace's blade leaves the equivalent of a paper cut in its wake, not even slicing deep enough to bleed.

"And if you stay quiet? You die. I don't want to kill you, but I will if I have no choice. So you better start talking."

Harry's eyes dart around, his mouth works soundlessly as he digests the instructions.

"I'm gonna give you to the count of three. Then I want to hear a name, or I slice your throat and leave your body here covered in the pictures of your victims for the cops to find. Talk to me, Harry. Say the name. One...."

"No wait!"

"Two...."

"Maybe we can work something out...."

"Three."

"Parker! Parker Shepherd!"

Micah looks up at Ben and sees the muscles in his body all go tense at once like he's getting ready to pounce or fight. They knew this was a possibility, for him to say a name other than Gabriel's, since the proof was there that there could have been other victims. It doesn't make it any easier to hear, though. None of the pictures they'd found on the drive they'd hacked into showed Harry with the boys, so they could have been downloaded pornography rather than snapshots specifically taken by Harry. The sound of the name voiced from the monster's lips validates everything they have feared.

"Parker Shepherd," Trace mimics. "You raped him?"

In the darkness behind the floodlight, Ben holds the microphone on the digital recorder toward Harry's face.

Harry fights, defiance starting to color his features.

"You raped him? You raped Parker?"

The point of the knife twists where it rests, opening the skin right above Harry's collarbone.

"AHH! STOP! Yes! YES! I did it!"

"How old was he when you raped him?"

"...I don't know... twelve? Eleven?"

Trace glances at Micah. "Well, Harry, that's not the name we're looking for. But I think Parker deserves some justice too, don't you?" He says to Micah, "Hold his left arm."

The pasty-white skin of the top of Harry's arm, wrinkled, loose and covered in age spots, covering lean muscle that hints at former strength that's been wilted by time and age, is overlaid with Trace's glinting silver blade. Working quickly and skillfully, the first three letters are done before Harry even feels what's happening and begins to scream. A rag is stuffed in his mouth, laced with a chemical to keep his muscles relaxed, his senses slightly dulled without diminishing his pain.

When Parker's full name is engraved on Harry's arm, Micah's gloved hand dips into the container of black ink. Getting a good dollop of it, he rubs it into the wound, coating the thin, deeply scrawling lines thoroughly; making sure they are filled before wiping the excess away and covering the strip with a narrow bandage.

"Okay," Trace growls. "Let's try this again. Those pictures we found? One of those boys was a member of my family. You raped him. Repeatedly. And scarred him for life. So I want to hear you say his name and *admit what you did to him.* And if you say the wrong name, guess what happens? If you say the *right* name, we leave, and you live. So what do ya say, Harry? Gimme a name...."

The phone rings two or three times where it's been stuck in the tray under the stereo in the rental car before Gabriel reaches for it and looks at the caller ID. Darrek is changing lanes and searching for their exit, so it falls to him to take the call.

"It's Kyle. Again."

"I'll call him back later," Darrek says offhandedly. "Let it go to voicemail."

"Nah. You said he sounded weird last time..." Gabriel flips open the phone. "Yeah, it's Gabriel."

"How's it going, Gabe? I've been worried about you guys," Kyle says from the other end of the bad connection.

"Well, it's been one of those days, ya know?" He slumps back in his seat and lays his head against the headrest, closing his eyes. Darrek glances over and his lips quirk in a pleased grin.

"So you saw him then. Did you say anything? Did he see you?"

"Yeah. To both. It wasn't anything like I thought it'd be."

"No, I guess not. Where you headed to now?"

"To see my mom. I think that'll be even harder. I was just a kid when I disappeared on her. Never even sent a letter to tell her I was alive. I feel pretty guilty about that, even if she did ruin my childhood."

"Damn. I don't even know what to say, man. Let me know how it goes, okay? I've been freaking out over here. Can't get anything done. Is Dare there? Can I tell him somethin'?"

"Sure. Hold on."

"Oh, and Gabe?"

"Yeah?"

"Good luck. We're all pullin' for ya."

"I know. Thanks. Here's Darrek."

He hands the phone over and Darrek feels the knot of anxiety loosen a little at the small glow of hope and strength on Gabriel's face.

"Kyle?" Darrek asks.

"Get him out of there if it starts to go south. Don't make him deal with that woman if she goes psycho on him. I don't care if she *is* his mother. She's done enough damage."

"You don't have to tell me. That's why I'm here. I'm gonna do what's best for Gabe, and that's it."

He can feel Gabriel looking at him, but Darrek keeps his eyes on the road.

"Look," Darrek continues, "I'm still worried about you. Everything okay over there? Is Ben around? Can I talk to him?"

"Nope. I'm alone. He's busy today. I guess that's why all I can do is sit here and worry about y'all. I'll let you go. I won't call anymore, but please let me know if Gabe's okay after all of this. I'd appreciate it. The other guys are all worried too."

"Sure. I'll do that. Later."

"Later."

The phone gets shut off and tucked into Darrek's pocket.

"No more calls 'til this is finished," Darrek says, turning on his blinker and merging onto the exit ramp.

"Yeah. Last thing I need is for Knox or Trace to start hounding me. At least Kyle is...."

"Sensitive to your feelings?" Darrek offers. "He is a well-trained sub. He knows how to make people he likes happy."

"I just never thought I'd be confiding in him like that. It's so odd. But just as odd as everything else today."

"Yeah," Darrek agrees.

"Maybe she won't be home. Maybe she's on vacation or works weird hours..." Gabriel debates worriedly, chewing at his lips and breaking out in a cold sweat. They round the corner, and pull down the street. There's a big old house on the far end with a cluster of mailboxes out front.

"That's it. She must live in one of those units. God, it's so small. Our house used to be huge. Guess the divorce took its toll."

Gabriel grabs the printout with the directions and folds it twice just to keep his hands busy. There's a car parked halfway up the cracked and fading driveway that leads around back to a wider paved area for the tenants to park in. The trunk is opened. The house's front door is ajar.

"That could be another tenant. It doesn't mean it's her car," Gabriel rationalizes.

"I can park over here and you can just sit here a while," Darrek suggests as he pulls over to the far side of the road diagonal from the house. "You don't have to confront her if you aren't ready. This is your decision."

The screen door swings out and an older woman with dyed-blonde hair comes walking out. She heads over to the opened trunk, the handles of some plastic bags sticking out of it. Gabriel bites his nails and makes a small, thick, desperate sound. He lets his left hand rest on the door's handle and leans on the door.

"That's my mom." The words are choked with emotion, and Gabriel's face crumbles the longer he looks at her. "That's her. It's her. She looks so old. And tired."

Darrek parks the car and shuts off the engine. The woman doesn't turn around or give any sign she sees them. He squeezes Gabriel's knee and rubs small circles there.

"What do you want to do?"

"I don't know," he breathes with wide eyes. Darrek can almost see the debate raging in Gabriel's head. Does he let her think he's gone for good? Do they drive away without saying anything? Would the pain from regret over inaction outweigh the difficulty of getting out of this car and going over there? Can he do this without dying a little inside?

"Dare, I need you to help." Gabriel looks back at him, seeming young and scared, his eyes huge and cheeks tear-stained. "I can't do this part on my own. It's different than with Harry. He's just a monster. She... she's my *mom*. And she didn't *protect me* from him...."

"Hey. All right. Hang on. I'm gonna get out, okay? I'll come around to your side."

Gabriel nods once. Darrek is out in a flash, and walks around to the passenger door. Gabriel's mother has retreated back inside but the trunk is still open. She'll be back out.

He opens Gabriel's door and Gabriel swings his legs out, holding on to the car's frame and staring at the darkened house. A fresh tear slides down over his cheekbone.

"Want me to talk to her first? You can just stay here, next to the car?" Darrek offers.

Gabriel cups his hands over his mouth and nose to mask the emotion spilling out.

He nods.

Helping Gabriel to his feet, Darrek shuts the door and turns to the house. Hands stuffed in his pockets, he walks slowly toward the driveway and the house beyond. Gabriel's mother emerges and sees him coming.

"Howdy," she says politely. "Help you with something?"

"Yeah, um... my name's Darrek Grealey. You don't know me, but I know your son, Gabriel."

She flinches, shocked. The color starts to drain from her face and her hands go to her mouth as she gasps.

"G-gabriel?!"

"Yeah. He's um... he's here. He came to see you but it's kind of hard for him."

"Oh my god! Gabriel?! He's *alive*?! Where is he? I need to see him! Where is he? Gabriel?! Oh my god. *Oh my god!* My baby. My son. I can't believe it." She's scanning the road with her eyes, and sees the man across the way, hugging himself next to the parked green sedan.

"GABRIEL?!"

She breaks into a run, dashing toward him clumsily, nearly tripping over a bush in the yard. Darrek chases after her. He can hear Gabriel's sob from almost forty feet away. Gabriel is a mess, thick cries wringing from him as he watches the mother who failed him so profoundly dash toward him.

When she's almost close enough to touch, he jumps back, inching backward around the car.

"Stop! Stay back!!" he shouts. Darrek runs faster, getting between them. He holds a hand up to Gabriel's mother.

"Give him a second," he tells her. "Give him some space."

"Don't touch me! Just... just stay there," Gabriel barks at her, sneering in defiance before his face twists with pained devastation.

"I thought you were dead," she gasps. "For so many years, I... I was sure of it.... And look at you! You're beautiful, honey. Oh, my Gabriel. Look at the man you've become. You look just like your father...."

Her hands go to her heart, pressing there like it might burst right out of her chest. She's crying too, but her face is alight like she's just been granted her life's greatest wish.

"I'm not *your* Gabriel," he says gruffly. Darrek steps closer to him and holds his shoulders as he tries to lunge for her. He's too pale, and Darrek can see it all affecting him. This was too much for one day, he realizes too late. Far too much. "You. You let him hurt me! You! You married that... that *thing*, that *child molester*. And when I tried to tell you... when I needed you to *help*, to *save me* from him, you called me a liar! How could you do that?! All of those years... it was YOUR fault! You were my mother and you did NOTHING. The *things* he *did to me...*" he sobs, shaking his head, lower lip quivering around the words.

"I know," she whispers, but it's a fearful, guilty sound. "I know that now."

"YOU DON'T KNOW!" he screams. "Your husband fucked me, over and over, in YOUR BED. He'd sneak into my room at night, like the boogeyman, and hold me down and RAPE ME. He threatened to kill me. Do you know *that*?! Do you?! Do you know that h-he held knives to my throat? H-he threatened to chop off my genitals. He burned me with cigarettes. And I was a *baby*! I was supposed to be *YOUR* baby! *How could you let it happen*?! Why didn't you DO ANYTHING?!"

"I didn't want it to be true. I was in denial. I never knew. Not really. Not until you left. And then it was too late. Years too late." She reaches out a hand to him, but he hangs on to Darrek and keeps his distance.

"I don't want to know you," Gabriel says with forced control. "I don't want you in my life. But I needed... closure. To let you see that I'm okay. I'm happy now – happier than I ever was before. It took thirty years of living, but I survived and I'm finally happy. Darrek loves me better than you *ever* did. He takes care of me, and I take care of him because he knows ALL about how family lets you down. *He's* my family now. I'm gonna be with him for the rest of my life, and we are going to be *happy*."

Gabriel's mother is crying hysterically, bracing a hand on the car. She doesn't try to defend herself, or ask forgiveness. Her heart breaks at the bitter words, but part of her heals at the knowledge that her child is alive, and has a good life.

"Dare, I want to go. I want to go, Darrek. All right? Let's go. I'm done. I'm done."

"All right," he says gently, feeling the muscles of Gabriel's shoulders and upper arms bunch under his hands. Hesitantly, he releases Gabriel, but Gabriel's hands are locked on him. He's staring at his mother as she gazes longingly over at him, wiping at her tears and crying into her hand. Backing away, Darrek peels Gabriel's hands off of him. He moves out from between the mother and son.

She sniffs and nods, resignedly. Then she backs away too, moving out of Gabriel's path so that he can get in the car. She moves to hug herself in an unconscious near-perfect mirror of the way Gabriel had been standing moments ago.

Time slows, drawing out as Darrek goes to the driver's side door. He opens it and stands there, watching the thick tension between the other two.

"It's okay Gabe. C'mon," he urges.

"It's why I divorced him," she tries. "I found out from the police. A neighborhood boy accused him, but then dropped the charges. It made me see the light, though. I kicked him out. But I'd already lost you. That's the greatest punishment anyone could ever give me."

Part of the car is between them, but at this new confession, Gabriel suddenly lashes out, seething and screaming. Drawing back his fist, he flies at her. "You BITCH!"

"No! Gabe, no!" Darrek just barely manages to get between them. Ms. Hunter recoils, yelping with fear as Gabriel's control snaps. "No!"

"You believed a stranger? A STRANGER?!"

Darrek holds him by the arms, using every bit of his larger size to restrain his lover who spits and claws, trying to get free of him in order to inflict some small measure of his pain on his mother.

"*Let me go,*" Gabriel rages.

"You know that I can't."

Gabriel's mother is shaking, her eyes wide with terror and desolation.

"No, it's okay. Y-you should hate me," she tells him, her voice hushed.

Gabriel sucks in a lungful of air and bellows, "I DO!"

"I missed you," she whispers in confession, trying to reach him somehow. "I love you, sweetie. I always will. Even if you hate me. You should hate me."

Gabriel sucks in a rough breath and breaks a little more. Gradually some of the fight begins to drain from him. When he tries to yank his arms free of Darrek's hold on them, it's with less violent urgency. Darrek knows it's not to get away, but to feel the connection and draw strength from him through it.

He continues to deflate in Darrek's arms, so with a steady, insistent look, deeply into Gabriel's eyes, Darrek asks him to end this.

"Take me home," Gabriel says quietly to him. "I'm done. We're done."

He presses a quick, soft kiss to Gabriel's temple and releases him. He is careful, however, to stay between them as Gabriel goes back to his side of the car and gets in.

Gabriel's mother looks frantically up at Darrek, and says, "Thank you. Thank you for bringing him here. I just want him to be okay. I want him to be happy. Take... take care of him for me."

Gabriel closes the door and folds in on himself.

Standing stricken in the middle of the road, she calls out, *"I love you Gabriel!"*

But he's not looking, not listening. Darrek nods once to her, and gets into his seat. He starts the engine and looks to Gabriel.

"Go," Gabriel rasps.

Shifting into drive, Darrek carefully pulls away, leaving Gabriel's mother behind to watch her son leave her a second time, with no idea where he's headed, or what may befall him there. All she knows is a new name, Darrek Grealey, and that her child is happy and safe at last. It's not much, but it's enough.

Chapter 45
Absolution

Kyle's phone rings. It's not Darrek. He can tell without even looking, and it's not because he doesn't hear the puppy-bark ringtone he set for when Darrek calls him. It's a generic ring, a shriller sound, because Ben is calling him from the disposable prepaid phone he'd bought before flying to Texas with Trace and Micah.

His hand shakes a little as it picks up the phone and turns it over.

"Yes, sir," he answers with, sounding even meeker than he'd intended.

"It's done. I'm coming home. The package will be picked up in a few hours."

"Yes, sir."

"The project went off without a hitch. So don't worry. I'll see you soon. How's Gabriel?"

"Wrecked. But he'll be okay, I think. He's moving on."

There's a pause in which Ben just listens to Kyle breathe. "What do you want to ask me?"

"Um..." Kyle murmurs.

"Go on."

"What was the total?"

"I don't think you want to know."

"Ben, *please*," Kyle begs.

"We'll talk when I get home. This line isn't secure."

"*Ben....*"

There's a loud exhale, then the distant sound of a metal door slamming shut.

"Seven. And not a single one was the one we were looking for."

There's a hollow *clack* and Ben can't hear Kyle anymore. Because Kyle set the phone down.

"Kyle! HEY! KYLE!"

"What?" he croaks, wrung out and just done with all of it.

Ben's voice is soft and low, a soothing hum surprisingly crisp given the miles upon miles separating them.

"I'm holding you. Can you feel me? My arms are wound around your back and no one can touch you. No one but me. I'm right there with you. Mm... you feel so warm. I'm just gonna hold you like this all night. Okay? I want you to go lie down on the bed and fall asleep with my arms around you. When you wake up, I'll be kissing your perfect lips and it'll be a new day.... So. Can you feel me?"

"Yeah," Kyle nods, letting out a shaky laugh in relief. "I love you," he whispers. "Come home?"

"I'm coming," Ben promises. "I love you too, Kyle. Now go and do what I asked."

"Yes, sir."

He hangs up.

There is a man, faceless to him, in a cold, dark room. His skin is carved up, inscribed with the names of seven of his young victims—innocent children he molested and abused more than once, more than twice. None of those names are Gabriel's.

This was why they had to do it. They had to mark him for anyone and everyone to see, so that they would know what he is. Kyle knows that the final act that they performed was to cut the words 'I rape children' into Gabriel's abuser's face, across his cheekbones. The recidivism rate for Harry's type of crime is astronomical. Even if you send them to jail, even if you give them treatment, even if they repent, even if you chop off their penises, *they will still keep doing it*. It's a compulsion they can never overcome. *Ever.*

So the logic of Trace and Ben was that if you cannot stop the criminal, except through death, then you at least give clear warning to potential victims. No longer will Harry be able to blend in and ascend the ladder of success at his law firm. No longer will he be able to approach a woman or a child without them being able to see on his face exactly what he is, no matter how charming he is, no matter what excuses he gives or lies he tells.

Kyle is glad they didn't have to resort to murder. They would have done it—Trace, Ben and Micah. Their anger was enough to push them over that line. Kyle is the one that acted as the voice of reason, afraid for their consciences, for the damnation of their souls. A murder is a murder, no matter the victim. He begged Ben not to go that far, to let Harry stand and be judged for his sins instead. Kyle simply didn't want to lose Ben. It was selfish, really. Perhaps he was putting his own interests ahead of those children's, but he couldn't take the chance that Ben would be caught, tried and convicted for his act of vengeance and justice for Gabriel.

Turning off his phone, he can still feel Ben with him—a whisper in his ear, a caress of his skin, a warmth in his chilled heart. He goes upstairs and curls up in bed, wanting to know more, to be with the others. He has played his part. Now the pieces must fall and land where they may.

Gabriel sleeps the whole way back to the rental car drop-off at the airport. He's on autopilot when they take the shuttle to the main entrance and then have to trek to their terminal to wait for the flight. After checking in at their gate and verifying the departure time, they go to a restaurant inside the airport's marketplace where they pick at their meals and Gabriel downs the two beers he orders without really tasting them or saying a word. There's a hockey game playing on a flat-screen monitor mounted to the wall over the bar, right in his line of sight. He stares at the action, fixated, when a fight breaks out and the players start beating each other bloody.

Darrek calls Kyle, and when he doesn't answer, leaves a message saying that everything went well and they're on their way home. He calls Ben and Trace too, at Gabriel's request, leaving them similar messages when they don't pick up. Little do Darrek or Gabriel know that Ben, Trace and Micah are at that moment in the very same building that they are, hurrying to another airline's departure gate as their flight is called for boarding.

As they go back to their gate to sit and wait for their flight to be called, Gabriel dozes off again with his head propped against Darrek's shoulder and his arms folded over his chest.

A few hours later, they are airborne and Darrek is the one that falls asleep. Gabriel listens to music on his iPod and replays everything in his head, dissecting, labeling and categorizing every second, every look, and every word.

They don't talk about any of it, except for when they've arrived at their destination and are climbing into Darrek's truck in the parking lot for the last leg of their tiresome journey, back to the comfort and safety of their home. Starlight and street lights shine down from above.

"You okay?" Darrek asks for possibly the millionth time. He asks mainly because the answer keeps changing.

Gabriel thinks it over as crickets chirp from the weeds lining the asphalt and an engine roars in the distance.

"Yes."

Darrek waits patiently, hoping for more.

Sighing, Gabriel admits, "I feel better now. I feel like I can separate the past from the present a little bit better. It's what I needed."

There is still an expectant look in Darrek's eyes, though. They sit in their seats and begin the last drive of the day, wiped out and emotionally exhausted.

When they are finally standing inside their own house, what seems like lifetimes later instead of mere hours, they go upstairs and pull clothes off of travel-weary bodies. Darrek isn't sleepy because he slept again in the car as well as on the plane. Gabriel isn't sleepy for other, subtler reasons.

Knowing instinctively and without a doubt what comes next, Darrek slips on some loose pants and watches Gabriel root through his gear.

He comes back with a thick leather collar connected to a leash and a set of wrist cuffs.

"Here," he says, holding Darrek's gaze and handing them over. "I need this from you. Just for tonight. Don't go easy on me, and don't hold back. Got it?"

There is want in his beseeching gray-blue eyes—so raw and

exposed that it's hard for Darrek to bear to look at—and a child-like defiance as well. Darrek knows the look. It used to be his. He knows what Gabriel needs—for that defiance to be taken from him through rough sex and pleasurable pain dealt with nothing but love and care. And Darrek is the only one that can do it for him, the only one he trusts that much. He's the only one that could possibly understand.

The collar is a tight fit around Gabriel's neck. When it's locked, Darrek pulls on the leash leading from the metal loop in the back of the leather band, testing the give. It constricts Gabriel's wind-pipe and he grunts softly. Eyes slipping shut in relief, he wheezes and thin trickles of oxygen slip through his lips. He holds his wrists in place behind his back, waiting for Darrek to shackle them there. Darrek pulls even harder on the leash and grabs both of Gabriel's wrists in one hand, twisting them up to his middle back. Darrek kisses tenderly behind Gabriel's ear as he strains and makes soft strangled moans.

One hour later, Gabriel is face down on their bed, his shoulders braced on the mattress, bearing his weight, his knees planted wide under him, and ass in the air. Following Gabriel's directions, Darrek hadn't added any more restraints, not even a blindfold since Gabriel was so specific with what he chose to wear when they'd started. But Darrek had been free to select the toys he wanted to use. There is an extra-long dildo stuffed up Gabriel's well-lubed hole, the pink, delicate skin stretched smooth around the flared base of the toy. It took Darrek a good half an hour to get it all the way inside. Dripping sweat pours from Gabriel's skin, slicking his hair, matting it in black curls to his forehead, temples and the nape of his neck. The moisture catches on his long, naturally curled eyelashes and soaks the sheet under him. There is a thick, weighted metal ring locked around his scrotum. It's circled with small holes into which metal spikes have been screwed. Right now the spikes have been tightened just enough that they are beginning to be driven into his sack. At first they had barely touched him, but slowly Darrek had tightened the screws and pierced him with the spikes more and more. As if this wasn't enough pain, metal clamps have also been fastened to his nipples and Darrek's index finger and thumb are currently circled around the base of Gabriel's shaft, holding him by the cock ring secured there.

Darrek touches the violet wand in his right hand to the dripping head of Gabriel's penis, and the stinging shock it gives him makes the muscles contract in spasms throughout his thighs and stomach. Gabriel tries to force himself to be still and just let it happen. Releasing his hold on Gabriel's dick, Darrek watches it jump and twitch at the next brush of the wand to the underside. Instead he takes hold of the dildo, pulling it slowly out of his captive before driving it ruthlessly right back inside with a snap of his wrist.

Gabriel is so hugely erect, so desperate with the need to climax that he thinks he might soon pass out from lack of blood-flow to his brain. Heavy and swollen nearly purple, his dick is so sensitive he cries a little even when Darrek simply drags the edge of a fingernail along it. Darrek rubs the wand over the tip, spreading the sharp shock over the area. A guttural moan bellows from Gabriel's chest.

With two fingers pressed to the base, Darrek keeps the enormous phallus where it is, impaling Gabriel and not allowing it be expelled by the inner muscles of Gabriel's rectum like it wants to whenever he lets go. Dropping the wand, he picks up a towel and mops the sweat from Gabriel's face. Then he feels for a pulse and listens to his lover's fluttery, shallow breaths.

As destroyed as Gabriel is in that moment—eyes rolling loosely back, mouth slack, skin blotchy, both pale and flushed—he is more at peace than Darrek has ever seen him. Part of it is the finality of his confrontations earlier that day, putting the demons of the past firmly back where they belong, and healing his broken heart. The other part of it is finding the strength to be weak—to let his lover take him apart and then be there to put him back together.

The instructions were specific. They were delivered when Darrek positioned Gabriel on the mattress and was selecting the things to use on him. Darrek is not to stop or relent until Gabriel either passes out or uses his safeword, whichever comes first.

Gabriel peers back at Darrek through heavy-lidded eyes and licks over parched lips between shallow gasps. He flexes his hands inside the cuffs and tries to stretch and rotate his shoulder muscles to work out a sharp kink that is forming there. They stare at each other.

The defiance is still there, though it has diminished quite a lot. He lets Darrek see it, challenges him to take it completely away, somehow.

Darrek cups his free hand under Gabriel's abused cock, straining up almost flush to his belly. Cradling it, he feels the heat baking off of it, the slickness of the pre-come oozing down its length. He lets his palm squeeze around it once, quickly, painfully, before relaxing again. Gabriel grunts and turns his face away.

"What do you want?" Darrek asks in a low, throaty growl.

"Doesn't matter."

He gives Gabriel's purple-red flesh a hard slap, causing Gabriel to whimper and buck, and then twists each of the thick metal screws further, driving them deeper into his balls. Then he slaps Gabriel's dick again and feels his own body ache with need at the shattered, muffled sob Gabriel makes into the bedding.

"What do you want?" he asks again, even lower, even harsher.

"*Fuck me,*" Gabriel rasps. "Fuck me like you hate me. Like I'm worthless piece of shit that deserves to be hurt. Do it!"

"No."

Getting a good grip on the plastic cock, Darrek pulls it completely out of Gabriel, eliciting a shuddering moan, leaving his hole gaping wide. Then he kneels between Gabriel's spread legs, and loops an arm under Gabriel's chest. In a swift movement, Darrek pulls him upright and back, sitting him right down on his dick. Giving a startled gasp, Gabriel writhes. Darrek made him take him all at once. Thicker in circumference that the toy, Darrek knows Gabriel can feel the added stretch and burn.

For a second Gabriel fights Darrek's hold and whines, his sphincter contracting against the new violation. A few tears slip from his weary eyes.

"Never," Darrek whispers to him. "I love you, Gabriel."

"*God.* Don't. *Don't,*" he whimpers. His bound hands press against Darrek's abs. A warm palm cups over his chest, over his jack-rabbiting heartbeat.

"I'm *so* proud of you. You are so precious to me. I would never do that to you. Ever. Not for anything. Not even if you begged me."

Guiding his legs farther apart though he's already straddling Darrek's thighs, the metal spikes in the weight encircling his balls get removed one by one with careful work of Darrek's hand, encased in latex. Gabriel's head bows.

"Don't move," Darrek warns when Gabriel shifts in discomfort. When the six spikes are all free, Darrek rubs some disinfectant under the ring. "Should I take it off?" he asks, working a single finger under the metal, over the delicate flesh.

Gabriel purses his lips. Defiance.

"Okay then." Darrek leans back, bracing his hands on the bed, leaving both rings locked around Gabriel's genitals. "Fuck me. Fuck me like you love me more than anyone else in the world."

He can't see the expression on Gabriel's face, but he can see the way his shoulders tense up, the way his head bows even more as if out of shame and hears the small, hitching cry he makes. Hate and anger are easy. Defiance is *easy*. Those things are all Gabriel has had since he was nothing but a child. Love? Love is so much harder.

At first he can't do it. He can't let go of the polluting negativity and bitterness. He just sits there.

So Darrek makes it easier. He takes off the weighted ring around his scrotum. He even takes off the wrist cuffs. Gabriel stares, unseeing, out into the darkness of the room and feels Darrek kissing over his shoulder as he reaches to remove the cock ring too.

"*Don't,*" Gabriel whines, trying to push away Darrek's hands. He's too quick, too determined. Darrek hugs Gabriel's back to his chest and throws the ring away. Then he fingers over the cigarette burn, the scar left by Gabriel's abuser.

"No more pain," he whispers in promise. Winding his hand in the end of the leash, Darrek pulls it snug and lets Gabriel feel the tension. Moaning, he arches his back and reaches up and behind his head to run his hands through Darrek's hair. Rearing up, he feels Darrek tug out through his rim. Slowly Gabriel pushes back down on him, taking him back inside.

"I wanna see you. Wanna see you holding the leash while I fuck you. Please? Let me see who I belong to."

Darrek gives him some slack, and Gabriel pivots without pulling off, turning in a circle. He twists to the side then gets his leg over Darrek's chest. Darrek moans at the friction, at the sight of Gabriel's blown-wide pupils and desire. Shifting to stretch out his legs, Darrek lies back against the bed and yanks on the leash playfully. Laughing, Gabriel leans down and catches his lips in a kiss. He breathes out over Darrek's mouth and starts to move in tight rotations of his hips, slapping his ass down in a building rhythm firmly onto Darrek's lap as they make love. Too far gone to hold back, it's desperate and rough and fast. Gabriel works himself on Darrek and stares fixatedly at the leash leading to Darrek's fist.

Knowing he's not going to last, Darrek reaches to give Gabriel some much-needed relief as well.

"*Don't,*" Gabriel begs, still moving, kissing Darrek's mouth and tongue-fucking him as he bounces on his dick. He bats Darrek's hand away. "You promised."

"No I didn't." He gets a good grip around the throbbing member and pumps it once, twice, and a third time. Gabriel makes a wrecked, keening sigh and unloads, splattering hot over Darrek's chest. Riding out the orgasm, he lets Darrek's hands lock on to his hips and hold him up as Darrek fucks up into his clenching opening, fluttering with the pulses of his heart and the spasms of his pleasure. They go until they're both spent, and then Gabriel collapses down onto Darrek's chest.

"We're not done."

Darrek laughs. "You're too hard on yourself, baby. And you know I'm not as much of a hard-ass as you."

"But I wanted...."

Darrek sighs and hugs Gabriel to him. "You wanted oblivion. Right? And torture. Or both. How about instead I hold you while you take a nap and then we'll get washed up and take Sierra for a walk. We can watch the sun come up."

There's no response, nothing more than caresses of Gabriel's fingertips in figure-eights over his nipple.

"I can't believe I really did it. I can't believe I stood up to them and got away, and that I get to... let them go, and... stop being so afraid and be here. With you. Makes me feel... lucky."

"Me too," Darrek smiles.

A few moments later, the fingers dancing over him go still,

Gabriel's breathing evens out in a regular, deep rhythm. His body relaxes and he melts into Darrek's arms, safe and utterly content.

Ben, Trace and Micah return from Texas and get right back to work at Diadem. Ben's appearance beside Kyle the next morning is all the reassurance Kyle needs. They get back into a routine and nothing more is said about what happened. Monitoring the news, mysteriously, Harry's story never appears.

The call was made to 9-1-1 a few hours after they left him, bandaged and bound in the basement of his law firm. But despite this fact, no story is printed in the newspapers, or reported on the television stations. Whether he paid off the reporters, or managed to slip between everyone's fingers and into anonymity, they are not sure. A call is made to his office the following week and they are told he no longer is employed there. They call his apartment and find the number has been disconnected. He is simply gone.

Nothing is ever said to Gabriel about their trip, and Gabriel doesn't say anything to suggest he has any inkling about what they did or that they were ever involved to begin with. Sometimes, when they catch him staring at one of them when they are hanging out in someone's backyard during a barbeque or when they go out for drinks on a Friday night, and Gabriel's sharp gaze is fixed to Ben or Kyle or Trace or Micah, they suspect that maybe, on some level, he knows what they did to Harry. Or maybe that's just their imaginations getting the best of them. Maybe Gabriel has never had any idea. They would rather not know. So they keep it to themselves. All that matters is the way Gabriel's eyes light up when he's with Darrek, the way his laughter, unfettered, fills the air around them, contagious and infecting them all with his happiness. Every trace of his guarded defensiveness is gone. He's nearly unrecognizable. A devoted and loving partner, a diligent and focused businessman as he begins the process of establishing his fledgling videography and tech support company, a grateful, forgiving and attentive friend, Gabriel is reborn from the ashes of his past.

And Darrek, who has only ever wanted to please, to make someone proud of him, is rewarded every day by something as simple and true as the smile on his lover's face. Building their life together, anything seems possible.

He still worries about Kyle sometimes, and the twisted nature of his life with Ben, but makes himself available whenever his friend needs him.

Inspired by Gabriel's bravery, Darrek continues to keep in touch with his own family. He realizes his interactions with them will never be ideal or the fairy-tale version of what family is supposed to be, but really? Family is never like that. And that's okay.

For a while, Gabriel and Darrek's sex life is nothing but normal, simple, uncomplicated and almost routine lovemaking. The toys and gear get stored away. The hooks get removed from the walls. The furniture gets locked up out of sight and out of mind in the unused, spare bedroom. And for a while that's more than enough for both of them.

Until one day, Gabriel gets home and comes through the front door to see Darrek waiting for him on his knees, hands behind his back, head bowed submissively. All he wears is the gleaming necklace bearing the lock inscribed with a G.

Gabriel drops his things, pulls off his jacket and his shirt. He walks up to the kneeling man and cups a hand under his chin, tilting his head back sharply, exposing the long, thick column of his neck and watching his Adam's apple bob as he swallows.

"What's your safeword?" he asks in a gravelly purr.

"Tundra. It's Tundra, Master. Thank you."

"So obedient. I think we should find out just *how* obedient you really are...."

"Yes, sir. Thank you, sir."

Gabriel smiles, and Darrek submits, again and again and again.

If you enjoyed this story, you can sign up for a free membership at ForbiddenFiction and discuss it with other readers and the author at the

Deliver Us story page at http://forbiddenfiction.com/library/story/LK1-1.000004.

We do our best to proof all our work, but if you spot a text error we missed, please let us know via our website Contact Form at http://forbiddenfiction.com/contact

Author's Notes

I began writing this book expecting that no one would ever see it. The idea sparked in my brain and it was born only because it was created without rules and boundaries, free of hindrances that may come when putting words to paper when you think you have a solid idea who it is that will be reading them. Like the event that sets Darrek's fate in motion, his story was formed from pure compulsion and curiosity, and it wasn't something I intended, initially to share.

The first chapter was written in one shot, one night, after being inspired by video footage of a real male Dominant and submissive couple together and wondering what the story behind the BDSM was. What were those people like? If you sat down with them at a bar to have a beer, how would the conversation go? How did they get involved in the D/s lifestyle? What were the motivations and emotions underneath the sexuality?

I incorrectly assumed, at first, that Darrek's first trip to Diadem was the farthest he could go. It was his extreme, or maybe even beyond his extreme, and that was all it was supposed to be—a short story of a first-timer's trip to a dungeon. But then a funny thing happened. That first spark was still there, but now it had shifted, and was burning between Gabriel and Darrek; something intangible that made me want to dig deeper, and keep going. And so, like Darrek, I fell down the rabbit hole into another world. The more I researched and learned about 24/7 Dominant/submissive lifestyles, and the people who live them, the more I grew to appreciate them and the astonishing level of surrender and power that takes place. To be made as helpless, as secure as a submissive, or as entrusted as a Dominant, is a gift overflowing with a freedom unlike any other.

There is a private bond there that I respect and I feel blessed that I was able to learn about those aspects of the human psyche. Maybe if more of us were brave enough to leave self-consciousness, fear and doubt behind, and indulge in that which our heart and our body tell us we need (with consenting adults), we as a society could be happier. Own yourselves, no matter what anyone else thinks, because you are exactly who you were supposed to be.

This book would not exist if not for the support and constant encouragement of my friends and readers. I am humbled and grateful for each and every one of you, every second of every day. With love, this is for you.

– Lynn Kelling

About the Author

Website: www.Lynn Kelling.com

Five years ago, **Lynn Kelling** spontaneously started writing and hasn't stopped since. It all started with the desire to take a closer look at behaviors and ideas lurking at the fringes of life—basically anything that people may hesitate to speak of in mixed company, but everyone wonders about anyway. She is drawn to that which some may consider to be taboo—the darker and wilder the better—in order to expose the humanity within it. Our most telling moments are conveyed through intimacy and that which makes us feel vulnerable, powerful, or both, and so what could be more intriguing? Lynn is an artist and lover of any form of creative self-expression that comes from a place of honesty and emotion, whether it's body art or opera. She works as a multimedia designer in the Philadelphia area where she lives with her husband and two children.

About the Publisher

ForbiddenFiction.com is a publisher devoted to writing that breaks the boundaries of original erotic fiction. Our stories combine intense sexuality with quality writing. Stories at Forbidden Fiction.com not only arouse readers through sensations, but also engage them emotionally and mentally through storytelling as well-crafted as the sex is hot.

ForbiddenFiction.com is also designed to be a social reading environment. You'll have fun even if just reading the latest post each day, yet you will have the chance for so much more. Readers and authors can be part of ongoing discussions of specific works and individual authors as well as more general topics.

Sign up for a FREE Membership at **ForbiddenFiction.com**